FERTILITY

A novel by

ADAM PATRICK FOSTER

978-0-6486464-7-1 (paperback)
978-0-6486464-8-8 (hardback)
978-0-6486464-6-4 (ebook)

Dedicated to

The woman who gave me life,
My moral compass,
My mother

Collette

CHAPTER ONE

LIGHTNING CRASHES

The air is so cold and dense that all sounds seem muted as if Glen can hear the silence reverberating around him like a dull buzz. A constant invisible electric charge that crackles loudly in his head as he treks on the middle of a vast frozen lake that stretches and winds through a wilderness valley. The surrounding abundant shrubbery filled with tall pine and Maple tree's bearing thick marshmallow-like globs of powdery snow from a fresh blizzard.

The distinct scrunching of soft layered snow meets rubber boot sole as Glen his older brother trudge across the serine ice sheeted lake, leaving two distinct trails of footprints winding all the way back to the shoreline some two-hundred yards back. Glen, eleven years of age, peers into the distance through waves of green and purple flashes through the skyline, oscillating all around him like an aurora bore-alis. Just nestled in the hills, Glen can make out a bright yellow house with white trimmings. He squints his eyes, thinking he can make out a figure standing on the house balcony watching he and his sixteen-year-old brother, Joe, walking across the lake. Glen stares hard at the figure, who looks like a man, but he's not sure. He turns his attention to his brother walking several yards ahead.

"Joe?"

"What?"

"I think someone's watching us."

"So?"

"Is this private property?"

"A lake can't be private. Unless it's government owned. Which it's not."

Glen looks back to the house. Only it's not there anymore. Glen stops, using his hand to shield his eyes to get a clearer eyeline to the source. Definitely no house. Glen blinks erratically. He could have sworn on his life there was a yellow house right there in the nook in the woods. Where could it possibly have gone? The aurora borealis now absent too, but he doesn't notice that and keeps walking.

CRACK.

Snaaaaap.

Joe freezes on the spot, spinning around to Glen, who is still walking in his own world of thoughts.

"Glen!"

Glen is staring off into the distance still obsessed with the house that isn't there anymore.

"Glen!"

"What?"

"Don't move!"

Glen stops in his tracks, a look of confusion on his face.

Joe says, "We hit a weak patch. The ice broke." He looks around wildly for the closest section of shore. He spots land about a hundred yards ahead, then points at it. "We have to-"

CRUNCH.

Joe plunges down through a fresh hole in the broken ice, water cascading all around it. Silence.

"Joe?"

Glen can't see now, because the mist around him has suddenly turned into a thick cloud.

"Joe!?"

Glen sticks his arms out and feels around in the hope of finding Joe. He takes small measure steps through the fog. His foot hits water and he almost slips over.

"Joe!"

Then Glen sees it. The hole in the lake ice. He dashes over to it and drops to his knees. He peers hard into the water but can't see anything except the lapping water. An arm punches out of the icy water and flails helpless around, trying to get a grip on the ice surface.

"Joe! I see you!"

Glen reaches out but can't quite grasp Joe's arm. The ice around Glen now cracking and snapping. He looks ahead at the shoreline, then back to his desperate brother. Glen slides slowly on his kneecaps closer to the edge of the broken hole. He almost has Joe's arm in his grasp several times but keeps missing it by an inch.

Joe's arm disappears under the water again. The air dead still again, except the gentle lapping of water.

"Joe! Please! I can't!"

Glen drops onto his stomach and slides to the very edge of the hole, diving his arm under the water. He wades it around frantically, the water so cold he can already start to feel his arm turn numb. Then he feels Joe's hand grip his wrist. Got him!

Glen pulls with all his might and heaves Joe up from the depths, groaning as he pulls his much heavier brother from the water.

The face of a grown man emerges from the water, frozen blue with wide eyes, white with frost. His mouth agape in horror.

Glen screams as the lifeless face bursts out of the water and consumes him.

Glen's eyes snap wide open and he sits bolt upright in his bed. His face mottled with sweat beads. Glen is in his mid-forties, with long brown hair streaked with greys. His eyes pale blue. He is still reeling from his frozen terrorized face in his nightmare.

Breathing heavily, he wipes his face and scratches his four-day growth on his sturdy jaw. His hands and wrists are littered with scars ranging from short and deep to large and long.

After a long moment of calming down, he pulls himself from his bed.

Glen puts on clothes draped over an old rocking chair in the corner of the bedroom next to a foggy window. After a few minutes he is rugged up in oil-stained mechanic's pants, a worn denim jacket and an old, knitted scarf wrapped around his neck. His thick hair pulled back into a ponytail. He walks into the living room with two leather La-Z-Boy recliners in the middle facing a widescreen plasma TV. Empty beer cans littered around one of the chairs. The walls have a few framed paintings of the Wild West frontier, several elk skulls and an old, framed picture of him as a young boy with his older brother Joe standing over a deer they had just shot. A large bay window looks out into the darkness of very early morning.

Glen pulls a Sig Arms hunting rifle from a gun rack mounted on the living room wall. The body of it varnished wood and has a scope fitted on the top. He slings the gun's strap over his shoulder and whistles loudly.

"C'mon Bullit."

An adult Alaskan Malamute trots up the house corridor to the front door and waits patiently for Glen.

Frost escapes Glen's lips as he locks the front door and strides on the snow around the side of the weathered pinewood house. It sits in the middle of a 40-acre property lined with pine trees on the cusp of a dense forest.

Glen now walking past a large dark green wooden shack twenty yards from the back of the house. The sturdy shack looks much newer compared to the old home. He takes a metal hook hanging outside the entrance to the shack and meanders into the forest.

Glen returns nearly two hours later with two dead rabbits and a beaver impaled on the hook. Bullit trotting proudly by his master's side. The first signs of sunlight starting to break over the horizon now. They pass a generator near the shack; a makeshift wooden grave cross next to it that reads "LILY".

After unfastening three heavy duty padlocks, Glen enters the shack. The inside of it is a hunter's wet dream. The walls are swathed with animal skins, taxidermy heads of previous hunting kills, collectors' knives and exotic blades of all sizes neatly arranged on one wall: guns and ammunition on another wall. Drills and other power tools, camping equipment and basic carpentry hardware neatly arranged in a corner. In the adjacent corner is a black 1976 Mustang with odd car parts strewn around it - a side project. Near the Mustang is a filthy old rug that is covering a trap door.

Glen hangs the hooks with the fresh dead animals on an overhead beam above a work bench. He unslings the rifle and gently lays it on a table littered with traps of all kinds. He stares at the traps for a long moment. He pries one of the small fox traps open. He closes his eyes for a moment, breathing deeply, then opens them again just before he slams his fist into the middle of the trap, setting off the spring and the sharp metallic jaws clamps around his upper hand and wrist. Glen howls with pain, causing Bullit to put his tail between his legs and take a few steps back.

Dark storm clouds roll into each other on the horizon.

Glen now at the rear of his silver Ford pick-up truck with all the off-road trimmings. He is loading the bed of the truck with five full navy colored gym bags. After the bags are neatly arranged side-by-side, Glen fixes a thick tarp cover over the entire back of the truck bed. With fresh bandages over his wounded hand, he ties the tarp down firmly, testing and re-testing the knots that are holding in place. He has a backpack over his shoulder that he places on the passenger seat of the truck as he hops in the driver's seat.

Glen starts the truck and drives down his property road until he reaches the barbed wire fence surrounding his property. He opens the swing metal gate, drives his truck out, then hops out and closes it. A homemade painted sign in the middle of the gate reads; "DEAR TRESSPASSERS. MY DOGS CAN'T WAIT TO MEAT YOU", with an oddly unsettling smiley face.

Glen drives along the remote woodlands road until he reaches a highway. After a while he passes a roadside sign that reads; "Thanks For Visiting Great Barrington, Massachusetts, Come Back Soon!"

Glen sips on his travel mug filled with drip coffee while listening to decades old Country & Western songs at mid-volume, tapping his fingers on the steering wheel to the music beats as he stares ahead on the long stretch of road and snow blanketed plains in the backwaters of Great Barrington. The odd car passing by from the other direction, but it's still quite early and there's not many people on the road.

An old blue Honda Civic materializes out of the morning winter haze a mile ahead of Glen's truck. The two vehicles traveling at a neutral pace toward each other. The Honda is now about to pass Glen's truck.

A rumble in the air.

CRACK.

A flash of bright white lightening snaps on the road between the two cars as they zoom past one another.

Glen lets out a load groan from the deafening clap of lightning that echoes in his head. He jerks in his seat and slumps over the steering wheel – passed out.

The Honda behind careens off the road and hits a large wall of snow powder, wedging halfway into the snow embankment.

Glen's truck rolls on down the road for several yards before coming to a gentle stop on the otherwise deserted road. Dusty Springfield now on Glen's truck speakers. Glen is still hunched flaccidly over the steering wheel. A moment, then his eyes flutter open. He winces in pain as a sharp ringing pierces his head. He sits up and nurses his head with his hands as the ringing changes back and forth between high and low frequency.

Glen heaves his truck door open and charily steps out onto the icy road. Wispy gusts of wind now starting to drown out the incessant ringing. Glen peers around at the desolate scenery of paddocks and forest all around the highway, then his eyes fix on the blue Honda stuck in the snow embankment about fifty yards down the road. Concern now growing for the driver of that car, Glen strides toward the Honda, shaking his head as the ringing refuses to completely subside. He is now ten yards from the car and stops in his tracks.

Glen looks back at his truck, specifically thinking about the bags hidden under the tarp in the back. He swallows hard. He looks back at the Honda, wiping his hand over his hair with frustration. His mind racing. Glen lets out a deep sigh of frost into the air, then turns on his heels and swiftly marches back to his truck. He swings himself back into the driver's seat, turning the ignition and roaring the engine to life. He accelerates off into the frosty haze, wanting badly now to distance himself from the scene of the accident.

CHAPTER TWO

FORBIDDEN SOIL

Frazzled strawberry blonde hair tied up careless in a bun is hunched over the steering wheel. A long drawn-out groan. The head belonging to the messy hair rises up. Sally blinks her wide hazel eyes, then creases them shut as her head fills with a dull ringing. She winces as the frequency sound reverberates in her head. She's in her late thirties with soft facial features, and wears no make-up of any kind, and if asked, she wouldn't be able to recall the last time she wore any.

Sally looks around the cabin of her car, breathing in short breaths with a visage of angst and confusion. The windscreen and windows around her are completely immersed in snow powder. She turns her head and looks over her shoulder, seeing a hint of highway through the back windscreen. She feels around her body to make sure nothing is broken or there's no blood. She's okay for now, she reasons.

Sally tries to conjure up her last memory before this happened. She vaguely recalls seeing a pickup truck on the highway, then a loud noise, and that's all she can remember. That damn persistent ringing in her head won't go away. She rummages around the passenger seat through the pile of take-out bags and food containers until she feels her phone.

She picks it up and lights up the screen. No service. She curses under her breath and languidly drops the phone back in the passenger seat mess.

She takes a deep breath, bashes the side of her head with her open palm a few times in some kind of attempt to knock out the dull ringing in her head, now oscillating between high and low frequencies. She leans over and jiggles the key in the ignition anxiously to get the car started. The brake lights flick on and off and the headlights doing the same, lighting up the snow covering her view. The car eventually powers to life and Sally throws the clutch into reverse. A few long moments of the tires spinning in the snow, then the Honda manages to wrench itself free from the embankment.

Sally backs the car out onto the empty road, turning the window-wipers to full power, eventually freeing most of the snow from the front windscreen. She powers the driver's window down, which takes off the snow in the process. She pokes her head out to look around. Not a soul in sight. Sally snorts frost out of her nose and powers the window back up. She maneuvers the car to face the way she was originally travelling and speeds off down the highway.

After thirty minutes Sally drives though a windy forest road with dips and rough terrain not meant for her little car: almost becoming bogged down in deep mud puddles a few times. She keeps an eye out for little red markings stuck on trees that she has previously placed there. She follows her own little trail until she pulls into a small clearing in the woods and stops the car.

Sally pops the driver's door open and steps out, stretching all her limbs out at once, looking to herself like a quivering starfish as she catches a glimpse of her splayed self in the car's side mirror. She puts on a green and blue woolen knitted cap adding to her shabby knitted purple sweater, washed out green corduroy pants and unlaced scuffed boots. Sally knows she has no fashion sense, but people have told her it's part of her charm.

Sally rounds the car to the trunk and opens it, pulling out a large case that resembles a medical kit. She slings the strap of the case over her shoulder and slams the trunk shut, then makes sure the car is locked. She muses to herself that no one is going to break in, because she's in the middle of nowhere in the forest. She shrugs, thinking it's better to be safe than sorry. Sally puts on a set of ugly multi-colored knitted gloves and trudges off into the forest.

Sally is at the base of a tall thick Northern Red Oak tree, the submerged roots caked with bright green moss. Around the globs of snow in the area she is are little laminated Post-It notes attached to long pins and stuck into the ground resembling mini flags, of various different colors. In the middle of the arrangement is a set of these flags fashioned into a ten-foot square. Sally kneels down beside the marked square and opens her kit. One half of the kit contains gardening tools, the other side houses an array of small bottles and laboratory vials with color coded labels on each one, from "Vinegar" and "Baking Powder", to "Dish Soap" and "Hydrogen Peroxide" and many other chemical compounds. She lifts out a vial filled with dark soil labelled "Coir Fiber" and twists the lid off. She can't help back take a little whiff of the contents. Sally loves aromas. The more pungent the better. She thinks it probably started when she was a little girl waiting in the car at gas stations, sneakily cracking the window to breath in the intoxicating petrol odor.

"Excuse me ma'am."

Sally squeals loudly and her heart feels like it's suddenly in her throat at the sound of another voice. She snaps her head around to find a man standing next to the oak tree. Mid 30's with receding blonde hair and a top-heavy boxer's build. He wears his perfectly ironed police uniform with fastidious pride. His police badge shined daily. It bears the name in small print, Officer Brian Sorenson, though Sally can't read that since she's a good ten feet away from him.

Sally clasps her hand to her chest, now visibly relaxing that he's a cop and not some deranged axe-murderer.

"My God, you scared the... sorry. You came from nowhere."

Brian takes a step toward her, his stature stiff and commanding. "What are you doing here?"

Sally makes awkward gestures to rise up and stand, grabbing and fumbling at trees that aren't there, and almost falling over. She gets there in the end, playing with loose strands of her wild hair nervously.

"Oh, um, I'm conducting, ah, an, ex, ex-experiment."

Brian peers at her kit, suspiciously eying the science vials. His eyes back to Sally now, looking her up and down in her unkempt appearance.

Sally is stretching her fingers on her right hand, back and forth, crunching her hand into a fist then spreading out her fingers as far as they will go.

"Ma'am. Are you engaged in the growing of illegal substances?"

"Wha-what?" Sally laughs nervously. "Oh. No, no, no. Well, I need... I mean, I'm trying with untreated soil in a natural atmosphere, to, um, slowly apply compound fertilizers with...," Sally stops, now looking Brian up and down with his neat uniform, trailing off on a tangent. "Y'know, I wanted a natural... y'know...," she blinks erratically and puts one hand on her hip. "I-I-I can prove it."

"Are you aware, ma'am, that this vicinity is a protected forest reserve?"

Sally's brows crease in confusion. "It's okay. I'm a horticulturalist."
Sally bunches a clump of her hair in her fist. "I wasn't doing anything bad, I was-"

"You're trespassing, ma'am."

"I'm sorry? I don't under... no, see, I, um-"

"Do you have a permit by the Massachusetts Department of Conservation and Recreation, to conduct experiments in this zone?"

Sally's lips are trembling. She's lost for words. Her hands are visibly shaking.

"Ma'am?"

"Look, officer. If this experiment works, it could be a medicinal breakthrough."

"Ma'am, I'll ask you again. Do you have the approval by the Departm-"

"No!" Sally's eyes widen and she clamps her hand over her mouth in shock.

Brian stiffens up and cocks one eyebrow up, running his tongue over his bottom teeth.

Sally says, "Sorry! I don't know where that came from. I've got this headache. I hit some snow before, and... look. I'll be done here real soon."

Brian exhales a long stream of frosty breath from his nose then reaches to the backside of his belt and takes a leather-bound notebook with a pen attached. He flips it open and starts scrawling.

"The time is approximately eight-twenty-five a.m. I am issuing you with a fine for trespassing on State controlled land, and vandalism."

"Vandalism?!"

Without looking at her, Brian languidly motions to the markers in the ground with his pen. "These markings, or whatever they are, are littered on a protected forest reserve."

Sally huffs a sigh and nervously fidgets her shaky hands. "I understand officer. And I'll pay the fine. But may I please wrap up what I'm doing here?"

"Absolutely not ma'am. I will be escorting you back to your car after you pick up all your belongings."

"I promise I'll take the right steps to get permission next time."

"You do that ma'am," Brian says still scribbling in his notebook.

"Can you please not call me that?" The irritation is unmistakable in her voice now.

For the first time since he started writing, Brian stops the pen and looks at her.

"Call you what?"

"Ma'am."

"Do you take offence to me addressing you as ma'am?"

"Yes. I do."

"Do you mind me asking why?"

Sally folds her arms across her chest defiantly. "It's condescending."

"It's a formal way to address a female. And I am formally addressing you."

"It's short for madame. Do I look like an eighteen hundreds British aristocrat?"

Brian taps his pen on the pad, staring at her with a deadpan expression.

"Well, then, tell me how you would like to be addressed. Is 'miss' appropriate?"

"What if I was married?"

"Are you?"

"No. But that's presumptuous of you. Again, with the condescension."

Brian looks like he's going to say something, then decides he shouldn't. After a moment, he calmly says, "Well, I was just coming to obtaining your details. So, let's start with your full name, and some identification."

Sally lets out a dejected sigh. She digs in a couple of pockets before finding her Velcro wallet, tearing it open. She pulls out her license and steps over to him with it outstretched in her hand.

"Sally Caroline Field."

Brian takes the license from her fingertips and positions it at the top of his notepad and begins jotting down the details.

Sally says, "This is actually a funded experiment. I work at a research facility for a major university. Harvard. Have you heard of it?" The last line coming out high, now wanting to sound condescending.

Brian continues writing and ignores her.

Sally continues, "Which means I can arrange a donation to your local council. For, um, charity. Yeah. Charity. And it will be a lot more substantial than a fine for littering."

Brian stops writing and shoots her a hard look.

"Did you just offer me a bribe?"

Sally's eyes widen and she swallows a hard lump in her throat.

"What?! No. God no. It's a gesture to your community for allowing me to conduct my serious work."

Brian snaps the notebook shut.

"Ma'am, I'm going to need you to come down to the station with me."

"Why?"

"I believe you just attempted to bribe a police officer. Which is most definitely a criminal offence."

"I wasn't! I was looking for alternatives."

"Well you looked in the wrong place. Now, are you going to come willingly, or do I have to put handcuffs on you?"

Sally takes a step back, looking horrified. Brian matches her and takes a step toward her. Sally whips her head around to look at her experiment, then back to Brian.

"These are my seeds!"

"And not your soil." He steps again at her charily. "Now, if you'll please come with me. I'll have someone come collect your things."

"This isn't fair!"

Brian points his index finger at her like she was a misbehaving child.

"I'm not in a position to say what you're doing is wrong, but I am in a position to state the way you have gone about it is wrong."

Sally's eyes are now welling with tears. "Do you use bureaucracy to pick on someone to, to, to, to justify your job?" Her face twists into a scathing visage. "I hope your dinner tastes like spite." Sally's face now going back to sadness. "I... I... I'm sorry. I just don't know...," she trails off. Tears now running down both her cheeks.

"You just crossed a line, lady," Brian says with a clenched jaw. He reaches to his belt and unclips the pouch housing his handcuffs and takes them out. "Turn around and place your palms on the tree next to you, then spread your legs. I am placing you under arrest, ma'am."

Sally fights more tears as she begrudgingly complies with Brian's orders.

"I'm sorry," she says.

Brian moves to her and starts reading her the Miranda rights as he cuffs her hands behind her back.

Chapter Three

NOT FOR SALE

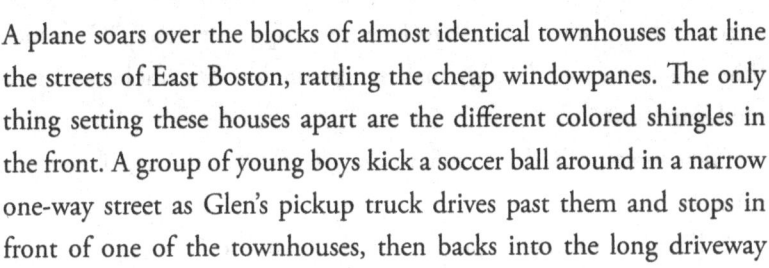

A plane soars over the blocks of almost identical townhouses that line the streets of East Boston, rattling the cheap windowpanes. The only thing setting these houses apart are the different colored shingles in the front. A group of young boys kick a soccer ball around in a narrow one-way street as Glen's pickup truck drives past them and stops in front of one of the townhouses, then backs into the long driveway leading to the rear of the property.

Teddy, a heavyset Latino man in his late forties, watches Glen back up the driveway from the living room window while sipping on a yellow mug of coffee that has a faded picture of Garfield on the side. A tribal tattoo sleeve covers his right arm and snakes up to his neck and the bottom of his face. His pride and joy is his well-manicured crowbar moustache, coated with glistening product oil. He turns and meanders down the corridor to the backyard.

The backyard is a mess of broken toys and mud patches in the dead grass. A paint-chipped wooden garage in the back corner of the property, where Glen has just parked his truck in the front of and shuts off the engine.

Teddy, wearing a tied bathrobe, no shirt, boxer shorts and slippers, ambles over to Glen as he hops out of the vehicle.

"Glen, my man. How the fuck is you?"

Glen takes Teddy's outstretched hand in his and they share a vigorous handshake. He looks down at Glen's other hand, bandaged from the bear trap earlier in the morning.

Teddy says, "Another hardware accident huh?" He sips his coffee and shakes his head with a grin. "Man, you gotta watch it with those tools, or get some new ones. Seems like you've had an accident every time you come here."

"I'm okay Teddy. Got a headache, but otherwise I'm fine."

"Oh shit. Can I get you something? I think the old lady's got Aspirin or some shit upstairs." He leans in with a suggestive look. "Or somethin' a little stronger." Teddy makes a gesture like he's smoking from a meth pipe.

Glen looks to Teddy's coffee mug. "Coffee's just fine, if you got some?"

"I'll get the woman to put on a fresh batch, bro."

"How's the family?"

Teddy shrugs haphazardly, taking another sip of his coffee.

"Oh, y'know man. Same fuckin' shit. Kayla's in the fifth grade, an' shit. Marly... well, he's fuckin' Marly. Nice of you to ask though, bro." Teddy takes a sip of coffee, and winces. Too cold now. He tosses the remainder of the coffee on the ill-kept patchy lawn, then motions for Glen to follow him to the house. "Let's get you a coffee. Then we'll see what you got, friend-o."

Glen and Teddy re-emerge from the house after fifteen minutes. Glen making small talk with Teddy's wife, Michelle, while she put on a fresh brew of coffee. Glen noticed the remnants of a black eye on her face. Probably done a couple of days ago by the look of it. Sometimes she has bruises on her face or arms, sometimes she doesn't. And Glen never mentions it. He knows damn well where they came from.

Now Glen and Teddy are at the old garage, Teddy unlocking the three padlocks on the doors. The garage has been converted into an office den. A desk at the back with an old desktop computer well past its prime. A few fake plants, a flatscreen TV with gaming consoles, a lava lamp and other novelty accessories. Posters of models in swimwear, skimpy trades outfits, and a couple outright nude. Every time Glen sets foot in the garage he likens it to a frat boy's college room.

Teddy moseys over to the desk and turns on a powerful swivel lamp above the desk as Glen brings in the gym bags from the rear of his truck, one by one until all of them are neatly placed on the brown leather couch facing the TV. He has the backpack from the passenger seat slung over his shoulder and leaves it there. Glen unzips one of the gym bags and opens it. The first one is filled with bags of assorted white and brown powders. Methamphetamines, Ketamine, Magic Mushrooms crushed into powder, and a few other uppers and downers. Inside. The next two bags are packed with dried marijuana plants. Glen picks one from the top and walks to the desk to give it to Teddy, who now has his robe off to reveal his naked upper body which is filled with Catholic imagery tattoos. A big crucified Jesus taking up his whole back. Teddy places the plant under the heat lamp and examines it with magnifying glasses while he smokes a cigarette. Glen is by one of the walls, sipping coffee while pretending to be interested in the trashy posters of under-dressed young women.

After a few minutes of studying the marijuana plant, Teddy looks over to Glen.

"This one's niiiiiccceee, bro. Not your usual hydro. What is it? A new strand of White Widow?"

"Nope. Cross pollinated a few various strains. This is the result."

"Good shit?"

Glen half turns and gives him a mindful look with a half smirk.

Teddy says, "Sorry amigo, I forgot. You know, you're my only client who doesn't, you know, enjoy the fruits of their labor."

Glen shrugs, swallowing a mouthful of coffee. "It'll do the trick."

Teddy grins. "I bet it does. Your stuff is way better than the dispensary shit. The legal weed is nowhere near as good as yours. My customers loooove it. If it weren't for you, man, I'd be slingin' just chemicals. You're keeping the green dream alive, hombre." He stubs the cigarette out on a mound of ash in a glass ashtray and stands up and shuffles in his slippers to a thick metal safe in the corner of the room. Teddy squats down and flicks the dial on the safe several times until the clunk sound, then opens it to reveal many stacks of cash piled up inside. Glen side glances and sees two guns sitting on top of one of the money piles, and quickly returns to feign interest in the poster girl dressed vaguely like a construction worker. Aside from the denim butt shorts and a tiny shirt barely covering her breasts, the only way to tell that's what she's pretending to be is the large mallet gripped in her hands.

"Now, please tell me that little back on your back has inside it what I think it does," Teddy says.

Glen looks over to find that Teddy is standing next to the safe with three large stacks of cash in his hands he places on top of the safe. Glen nods and takes the backpack from his shoulder and tosses into Teddy's waiting arms. Teddy immediately unzips the bag and peers inside at smaller, tighter bunches of marijuana in two vacuum sealed bags. He picks one out and pries a little hole in the top. He brings it to his nose and takes a deep measured sniff, closing his eyes and basking in the aroma like he was a Sommelier tasting the bouquet with his nostrils. After a long moment, and a little too dramatic for Glen, Teddy opens his eyes and a smile creeps on his face, raising the sides of his mani-cured moustache.

"You couldn't put the Mona Lisa in a plastic bag and make it look good. But this, amigo, is art in a fuckin' Ziploc."

Glen shrugs modestly and pretends to take a long sip of the coffee he has already finished, unsure what else to do to pass the moment.

Teddy says, "Have you thought about my proposal?"

Glen stares at the lava lamp a moment, watching the globs float around in the purple lit gel water. Trying to calm himself a little and mask his fresh irritation at Teddy.

"Sorry Teddy. But I ain't cloning Frostbite."

Teddy expecting that answer and is quick to follow up. "You know how much I pay for this, and I know you know how much I charge for it. All I'm sayin' is, we mass market this, we're sittin' on a fuckin' goldmine bro."

"I'll think about it," Glen says flatly.

Teddy takes a deep breath with glowering eyes on Glen, then lets out an openly frustrated sigh.

"Yeah, you always thinkin' about it, hombre."

There's an awkward tension in the stuffy air now, and this is not the first time regarding this particular issue. Glen takes a sip from the empty coffee mug again.

Teddy drops the bag of Frostbite marijuana back in the shoulder bag and zips it up, tossing it in front of the safe with a little more emphasis than needed. Glen figuring he did that so Glen's eyes would go to it, then to the stacks of cash behind it to make a point, and more importantly the guns clearly visible on top of it.

"I just think it's a waste, man. But you got your reasons I guess. And I gotta respect that."

"I'll see if I can bring a little more next time, seeing as how it's good for your business."

"What are those reasons?"

"Huh?"

"All the times I asked about why you won't clone it to make shit tons more money, and you still haven't given me no reason."

"I make enough money, is one reason."

"Yeah? Well I don't."

"That's none of my business, man."

"But it is. You are part of that business, bro."

"You shouldn't rely so much on me. What if I died tomorrow? I mean, just this morning on my way here I nearly had a serious car accident. Passed out at the wheel and everything."

"There's more ways to die than a car crash."

Glen knowing full well that the last comment was a veiled threat. Glen not too intimidated by Teddy. Sure, he's a mean looking son-of-a-bitch. But Glen is taller, scrappier, not as muscular as Teddy but has broader shoulders and more weight than him. Most importantly, though, Glen is no stranger to pain and often welcomes it. Glen can tell Teddy is mostly show. The whole 'gangsta' thing is primarily theatrics. If Teddy went for one of those guns right now, he would have a lava lamp busted over his head faster than he could grip the butt of a weapon. No, it's not Teddy he's worried about. It's his associates. Glen knows this chump is a middleman who works for much bigger hitters. And it's precisely that reason Teddy wants his prized Frostbite to excel his interests to take the top tier of the industry.

Glen pretends to take the last gulp from the mug and places it on the coffee table in front of the couch, coated with ash and weed smoking paraphernalia.

"We good?" asks Glen with a polite disposition.

Teddy hovers his eyes ominously at Glen a moment, then straightens his posture and exudes a friendly smile. "Yeah, we good. Hunky dory as you country folk like to say." Teddy picks up the backpack from the floor and takes out the bags of Frostbite. He places them on the safe and proceeds to fill the bag with the three stacks of shrink-wrapped cash he previously took from the safe then apathetically tosses the bag to Glen.

"We talked last time about new inflation. With Frostbite," says Glen.

"Ahhhhh, yeah. We did." Teddy reaches down into the safe and takes a wrapped bundle of cash, pulling it out so vigorously one of the guns topples off the pile and falls onto the shag carpet. Teddy deliberately lazily throws the cash to Glen so he misses the catch and has to stoop down to collect it.

"Sorry 'bout that," says Teddy as he strokes his moustache.

Glen just smiles as he grabs it and rises back up.

Teddy bends over and picks up the fallen gun. Teddy not putting the gun back in the safe right away, now just holding it menacingly to his side, tapping it on his thigh as he watches Glen stuff the bundle in the backpack with the others and zips it up.

"You never count it, huh?"

Glen gives him a mindful little grin. "You know anyone else who got Frostbite?"

Teddy smiles. "Nah man. I guess I don't."

Glen shoulders the bag and moseys to the garage door and opens it. He turns his head and says, "Thanks for the coffee."

"Anytime, hombre," Teddy says, using the gun to salute Glen.

"Give Michelle my best."

"I'll give her my best alright," Teddy says with a sleazy grin showing his stained teeth.

Glen is out the door and closes it. Teddy listens as the pickup truck starts and drives down to the street. He lights a cigarette from a pack on the coffee table, his face now full of indignation.

"Fuckin' stupid ass hick."

Glen stops in for a bite to eat at his favorite Boston diner, a rockabilly 50's inspired décor with the standard pictures of old school entertainers like Marilyn and Elvis. Best burgers in town to him. He always sits near the jukebox that spins out Buddy Holly and the like. He finishes up, then decides to go catch a flick at the cinema. Some shitty action movie with an older actor he recognizes. He rarely comes into the city, only to deliver to Teddy, so he tries to make the most of it when he does.

Late afternoon now, Glen is halfway home and now driving through small towns. It's half raining, half snowing. Slush all over the road. Glen listening to a country and western radio station. He's got his own selections but sometimes likes to zone out and let some DJ at the radio station make the selection for him, and listen to news updates, especially about baseball.

Glen passes by a large power station on the outskirts of Springfield. As the truck drives past the massive maze of electrical towers and power lines on the property, the ringing in his head from this morning makes a deafening comeback. Glen clenches his jaw in pain, his knuckles white from gripping the steering wheel so hard. The ringing now morphing into a frequency signal, the popping and cracking changing from extreme highs and lows like someone is changing the radio dial up and down in his head.

Glen lets out a drawn, frustrated groan. His head pounding and the headlights whizzing by him distorted and blinding. During the frequency, he can hear the distinct sound of woman sobbing loudly. That kind of blubbering that causes the nose to drip with snot.

Glen slams his foot down hard on the accelerator and burns past the power station as fast as he can, having to sloppily overtake two cars in the process, thinking he must look like a drunk driver to the occupants of the other cars. The deafening frequency now becoming fainter and fainter the further he gets away from the electrical towers and power lines. He wipes sweat from his face and blinks erratically to try and focus on the road. The ringing dissipates until it becomes somewhat unnoticeable as he continues the drive home.

Chapter Four

AS THE UNIVERSE INTENDED

Sally pushes through the front doors of the Great Barrington Police Headquarters, hurriedly walking down the ice-laden cement stairs. She almost slips over on a puddle of frozen water, having to grab the rail for support and dropping her horticulture kit in the process - several vials and bottles clattering out and falling down the stairs. She quickly collects them back up and carelessly stuffs them back in the kit she had to collect from the evidence room twenty minutes ago.

Sally looks for her car in the parking lot where she was told someone parked it during her police interview. There it is, right in the corner. She half runs, half walks to it, fearing another slip accident on the way. She jiggles her keys furiously, taking longer to get the key in the door because she is panicking and just wants to get the hell out of here.

Sally now on the road, frequently catching herself speeding down the highway and having to soften her foot on the accelerator. The last thing she wants right now is a run-in with another cop. The car headlights illuminating the falling snow, looking to Sally like glowing confetti before the high volume window wipers scrub them out. She's listening to a Kate Bush album, singing along with the words she knows and hums the rest.

That cop's face now in her mind again. The word "ma'am" reverberating in her head. She beats the steering wheel with her fist. She can't shake it. Sally sharply swerves the car off the side of the road into a rest area and turns off the engine.

She turns the music off and sits in silence for five minutes. Without any kind of warning from her body, she blurts out a hail of projectile vomit all over the dashboard and windscreen. Chunks of half-digested bagel and pesto dripping from the steering wheel. Sally tightly grips the wheel with both hands, leaning forward to press her forehead on the top of it. She feels the warm bile of her vomit on her upper face, but she doesn't care. Sally starts weeping quietly as headlights zoom past her on the highway several yards away. After a minute of trying to keep the tears at bay, she bursts into uncontrollable sobbing. She moans loudly with her mouth agape, gripping the steering wheel so tight her hands are turning numb. She inches her head to the side and bites down so hard on the wheel a voice in her head is telling her that her teeth will crack. She continues to groan and wail as tears stream past her snot dripping nose.

After several minutes, Sally pulls herself back together and wipes her eyes and nose with the sleeves of the green cardigan she's wearing. Glistening wet snot all over the cuffs now. She rustles through the discarded food wrappers on the passenger seat until she finds unused napkins and uses them to clean the vomit from the windscreen, only making it smudgy. She reaches around in the backseat and finds a woolen scarf, using that to mop up the rest of the puke.

Sally turns the music back on and sings along to it in a soothing voice to herself. She checks her phone for the first time in hours and sees seven missed calls from 'Larissa'. She thinks about dialing back, but opts to send a text instead, saying she is fine, just got waylaid and will be home soon. She starts the engine, and with a face full of determination, she sets the car in motion and is back on the highway.

⁂

Laughter reverberates around the ostentatiously decorated dining room. Four women sit around an ornate mahogany dining table, holding lipstick-stained wine glasses containing Chilian red wine. They are all in their late thirties, early forties. Dressed in a mix of power suits and chic bohemian. The décor around them a juxtaposition of carefully manicured flowerpots and impressionist art prints, with bleak industrial sculptures and Roman-inspired busts.

The woman refilling her wine glass, Larissa, has short boyish black hair with deep red highlights through it that pair well with her dark skin. She is wearing a trendy high-collared shirt and tailored vest with embossed gold vines stitched all over it.

"I mean, seriously, how gross is that?" Larissa says as she carelessly slams the wine bottle in the middle of the table.

Roz, a plump brown-haired woman with a perm, snatches the bottle to refill her glass which is still a third full.

"I wish I had that problem."

Larissa cocks one eyebrow. "What? Having some inconsiderate bitch leaving her coochie sweat all over the seat?"

The others laugh.

Roz says, "No, having time to even got to the gym."

A woman who frowns too much and is wearing a Boho Kimono, Lynne, puffs on a vape. A cloud of blueberry scented smoke escapes her lips as she speaks. "Gyms are full of posers. It's a glorified pick-up joint under the guise of social superiority."

Chantel, the oldest of the group and dressed conservatively in a fitted light blue suit, takes the wine bottle from Roz's hand the second she finishes filling her glass, and proceeds to do the same with hers. "Even at the women-only gyms, everyone's all dressed up like Gucci mannequins."

Lynne says, "Ugh. I wouldn't set foot in a regular gym. All those lecherous men staring for the moment they can spot some kind of cleavage, above or below."

Lynne tries to suppress a laugh that comes out a snort from her nose.

Roz says, "Cleavage from below?"

Lynne raises an eyebrow and nonchalantly says, "Camel toe, dear."

"Oh."

Larissa swills the wine around in her glass and says, "I'd like to go into a normal gym. Walk right to the beefcake weight area, catch a guy's attention. Share a flirty smile, and get his hopes up, then drop chainsaw fart, and maintain eye contact the whole time."

They all laugh boisterously.

Chantel says, "That'd probably turn them on. Make 'em think of anal sex or something. And what's with all this 'eating ass' trend? Everyone's out there licking each other's shitters according to the internet."

Roz screws up her face in disgust. "Come on. I'm trying to digest food here."

"Where do you think that digested food ends up?"

Raucous laughter from the whole table.

Lynne says, "Seriously through, the easiest thing next to dunking a tea bag in hot water is getting a man to blow his load."

They all laugh.

Roz turns dunking a tea bag gesture into a blowjob insinuation. "When's the last time you dunked your tea?"

Lynne sucks on her vape and gives Roz the middle finger with a deadpan expression.

Chantel says, "The last time I did that, Hotmail was still a thing."

Roz and Larissa chortle.

Larissa says, "Actually, I once blew this dude in a movie cinema. I can't exactl-"

"Ahem!" Roz cuts her off and narrows her eyes suggestively to Larissa, then flicks her eyes to the side in a warning that someone is behind her.

Larissa twists around in her seat to find Sally standing in the dining room doorway. Her hair a wild mess and her disheveled clothing a stark contrast to the ladies around the table.

"It's only Sally. Finish the story," says Lynne apathetically.

"Hey Twinkie. Come join us." Larissa motions for Sally to grab a spare chair under the baroque mirror on one of the walls.

Everyone waves genially to Sally, except Lynne, whose wave is half-hearted at best. Sally meekly waves back to the group, eyeing off Lynne smoking huge puffs from her vape the clouds the air around her. Sally's eyes flick to her with creased eyes for a second.

"I've been trying to call you," says Larissa.

Sally looking back to Larissa. "Didn't you get my text?"

"Yeah. But you didn't answer your phone all afternoon."

"Um, yeah. My phone died."

Larissa furrows her brows. "But it rang out every time I tried."

Sally tugging at the back of her hair anxiously. "Oh, right. Yeah. That was before it died."

Lynne grins quietly to herself, loving watching Sally squirm her way through an obvious lie.

"Okay," Larissa says with obvious doubt, but not wanting a full blown argument to happen in front of her friends. "Have you eaten?"

Sally nods, now wondering if there's any crusted remains of her vomit on her face or clothes from earlier. She unobtrusively strides over to the mantle on the opposite wall from the mirror and takes a lavender scented incense stick from a long wooden box, places it in the holder and lights it up with trembling hands.

Larissa glances at Lynne smoking her vape and immediately knows Sally is passively aggressively telling her to stop by lighting the incense. She is about to say something to Lynne, but remembers she gave her the okay to smoke at the table two wine bottles ago.

"We ordered Thai, Twinkie. There's heaps of leftovers if you wanna grab a plate in the kitchen," says Larissa.

"I'm good, thanks." Sally walks over to Larissa and gives her a peck on the lips. She looks over to see Roz's wine glass is on the bare table and not on the coaster next to the glass. She thinks about correcting the situation but knows that her effort will make her seem bitchy. Sally straightens up and clasps her hands together, giving her best fake smile.

"Well. It was nice to see you all. I, ah, have to go over the results from today's experiment. Sorry I can't stay and hang out."

The ladies all give her courteous smiles, except of course Lynne, still sucking on her vape. Larissa takes Sally's hand in her and gives it a squeeze, then blinks her eyes shut tightly with a loving smile.

"We won't be too loud."

Sally nods, then sheepishly scurries out of the room.

Larissa says, "What were we talking about again?"

"Blowjobs and men in movie theatres," says Lynne.

Larissa takes a deep breath, then says, "Who wants some cheese?"

◦※◦

Shubert's Symphony No. 1 in D Major plays on a portable speaker next to Larissa while she hand-washes the fine China plates in the kitchen sink. Clay pots growing herbs, from cilantro to parsley, hang from long chains all around the room. The black marble countertops perfectly match the black and white tiles. Display cases housing Larissa's proud collection of fine China and Moroccan dishes and cups. A chilled wine fridge filled with white, a large multi-level wine rack next to it houses the reds.

Sally silently appears in the entrance to the kitchen that shares the same space as the informal dining area where the two of them usually eat breakfast on the quaint round wooden table. Sally is in her old plush khaki bathrobe with frayed ends from having gone through the dryer too many times. She's hugging her favorite red mug to her chest, cupped with both hands. She watches Larissa wash the last of the coffee cups, taking in the classical music a moment, then glides over to the stainless steel kettle and flicks it on.

Larissa hears the kettle firing up and looks up into the window's reflection in front of her to see Sally behind her pulling a cannister of loose-leaf tea out of the pantry.

"Hey you," says Larissa.

Sally notices a bunch of pink roses on the counter, sitting in a crystal vase. She screws her face up.

"Ugh. Pink roses. Who gave them to you?"

"Some new sleaze at the firm who hasn't figured out I'm a rug muncher yet."

Sally reaches over to a hanging pot and plucks a sprig of fresh lemongrass and drops it in her mug.

"How was dinner with the girls?"

"You mean the bitch session? Roz broke up with Amanda, again. You know how it goes."

Sally nods, staring at the boiling kettle blankly.

Larissa says, "I thought you were going to join us for dinner."

Sally spoons tea into a metal strainer, not saying anything.

Larissa rolls her eyes to herself, sighing silently as she pulls the plug from the sink. "How did it go today?"

"Huh?"

"Your project."

Sally fidgets with the now filled tea strainer. "Oh. Um. Yeah. I mean, no. It's not going as well as I'd hoped."

The loud sucking sound of the last remnants of water swirl down the sink. Larissa flicking the excess soap suds off her hands into the sink, then grabs a tea towel to dry them.

Sally gently places the strainer in the mug, then turns around slowly to look at Larissa who takes a sip of wine from her glass on the counter.

Sally purses her lips a moment, then says, "I did, sorta, get into a little car accident today."

Larissa slams the wine glass on the counter harder than she meant to, almost shattering it.

"And you didn't tell me until now?!"

"There was no reception out there. And later, you had your friends here."

"Fuck them. Honestly Sally." She shakes her head and rubs the bridge of her nose.

"I'm okay."

"For fuck's sake. Why didn't you call me?"

"I was out in the sticks. I said, there was no service. I said I'm fine. The car's fine. I just went off the road into a snowbank. The only damage was a little headache."

The kettle finishes boiling and snaps off.

Sally says, "Anyway, did you really need me to be here? I mean, they talk over the top of me all the time. And I'm pretty certain Lynne hates me."

"Why do you think that?"

Sally cocks her head and gives her a mindful look.

Larissa shrugs. "Well, you kinda insulted her little princess Elenore."

"No I didn't. I said she should have adopted, not gotten her from a puppy mill."

Larissa takes another sip of wine and shrugs. "Look, Lynne doesn't like anyone except herself anyway. So I wouldn't get your panties in a twist."

"I didn't. I'm just saying that my presence wasn't missed."

Larissa places the glass down gently this time and steps over to Sally, placing her hands on either side of Sally's cheeks affectionately. "I missed you." She gives her a soft, lingering kiss on the lips, then pulls back and looks into Sally's eyes with a little concern. "Did you have one of your... fits?"

Sally lets out a deep sigh and looks away. Larissa gently forces her face to look into hers again.

"Oh Twinkie. I don't care if you can't make it to dinner. I just wanna know you're safe, is all. I don't like you driving out in the middle of butt-fucksville by yourself. Y'know, with your anxiety and all. And the fact you've been off your meds."

"You agreed it was a good idea to trial it."

"I know," Larissa says using her thumbs to massage under Sally's eyes.

After a moment, Sally breaks free of Larissa's tender touch and reaches over to pick up the kettle. "I'm sorry. I was a bit shaken. And, I needed some... I dunno... clarity. I was in the woods, and, and...," she pours boiling water into the mug and slams the kettle back down, now looking at Larissa with fierce determination.

"I want a baby."

Larissa lowers her head to look at the floor a moment, a slight grin sprouting. She reaches under the counter and pulls out a white metal stool to sit on.

"I know you do, beautiful. And I've applied to all the best agencies. We're in the waiting game, and it takes time. We've discussed this."

Sally shakes her head and gently rubs her tummy.

"No. I want to grow it." She picks up the hot mug and takes a sip. She winces in pain. Too hot. She places the mug back on the counter. "And my clock's ticking."

Larissa shrugs, throwing out her arms in a gesture of agreement. "Okay. Alright. But I thought you said the artificial way was too sterile."

"It is." Sally starts playing with hair on the back of her head. "That's why I want to do it... naturally. With a partner."

"Naturally?"

Sally picks up the mug again, knowing it's too hot, but it gives her something to focus her anxiety away from. She brings it to her mouth and blows on it a few times while Larissa blinks, trying to figure out what Sally means. She notices Sally's shaky hands. Then it hits her.

"Honey. Do you have any idea what you're...," Larissa stands up so they are once again face-to-face, pushing the stool aside. "No. No fucking way."

"I need to do this."

"I? No, we. And this is fucking ridiculous. You've never even been with a man before. Hell, you've never even kissed one."

"Yes I have."

"Your brother doesn't count. You two were dumb kids experimenting. You can't just-" Larissa bunches her fists and makes an angry growl sound, stamping her foot. "I swear you live on another fucking planet sometimes, Sally!"

Larissa paces back and forth for a few moments. She stops after being hit with a bolt of realization. She spins around and points at Sally with an accusing finger.

"This is about before, isn't it?"

"What?"

"The fucking blowjob comment."

"Don't be stupid."

"Does it make you feel left out that you've never fucked a man before?" She scoffs, giving Sally an incredulous smile. "Poor little inexperienced Sally. Never ridden a cock."

Sally slams the mug on the counter, hot tea spilling everywhere.

"I don't want a fuck, you selfish cunt!"

Larissa's eyes bolt wide open in shock. She's never heard Sally use that word before.

Sally says, "This baby is going to be mine. Because it's my body. My eggs." Her eyes welling with tears. "No stupid policeman can accost me. No arbitrary laws can take it away."

"Policeman? What are you-"

"No more agencies. No test tubes. No, no, no, illegitimate third parties. It should be conceived from the substances, that, that, that, the universe, that, that, creation intended. It's my right!" Sally slams her closed fist on the counter.

"What about my rights, Sally? I'm your partner. Your lover. Doesn't my say count for anything?"

"You don't even want a child."

"Fuck you. When did I say that?"

Sally huffs aggrievedly and storms out of the room.

Larissa calling after her. "When did I say that?!"

A door slams somewhere in the house.

Larissa shouts at the top of her lungs. "Okay, great. Archetypal Sally fashion it is! Just walk away when she can't handle it. Who's the selfish cunt?!"

Larissa strides to her wine glass and necks the rest of the glass. She wipes her mouth angrily. She picks up a set of keys from a ceramic bowl on the counter and pitches them across the kitchen, hitting the back door.

"Bitch!"

Moonlight pours through the French bay doors in the living room, casting a waxen glow over the ornate matching leather upholstery.

Sally is lying on the couch, snugged up in a thick blanket and playing with a sunflower, twirling it around in her fingertips. Her eyes red raw from crying on and off the past hour.

A silhouette appears in the main doorway. Larissa standing there in an old blue business shirt and her white knickers. Her arms folded. She takes a deep breath and unfolds her arms, dragging her feet to mosey over to the couch to stand over Sally.

"You awake?"

Sally clears her throat to let Larissa know she's awake.

Larissa looks around the room at nothing in particular, trying to stop herself from crying.

"I'm sorry."

Sally sniffs and wipes her wet nose.

Larissa says, "I'm sorry I insinuated you were jealous… or selfish."

Sally breaks out with a little giggle.

Larissa stomps her foot softly. "Don't laugh at me. This is hard."

Silence. Larissa sighs, throws her hands up in defeat and starts to walk away.

Sally says, "I'm sorry Bunny. It's just… you know how it's funny when it's absolutely not supposed to be."

Larissa stops at the doorframe and grumbles incoherently under her breath. Sally sits up and lifts the blanket up as an invitation. Larissa hesitates a moment, then moseys back to the couch and plonks down next to Sally, who wraps the blanket around them both. They both lie down so Larissa is the little spoon.

Sally says, "I'm sorry for calling you a cunt."

A moment of silence, then Larissa says, "You better be, bitch."

Their bodies vibrate together as they both chuckle. Larissa feels under the blanket and finds Sally's arm, bringing her hand to her mouth and gives it a kiss, then arranges it so her hand is cupping one of her breasts.

"I'm in," says Larissa.

"In what?"

"With your… fucking…," Larissa breathes out calmly, squeezing Sally's hand. "Make me a mommy."

Sally breaks out crying. Larissa maneuvers with a few grunts to now face Sally. Each feeling the other's hot breath in their face. Larissa kisses Sally on her snot dripping nose.

"I love you Twinkie. And I'll do whatever it takes for you to be happy. Even if I don't entirely agree."

"You don't?"

"It's… complicated. And sudden. But I'll come around to it."

"Thank you," says Sally, tasting the salty tears streaming into her mouth.

"Just the thought of you holding our child. Smiling. Cooing it. I can see it. And it fills my cold heart with joy."

Sally bursts out laughing. Larissa smiles.

"So, we'll do it. In the way that you need it to be done. I've got your back, baby. So let's make a baby. And we'll mollycoddle the little shit so much he or she will resent the shit out of us when they talk to their future therapist."

Sally laughs again.

Larissa sighs. "An emotionally fucked up botanist and a cold-hearted lawyer. Can't, fucking, wait."

Sally smiles and wriggles her arm from between them to stroke Larissa's face lovingly.

"You're gonna make a great mom."

Larissa pulls the blanket so it's much tighter around them. They cuddle tightly until they both fall into a deep slumber.

CHAPTER FIVE

CRYING OVER SPILLED MILK

Light snow falls around the cigar-shaped one level concrete building with a fluorescent sign above the entrance that reads: "Cove Bowling Lanes". A smaller blue neon sign next to it reads; "Miller's Now on Tap!" – the 'o' and the 'a' bulbs shorted out long ago. The parking lot half full in one of Great Barrington's signature recreational hangouts.

Glen is in the cabin of his pickup truck in the passenger seat, parked on the outskirts of the lot. Music at medium volume, playing Def Leopard. A permed blonde woman in her early thirties is bouncing on his lap, her panties pushed aside in the rush to get into the action fast. The reason she wore a skirt tonight, despite it being five degrees outside, is for this very scenario. She's moaning and grinding, giving it all she's got. Glen's face is devoid of any emotion. He may as well be hanging laundry. He's only a few beers deep, so it's not the alcohol preventing him from orgasming. He's just not feeling it tonight. Like most sexual interactions he's had in the past couple of years, it's like a chore he feels he has to do to stay relevant. Denise is a nice girl, and this isn't their first rodeo. She's always been nice to him, and right now he feels like he's simply doing her a favor. She climaxes. After a few awkward minutes of trying to release, Glen realizes it's just not going to happen and fakes it.

Denise gets off him and sits in the driver's seat. She readjusts her underwear and pulls a pack of menthol cigarettes, lighting one up, then cracks the window an inch for the smoke to escape.

"Why do I have a feeling that was all for my benefit?" Denise asks.

Glen does his pants and belt up, picking up his half-drunk bottle of beer from the middle compartment in the car.

"What? I came."

Denise huffs a little chuckle, blowing a lungful of air out the window. "Okay," she says, clearly not convinced. "Want one?" she holds out the cigarette packed to him.

"Nah, I'm good. Tryin' to quit."

"And how's that goin'?"

"Pretty good. But, I mean, if those weren't menthols I'd cave right now."

The worn and stained maroon carpet in the bowling alley hasn't been changed in nearly two decades, and neither have the arcade games and pinball machine in the offshoot arcade parlor in the corner near the entrance, where kids and teenagers hang out on their smartphones. Seven of the eight bowling lanes are occupied by families and groups of friends. The TV monitors showing the scores have the software layout burned onto the screens from not having been replaced or turned off in many years.

Denise enters the main glass front doors and rejoins her girl squad in the middle of their bowling game.

Glen comes in a few minutes after Denise and idles up to the bar in the front corner of the building, adjacent to the arcade room. Tables and chairs neatly spaced out in front of a bay window that overlooks the parking lot. The vinyl tablecloths are red and white checkered. Several people scattered through the seating area; a couple of old men drink silently while watching football on a mounted TV screen above the bar. A section of one wall dedicated to old bowling legends of the town for the last 50 or so years. Christmas lights adorn the shelves of liquor bottles, with kitsch décor hanging around, mostly novelty street signs, beer advertisements and wagon wheels.

A pretty woman in her mid-thirties comes through the building's entrance and spots Glen sitting at the bar by himself. She has a little girl in a puffy pink jacket by the hand. She tells her daughter she just wants to speak with a friend quickly, the six-year-old girl rolling her eyes.

"Hey Glen."

Glen turns to find the woman and the girl standing behind him.

"Oh. Hey Lisa."

The two adults have the stiff politeness of two people who have been intimate before. Even Lisa's daughter knows something is up.

Lisa says, "Me and Lexy here are gonna knock the crap outta some pins."

Glen smiles and nods.

After an awkward moment, Lisa says, "If, ah, you wanted to come join us, you're more than welcome."

Glen waves at Lexy. The kind of fingertip waggling wave people tend to give three-year old's. Lisa gives her daughter a nudge and she gives a shy uninterested hello back. Glen looks back to Lisa and takes a deep breath, shrugging helplessly.

Glen says, "That would be great, 'cept I gotta sit for Janeen's kids tonight."

Lisa smiles, though clearly hiding her disappointment. "Well, alrighty then. If things change, you'll know where we'll be."

Glen smiles and nods. "We should definitely do it again sometime." He swallows hard, instantly realizing how that sounded. "Bowling, I mean."

Lexy watching the two adults awkwardly touching their hair and darting their eyes around.

Lisa, now brandishing a reddened face, says, "I'd love that." She pulls Lexy. "Come on, let's go see what ya got kiddo."

The two of them head off to the main desk by the entrance.

"Sittin' for my kids, huh?"

Glen turns his attention back to the bar where a fresh glass of beer has just been placed on the faded Coors beer mat in front of him. The person who delivered it is Janeen, a plump-hipped woman in her late thirties. Her hair is curly matted orange. She has firm blue eyes just like Glen's, and a no-nonsense air about her.

"Well, I am, ain't I?" says Glen.

"I don't knock off for another half hour. You could have fit in a game with her."

Glen sighs, his eyes fixed on the bubbling amber beer.

"I don't want it anymore, Jan."

"Well tough tiddies. It's poured now. So shut up and drink it."

Janeen picks up a wet cloth and wipes the condensation off the beer tap closest to her.

"Everyone was harkin' on about getting more beer on tap. So I finally listen. And not a damn soul drinks the shit." Janeen tosses the rag down the inside of the bar. "Don't I look like the donkey's ass."

Glen takes a long sip, then wipes the foam moustache from his upper lip. "I'm drinkin' it, ain't I?"

"You don't have a choice," Janeen says with a crooked grin and piercing stare. Her eyes then fix on Glen's bandaged hand, then back to his face. "When are you gonna get a woman, Glen?"

Glen takes another long sip of beer to delay his answer.

Janeen says, "And I'm not talkin' about a floozy like Denise over there."

Glen gives her a faked look of confusion. She cocks her head with a deadpan expression.

"Come on. You think you're some secret spy, the two of you sneakin' out to your truck like you was back in high school?" She shakes her head with a smirk. "May as well fuck in the disabled bathroom. Save the two of you some time."

"Alright, alright," says Glen, rolling his eyes. "Floozy? What is this, the nineteen-fifties?"

"Don't try and be cute. I mean it. It's time. You ain't getting' younger. And Lisa's the real deal. She's the kinda woman who would take good care of ya."

"Not now, Jan. I ain't in the mood getting' into this shit."

"You're sittin' in my bar, in my alley, you'll listen to what I have to say. Now, you've been bangin' every short skirt that comes your way. And that's cute if you're a fuck boy. Thing is, you're in your forties. Sure, you still look good. But one day you're gonna wake up and look like Father Time whooped your ass UFC style. There's plenty of good, caring women in this vicinity. But you're either too stupid, or, well, too stupid, to let one of them take care of ya like only a devoted partner can." Janeen's eyes flick to Lisa and Lexy now putting on their bowling shoes by the main desk. "You sit up in your lonely old house, dwellin' on the past day and night, like you can actually do anything about it. You're hurtin' big bro. You need a family."

Janeen puts her closed fist on either of her hips, staring at Glen irately.

"Jesus, Jan. Lay off, would ya?" He takes a sip of beer and slams it back on the mat. "Besides. You're family ain't ya?"

"I'm your sister. We're family by default. I play therapist to my husband and nurse to my three kids, and that's enough for me to handle. Plus running this joint. Which hasn't been easy. I got it cheap, thanks to Covid, but when I finally fix something, another thing breaks. Still, it's doin' good enough." She makes a prayer symbol with her hands and looks up to the ceiling. "Thank you Covid."

An older man a few seats down the bar gives Janeen a greasy look. Janeen turns her body on his direction. "Christ Dale, I was joking."

Dale scowls and sips his bourbon, looking back up to the TV screen above him.

Janeen leans over the bar to Glen and lowers her voice. "I wasn't joking," she says with a wink.

Glen smiles and nods.

Janeen raps her knuckles on the bar top next to Glen's bandaged hand.

"Anyway, the point is, you gotta stop cryin' over spilled milk, and find that special someone to help you clean it up."

"Okay, alright. I got your point. Think everyone else in the bar did too. Are ya done?"

Janeen sighs and waves him off. "I fuckin' wish."

Janeen turns sharply and moseys down the bar to attend to a new customer. Glen leans forward and hunches his shoulders, sipping on his beer.

Three kids, from five to eleven, come bounding through the front entrance to the alley, bouncing off the walls with energy. They are accompanied by a man in police uniform. Brian.

"Go see Jerry at the desk to get shoes. And make it quick. We got time for one game, okay?" says Brian to his children.

They all give him assurances and dash off to the main desk, cartwheeling and skipping their way over.

Brian ambles over to the bar and eases on the stool next to Glen.

"Hey Glen. How's it hangin'?"

"Not bad Brian. You just clock off now?"

"Yeah, had to pick up the kids from school and take them back to headquarters to fill out a mound of paperwork."

"Got yourself a big fish today, huh?"

"Nah, pretty far from it. Some city lady obsessed with plants. Caught her out in the Berkshires in a state-run forest, doin' some weird experiments. Would've let her off with a small fine, but she kept on fightin' me, so I hauled her ass in with some charges."

Glen nods slowly, sipping on his beer. Janeen appears with a bottle of soda for Brian, not saying a word to her husband, then meanders off down the bar again.

"Say, Glen. You know anything about plant soil?"

Glen shakes his head aloofly, running his fingers down the beads of water on the outside of his beer glass.

"Not really. Why?"

"Nothin' really. You're an outdoors kinda guy." He sips his cola and waves Glen off like it's no big deal. "Ah, forget it."

Janeen is back in front of them, hands on hips.

"Our first date night in months, and you can't be bothered gettin' dressed for it?"

"Honey, I got kept behind at work. Big fish today, y'know?" Brian's eyes flick to Glen a moment, then back to his wife. "You're lucky I'm even on time."

Janeen scoffs, shaking her head in amazement. "I'm *lucky?*" she says with bite.

Brian again glances at Glen for some kind of support. Glen simply raises his hands defensively.

"You two have fun now," says Glen standing up from the stool. He knocks back the rest of his beer. "I'm gonna take the kids and grab pizza. See you two at home later. Have fun, lovebirds."

Glen tries to a smart-ass grin but isn't very successful. He leaves Brian with a toe-tappingly irate Janeen.

"Can I have some strawberry ice cream?" says Alex, the youngest of the three siblings at five years old, as he marches into the rumpus room in his house.

"You had some after dinner," says Glen as he connects Lego pieces together.

Kaylee, eight years old, has been putting together a Lego set of a fairytale castle, and now Glen the babysitter is her assistant.

Alex holds his arms together and sways side to side in frustration. "But that was before."

"And now we're in the after," says Glen.

"So?" Alex giving Glen a forlorn look, even though Glen is concentrating on building the castle and paying him no attention. "You only have us three scoops. Mom gives us...," he thinks a moment, "Mom gives us six." He holds out his fingers and slowly counts to six.

Glen chuckles under his breath and shakes his head. "No she doesn't."

"Yes she does," Alex says, now pouting.

The warbling sound of radio frequency changes can be heard in the living room next door. Braden, the oldest sibling at eleven, is playing with Brian's old police Walkie-Talkie, trying to tune it so he can hear someone on it talking somewhere, be it a truck driver or cops.

"Did you know the first people to build castles were called Normans?" says Kaylee.

"Really?" Glen says with feigned interest.

"Yep. And they built them on hills so they could see the enemy coming," Kaylee says with pride.

"That's cool." Glen finishes the stable he's been building and places it on the set next to the castle under construction. "Who are the Normans?"

"Huh?" says Kaylee, her pride now evaporating.

"You said these Norman guys were the first. Who were they?"

Kaylee shrugs, now pouting, and says quietly, "I dunno."

Glen now realizing he accidentally stole her thunder. "Well, that's a cool fact anyway."

"Pleeeaaaasssseee, can I have some ice cream?"

"I said no, buddy. But maybe I'll make us all some cocoa before bed."

"I don't want cocoa. I want strawberry ice cream."

"Look Alex, I'm letting you guys stay up later than you're allowed. Cut me some slack, okay?"

Alex furrows his brows, still holding his arms together behind his back. "What's slack?"

"It's… um… like when you have rope, and you…,' Glen trails off, not sure how to explain it to a kindergartener.

The radio frequency now becoming louder in Glen's head. The high and low pitches feeling like a knife cutting through his brain.

"Hey Braden, can you turn down the volume on that thing?"

"It's already low volume," Braden calls out.

The static and warbling piercing Glen's mind so much he can't hear anything else. Kaylee is reading out facts about the Normans she just googled on her smartphone, but he can't quite hear her words over the Walkie-Talkie sounds. Alex is stomping his foot and begging for ice cream, but Glen can't hear him either. Glen opens his eyes as wide as he can, the high pitches are causing the back of his eyeballs to feel like they're being pushed out of their sockets. Then he hears a voice. A female voice. It starts off low and the words unrecognizable to Glen, but then the clarity becomes sharper. He hears "I don't want a fuck you selfish cunt!" boom in his head.

"Braden! Turn that thing down!"

"I told you Uncle Glen, it's on the lowest setting."

"I can hear a voice on there loud as hell."

"I don't hear any voices. It's just static."

Glen groans and puts his face in his hands, rocking back and forth in his bow-legged sitting position. "No stupid laws can take it away! No agencies, no test tubes, no, no, no illegitimate third parties", the female voice now echoing in his mind like she's in an acoustically padded room. "The, the, the universe, that, that creation intended. It's my right!" The last words pounding in Glen's head so harshly it feels like his skull is about to burst open.

"Turn that fucking thing off!" Glen screams at Braden at the top of his lungs.

The three children freeze. Eyes wide. Kaylee's jaw dropped.

Braden quickly switches the power knob on the Walkie-Talkie off.

The radio frequency waves now quickly dissipate in Glen's mind. He breathes out a long exhale of relief. The pain in his head subsiding. There's still a remnant of a headache in Glen's mind, but he can hear his surroundings again. He quickly rises and steps over to take the shocked Alex up in his arms.

"Hey buddy. Y'know what. Let's have some ice cream." Glen looks to Kaylee, then to Braden sitting in the armchair through the doorway to the next room. "How about we all have ice cream?"

Kaylee nods, fighting back tears, staring at the Google results on her phone screen. Braden sheepishly places the Walkie-Talkie on the coffee table in front of him.

"That'd be great, Uncle Glen."

"I'm sorry about the swear word. And the yelling," Glen says as he bounces Alex in his arms. "Tell you three what. If I give you guys another bowl of ice cream, you don't tell mom or dad about that, okay? Deal?"

They all nod their heads in unison.

"Good," says Glen with a beaming smile he has to force.

"The Normans come from France. It's a place called Normandy."

"Oh, cool, Kaylee" says Glen. "The place the soldiers landed in World War Two." Glen looks to Alex, who has calmed down now. "Wanna help me prepare the second dessert?"

Alex nods, starting to smile again. Kaylee now typing away in Google, 'Normandy World War Two' and reading the results.

CHAPTER SIX

THE GARDENER AND THE HUNTER

Sally wakes on the couch flustered and hot. She has been in and out of sleep for the last few hours. Sometimes Larissa's leg kicks hers. Sometimes a street noise like a car horn or loud passers-by. This time because Sally's throat is parched, and her skin feels like it's on fire. She figures it must be menopause coming on. Her heart beating faster thinking about that. No, she can't have her reproductive hormones starting to decline now, not now of all times. She has read that it can onset in one's thirties. She carefully climbs over Larissa's passed out body. Her mouth agape and a pool of saliva on the pillow next to it.

Sally goes to the downstairs guest bathroom and splashes her face with cold water and cups her hands under the running faucet, leaning down to slurp the water. She takes a long moment to look at herself in the mirror. Focusing on her crows-feet and other wrinkles she's never noticed before. She asks herself why she had to wait this long to decide to have a baby naturally. All those young healthy years wasted. Sally opens the mirrored cabinet above the sink and takes a bottle of heavy-duty sleeping pills. She pops a couple in her mouth and slurps water from her hands again to wash them down. She'll get on it first thing in the morning. No time to waste now. But first, she needs a decent night's sleep.

Sally navigates her way through the dark rooms in the house. She doesn't want to wake Larissa on the couch trying to climb in and get comfortable. Moonlight coming through windows giving her guidelines to follow until she reaches the master bedroom. Their bed upstairs still neatly made. Sally tosses the decorative pillows from the bed and slides into the welcoming cool sheets that feel amazing on her hot skin. She takes one of the pillows and shoves it down so the bottom of her feet rest on it. She splays out her arms and tries to relax, despite the menopause possibility running through her head. She tries to change her mind's subject. She pictures a deer's face, chewing slowly on grass. It's not working, so she imagines a big brown grizzly bear eating fresh honeycomb with angry bees buzzing around it. That's better. She does all she can to keep that scenario there. She concentrates on her breathing. The pills starting to kick in now. She slowly drifts off into a deep slumber, then her body enters REM.

A rolling field with rows upon rows of bright purple lavender as far as the eye can see. Despite it being daytime, the light blue sky bleeds into another violet night sky above it. A massive ringed planet resembling Saturn hangs in the second sky, the bottom end of the rings dipping into the blue day sky with a dazzling array of stars twinkling around the planet. The forever appearing lavender field bears a small green lonesome tree, poking out amongst the dizzying purple plants. Small flickers of light dance around the tree trunk like drunken fireflies, some of them shooting out into the lavender field and frolic on the tops of the plants.

Sally steps out from behind the tree. She's wearing a flowing white silk dress and carrying an old-fashioned red watering can. Her feet bare, she walks on the soft fertile dirt. She moseys through the rows of lavender, sprinkling them with water from the metal can. She has a lighthearted smile on her face, completely in her element.

A small flame bursts out on a lavender plant several yards from her. She blinks a moment out of confusion, then drifts over to the fire quickly and douses it with water. The flame now gone, Sally resumes her smile like nothing happened. A 'whoomph' sound behind her. She turns around to find another flame has erupted on a lavender plant ten feet away. Without hesitation she dashes over to it and tips water on it until the fire is out.

The unmistakable sound of dogs barking, somewhere in the distance. Sally peers around at the horizon in all directions but cannot spot any dogs.

Another flame erupts further down the field. Sally groans and runs to it, her white dress ends flailing out behind her. Before she reaches it, she catches another fire burning in her peripheral vision from another direction and she skids to a halt in the dirt, which now feels a little crusty as opposed to the softness before. She frantically looks between the two fires, trying to decide which one is closer and which to go for first.

The barking dogs turn more ferocious. Snapping their jaws and gnarling with bloodlust. It seems to Sally there's more dogs this time. She again tries to locate them but can't see any living creatures in her view.

Sally desperately races to one of the flames, tripping over on her dress and sprawling forward into lavender plants. She rolls over, reaching out for the watering can on the ground nearby. A big puddle of spilled water all around it. She picks it up. It's empty.

"No!"

Sally crawls frenziedly to the nearest flame on her hands and knees. She reaches it and tries to bat it out with her bare hands. The flame sizzles her skin forcing her to recoil in pain. She looks at the palms of her hands which have third-degree burns on them. She wails, then tries to put the fire out again with the backs of her hands, only burning them too. She picks up the watering can and desperately starts hammering the flames with it, only making it grow and worsen.

The flames now several feet high and growing. The heat from the towering flames force her to scurry backward. Her skin burning all over just like her hands. She lets out a cry. Then she sees a figure through the sweltering haze. She peers closer to discern that it's a woman. Sally can't see her face, but she can see that she's wearing a sexy figure hugging bright yellow dress and holding the leashes for seven huskie dogs. All of them ravenously barking and snarling at Sally with foaming mouths.

Sally is frozen with awe and wonder. While absolutely terrifying to her, she is aloofly entranced by the shimmering colors and the majestic woman keeping the dogs from ripping her apart.

The woman suddenly vanishes, along with the canines. The flame poofs out of existence. The blue sky is gone and replaced with a star speckled night sky. A full moon casts a metallic glow on the lavender field, the plants now all encrusted with a layer of thin ice. Sally's breaths now turn to frost in front of her eyes.

BANG!

The clack sound of a gunshot echoes out over the valley. Sally whips her head around in all directions. She can't see anyone. She turns around again. Where there was nothing but small hills of lavender there before, is now the lining of a thick pine tree forest. The tree branches coated with snow.

Sally scans the edge of the forest. Then she sees it. A figure emerging out of the foliage. She can discern that it is a man now, by the way he lumbers as he walks. He has long hair pulled back into a ponytail. Sally also notices he is carrying a long hunting rifle, the barrel exuding smoke from recent discharge. The man stops twenty or so yards from her and raises his rifle to aim at her, staring intently through the target scope.

Sally freezes in terror. Nowhere to run and hide. This is it.

Looking through the target scope at a deer in the middle of an icy lavender field, Glen readies his trigger finger to shoot the animal. The deer is looking right at him. Glen blinks a moment, wondering why the deer hasn't decided to make a run for it. He lowers the scope to stare at the animal with his naked eye. He slowly takes another look at his surroundings. He's now back deep in the forest. Towering pine trees all around him. The forest floor is bleached with snow. Odd lavender plants poke up through the powder. Glen's face twists with confusion. Didn't he just step out into a field? What is he doing back in the forest?

Now there are colorful flowers of all kinds popping up through the snow. Lillies. Orchids. Roses. Sunflowers. Carnations.

Glen looks ahead where the deer was. Now it's a woman. Standing there in a forest clearing in a long white flowing silk dress stained with dirt. Her strawberry blonde hair wild and free like a lion's mane. She's looking right at him with an expression of helplessness and fear. Glen brings the rifle up to his face again and peers through the scope. The target now has the deer in sight again. Without hesitation Glen pulls the trigger.

BANG!

Sally's eyes bolt wide open with shock. She looks down to find a burnt hole in her dress right above her naval. Smoke wisps up from the fresh wound. Sally quickly clamps her hand over the gunshot wound. She expects blood to start gushing out at any moment. Sand starts pouring out through the cracks in her interlocked fingers.

Sally looks up to find the hunter marching purposefully toward her now. She turns and runs toward the green tree in the middle of the lavender field as pine trees start appearing out of nowhere all around her, forcing her to weave and duck under branches and around tree trunks. The pear tree now becoming obstructed from her view by the newly appearing pines. She realizes she is not moving fast at all. Her legs seem to be moving but it doesn't feel like she's gaining much ground.

Frustrated, she keeps slogging through the forest, but it feels like her legs are heavy weights. In an effort to change her strategy, she turns around and tries running backward. She can see the hunter gaining on her, striding through the forest like a determined machine. He's getting closer and closer while she feels like she's becoming slower and slower. The sand still oozing out of her weaved fingers over her belly.

Sally stops and hides behind a massive tree truck. A few moments go by and she carefully peers around the side of the tree. The hunter seems to have vanished. Sally looks around in all directions. Just a dense, quiet forest. Then something catches her eye. The woman in the tight yellow gown moseys through the trees in the distance. Sally squints to see her better but can't get a decent look as the mystery woman disappears behind a thick bush. She looks down to find the sand has stopped pouring out. She slowly removes her hands to reveal there is no longer a gunshot wound. Her dress immaculate again.

Sally again turning around to stare intensely in all directions. Then she spots the hunter again. He's not coming at her now. He's kneeling down several yards away, hunched over and facing away from her in a patch of lavender plants. She cautiously takes a few steps toward him, now intrigued rather than afraid. She can hear the wailing of a baby. Sally watches as the hunter lifts an infant from the lavender patch in the snow. The baby covered in rich dark soil, falling of it like crumbs from a chocolate sponge cake.

Sally breaks into a run toward the hunter and baby.

"Is that my baby?" she calls out.

The hunter is staring at the baby in his hands with consternation.

"Is that my baby!?" she repeats, hiking up her dress as she dashes barefoot through the powdery snow blanketed forest floor.

The hunter slowly turns to look at Sally running at him. He now looks lost, and slightly afraid.

"Is that my baby!?"

"I... I don't know," he says.

Sally reaches him with her arms held out desperately.

The hunter hands Sally the baby gently. She takes it in her arms and cradles it to her chest. Sally looks at the man with tears of joy welling in her eyes. He stares back, eyes blinking slowly from feeling overwhelmed.

Sally looks back down at the baby in her tight grasp. It's not a baby anymore. She's cradling a big heap of thick dirt and fertilizer. Out of shock, she opens her arms and the dirt slowly breaks apart and crumbles to her feet.

Sally looks back at Glen and lets out a bloodcurdling scream.

Glen jumps to sit bolt upright in the armchair he fell asleep in. His face shiny with sweat and his breathing heavy gasps. He drags a palm over his face to collect as much sweat as he can and clears his throat.

Janeen is standing five feet away with folded arms, staring at him with knitted eyebrows of puzzlement.

"Is that my baby?" she says with a confused visage.

CHAPTER SEVEN

MUMBO-JUMBO SPECIALIST CRAP

Brian opens the freezer in the kitchen and pulls out the tub of straw-berry ice cream. He removes the lid to find the tub is nearly empty. He peers through two doorways where he can see his wife conversing with Glen, still seated on the chair where he was passed out when they came back from their date night five minutes ago. Brian is a mixture of confused and disappointed at the lack of ice cream. He deduces Glen must have had a few too many and got the drunk sweet tooth. Brian picks up a slightly dirty spoon from the dishwasher and wipes it on his pants, knowing they are going straight into the dirty clothes hamper, and starts eating what ice cream is left out of the tub.

Glen wipes his face again to collect what sweat is still on his face from the intense dream.

Janeen says, "You were tossin' and turnin' like you were bacon fryin' in the pan."

"A bad dream is all."

"It's called a nightmare."

"No. It wasn't. It was just weird. Like it wasn't even my dream, or...,' Glen now deep in thought trying to think to even himself how to describe it. He looks up at Janeen standing over him, he shakes his head and shrugs, then stands up. "Never mind. It was just a damn dream anyway. Means nothin'." He sticks his thumb out and points it to the ceiling. "The kids are in bed and sleepin' sound."

"I think you were sleeping sounder than they are."

Glen collects the few empty beer bottles from the coffee table that he left there before passing out.

"Did you get a girl knocked up?" asks Janeen.

"Huh?" Glen staring at her incredulously. "No. What kinda question's that?"

"You kept sayin', 'is that my baby?', 'is that my baby?', over and over again."

Glen strides to the kitchen, Janeen immediately following him.

Janeen says, "What baby?"

"I told ya, it was a stupid God damn dream. It means fuck all."

Glen now at the sink and opens the cabinet underneath, dropping the empty beer bottles in the recycling trash can. They tinker and crash with several other empty beer bottles he put in there earlier.

"Hey. You'll wake the kids," Janeen says in a hushed hiss.

"Sorry."

"What happened to all the ice cream?"

Glen and Janeen look over to find Brian in the corner, police uniform still on and ice cream tub in his hands with pink stains around his mouth.

"Ah, yeah. I'll leave you some cash."

Brian says, "I thought you didn't like ice cream."

"I don't."

"But it's all gone. Most of it anyway. I just picked this up the other day."

Glen scratches his head. "I had a few beers. Y'know how it goes."

Brian grins. "I knew it."

Glen rubs his chin and flicks his eyes between his sister and brother-in-law. "How was your date, anyway?"

Janeen takes a deep breath and eyes Brian with a plain expression.

"Why don't you tell him how it went, dear?"

Brian calmly puts the empty ice cream tub on the counter and wipes the residue from around his mouth.

"The place she wanted to go was booked out. So we went to Bridie's instead."

Glen nods with a feigned expression of interest. "Can't go wrong with Bridie's."

Janeen scoffs and shakes her head. "Bridie's is a fuckin' bar."

"They serve food don't they?" says Brian pleadingly.

"The steaks there are actually really good," says Glen meekly. "Best in town in my opinion."

"I told him I ain't been out in months. I want to go to Fratelli's. I want somewhere fancy. He says, 'sure babe, anything you want'. Then the blockhead doesn't book ahead. On a damned Friday night. You can't just waltz into a place like that as you please on a busy night and expect them to have a table ready."

"I'm sorry. It was a busy week. I was gonna call, sweetheart."

"Busy week? Don't get me started, Brian. Did you help the kids with their homework this week? Did you build a fuckin' model volcano for Kaylee's science project? Did you rack your fuckin' brains pretending to know calculus for Braden? Did you have to fuckin' sew a whole giraffe outfit for Alex's play?"

Brian is staring at the floor. "Alright. Okay."

"No, don't you alright me. I asked you to do one thing. One fuckin' phone call."

"Keep your voice down, honey. The kids."

Janeen puts her hands on her hips and lets out a long guttural groan.

"I'm sorry honey. I'll make it up to you. I promise. We'll go to Fratelli's next week."

"I'm busy next week," Janeen says before storming out of the room.

Glen and Brian share a sheepish look for a moment, then Brian wipes his hand on a tea towel. "I gotta get outta this uniform."

"No probs, man. Good seein' ya."

"Yeah, you too, Glen."

Brian nods, clearly embarrassed, and strides out of the kitchen to the carpeted staircase leading upstairs.

Janeen reappears in the kitchen with a hamper filled with a load of laundry that had been sitting in the dryer. She sighs, walks over to the counter where Brian left the empty ice cream container. She angrily snatches it and marches to the recycling and shoves it in.

"I was lookin' forward to some nookie tonight. But I don't wanna be doin' that lazy bastard any favors."

Glen claps his hands together and rubs them frenetically. "Right. Well, I best be goin'."

Janeen places the laundry basket on the counter. "I'll walk ya out."

The two of them make their way to the front door via the main carpeted hallway. Glen takes his rugged old jacket from the collection of jackets on the wall next to the door and puts it on, zipping it up. He pulls out his wallet and fishes out a few bills.

"What's that for?"

"For the ice cream."

Janeen waves her hand at him. "Don't be stupid."

Glen shrugs and puts the money back.

"Besides. I know you gave it to the terror trio." She's grinning now. "I know you too well, that even on the drunk munchies you wouldn't touch strawberry ice cream."

Glen smiles, nodding while looking at the floor. "Ya got me."

"About that dream."

"Jan, I told ya, I-"

"Just hear me out."

Glen sighs and places his hand on the wall next to the coats. "Here we go."

"Jackie Gainsbury. She runs the children's clothes shop in town."

"Yeah, I know who she is."

"She goes to Boston once every two weeks to see this therapist."

Glen scoffs and shakes his head. "A fuckin' shrink? Jesus Jan."

"Shut up and listen. She's not just any therapist. She specializes in sleep. Dreams and all that. Jackie says it's been turnin' her life around. She's got recurring nightmares, like you. She said this Yvonne lady listens to her. Even puts her under hypnosis sometimes."

Glen chuckles, looking into thin air. "She do magic tricks too? Y'know, bunny rabbits and shit."

Janeen ignores him and says, "She takes notes and gives you activities to do that focus on your subconscious issues. Those dreams about Joe. She can help with that." Janeen makes it painfully obvious to stare at his bandaged hand. "You could use it."

Glen pushes off the wall and tugs his coat forcefully. "I'll be fine. I certainly don't need a spell cast over me by some wacko shrink."

"It's a legit field of study, Glen. And it's for people like you."

"I bet it's legit alright. Legitimately expensive. I'm guessing this woman charges more than a regular shrink, because of all the specialist bullshit."

"What the hell are you on about?"

"See, the thing is, you can find a shrink for a good price. Because there's so many of 'em. They have to be competitive. Like fast food joints. But when you throw in all this mumbo-jumbo specialist crap, they corner a market. And believe me, I know customers pay a lot extra if they have trouble finding what you're selling elsewhere. It's basic business one-o-one."

"Customers? What the fuck do you sell that's so special?" She laughs. "Rabbit skins?"

"Alright. I'll be seein' ya," Glen says as he lightly brushes her to move aside so he can get to the front door.

"Do one thing for me, Glen. And consider it even with the ice cream if need be."

Glen stops, raising both his eyebrows in fake interest.

"Think about it. Would ya?"

"Think about the therapist?"

"No. The steaks at Bridie's. Of course the fuckin' therapist."

"Yeah. Sure. Fine." Glen not sounding convincing in the slightest.

"Alright, you can fuck off now. Drive safe and whatnot."

Glen opens the door and leaves with a backhanded wave.

Glen is standing naked in front of the fog swathed bathroom mirror. The steam still thick from his morning shower. He rubs his good hand over the mirror creating a small hint of his reflection through the beaded moisture now there.

The faint ringing echoing in the back of his head. It hasn't gone away since the other night's Walkie-Talkie incident. It hasn't grown worse, but it's not gone away either.

Glen opens the mirrored cabinet and finds a switchblade razor. He opens it and places it under the faucet, turning on the hot water. After searing the blade either side for a minute, Glen turns the water off and pulls a small wooden stool from under the sink. He places one foot on it and splays his leg open to bare his thigh. On the inside of his thigh is a collection of twenty or so scars. Small slits in the skin running from the top of his knee to the top of his thigh. Glen places the hot blade on the inside of his thigh and nicks the blade so it creates a fresh slice in his skin. He makes a painful sound sucking skin through his clenched teeth. Blood immediately starts running from the new wound and drops onto the white tiles below. Glen reaches over and grabs a towel off the rack next to him and suppresses the bleeding with it. He tosses the razorblade into the porcelain sink with a clunk sound and holds the towel hard on the wound for a few minutes. He checks to see if the bleeding stopped. Nope. He holds it again for another five minutes, then checks again. It's stopped now. He tosses the towel in an overfilled laundry hamper and half limps, half walks out into his room and puts on some clothes.

Glen feeds Bullit and makes coffee. Bullit seems to like the new dog food Glen picked out for him. He doesn't normally care for organic this, organic that. But Glen thinks the dog should have his diet changed up here and there for variety. Glen eats mostly the same heat-up meals every day and has been for years, and he knows how boring it can be. He doesn't mind the monotony so much, but he figures Bullit shouldn't have to be a depressed old bastard like him.

Glen finishes his coffee and watches his news channel, then meanders outside, trudging through the fresh snow powder to the shack at the rear of the house. After unlocking all the thick padlocks and turning off the alarm system, Glen ambles over to the rug on the floor near the partially restored Mustang. He pulls the carpet back to reveal a trapdoor. He unlocks the two locks on it and pulls the wooden door open.

Glen climbs down the ladder to the basement room below that once served as a bomb shelter. Otherwise a plain cemented room, it's also a professional looking operation with methodically arranged planters growing five-foot-high marijuana plants. Around fifty of them in various stages of grooming. Glen walks by the long metal sterile table bearing the plants, checking temperature gauges and feeling the leaves to ascertain the texture.

A large generator at the rear of the room gives energy to the lights and heat lamps over the plants. A long line of paint buckets housing different types of fertilizer. Glen has started experimenting with different soils and even cross-pollinating. What was once a small business idea has become a hobby. He is proud of his plants, despite the fact he doesn't smoke the shit. He simply loves growing them and gets a kick from the feedback he gets from Teddy. Glen figured that business would rapidly decline after weed became legal in the state years ago. But it hasn't really affected it much. Teddy's customers prefer his stock over government subsidized pot. People complain that it's too expensive. Makes you too paranoid. The feedback from Glen's weed is that it's super chill stuff. A nice floating high, they say.

Glen picks up an old-fashioned water can and fills it in a large sink at the front of the room. He turns on a beat-up old clock radio and country music blares through the room. Glen goes to each plant and delicately waters them.

CHAPTER EIGHT

UNEXPECTED RAIN

Microscopic organisms dance together on a glass microscope casing. An infusion of aerobic bacteria and cyanobacteria that Sally has been working on.

Sally is hunched over and peering intensely through the microscope ocular lens, occasionally adjusting the diopter as the bacteria swell and shrink in front of her eyes. She's wearing a lab coat and face mask. Her hair tightly pulled back into a bun and under a protective cap.

The laboratory she's sitting in is the opposite of Glen's bunker lab greenroom. It's white, sterile and filled with high tech equipment. Digital incubators. BOD analyzers. Blast oven. Multi-purpose computer Sanheng electrophoresis. All the plants are tagged, some in freezers, others in sterile holding cases. Two other lab assistants are busy at work around her. Everyone silent, just the way Sally likes. The face masks make it hard to have a conversation anyway, but to Sally the lack of speaking to her co-workers is bliss. She doesn't much care for them. Matthew is into Dungeons & Dragons type of roleplaying games which Sally doesn't know much about and wants to keep it that way. And Beth likes to overshare her sex life. Sally doesn't want to know much about that either, but Beth finds ways to fill her in anyway. It's why Sally times her lunchbreaks after the other two have taken theirs, so she can sit in the university cafeteria alone to read a book or people watch.

The door opens and Marcus briskly strides in. A man with authority about him. The posture and way he walks denotes his authority over everyone. He picks up a face mask, slips on disposable gloves and cap, and looks over the shoulder of Matthew and Beth for a few minutes each, not saying a word, then finally approaches Sally.

"Hello Sally."

"Hello Marcus." Sally says, clearing her throat under the mask.

"How are you today?"

"I'm fine. It's your project I'm concerned about."

"Which one?"

"The sub-zero nettles one."

"Oh. Um. Yeah. I know it's been stagnant, progress wise. But I remain confident."

Marcus folds his arms, talking muffled through his mask. "The university board doesn't share your enthusiasm. When we start getting lavish bills for arctic corals and Peruvian mountain soil, they understandably start asking questions."

"You said I'm funded."

Marcus smiles under the mask, but Sally can see his eyes grinning. "Yes, but within reason. The materials you are ordering are starting to breach the funding."

"Well, I can't experiment with the materials we have. So I have to order more appropriate ones, as exotic as they may be."

"The board, and myself, are starting to wonder if you can really grow tropical plants in sub-zero climates. And as intriguing as that might be, and it may get us some headlines if it works, but the overall use of it is now being scrutinized for the money being spent on it."

"It was all in my pitch report, and the updates I have been sending. Have you not been getting my emails?"

"Yes, yes. But the point is, you're making very little progress."

"I think I almost had a breakthrough last week. I have been growing nettle seeds in untreated frozen soil."

"I told you, I read your emails. But you're detracting from the main issue again. The words 'think' and 'almost' don't fill me, or the board, with any kind of enthusiasm."

Sally is becoming flustered now. She wants to pull at the back of her hair, but it's under the cap, so she simply pretends to.

"I was close the other day, Marcus. I mean really close."

"So, what happened?"

"There was, was, was, a negative influence. A, uh, an external influence. I need a little more time to set the experiment up elsewhere."

"What do you mean, external influence?"

"There was, a, um, look. Just an issue about a permit. That's all."

"A permit?"

"It turned out to be state owned land. Look, Marcus, I know what I need to do. I just need to set it up elsewhere."

Marcus sighs and uncrosses his arms. "Sally, if there's no promising results soon, and I mean real soon, we're going to have to label it unsuccessful and move you on to other projects. Do you understand?"

Sally lowers her head and nods, swallowing a dry lump in her throat and trying to hold back burgeoning tears.

"Sally, do we understand each other?"

"Yes." She looks back up with a fake smile and tired eyes. "Thank you."

Marcus nods sternly with pursed lips, then turns on his heel and beelines for the door. A minute later the door reopens slightly and a mousy lady with circle classes pops her head through.

"Sally?"

Sally, now wiping her wet nose with the back of her gloved hand, looks over with a sullen expression.

"Yeah, what?"

"You've got a visitor."

Sally sighs, still fighting back tears. "Tell them I'm busy."

"She said she would wait as long as it takes." The mousy lady licks her lips, and hesitantly says, "She told me to tell you that she's come to rain on your... expletive, um, parade."

This makes Sally stiffen on her seat. Her eyes now full of anxiety. She exhales loudly from her nostrils.

"Tell her to wait at the greenhouse. I'll be ten minutes."

Sally briskly walks through the glass doors of the newly constructed greenhouse, situated next to the Harvard University Herbaria. Lab cot off now, she's wearing a vintage blue shirt with buttons done up all the way to her neck, and a thrift store seized brown skirt that goes down to her white sneakers.

Two rows of the greenhouse run parallel to each other and are filled with a cacophony of plants, from the yellow spiked Golden barrel cactus to the lush green ferns of the Vascular plant. The air is humid and moist and smells stuffy and wet. Despite there being so many different kinds of plants, the aroma is overpowering dirt and fertilizer. Sally checks one aisle, seeing nobody, then goes to the next one. She spots a woman browsing a collection of Bromeliads. A portly mid-forties woman with rosy cheeks and long graying brown crimped hair interlaced with sporadic dreadlocks.

Sally puts her hands on her hips. "I wish you'd call before you visit, Rain."

Rain turns with her whole body to face Sally. The ten necklaces she's wearing jingle together with their shells and talismans as she moves.

"Oh boo-hoo. Come here and give your big sis a hug, stroppy Sally."

Sally doesn't move, prompting Rain to sigh over-dramatically and march over to her sister, giving her a bear hug so hard Sally's feet momentarily lift off the wet cement greenhouse floor. Sally awkwardly reciprocates a moment, then pats Rain's back in an effort to show her the physical greeting is over. Rain lets go of Sally and stands back, throwing her hair over her shoulder.

Sally steals a glance at Rain's collection of necklaces, lamenting that there's more hippie trinkets than when they last saw each other, and thinking it's a tad over-the-top.

"I love your, um, new jewelry."

Rain proudly lifts some of them up in her hands and lets them fall back down on her buxom bosoms, tinkering together again.

"Thanks. I picked up a few on my hike through Greenland last year." Rain pauses and thinks, screwing her face up. "Or was that the year before?" She thinks hard another moment then her face lights up. "It was the year before. Last year I was in Mongolia." She looks down, chin to her chest, and selects one particular leather woven necklace with a cherry pink stone encased in silver wire. "This is a tugtupite stone. Only place in the world you can get them is Greenland."

Sally smiles. She thinks the necklace itself is gaudy, but the pink stone is pretty. "Huh. It's really nice." She watches Rain admire it herself with a lazy grin on her face. Sally becoming anxious and says, "The same color as my favorite tree, the cherry blossom."

"Oh yeah," says Rain distractedly, still looking at the stone.

Sally knows that aloof behavior all too well. She knows her big sister is stoned right now.

Sally says, "So, how long are you here for this time?"

Rain lets the necklace drop from her fingers and gives Sally a smarmy smirk.

"I'm not even here five minutes and already you wanna get rid of me."

Sally touches the side of her hair, patting it gently with her fingertips. "No, no, I... no. I was just-"

"Don't worry stroppy, I'm not gonna cramp your style," Rain says as she places her hand on Sally's shoulder. "I'm staying with a friend this time." Rain winks and nudges Sally with her elbow. "Well, he's more a friend with benefits."

Rain bursts out laughing boisterously. Sally's lips curve in and out of a smile. Her hand now at the back of her hair and tugging on a few loose strands.

Sally says, "I didn't mean to be rude. I was, just, y'know... it's a weird time. Y'know, for me."

"Oh hun, everything okay? Did you break up with...," Rain stops and racks her brains.

"Larissa."

Rain snaps her fingers. "I was just about to say."

"We're still together."

"Great," Rain says with an empty smile.

Sally fidgets her hands together. She just remembered that the last time Rain visited her she stayed in their home and her holistic antics annoyed Larissa so much they had a massive argument which led to Rain being kicked out.

Rain gently takes Sally's wrist in her grasp.

"Let's walk and talk. It's a beautiful day out, and our heart Chakra's should soak it up."

Rain was right, it is a beautiful day. Sun rays gleam off small patches of snow on the grass surrounding a lake in the middle of the park. People are jogging by as Sally and Rain stroll along the path next to the water holding take-out coffee cups. Rain reaches into her colorful Himalayan yak wool jacket and produces a long joint. She snaps open a Zippo lighter with Betty Boop on the side and lights the joint.

Sally sighs. "That's why you really wanted to come outside, isn't it?"

"Guilty as charged," Rain says as she blows a lungful of smoke out the side of her mouth. "So, back to what we were discussing." She sucks in smoke from the joint, her voice squeaky as she holds the smoke in her throat. "You're really gonna go through with it, huh? You're finally gonna get boned by a cock."

Sally snaps her head around with a baleful expression, breathing angrily through her nostrils.

"I'm kidding, Stroppy. I'm kidding."

Sally sips angrily on her coffee a moment and calms herself. "It's been something that's been weighing on me. I had this weird dream the other night. It felt so... lucid. Y'know? I was being hunted by a man with a rifle. And there was some woman there too. She looked like me. With these ferocious dogs."

"The hunter represents your primitive driving force. The rifle could be seen as phallic."

"He shot me in the stomach."

"Definitely phallic."

"I ran, but then he had this baby. I was sure it was mine. I was desperate to have it." Sally clasps her hands over her stomach, recalling the dream. "I know this is something I want to do. But my subconscious ethereal state was telling me otherwise."

"You seem to know about dream landscapes. A little more than previously, anyway."

"Yeah... I'm seeing this therapist."

Rain turns to look at Sally with a smile. "Good for you."

Sally lets out a deep exhale and interlocks her fingers, stretching her arms out and twisting them around like a contortionist.

"Does it hurt?"

"Does what hurt?"

Sally, shy, looks at the ground. "You know...,"

It takes a few moments, but Rain gets it. "Oh, the dick. Right. Ummm, it depends. Everyone's different. I mean, I don't know the details of your sex life with Larissa." She looks at Sally mindfully, "And I don't want to. But if you guys are into pegging, or y'know, the like."

"What's pegging?"

Rain laughs, joint smoke wafting from her mouth. "Oh, my sweet summer child." She shakes her head. "Well, that's off the table then."

"What's pegging?"

"You know what. I'm gonna let you Google that one."

Rain laughs again, this time she chokes on smoke and saliva caught in her throat and erupts into a loud coughing fit. Two women pushing prams walk past, their nose screwed up in disgust at the joint smoke and Rain's guttural coughing. Sally makes an apologetic face at them then looks the other way at the lake out of embarrassment. After what feels like an eternity to Sally, Rain gets it all out and clears her throat several times. She looks at Sally with watery eyes and nods like they're good to go. The two of them continue strolling.

"You didn't answer my other question," says Sally. "Is it painful, in any way? The first time you did it."

Rain makes a 'prbbbrrrrrtttttt' sounds with her lips. "Good Lord, that was a million years ago. I can't even remem-" she stops to think. "Oh yeah. Robbie. He was terrible. But from what I know, most first time usually is."

"So it hurt?"

Rain shrugs one shoulder. "Physically, a little, I guess. But, it's a good kind of pain. If it's invited."

"Of course I'm inviting it."

"No, no. I mean, if you're attracted to the person. If you...," Rain glances at Sally with a hint of pity. "Look, hun. Aside from reproduction, sex is for pleasure. Making love is, well, a connection. You both need to be on the same page. That part is the most important." She opens the lid to her coffee and dumps the butt of the joint into the dregs at the bottom. "That, and the size of his ding-a-ling." She looks to Sally with a cheeky grin.

Sally shakes her head and rolls her eyes. She flexes her fingers in and out of a closed fist to a flat palm over and over.

Rain notices her involuntary hand flexing.

"Your hand still giving you grief after all these years, huh?"

"Only when it gets too cold."

After a long pause of ruminating, Rain says, "Sorry, Sal. I never thought I'd ever have this conversation with you. I can finally be a big sister about the sex stuff." She thinks a moment, her expression full of remorse. "The way I should have been." Rain now looking downright dejected. "The way we all should have been."

Sally waves her hand dismissively at Rain. "It's fine. Let's not get into that right now."

Rain stops in her tracks and peers intensely into Sally's eyes.

"This natural pregnancy thing. It's not because you felt left out, is it?"

"Left out of what?"

"Sally Caroline Field, don't you dare be coy with me. I'm not Star, or Leaf, or Summer. You can talk to me."

Sally goes to bite her fingernails, but Rain tosses the coffee cup to the ground and clasps Sally's hands tight with hers, pulling them down to their waists.

"There was a time we talked. Remember?"

Sally nods and breaks her hands away from Rain's. She stuffs her hands in her pockets, rummaging around until she finds her ugly knitted gloves and puts them on.

Rain says, "Now, is this a biological issue? Because mom and dad always accepted you as one of their own. Hell, the reason we all gave you a hard time is because we thought you were their favorite. You were the baby. Everyone just loooovvveees the baby." Rain reaches over and pinches Sally's cheek. "And you're still the baby."

Sally smiles bashfully and sways side-to-side on the spot awkwardly. "No." She shrugs. "I mean, yes, I did feel like you all ganged up on me all the time."

Sally spots a birdbath several yards behind Rain and meanders over to it, Rain following her. Sally plays with the snow lumped inside the birdbath, sculpting it with her hands.

"But that's not the reason I'm doing this. I've spent most of my life learning how to grow life that doesn't belong to me." Sally looks at Rain with a gentle smile. "Now I want to learn… for me." Sally twists her lips in an embarrassed way. "Is that a selfish thing to say?"

Rain beams a smile and saunters to join Sally at the birdbath, looking down at the little snowman Sally has been fashioning with the crunchy snow. Rain helps Sally's efforts by smoothing out the base of the sculpture.

"It's a brave thing to say, Sal." Rain stoops down to collect more snow from the ground, dumping it next to the snowman so they now have more material to enhance it. "You have always spent so much time trying to please other people, you forgot the one person that really matters." Rain flicks snow at Sally, hitting her in the tummy.

Sally chuckles, then flicks a little at Rain in retaliation. Rain takes a lump of snow and starts rolling it around in her hands.

Rain says, "I'm here for the time being. And I wanna help you in any way I can."

Sally smiles warmly. "Thank you."

Rain pitches a snowball at Sally, hitting her in the face.

"Hey!"

Rain bends down and cups more snow in her hands. Sally now sports a devilish smile, dropping to her knees to collect more snow to make her own snowballs.

"Are we on?" says Rain.

"Like Donkey Kong."

CHAPTER NINE

THIS ISN'T REAL

A doe nibbles on grass at the base of a thick oak tree in a small forest clearing. She daintily steps through the snow to another patch of grass nearby. The reposeful sound of trickling water from a stream twenty feet away. Another twenty-five feet beyond that is Glen, lying on his stomach on top of a military style light green blanket. His right eye pressed to the scope of his hunting rifle; the doe's torso perfectly centered in the scope's reticle.

Bullit patiently waits by Glen's side, lying all the way down like Glen is. He too is fervently watching the deer.

Glen slowly wraps his index finger around the trigger. He couldn't be in a better position to take the shot right now. His finger stops squeezing and freezes. He watches the deer munch on the long grass peacefully, and blissfully unaware that she's about to receive a bullet in the heart. Or is she? Glen swallows hard. He can't seem to go all the way right now. It's confusing the hell out of him, as he has never paused like this in all his life of hunting. And that goes for humans too, when he was stationed in Afghanistan during the war.

The doe takes a step forward; rendering it now not perfectly centered in the crosshairs. Glen doesn't adjust it. He simply stares into the scope wondering why he's not following through. The deer from the dream he had, the one which turned into a woman. He can't stop picturing it, or rather, her. The two of them inextricably linked right now. The vivid imagery unlike any dream he's had before, now manifesting his conscious mind for reasons he cannot understand. Emotions of such kind are usually alien to Glen.

Bullit sits next to Glen. Watching the deer, then watching Glen. Even Bullit is confused that Glen is withholding shooting the animal.

Glen's phone rings with a generic electronic tune that was the default setting when Glen bought it years ago.

The deer hears the phone and jerks its head up in Glen's direction. She sniffs the air, then spots Glen as he rolls over to pull the phone out of his thick rainproof jacket. The doe leaps into a sprint and is out of sight within moments.

"Jesus-H-Christ!" Glen yanks his phone from a pocket, not being able to comprehend why he didn't turn the phone off, or even leave it at home, as he often does.

"Yeah what is it?" Glen says irately into the phone.

"What got your panties in a bunch?" says Janeen on the other end.

Glen sighs, getting to his knees. "I was about to shoot a deer."

"You took your phone out hunting with you?"

"Yeah. I guess I wasn't thinkin'." Glen rubs his forehead. A buzzing sound now echoing in his head. "I ain't really been myself lately."

"I'll say. You were acting kinda weird the other night."

The buzzing now turning into a dull ringing in Glen's head, making him wince as he uses the tree next to him to help him rise up to stand.

"You okay?" asks Janeen, hearing Glen's pained grunts.

"Yeah... I think. Just a little...," Glen clears his throat and tries to override the pounding in his mind. "What did you ya want, anyway?"

"I was just askin' for a favor. Can you watch the kids this Sunday? Brian has to go to Boston for work, for some stupid reason he won't elaborate on. And I'm understaffed right now, so I gotta do a double shift that day."

The ringing and buzzing intensifies to a point where Glen's vision is being filled with white spots. Glen's vision is now going blurry.

"Hey, you listening?" says Janeen.

Glen's legs suddenly buckle and wobble. His eyes roll back and he drops to his knees, then falls face-forward onto the snowy ground. The phone falls from his grasp as he passes out. Janeen's concerned comments over the phone is the only sound in the otherwise quiet forest.

Bullit whimpers, walking distraught circles around Glen, occasionally nudging him with his nose.

Glen stands at the bottom of a deep old stone well. He's wearing his brown leather jacket over a white hospital patient gown. He tries to move his feet, but they are submerged in thick, slimy sludge up to his kneecaps. He shivers from the cold and hugs his arms tight into his chest. Glen peers up. About fifty feet up is the opening of the well and the grey overcast sky above it.

"Hello?" he calls out. "Is there anyone up there?"

Nothing but silence. Glen fiercely rubs his upper arms, shivering from the freezing temperature.

"It's fuckin' cold down here," he says to himself. Then he wonders how he ended up down here in the first place. Wait, where is he exactly?

The buzzing sound in his head again, this time much louder and way more intense. He clasps his hands over his ears and growls with pain.

"Stop it! Stop that fucking noise!"

The noise grows even more abrasive. Glen claws at the crude stone bricks all around him in a desperate effort to climb up and out of the old well.

"Somebody, please! Make is stop!"

Glen can't get a hold on the stones. He has no fingernails, and the stones are wet and slippery all the way up.

The loud buzzing turning Glen insane now. He roars at the top of lungs. He drops to his knees in the muck and starts digging into the filth by plunging his arms in and feeling around for something. Anything. Then his hands find something solid. He grabs it with both hands and pulls it up. It's a human skull attached to a thorny plant. The skull is where the flower pistil should be and is dripping sludgy black goop. Glen pulls the plant further from the muck, but the stem keeps coming. He pulls and pulls, the stem now bearing sharp thorns. Glen ignores the stinging on his hands from the thorns and keeps trying to uproot it. The more he pulls the plant from the depths, the more the buzzing in his head dissipates. He finally manages to rip out the roots and all.

The buzzing stops.

Sally moseys through a healthy grassy windswept field wearing a light blue robe fastened with a matching belt. Birds flutter to-and-fro in the sky above. Bees sail between the sporadic sunflowers on the green plain. Sally carries her old-fashioned red water can, sprinkling a little on flowers she passes. She stops, craning her neck to the side. She can hear a faint voice somewhere in the distance. Curious, she makes her way to a hill in the middle of the field that she hadn't noticed until now.

As she nears the small hill, she can now see an old stone well poking up from the top. There's a wooden bucket attached to a rope sitting on the well's surface. The closer she gets, the more the voice she hears becomes distinct. A young boy.

"Get me out of here! Please!" the voice cries.

Sally reaches the top of the hill and peers down into the depths of the well. She was right on her intuition. It is a young boy. A very scared young boy standing in mud at the bottom. A long plant stem snaked around him.

"Hello!" cries Sally.

Glen hears someone call 'hello!' and immediately fixates on the opening of the well above. He can make out a person. It looks like a blonde woman.

"Help me, please!" Glen shouts up the well.

"Hang on!" the woman shouts back.

A wooden bucket is being lowered down via a rope. When it reaches him, Glen grabs the rope and gives it a few good tugs to let her know he's ready. A moment later and the rope starts to pully up. Glen holds on tight as he slowly ascends to the daylight above, using his legs to climb vertically. He reaches the top and an arm lowers down. He reaches out and takes the wrist with one hand. After he feels confident enough, Glen lets go of the rope and grasps the wrist with both hands.

Grunts can be heard as the person outside hauls him out, his legs kicking the stones in the well for increased traction. They work together until he pulled up and out.

Sally pulls the boy from the well and they both tumble down the grassy hill together. The two of them land on hard ice with a thud, and slide across it a few moments. When Sally collects herself, she looks over to find that the boy isn't a boy at all – he's a middle-aged man. She squints at him, thinking she's seen him somewhere before. He sits up and dusts pieces of snow from his leather jacket. Sally now realizes the two of them are in the middle of a frozen lake.

Glen looks over to acknowledge his rescuer. A grown woman in a silk robe, who is scanning the environment with awe. Her eyes wide as her head swivels this way and that like she's just landed in a whole new place. The stone well now in the distance, punching up through the lake's ice. Glen's feet are covered in mud, and he awkwardly maneuvers on the slippery ice surface to stand. He knows this lake. It's the one from his dreams. The one where Joe perished all those years ago. Glen looks back to Sally, watching her try to stand, but she's also bare foot and having a tough time. He steps over to her and offers his hand for support. She stops and looks at him. Fear in her eyes and unsure whether to take his hand.

"It's okay," says Glen. "I ain't gonna hurt ya."

Sally looks at him and his hand skeptically for a moment, then she accepts the offer and he pulls her up to stand next to him. She takes a couple of steps away from him, still watching him with strong dubiousness. She clasps her arms around her, her whole body shivering from only wearing her satin robe.

Glen takes off his leather jacket and holds it out for her. Sally's eyes dart back and forth between him and the jacket. She wants to take it badly, but she's still scared of him. Now she recognizes him. He's the hunter from the lavender field. And he now recognizes her. The woman who he shot in the stomach in the forest dream.

"Go on. Take it. I don't mind the cold as much as you."

She swallows hard, her teeth chattering and her skin turning blue.

Glen takes a slow, wary step toward her. Sally doesn't back way, so he gently uses both hands to hold it out and takes another step, carefully bringing it around to drape over her shoulders. Once the jacket is hanging off her, Glen takes a couple of steps back. Sally takes hold of the jacket shrewdly and pulls it tightly around herself. It's big on her small frame and the cuffs are several inches too long, but she's already feeling snug in it.

"Thank you," she says in a low raspy voice.

They both awkwardly eye each other up and down a moment, Sally looking away and back again a few times, then she says, "I know you."

Glen stands there sheepishly, hugging his arms tight into his chest.

She says, "You're the man who shot me."

"I'm sorry," Glen says with an ashamed disposition. "I thought you were a deer. I swear I wouldn't have if I had known you were a person."

"Why would you shoot a deer?"

Glen now looks confused. "I'm a registered hunter."

"That doesn't answer my question. Why would you kill a defenseless animal?"

"You'd rather I kill defensive animals?"

Sally cocks her head with a dry visage. "You know what I mean."

"I don't, really."

"We live in a society where you can drive to a supermarket to buy meat, if you're that way inclined. You don't need to go into nature and kill it yourself. And if you're going to play the culling card, deer numbers have been on the decline for years. The only reason you would do it is for fun. And that makes you an asshole."

Glen slowly closes his eyes to show that he's unperturbed, then opens them again with a droll expression.

"I don't just kill 'em and eat 'em. I sell the heads for taxidermy, and I sell the pelts for clothing. If you wanna sling shit, how about the people that buy it? The ones who have 'em mounted on the wall, spread across their living room floors, or wear 'em as fashion. Where there's a demand, there's people out there filling those demands. If there weren't a market, I'd be killin' less of 'em. I sell some of the meat also to those markets you're on about. Again, go tell them they're assholes. I eat the rest, and my dog Bullit loves the bones. They're good for his teeth." Glen's eyebrows furrow as a thought drops on him. "Hey... where is Bullit?" Glen looking around in all directions. "He was just here with me a moment ago."

Sally joins him in scanning the environment. They are in the middle of the frozen lake. Nothing but thick forest bordering the lake miles away in every direction.

And thousands of colorful flowers of all kinds all around them in the snow. Daisies. Dahlias. Tulips. Roses. Gardenias. Marigolds.

"Weird," says Sally.

"What?"

"I could swear I was somewhere else. Just before I found you in that well." Sally now outright confused at the new surroundings for the first time since she pulled him out of the well. "Where is this?"

Glen is now looking at a six-foot hole in the ice just several yards away. Cracks all around it, as if someone had fallen through.

"We shouldn't be here," he says stepping back and swallowing a fear induced lump in this throat.

Water lashes around the ice hole as if something is thrashing around under the surface.

"I don't wanna be here," Glen says, looking around for a way out or a direction to go. He sees a figure in the distance. It looks like a teenage boy, just standing there watching Glen and Sally. The same clothes as his brother Joe. His face and hands are light blue as if he's frozen. Glen turns to Sally. "Can you take me back to where you came from?"

Sally blinks in confusion for a moment. "I… I don't know how I got here."

Glen looks back at Joe, only to discover he's shorter and younger now. It's not Joe anymore. It's an eleven-year-old Glen standing in Joe's place. Tears welling in Glen's eyes, his face turning a rageful red.

"Why didn't you help me?!" Glen says with tears running down his face. "Huh?! Why!"

"Who is that?" asks Sally through chattering teeth, hugging the leather jacket as tight as she can.

Young Glen turns and runs off in the other direction. The forest hill he's making a dash to now has a yellow house sitting amongst the pine trees.

"Come back here! You coward!" Glen cries out and launches into a sprint after the child.

Sally is uncontrollably shivering now. Her teeth loudly chattering and her whole body convulsing. She closes her eyes and tries to drown out the thoughts of how freezing she is. She concentrates on her breathing, slow and calm.

"A fire would be nice," she says quietly to herself, picturing a flame filled fireplace. "A nice, roaring fire."

Glen slips on the ice and falls hard onto his stomach. He looks up to see where his younger self is. Only he's not on the ice lake anymore. He's in a room. A cozy redwood log cabin. He's face down on a thick black bear rug. The walls of the cabin are fashioned from logs and have Native artifacts on them ranging from tomahawks to bows and arrows. The room is lit with the flames from oil lanterns hanging from the beams under the ceiling. A large stone constructed fireplace is at the front of the room, a healthy log fire raging inside it. Sally is standing next to the fire, still in her silk robe with the leather jacket pulled around her. She opens her eyes and looks around the new scene with wonderment.

"How did…," says Glen, "What the hell?"

Sally looks over to him sitting up on the bear rug scanning the cabin.

Glen says, "Hang on a minute. Somethin' ain't right here."

Sally spots a thick knitted wool blanket draped over a plush velvet armchair facing the fire. She drops the jacket to the floor and marches over to the chair and whips the blanket from it, wrapping it around herself from neck to feet. Her spine tingles from the warmth and security of the blanket. Her whole face smiling and rosy in an instant. She glances over at the other side of the cabin and notices a small trickle of water coming from a gap in the wood slat roof, dripping onto the varnished floor.

Without hesitation, Sally beelines for the kitchenette in the far corner of the cabin. Glen watches her with a bewildered expression as she strides to the long wooden kitchen counter with five cupboards above it. Sally immediately goes for the cupboard above the sink, opening it to find it is full of pots and pans. She tales one of the saucepans out and looks it over.

"We weren't here a moment ago, I swear it," says Glen. "Am I drunk? How did I get here?"

Sally ignores him and dashes over to where the drops of water are hitting the floor and shoves the pan into the middle of the small puddle so the drips from the ceiling now fall straight into the pan. She rises and puts her hands on her hips, content with her work.

"Are you listening to me?" Glen says stepping around an oval shaped wooden dining table. "I said how did we get here?"

"I don't know how we got here," Sally says aloofly.

"But you know where we are, right?"

"Huh?"

"You went and found that pan in the kitchen right away. You knew where it was."

Sally scratches her head thoughtfully, still staring at the water drops hitting in the pan. "I did, didn't I?"

"What did you do? Did you bring me here?"

Sally now gazing around the cabin a daze. "I... I just thought about here... and then I was here."

"That don't make any sense."

"It doesn't. Yet...," she trails off, noticing another trickle of water dropping from the ceiling in the adjacent corner of the room.

Sally growls under her breath and marches past Glen back to the kitchen. She opens the pot cupboard again and takes out another saucepan, then deftly zigzags between the furniture to the new leak in the roof and sticks the pot in the right position to catch the water droplets.

"And none of this strikes you as odd?" says Glen while he watches Sally stare wide eyed around the room to see if there's any more leaks.

"What?"

"Will you pay attention to me. I'm fuckin' serious. What the hell is going on?"

"I know this place," says Sally with a smile starting to form. "This is my grandfather's lodge in Maine."

Drip. Drip. Drip.

Sally can hear more water but can't see where it's coming from and whips her head round to find the source, her eyes wide and crazed.

"Can you hear that?"

"Hear what?"

"That... dripping. The water."

Glen strains to hear a moment, then shakes his head. "I don't hear a goddam thing."

Sally dashes back to the kitchen and opens the pot cupboard again, springing up on her tiptoes to reach further into the cabinet. She finds a handle and roughly pulls out another pan, bringing several others with it. Pots and pans fall and clatter loudly all around her.

"You're a bit crazy, aren't ya?"

Sally ignores him, peering intensely around the cabin. There it is. Another leak from the ceiling near the fireplace. Sally growls loudly and stoops down to grab another so she now has one in each hand and races over to the leak, her leg snagging a little coffee table stool that sends her sprawling forward and crashing into an armchair.

Glen shakes his head as he watches the maniacal woman in front of him quickly stand up with her two pots and reaches the dripping water, placing one of the saucepans under the leak. She spins around, breathing heavily and waiting for another leak to appear with her other pot ready to go.

"So, we're at your granddaddy's place. But how did we get here? Did you drug me?" Glen pacing back and forth now, racking his brain for answers. "Wait. Where were we before here?"

"I don't know," Sally says in a daze as she continues to scan the room.

"Would you stop that shit for a second and talk to me?!"

Sally swivels her head robotically to stare at him with glazed eyes. "What?"

"Don't you find this weird? All this. We were someplace else. Cold. Snow. Somethin' like that. And now we're in your family cabin in fuckin' Maine."

Sally is side eyeing the walls.

Glen marches over to her and stands right in her space.

"Hey! Focus. One thing at a time. You can't control every leak."

Sally's face now turning alarmed and frightened. "I can't?"

"No, you can't."

Sally's face quickly turns into a resentful scowl. "Yes, I can."

Sally pushes past him using her shoulder to barge him out of the way and runs to the center of the room where the dining table is and sees tiny droplets of water falling on the surface. She grins wickedly.

"Gotcha, you little bastard!"

Sally puts the pot on the table to catch the falling water. She stands back and makes a little triumphant grunt.

"Just slow down and think. What are we doing at your grandfather's lodge?"

"I haven't been here since I was a teenager."

"Look, I don't know you lady. Why would I be here? Why would you bring me here to this decrepit old cabin?"

Sally spins around to face Glen with an incredulous expression.

"What do you mean decrepit? He built this with his bare hands. Who the hell do you think you are, coming into my family cabin and making fun of it?"

"I didn't fuckin' come here. You brought me here!"

"No I didn't."

"Jesus. How do you think I got here? I've never met you before. How would I know where it is?"

Sally now looks at the doors and windows, then back to Glen.

"Did you break in here?"

"Oh for fuck's sake lady," Glen shakes his head vigorously. "I'm getting' the fuck outta here and away from your crazy ass."

Leaks start dripping from all over the ceiling. Six of them in every part of the cabin. They quickly turn from drops into gushing water.

Sally looks around in horror, knowing there's no way she can attend to every one of them.

"Wait!" Sally calls to Glen as he reaches the front door. "Help me, please."

Glen turns and glances at the running water cascading all over the floor and furniture.

"Listen, lady, I-"

"Stop calling me lady."

Glen raises his hands defensively in a borderline mocking manner.

"Alright, sorry. But this place is stressing me out. You, are stressing me out. And I don't think there's enough pots to save this mess."

Sally steps toward him, her expression earnest. "Can I come with you?"

Glen sighs and shrugs. "Sure."

"Where are you going?"

"I dunno. Anywhere that's not here."

Glen opens the door and a cold gust of icy wind hits him in the face causing him to clamp his eyes shut. After a moment he opens them again.

He's standing on the frozen lake again. Water drops start hitting his face from blackened rain clouds above. He turns around to find Sally behind him, clutching her knitted blanket around her. She's blankly looking around, realizing that they are back on the cold expanse of the lake. She feels the rain and peers up at the foreboding sky. Flashes of thunder and lightning raging in the dark clouds.

"You brought the goddam water with you, lady!" says Glen.

"Why are we back here again. What happened to the cabin?"

"I have no idea. But I don't wanna be here."

Cracks start splitting through the ice around them with loud cracking sounds.

"Take us back to the cabin!" says Glen with fear in his voice.

"I... I... I do-do-do-don't know h-h-h-how we got th-th-th-there in the f-f-first place," Sally says as she tries to control her stammer.

The rain now cascading down in a torrential downpour. The ice beneath Glen's feet splitting into zigzags in all directions. Glen tries to yell at Sally to find a way back to the cabin, but the sound of the rain and thunder drown him out.

Glen looks down to see a corpse floating underneath. Joe's hauntingly frozen face staring right up at him.

Glen lets out a scream of pain and anguish.

Sally can hear his cry but can't see him through the harsh downpour. She lets the sopping blanket fall from her shoulders to her feet. The rain not feeling cold to her. In fact, it feels warm and almost comfy.

The rain stops in an instant. Not even a drop. The dark clouds have disappeared to give way to a bright blue sky. Sally looks around to find Glen has gone. The cracks in the ice vanished with him. She turns to look behind her. A solitary fireplace sits on the ice sheet several yards from her. It's the same stone fireplace from the cabin, complete with roaring fire inside.

Sally blinks erratically, trying to figure out what a functional fireplace is doing out in the middle of a frozen lake like this. A bolt of realization snaps her mind.

"This isn't real."

CHAPTER TEN

A POSSIBLE SUITOR

Sally's eyes open quickly, and she takes a sharp breath in. She looks around to find she's in the little indoor sunroom attached to her and Larissa's house. Tempered glass windows and roofing allow sunlight to wash over the lush green plants all over the room. The floor is black and white checkered, with a long cane couch and two wicker peacock chairs, one of which Sally is sitting in with an open book in her lap that she was reading before dozing off.

"You never talk in your sleep."

Sally gasps and nearly jumps out of her skin at the comment, looking around wildly to find Larissa standing in the doorframe leading into the house. She lets out a droll sigh of relief and reaches over to the couch to pull a blanket over to her and wraps it around her lower body.

"I wish you wouldn't watch me when I sleep like that. It's kinda weird."

"Awwww, Shnookums," Larissa says with mockingly pouted lips as she moseys over to Sally and kisses the top of her head. "Did we have a nasty wittle dweam?" Larissa knowing Sally hates the baby talk as she tries to pinch her cheeks playfully.

Sally bats Larissa's hands away with an irritated expression.

"Fuck off."

Larissa giggles. "You just look so peaceful and cute when you're in a deep sleep."

"How long were you standing there?" Sally says as she pulls the blanket up further around her, turning in her chair to point her body language away from Larissa who remains bent over in front of her.

Larissa shrugs, "I dunno. A few minutes."

Sally can smell the white wine on Larissa now.

"Ugh. You smell like a brewery."

"A vineyard."

"What?"

"I drank wine. So, it would be more appropriate if you said I smell like a vineyard."

"It would be most appropriate if you took a shower."

Larissa laughs. She rises her upper body to stand straight. She suddenly blinks erratically and slaps a hand on her forehead.

"Wooooo, head spin."

Larissa shakes her head like a wet dog to will the dizziness away. Sally pulls the book in her lap to rest on top of the blanket and pretends to read so Larissa will leave her alone.

Larissa, now having rid of the head spin, puts one hand on her hip.

"Okay, so I did have a few Chardonnays. But, for a cause."

Sally ignores her and traces her fingers down the page to find the last sentence she read before falling asleep.

"Did you hear me Twinkie? I said I had a few drinks to celebrate."

Sally doesn't look up from the page and couldn't sound less interested. "Oh yeah? What did you celebrate? Let me guess, someone you don't like at your firm got fired."

Larissa shakes her head slowly, her smile broadening.

"No, my pretty. We got you a donor."

Sally snaps her head up to stare into Larissa eyes.

"What do you mean a donor?"

Larissa doesn't say anything, she simply holds her gaze and smile at Sally. It takes a few moments for the realization to kick in, but Sally gets there.

"Wait. Are you serious?"

"Serious as a suicide bomber."

Sally covers her mouth and looks out the window to the small backyard lined by a tall wooden fence and Sally's impressive herb garden. Sally not sure why she's hiding her nervous smile from her love. She takes her hand away and looks at Larissa with a proper demeanor.

"Well, where did you... um... I mean... who? How?"

Larissa stoops down to pick up her brown leather work case sitting just behind the doorway.

"A paralegal at my firm." She rolls her eyes with a curt grin. "Alright, his name is Brad. I know you hate that name. But he's a real doll. He likes soy decaf latte's, pug dogs and Thunder From Down Under."

Sally turns around with a curious visage.

"That's right Twinks, he's as gay as you and me." Larissa rifles around in her bag a moment then whips out a manila envelope. "I thought it might make it easier, if, y'know, it's the first, uh, 'straight', time, for both of you."

Sally purses her lips and thinks a moment. "That's... thoughtful. I guess."

"Trust me, you don't want a salivating bro just wanting to stick his ding-a-ling in you for kicks. You're a hottie, Sally. A fuckin' grade-A piece of ass. We gotta weed out the horny douchebags and whittle it down to the inexperienced curious cats."

Sally touches her hair and smiles, looking bashfully into her lap. She likes compliments, but with the way she dresses and acts, she doesn't get them very often.

Larissa says, "Plus he's super clean. Like, stereotypically flaming gay guy obsessed with his appearance kind of clean. He hardly drinks, doesn't do drugs, and has good genes." Larissa smiles to herself, tracing her index finger along the doorframe. "Not that you really care, but for all intents and purposes, the dude is smokin' hot. Which means, with your DNA combined, we're gonna have a future heartbreaker on our hands."

Sally rolls her tongue around her mouth back and forth, dislodging a parsley leaf in the back from an earlier sandwich. She takes a slow deliberate breath in, gathering her thoughts and trying to imagine what this Brad guy looks like. Sally pictures a few pretty boy actors in her mind, and it's starting to gross her out, so she wipes it clean to focus on the business of this.

"What's the, um... what does he want?"

Larissa holds up the envelope above her head and jiggles it a few times.

"Don't worry your pretty little head. I drafted the agreement myself. The kid will be a hundred percent yours."

"Ours."

"Yeah. But technically...," Larissa trails off in thought. A conversation piece she doesn't want to have right now. "The kid will be ours. Don't worry. Just look over the documents a few times. Make sure it's all hunky-dory. Now, my lawyer fees are usually quite high. But since you fall under family and friends, I'm prepared to offer a sizeable discount." Larissa smiles and winks.

Sally nods but is not in the same drunken playful mood. "Yeah, okay. But what does Brad get out of this? Surely he doesn't want to... y'know... if he exclusively likes men."

Larissa now fans herself with the envelope. "Let's just say the wonderful world of legal and business works on favors and misguided principles."

Sally gives Larissa a war glance, then reaches to the back of her head and starts twirling hair around two fingers. Larissa knows every anxiety induced mannerism of her love.

"I told you, don't worry Twinkie."

"I do worry."

"I know you do. Look. He's getting a lot out of this. Firstly, he's getting a handsome payment. All taxable and on the books. No shady stuff. Second, I've, uh, kinda promised him some... um, new, work opportunities."

Sally rises up from her chair, the blanket and book toppling onto the floor.

"No shady stuff? You're promising him a raise?! That's about as shady as it gets."

Larissa meanders to Sally, putting her hands on her hips.

"Hey. Brad is a hotshot at the firm. It's not going to be long before he rises the ranks anyway. It's fine."

Sally looks everywhere but Larissa's face right in front of hers. "It's not right. He's only having sex with me because he's been offered a promotion. It... it doesn't feel right. It's like, blackmail, or extortion, or something like that."

Larissa places a few fingers on Sally's chin and gently guides her face so they are eye to eye. "Sally, it's nothing like those things, okay? Those are threats. I'm not saying to him he'll be fired or demoted for not taking part. I'm saying I'm in a good position to refer him to the top brass. It's not even my final call. It's just a letter of recommendation. I mean, fuck. I've seen people climb the ladder for way more dubious means. You remember Kate Littleton, right?"

Sally shakes her head with a pout.

"You met her at least a couple of times at a few work things." Larissa thinks a moment. "At the marathon last year for one. She wore that awful matching Gucci outfit. Even her fanny pack matched her ugly ass sweats combo."

Sally nods. "Oh, yeah. Ugh. I hated her. That shrill voice."

"Yeah, that fake bi-atch. She's my fucking peer. Promoted three months ago. Remember? I came home drunk and was ranting."

"Like every other day?"

Larissa cocks her head and darts Sally a dry smile with seedy eyes. "Alright smart-ass. Shut up." Larissa lovingly strokes her finger across Sally's cheek. "Anyway, have a guess how that botox addicted cow got to be where I am without the years of hard work in the boys club?"

Sally shrugs.

"Oh come on now, don't be coy. You know damn well I'm about to say she fucked one of the partners. Everyone knows it."

"So, wait. You're telling me you condemn the behavior of her using sex to get a promotion, but it's also okay for Brad, lover of pugs and soy latte's, to do the same thing?"

Larissa recoils back with an incredulous smile. "You've got some sass on you today, girl."

Sally takes a deep breath. "I had an intense dream before."

"Sally, listen to me. There is nothing illegal, barely even morally wrong, about this. Everyone is consenting. Except you, it seems."

"I need time to think."

Larissa makes a stupid expression and contorts her face. "Well, DUH!"

Sally sniggers and covers her mouth with her fist, knowing her breath probably stinks having been asleep before and downing that coffee and sandwich.

Sally says, "What's he look like?"

"Who, Brad?"

"No. The King of Spain. Of course Brad."

"Ohhhh, you got some real attitude today, Twinkie. And you haven't even had a drink yet."

"I think I need one. Or five."

"My thoughts exactly."

"But I do wanna know what he looks like. I'm curious."

"Of course you are," Larissa says as she removes her hand from Sally's hip and takes a couple of strutting steps back with a confident smirk. "So come and see for yourself."

Sally's eyes bolt as wide open as they will go.

"What?"

Larissa doesn't say anything, she just holds her smug smirk on her face.

"Wait. Here?"

Larissa slowly nods her head. Sally races to the doorway and covertly peeks into the living and dining rooms inside.

"He's in the front room drinking a green smoothie."

Sally uses the faint reflection in the windowpane to frantically fix her mop of blonde hair with her skinny fingers.

"Jesus Christ, Larry. You could've said. I look like an old maid. I look like a chimney sweep from a Dickens novel."

"What are you so worried about? He's gonna fuck you no matter what you look like."

Sally spins around and glares daggers at Larissa, who sighs regretfully and offers out her hands apologetically.

"I'm sorry sweetie. I know we shouldn't joke about it. But this whole situation is kinda... abnormal. Don't ya think?"

Sally becoming more and more wound up. Her hands are shaking and she doesn't know what to do with them. She grabs at her hair, her crinkled sundress, her face. She licks her lips incessantly and starts to pace on the spot, breathing in and out quickly and harshly.

Larissa charily steps over to Sally and gingerly offers her hand out. Sally doesn't see the gesture, too much in her own world of anxiety, so Larissa moves behind her and hugs her from the back. She can feel Sally's body quivering all over.

"Shhhh. Calm down. It's okay, baby. Y'know what? You two should save it for the actual night. It'll be more... well... romantic. I guess."

"Really?"

"Sure. Mystery is a harbinger to adventure. And this is an adventure. For all of us. Our baby is going to be conceived with sparks."

Larissa leans her head around and kisses Sally softly on the ear, right where she likes it. Larissa feeling the happy shiver running up Sally's spine and she smiles. After Sally's nervous shakes start to dissipate, Larissa lets Sally go and steps back, not being able to resist smacking her on the bum.

"I'll go see him off. You go get dressed. We're going out for drinkypoo's and boogie-roo's."

Sally smiles. "I don't think you need much more."

"I think you need to get to my level, is what I think," Larissa says as she moseys to the doorway. She picks up the manila envelope from the top of her leather case and holds it out to Sally.

"Put this somewhere so you can read it tomorrow. And let's set the date for when you're peak ovulating. We only got once shot at this."

Sally nods and takes the envelope, then Larissa strides out the door.

"Wait," Sally calls out.

Larissa reappears in the doorway with raised eyebrows.

"You said I was talking in my sleep before."

"Uh-huh."

Sally clears her throat nervously. "What… ah, what did I say?"

Larissa looks away a moment to conjure up the memory, then looks back to Sally and says, "You said 'where are you going?' and 'can I come with you?' Then you said something along the lines of 'I don't know how we got here', and something else, but I can't remember right now."

Sally nods, looking at the floor with creased eyebrows.

Larissa says, "Why?"

Sally shrugs. "Just… the dream was very vivid. It felt more real than normal. Like that one from last week I told you about. The hunter and the baby."

"Oh, yeah, that's right," Larissa now remembering.

"He was back."

"Who was back?" Larissa says, now pumping her legs on the spot.

"The hunter guy."

"Did he shoot you again?"

"No," Sally says with the slightest hint of a smile. "Actually, he apologized for shooting me."

"That's nice of him," says Larissa still half jogging on the spot.

"And then we were in my grandfather's old cabin. The one I showed you pictures of."

"Twinkie, I love you, and I can't wait to hear all about your dream, but I gotta piss something chronic, and I've gotta see our guest off. Get changed. Drinks."

With that, Larissa pushes off the doorframe and dashes through the house to the bathroom holding her crotch.

Sally looks down at the envelope in her hands with a foreboding expression. She can't believe this is actually happening. There's legal documents to sign and everything. Then one day really soon, she'll be growing her own baby in her own tummy. Sally feels a rush of adrenaline wash over her with a dash of anxiety. 'It's not too late to back out', Sally thinks to herself over and over. She goes to bite one of her fingernails but stops. No, she's not going to take up old bad habits. First it starts as just one. Then before she knows it she'll be smoking again. No. She's got to set a good example from now on. After all, she's going to be a mother soon.

Sally smiles and hugs the envelope to her chest.

CHAPTER ELEVEN

BEAKY THE PENGUIN

The hospital's automatic doors whisk open for Brian in his neatly pressed police uniform. He carries a brown paper bag in one hand, the other hand on his hip with his thumb hooked on his belt. He strides for the main desk, but his peripheral vision catches sight of a collection of loud colors. He glances over to find a small gift shop nestled in the corner of the foyer and he slows his gait to a stop.

Brian changes trajectory and marches over to the kiosk surrounded by shiny 'Get Well' balloons, cute little plush teddy bears bearing stitched in wellness sentiments, and an array of flower bouquets mostly consisting of violet button poms and golden sunflowers. The kiosk is a mirage of color in the otherwise drab and sterile white hospital entrance. Brian reaches a stand bearing flower bouquets and stares at them a moment before touching a white monte casino flower petal gently with his fingertip.

"Do you need a hand?"

Brian looks over to find a twenty-something girl with brunette bangs wearing a cheap white apron over denim overalls, sitting on a stool behind the tiny kiosk counter. She stops scrolling through Instagram and shoves her phone in her pocket and stands up to greet Brian professionally.

Brian points to the flowers and says, "Did you make these?"

The kiosk girl tries unsuccessfully to mask her confusion and says, "Uh, they're real. If that's what you mean."

"No, no. I meant, did you grow them?"

Now she's not trying to hide her confusion. "You mean, did I plant them myself?"

"Yeah."

The girl holds her gaze on him a moment then shakes her head slowly, now eying his impossibly clean-cut police uniform.

"No, sir. But they're legal." She thinks a moment, darting her eyes around, purses her lips, then says, "Aren't they?"

Brian knows that fear in her eyes. The fear of the uniform and badge that is elicited more from law abiders than actual criminals. Behind those vacant eyes the mind is running through all the possibilities of breaking the law, either right now or anytime in the past. Brian deals with that look every day, knowing in that head of hers she's thinking 'did I leave drugs in the car?' or 'did I steal something from the supermarket without realizing'. It amuses Brian to no end that people react this way to the law enforcers. At some point in their life most people have broken a law, whether it be jaywalking or going slightly over the speed limit while zoned out. This girl caught off guard while incapacitated by her social media and now wondering if these flowers she's selling are in some way illegal.

"It's nothing like that," says Brian, waving his hand aloofly. "I was just wondering if these flowers are grown locally, and if so, where they're from."

"I…. I just work here a couple of days a week, officer."

Brian fighting back a smile after she said 'officer'. She's definitely a deer in his headlights now. Usually he would purposely screw with her like he does to others who become putty in his hands like this. But right now, he doesn't have time.

"I'm not asking as a policeman, ma'am. I'm just curious as to how...," Brian stops himself, then smiles and says, "You know, never mind. I don't even know why I was asking that."

The kiosk girl now staring at him in a mixture of fear and discontentment. Brian himself feeling a little uncomfortable for asking this girl about those flowers when she probably works minimum wage and has no idea where the damn flowers originated, so he picks up a stuffed white and grey penguin with a little blue ice pack on its head that says, 'Get Well' and places it on the counter.

"How much is this?"

"Sixteen."

"Sixteen bucks for this?"

"Uh, yeah."

"What's it made from?" Brian huffs a little chuckle in anticipation of a funny punchline, but he can't think of any expensive materials on hand right now, so he tries to save the effort. "Must be drugs in there or something, right?"

The girl forces an awkward smile, though her eyes are screaming utter discomfort.

"You know, like a drug smuggling operation," Brian says with jest. "Why the damn toy is so expensive."

The girl smiles to show her teeth now, in a desperate attempt to placate him he reckons. It's the most unnatural smile he's ever seen. Brian quickly pulls out his wallet and opens it to grab a twenty-dollar bill and places it on the counter next to the stuffed toy.

"I can gift wrap it for an extra three dollars."

"No, it's fine as is," Brian says as he snatches the penguin from the counter.

The girl hastily counts out his change and hands it to him.

Brian quickly turns on his heel and briskly marches to the hospital front desk. He tells the woman behind the counter who he's here to see, and after some keyboard punching and a phone call, she tells him to head up to level four and gives him the room number, then tells him a few rules and policies, skipping over a few because of his police uniform.

Brian holds up the paper bag he's been carrying and asks if he's allowed to take beer upstairs and she tells him it's against the rules. He asks if he can leave it with her until he comes back down, and she tells him 'sure'. Brian thanks her and heads over to the elevator and presses the button on one of the panels. The elevator taking an eternity to Brian. He steals a glance over at the kiosk. The girl is tapping away on her phone and looks up, locking eyes with Brian, who quickly looks away. He goes to the other panel and wildly presses the button, telling the elevator to hurry up over and over under his breath. Ding. One of the elevator doors opens and Brian hurriedly enters, pressing the level four button erratically to hurry the doors to close. He looks over again at the kiosk girl who is no longer in sight, then the doors close. Thank fuck.

Glen is lying in a hospital bed in the center of the room, his hair loose and down, splayed out all over the pillow he's propped sitting up against. A cramped little room with a window overlooking the parking lot, and a television mounted on the wall in front of the bed. Janeen walks out of the small bathroom in the corner of the room, the noise of the toilet water refilling as she exits. She closes the door as to not inflict the smell in there on the current occupants of the hospital room.

"Alex, quit messin' around with that," Janeen says as she spots her son wheeling the IV drip pole around in circles.

"Kaylee did it first!"

"Would you jump out that window if Kaylee did it first?"

Kaylee is sitting in an uncomfortable plastic chair in the corner and looks up from her computer tablet playing a cartoon, the screen smudged with dirty fingerprints. She has a finger up her nose and wiggling around to find the elusive snot ball she knows is up there.

"What momma?"

"Nothing," Janeen says as she takes her seat next to Glen's bed. "Where's Braden?"

Glen says, "He went to look around out there."

Janeen sighs exhaustively. "Why'd you let him do that?"

Glen shrugs. "Maybe he might like what he sees. Maybe he'll wanna become a doctor or somethin'. Imagine that, a doctor in our family."

Janeen has on her best resting bitch face. "More like he's wanting to check out the young nurses."

"'Hey. A healthy interest in girls never hurt anybody."

"Great," Janeen says flatly. "He can be a womanizer just like his uncle Glen."

Glen manages a little chortle and glances at the TV which is playing some 90's movie with Meg Ryan in it. Glen not sure if he's seen this one.

The door to the room opens and Brian moseys in.

"What took you so long?" Janeen asks apathetically.

Brian goes to answer but she cuts him off.

"Never mind. Did you stop by the store like I asked?"

"I got your new iron."

'Did you get the right one?'

"Read your text about three times to make sure I did."

Janeen looks past him to the Meg Ryan movie.

"Did you get me beer?" asks Glen.

"The lady at the front desk said it's against the rules."

"Well of course it is. That's why you don't ask."

Janeen looks to Glen with a knowing look. "Now why would you ask mister top cop here to break the rules? Should've asked me."

"You were here before I woke up, else I would have."

Brian holds out the stuffed penguin. "I got you this though."

"What the hell is that?"

Brian looks at it a moment, then back to Janeen with confusion. "It's a penguin."

"I can see it's a fuckin' penguin."

"A dollar for the cussing jar, mom," says Alex proudly as he inspects the chest of drawers in the corner next to where Kaylee sits.

"Yeah, yeah," Janeen says to Alex, then rolls her head to look at Brian still holding out the plush toy. "Why'd you bring Glen a stuffed toy?"

"I dunno. They were sellin' stuff of the like downstairs. Thought, I dunno, it might cheer him up."

Janeen looks to Glen. "When's the last time you had a teddy bear."

"I don't remember." Glen is smirking a little, and says, "But I do remember Joe and I used to hide your Barbie dolls until you hollered so much mom saved the day."

Janeen rolls her eyes. "Yeah, I remember you buried them in the backyard once. Took me days to comb the dirt and mud outta their hair." She glances at the penguin, then her eyes meet Brian's. "How much did it cost?"

Brian swallows hard, trying to think of a way to divert the subject to something else. "Y'know what, I'll leave him over here." He strides over to the bedside table and rests the penguin next to the empty glass vase on the surface. Brian turning his attention to Glen. "Maybe Bullit would like it."

"If he don't tear it to shreds, maybe," Glen says with a lazy smile.

"I'll leave the six-pack downstairs so it's there when you're discharged."

"Thanks buddy."

"You didn't answer me, Brian. How much that thing cost?" Janeen sticks her thumb out in the direction of the penguin.

"Doesn't matter, does it?"

"Yeah it does, that's why I'm askin'."

"I don't mind it," Glen says as he looks over at it. "It's kinda growing on me already." It really isn't, Glen's just trying to do Brian a favor. That, and he's not really in the mood for one of their little verbal boxing matches. Or rather, Janeen cornering him in the ring and belting him until he's KO'd, like always.

"I'm just interested to know why Brian would buy a toy for a grown ass man."

"Two dollars for the cuss jar," Alex calls out beaming a smile.

"Ass ain't a cuss worthy of the jar," says Janeen.

"So I can say it then?" Alex says with a cheeky grin.

"No you certainly cannot. Now quiet." She turns her attention back to Brian. Before she can ask again Brian answers.

"Sixteen dollars."

Janeen's eyes widen and she opens her mouth in disbelief. "Sixteen dollars?"

"I got talkin' to the girl at the kiosk. She was real nice, so I made a snap decision. That's all honey."

"That's all," Janeen scoffs, shaking her head. "We were only talkin' the other night about Braden's college fund, and how we need to cut back on shit like your train stuff."

"You said shit! Shit's a cuss jar word!" Alex cuts in.

"Hey!" says Janeen and Brian in unison to Alex sternly.

"You know you're not allowed to repeat them," says Brian. "You're goin' to bed an hour earlier tonight. And no TV."

Alex pouts his lip and drops his head down to look at the floor in anguish.

"Same should go for you," says Janeen with a scowl. "Sixteen dollars."

"I can take it back for a refund," says Brian fidgeting with his fingers.

"So you can go talk to the pretty girl at the kiosk?"

"I never said she was pretty. I said she was nice."

Janeen dismissively waves her hand at him. "Same thing."

"No it isn't."

"You should go join your son out there, chat up some nice nurses with him while you're on a role."

"Not in front of the kids, honey."

Janeen wants to take this further, but she knows he's right. She simply aggressively stares at him, waiting for him to say something stupid.

Glen shifts in his bed, growing uncomfortable with the rising argument, looking at the TV as his only respite right now.

"Do you know what this movie is?" Glen asks. "It's been bugging me."

Janeen looks at the TV with a blank expression. "You've Got Mail."

"Huh?"

"That's the name of the movie."

"Oh."

Brian says, "So, I'm a little out of the loop. What exactly happened to you that you ended up here?"

Glen shrugs. "I passed out, is all."

"Passed out? And you're admitted to hospital?"

Janeen cuts in. "I was on the phone to him at the time and he just keeled over. I knew something was up so I had Denny cover for me while I went over. House was empty, but Bullit was barkin' like crazy by the forest. Led me right to him." She softly smiles. "Damn mutt saved your life. Much longer and you'd have gotten frostbite. Turned into a human popsicle, you would have."

"Can I have a popsicle?" asks Alex hopefully.

"No," says Janeen without missing a beat.

"Why'd you pass out?" Brian asks, then drinks an imaginary can of beer. "You on the sauce?"

"I never drink when I go hunting. I've had these headaches since the other week when my car damn near got struck by lightning. Doctors are lookin' into it. They say it should be fine."

"When they lettin' you out?" asks Janeen.

"In the next couple of days, I think."

"Why a couple of days? It's just a dizzy spell, ain't it?"

Glen sighs. "You know hospitals and their legal nuts and bolts."

"Yeah, been in and outta this place more than I care to, thanks to these crotch goblins," Janeen says and darts her eyes to her kids in the corner. "But you're as fit as a fuc-" Janeen having to stop herself shy of another dollar for the jar. "You're as fit as a fiddle. Shouldn't you be okay to leave today? What more tests they gotta do?"

"I dunno. Gotta dot the I's and cross the T's an' all that I 'spose. One thing's for sure. I've only been here a day and I already miss a proper meal."

"We'll have you over for dinner as soon as you're good," says Janeen.

"Oh, you asked me to sit for this kid's this Sunday, didn't you? Right before I, y'know."

"Don't be silly. I'll get Kelly or Simone to do it. No problem. You rest up." Janeen stands up, brushing her worn grey sweater down the front. "We'll leave you to your romantic comedies." She motions to the TV with a smile.

Glen grins back at her. "Gee, thanks."

"Come on kids, get your things together. We're gonna let Uncle Glen get better."

Alex and Kaylee collect the toys they brought with them, scattered all over the floor, and stuff them in the designated piece of luggage reserved for playtime on the move.

Janeen looks to Brian impassively and says, "Can you go find Braden. Actually, you're coming home now anyway. He can ride with you."

Brian nods assertively.

Janeen can't help herself. "And if ya can, don't buy any more stuffed animals from the cute girl on the way out."

Brian takes a deep breath, then looks to Glen. "Great seein' you buddy. Get well and all that."

Glen reaches over and picks up the penguin. "Of course I will. I have...," he stares at the toy a moment, then says, "I got Beaky here to ward off the sickness fairies."

"What's a sickness fairy?" says Kaylee, now by Janeen's side.

Janeen ruffles Kaylee's hair endearingly. "The visitors you're gonna get if you don't keep washin' your hands like momma keeps askin' ya to."

"But I like fairies," Kaylee says with confusion.

"Not these ones. Alex, take your sister's hand. C'mon. We're leaving. Your mom's gotta get dinner started."

Brian is at the door now. He gives Glen a little salute. He looks to Janeen to give her a loving sentiment, but she's too focused on making sure the kids didn't leave any toys behind. He gives up and exits the room.

Janeen gives Glen a dry kiss on the forehead, then tells Alex and Kaylee to say goodbye to their uncle and say they love him. They do. Glen leans over and gives both of them a hug. After a minute they're all gone. Glen stares at the TV for about ten minutes. Just when he thinks about changing the channel, a doctor enters the room carrying a clipboard.

"Hey Glen, how are you feeling?"

Glen sits up a little, feeling vulnerable in the hospital bed. "Yeah, I'm good."

"No headaches today?"

"Just from my family."

The doctor smiles as he looks over the charts in a tray at the end of Glen's bed. Adrian Thomas, a half-Asian, half-Caucasian man in his late 30's, handsome and clean cut except for a five o'clock shadow on his jaw. He places the clipboard of charts back into its slot and folds his arms.

"We're going to run some more tests tomorrow."

Glen nods.

Adrian says, "Did you tell your family about the tumor?"

After a few moments, Glen shakes his head 'no'.

CHAPTER TWELVE

TREE BABIES

The train rattles along the Forest Hills line while Sally sits slumped in one of the chairs, her head reverberating on the window while she's in a deep slumber. She takes the train to and from work most days, partly for environmental reasons, but also because the commute gives her more time to read a book. The train wheels squeak shrilly as the brakes are slowly applied coming into Ruggles station. It's not that sound that abruptly wakes Sally from slumber, a sound she is very much accustomed to after all these years of train commuting. It's the sudden violin crescendo of the Chopin string quartet track she's listening to through her headphones.

Sally groggily opens her bloodshot eyes. She wipes fresh drool from the side of her mouth with the sleeve of her lime green cardigan. She looks over to find the doors opening to the train. An older man is looking right at her with perverted grin plastered on his face. A few people enter the carriage, avoiding the man who is reluctant to get off the train. He just keeps on eyeballing Sally. The lingering creepy smile making her really uncomfortable now. As a woman she's used to being leered at. Even though she's hardly ever dressed provocatively in any sense, wears no makeup and her hair is perpetually messy, it doesn't stop creeps from ogling her like she'll suddenly be turned on and invite them for a chat that in their mind will invariably lead to sex. Ugh. Men. Sally is always grateful that she's been gay since she can remember. To have to sort through the minefield of gross men to find an acceptable one like some of her hetero female friends are always complaining about, would skyrocket her anxiety to a new stratosphere. Though some seem to enjoy the hunt and even the disappointments that come with it, like her co-worker Beth. Always telling Sally dating disaster stories with a kind of relish. She supposes it's because a lot of people welcome drama and chaos into their lives. And that's the last thing Sally wants.

Sally has been staring out the window at a pigeon strutting around the station platform. She's imagining the bird can hear the virtuoso violins in Chopin's melody, and it makes her smile. She looks back to the door to find that the man is still looking at her with that gross smile still intact. Sally looks around the carriage to make sure there are witnesses in case something awful happens. She looks down at her lap where the book she was reading before she fell asleep is still open in her lap. 'Ecstatic Ritual: Practical Sex Magic'. The pages facing her feature black and white photography of men and women in the throes of graphic passionate lovemaking.

Sally now realizing that the pervert must have been sitting behind somewhere and saw her reading material as he made his way to the doors. Great. Now he probably thinks she's some sexual freak and wants in on that action. Sally slams the book shut and gives him a subtle scowl, screwing her nose up at him. She wishes she had gas so she could fart loudly at him. But then she quickly realizes that she is not capable of that. Not in front of people. It is, has, and always will be a fantasy to act that bold. Her visage must have been enough though, because the doors start beeping and the man quickly hops off the train just before the doors slam shut and the train begins to move again.

Sally once again tilts her head to rest on the window again, slowly closing her eyes and drifts off to sleep listening to the peppy violins on the Chopin track.

The lavender field from Sally's previous dream that stretches for miles in every direction. Only this time there's no ringed planets in the sky, nor stars. It's just black space bleeding down into blue sunny skies. The environment is like a giant fishbowl with sunbeams vibrating in the air like heat waves.

Sally is dressed like an old-fashioned outdoor gardener. Baggy green ripstop nylon overalls with a large, embroidered sunflower on the right leg. A large, brimmed straw hat on her head and black gumboots on her feet. She is kneeling on the dirt amongst the purple plants using a gardening trowel in one hand, digging into the soft soil to loosen it.

Sally is humming a lullaby tune that her mother used to sing to her before bed when she was a child. She carefully pulls out one of the lavender plants from the row she's working on and gently lays it down in a wicker basket by her side.

Her ears prick up. Sally can hear the cry of a baby somewhere close by.

Sally looks around her immediate space, shifting around in a circle on her knees until she's done a full 360-degree turn. The baby's cries sounding to her like it's right here somewhere. Then she sees a tiny infant arm reaching up through a clump of lavender plants. Sally quickly walks on her kneecaps over to the arm and uses both hands to separate the plants around it to reveal a baby girl half submerged in the soil. The little girl flailing both arms as if wanting to be picked up.

Sally uses the trowel to dig ever so carefully around the child, loosening the dirt to make it easier to pull her from the earth. Sally continues to hum the lullaby as she works. Satisfied, Sally reaches over and gently wraps her hands around the baby's torso, then pulls her up from out of the soil, flakes of dirt falling from the infant as she kicks her free legs around in glee. Sally tenderly lays the baby girl in the wicker basket on the soft bed of lavender plants inside.

The sound of snarling dogs. Several of them. Vicious and bloodthirsty.

Sally stiffens with fear and looks around.

Behind her, about ten yards away, is the woman dressed in her deep red cocktail dress with matching heels and bright red lipstick. Her face still fuzzy. An ethereal circle of white light behind her. She holds the leashes to six huskie dogs, snapping and growling with foam dripping from their mouths.

The cloudiness around the red woman's face dissipates. Sally's eyes widen. It's herself. Her blonde hair pasted down with product and shimmering from the sun waves. Her eyelashes long and blackened with mascara. Smokey eyes from thick eyeshadow. Her cheekbones accentuated with foundation. Sally has never in her life worn make up this classy. Sexy, even. She stares with awe at this dolled up version of herself, while the alternative Sally stares back at her with a confidently playful smirk.

Sally wants to speak to her but can't find the words. The red dressed Sally lets the dog leashes go and the huskies start sprinting for her, barking and snarling as they kick up mangled lavender plants behind them.

Sally spins around and picks up the wicker basket with the child and bolts across the field. There's nowhere to hide. No place to sprint to safety. So she runs, hugging the basket to her chest with a face full of desperation. She looks behind her to find the dogs are gaining on her, leaving a trail of destroyed plants behind them.

Red Sally laughs wickedly.

"Stop them! Why are you doing this!?" Sally calls out between exasperated breaths.

Red Sally only responds with her low, deep throated laugh.

The night air is still and coldly thick in the pine tree forest. Moonlight reflecting off the snow-covered forest floor. Glen trudges through the fresh powder, wearing only a hospital gown and black workman's boots. His hair is free and falls halfway down his back. He carries a rifle gripped in both hands at the ready.

Glen stops. He feels the presence of another. He slowly turns to find the boy version of himself is standing behind, wearing a puffy jacket and knitted cap. He looks afraid and lost. His lips trembling and eyes sad. Glen ignores the child and keeps stalking forward through the maze of trees.

Glen stops again, spotting something running through the forest ahead. He brings the gun up so he can peer through the targeting scope. A deer. Glen notices dark shapes several yards behind her in pursuit. He uses the scope to zoom in. Big dogs on the hunt for the doe. They almost have their prey. Glen brings the gun down and breaks into a run after the animals.

Sally is dashing through the lavender field. The sunlight vanishes in an instant like a light was just switched off. The sun replaced by a full moon directly above. The sounds of the dogs gnashing teeth and bloodlust snarling growing nearer and nearer by the second. She can feel the warmth of their breath on her back. The baby in her basket now wailing loudly. Her face red and arms reaching out for help. Sally can hear crunching under her boots as she runs and looks down to find globs of snow intermittently all over the lavender and dirt.

Sally notices someone else running toward her from the side. She snaps her head to look over and sees that it's Glen full pelt sprinting at her with his rifle clutched to his chest.

"Help! Shoot them!" Sally screams out to Glen.

Sally now seeing a pear tree several yards ahead and uses all she has to quicken her pace toward it. Flowers of all kinds and colors pop up through the snow she runs.

"They're trying to take my baby!" Sally calls out.

Sally reaches the tree and uses one hand to reach up for a branch while the other holds the basket handle. She manages to grab hold of the lowest branch and plants her foot on the tree trunk, pushing upwards. She manages to hoist herself up onto the branch just as one of the dogs nips the back of her foot. Sally climbs to the next branch up and nestles the basket with the screaming baby into a hole in the trunk. She looks down to find the dogs circling the base of the tree, barking and trying to jump up to get to her.

"Hey, what's going on here?" Glen calls up to Sally.

"They're going to kill me and my baby. Shoot them!"

Glen arrives at the tree and stops, looking at Sally then at the ferocious beasts. He casually walks up to the huskies. Sally watches with terror in her eyes, thinking the dogs will tear him shreds.

As Glen moseys to the trunk of the tree the dogs surround him. Their barks and snarls turn to happy whimpering noises. Their tails wagging gleefully.

"They're not gonna hurt you," Glen says as he starts petting the dogs vying for his attention. He shoulders his rifle and drops down to one knee, letting the dogs lick his face. All of them climbing over each other in a happy frenzy.

Sally watches the scene below with amazement. She looks over to the basket to make sure it's still safe. The baby has stopped crying, now just making soft baby gibberish noises.

Glen looks up to Sally with a big dumb grin on his face.

"See? They just need some attention."

Sally looks across the field to locate her red dolled up alter ego. She's nowhere to be seen.

"They're hungry fella's, ain't ya," Glen says as he scratches them behind the ears. He looks up to Sally. "Come on down."

"Is... is it safe?"

Glen laughs, pushing one of the dogs over and scrubs his belly. The dog clearly loving it.

"They might lick you to death, but that's a risk you should be willing to take."

After a few moments, Sally reaches over to the hole in the tree and takes the basket out. She carefully climbs down to the next branch and lowers it down toward Glen.

"Little help?"

Glen rises up and carefully takes the bottom of the basket with both hands. Sally dangles her legs down from the branch and pushes off.

Sally's feet land in two feet of fresh snow. Phoomph. She shivers and looks around to find she's now in the thick of the woods. Not a lavender plant in sight.

"Where are we?" Sally asks.

Glen looks around, wondering why she's confused. To him, they have always been here. But all the colorful flowers were not there before. All the daisies, sunflowers, dahlias, roses and carnations.

Sally remembers now that there were dogs here just moments ago, but now there's no sign of them.

"What happened to the dogs?"

Now Glen is confused with her. He remembered the dogs being here but have vanished. He scratches his head, gently laying the wicker basket on top of a tree stump next to him.

"I dunno. They must've run off?"

Sally crosses her arms. The summer overalls she's wearing and lack of jacket making her increasingly cold.

"You always bring the cold with you," she says to Glen matter-of-factly, eying him off in his hospital gown and boots, wondering why he's not freezing like she is.

A twig snaps in the forest nearby. Sally peers through the mélange of trees and shrubbery. She spots young Glen skulking around with aa pout on his face and his hands stuck deep in his pockets.

"Who is that child? I've seen him before."

"He's no one, lady. Never mind him. He'll go away," Glen says as he stares contemptuously at his younger self.

Sally's eyes fall on the basket. The baby! She dashes over to the stump to grab the basket, but when she arrives, her jaw drops and her visage turns to devastation.

The basket is empty.

"What?! No, no, no, no, no, no!" She turns to look at Glen with horror in her eyes. "Where is she?" She starts pulling at her hair anxiously.

"Where's who?"

Sally picks up the basket with both hands and inspects it closely, as if the baby will suddenly reappear. She shakes the empty basket with desperation.

"The baby! Where is she?"

"There was no baby."

Sally drops the basket to the snowy ground, and it topples on its side.

"Yes there was. There was a baby girl when I handed you the basket. I'm telling you there was, you bastard!"

"And I'm telling you there was nothin' in it when you handed it to me."

"Bullshit!"

Sally marches over to the pear tree and climbs up to the lowest branch, then to the next one up. She clambers to the hole in the trunk and peers intensely inside. Nothing. She sticks her hands in and feels every part of the enclosure. Nothing.

Sally frantically tries to climb higher in the tree, thinking there might have been another hole in the trunk she may have placed the child. The next branch up is too high for her to grasp, and she almost loses her footing twice.

"Careful, you're gonna fall."

"She has to be here somewhere!" Sally grunts trying to scale the side of the tree.

Glen mindfully glares at boy Glen still pacing around the trees nearby.

Sally loses her footing and squeals, falling off the branch and tumbling to the ground. Glen is quick to react and catches her in his arms. She gives him a look of bewilderment for a few moments while cradled in his arms, then scrambles to get out of his hold.

Sally is wild eyed and manic. "There was a baby girl. I just had her. I picked her myself from the field."

"Picked a baby? From where? What field?"

"There was a baby. I grew her. I handpicked her from the lavender. She was mine. She was mine!"

Sally lunges forward and shoves Glen harshly in his chest, sending him stumbling a few steps back.

"Hey lady, what's yo-"

"I've told you! Don't call me lady. It sounds condescending."

Glen stares at her with a blank expression for a moment.

"Alright... uh, flower girl."

"Flower girl? That somehow sounds even more condescending." She folds her arms with attitude and looks away a moment, then looks back at him. "Why flower girl anyway?"

"Every time you show up there's flowers an' shit."

Sally can't help but grin a little.

"Okay, fine, bullet man."

"Let me guess. Because I've got a gun?"

"Well, you shot me, more to the point."

Glen rubs his chin and nods. "Oh, right."

"Anyway. Help me find the baby. She has to be here somewhere."

Glen wants to remind her that he saved her from falling just moments ago but figures this crazy woman won't care about that. He watches her parade around all the neighboring trees searching for this elusive infant. Glen chuckles. The chuckling turns into laughter, which soon becomes full blown hysterics. He can't breathe he's laughing so hard. He bends over and slaps his knee.

Sally stops and glares at him with a mixture of disdain and confusion.

"What's so damn funny?"

Glen tries to speak but is having trouble talking while laughing. "You're... as... loony as a... fuckin' toon!"

"Come again?" Sally takes a step toward him with clenched fists.

"Babies growin' on trees? Damn. I ain't never heard anything so ludicrous. I mean, the stork thing was always stupid. But God damn woman, I haven't laughed so hard in years. You gotta show me what you've been smokin'. I thought my Frostbite was the bee's knees."

Sally breathes heavy, angry breaths. She storms past Glen and picks up the empty basket from the ground, giving it one more hopeful look inside. Still empty.

"You know. You're right, Glen. Joke's on me."

Glen's chortling now subsided, he wipes laughter tears from his eyes. "What do you mean? What joke?"

A tear rolls down Sally's cheek as she stares at the empty basket in her hands.

Glen now looking remorseful. "I... I'm sorry, Sally. I didn't mean to...," Glen doesn't know how to finish that. He's never been good at apologizing. He wants to give Sally a hug. But he's never been very compassionate either.

"No, it's okay. Sometimes you think things are going your way for once. Then you realize it's just another stupid dream."

"Dream?" Glen's eyes furrow.

Sally lets the basket fall to her feet, and she turns and starts to walk away.

"Hey. I'm sorry. I just don't know what to make of this."

Glen turns around to look at his younger self, only he's gone now. Glen looks back to Sally. She's gone too. He starts to wonder what she meant by that dream comment. He bends down and picks up the basket and inspects it himself.

He can hear a thumping sound. Rhythmic in short little bursts. After a few moments he recognizes it as knocking. Someone pounding their fist on a door over the sound of a barking dog.

CHAPTER THIRTEEN

THE CULPRIT

Knocking at the door wakes Glen up. That and Bullit barking. He wipes his hand over his face, his eyes groggy and mouth dry. Glen sits forward in his recliner. Confusion quickly washes over him. He realizes he has his rifle slung over his shoulder. What the hell? He passed out watching TV and hasn't been out hunting since the fainting incident in the woods several days ago.

Knocking at the door again. Glen stands up and mounts the rifle on the wall where it belongs. Knocking again, driving Bullit nuts.

"Quit it Bullit!"

Who could this be? Glen hasn't expected anyone today, nor in the last few years. Must be Janeen.

Glen, wearing a bath robe and slippers ambles to the front door and tells Bullit to scram. The dog obeying his master and trots halfway up the corridor and sits obediently and quietly.

Glen opens the door to find a woman in her 50's standing on the front porch. She's got long chestnut hair with the odd grey hairs. Hazel eyes and genial smile. She's wearing a silky frilly blouse with a gold owl brooch, a long navy blue Burberry trench coat and dark plaid skirt that ends at her trendy black leather boots. Glen's eyes fall on the professional leather case she's carrying in one hand.

"Are you Glen Bourke?"

Glen scratches his head. "Uh, yeah?"

She sticks her hand out to be shaken. "I'm Yvonne Pettigrew."

Glen hesitates, then shakes her hand, looking at her with puzzlement.

Yvonne says, "I must apologize for showing up unannounced without calling first. It's not very twenty-first century of me, I know. But your sister, Janeen, said you would never have felt otherwise disposed."

Glen's first instinct is to ask her how she bypassed his property's front gate lock, but after looking over her shoulder he can see Janeen's car driving away in the distance. He realizes immediately that Janeen let this woman in with her spare keys.

"I'm sorry. But agreed to what?"

"Janeen said she had briefly spoken about myself and my profession a short time ago. I'm a psychologist whose expertise is dream analysis and therapy."

Glen sighs and rubs the bridge of his nose with closed eyes a moment. Dammit Janeen. He opens his eyes and crosses his arms.

"Listen, Aylon."

"Yvonne."

"Yvonne. I'm goin' through some shit. Sorry. I mean, I'm goin' through some stuff right now, and I'm not really up for this, uh, kinda thing, right now."

"And what kind of thing is that?"

"Look, no offense, but I don't need a shrink."

"Well, you're in luck. Because I'm not a shrink. I'm not here to listen to your day-to-day problems. I really couldn't give a fuck about that."

Glen taken aback by her candor.

Yvonne says, "I'm just coming to chat about your subconscious and what it's trying to say to you. Have you been having vivid dreams lately? More so than usual?"

Glen sucks in a deep lungful of breath through his nose, staring at her complacently in order to give her no indication he is interested in what she's saying. Though, after her cussing and being up front with him, he is sort of interested. Sort of.

"Maybe. A little. Yeah."

Yvonne smiles. "Cool. So why don't we cut the shit, and you invite me in for a tea and you can tell me a little about it. I drove a long way, and, it's pretty fucking cold out here."

"I don't have tea."

"Whatever you got is fine."

"What time is it?"

She checks the gold analog watch strapped to her wrist. "Nearly two-thirty."

"How about bourbon?"

She grins. "Even better."

Glen moves out of the way for her to enter. She takes a step inside and notices Bullit up the hallway and stops in her tracks.

"It's okay. Bullit don't bite."

"He's a big dog."

"And an even bigger softie."

"Why bullet?" Her eyes flick to the rifle mounted on the wall. "Because you like to hunt?"

"Not bullet. Bullit, like the Steve McQueen movie." He shrugs. "I love Mustangs."

Yvonne nods curtly and continues in, Glen shutting the door behind her. Glen motions for her to follow him as he turns right into the living room. Glen notices the empty beer bottles around his recliner and makes haste to clean them up.

"Sorry. I wasn't expecting anyone." He has the necks of six bottles clenched in his fingers, the glass tinkering loudly as he bends over to scoop more up with his other hand. "In fact, I never have visitors over. 'Cept my sister and her cronies."

"That's okay," Yvonne says as she eyes off the decorations in the room to ascertain some kind of insight to his personality. The elk skulls, Western frontier paintings and pictures of Middle Eastern desert give her a little idea.

Yvonne spots a picture frame on a small table next to one of the armchairs and steps over to peer down at it. The picture inside is of Glen wearing military fatigues and holding what appears to be a kelpie puppy.

"You were in the service?"

"Yup. Two tours in Afghanistan."

"And who is your little friend?"

Glen looks over at the picture. A soft, melancholy smile appears for a moment.

"That's Lily. I found her in a village we liberated. A lot of houses in that area got bombed pretty bad. I heard her crying in some rubble. Pulled her out. A few of the guys said I should put her out of her misery. I did the opposite. I took her with me for the rest of my tour, then brought her back here with me."

"So she's here?"

Glen's eyes furrow. "Out back."

Yvonne is about to ask if she can meet her but quickly realizes by the stern look on Glen's face that it's probably not a good idea.

Glen dumps the empty beer bottles into a wastebasket in the corner. "Take a seat," Glen says, pointing at the second leather recliner that Bullit usually curls up on. Glen realizes there's noticeable dog hair on there and quickly picks up a scarf from the coffee table to dust the chair off.

Yvonne smiles politely and daintily sits on the recliner, placing her leather case next to it. Glen darts away for a couple of minutes. Yvonne looking over to the corridor doorway to find Bullit sitting there, watching her with innocent interest, despite the fact she is sitting in his special chair.

"Hello," Yvonne says to Bullit, even giving him a little feminine wave.

Glen returns with two mismatched glasses and a bottle of Jack Daniels. He pours them both a hefty glass and hands her one, which she gingerly accepts.

Glen says, "You want ice, or...,"

"Neat is just fine, thank you," Yvonne says as she crosses one leg over the other.

Glen nods and takes a seat in his recliner. "First off the bat, my sister did mention you. She said you're based in Boston."

"That's correct, yes."

"You drove all the way out here?"

Yvonne takes a sip of the bourbon and nestles the glass comfortably in her lap.

"I did. But before we begin, I need to tell you that house calls are not in my repertoire. In fact, this is the second time in my twenty years of my practice that I've done this. The only reason is your sister is quite concerned about your welfare, and on top of my hourly fee she covered the cost of my travel time and expenses. Now, before you say something along the lines of, I'm not paying a fee for which I did not ask for, it's all taken care of. Janeen has covered our session today. Beyond that, it's up to you if you want to continue with further sessions. In other words, you don't pay a dime for my services today."

Glen sips on his drink taking all that in. He nods and says, "She shouldn't be doin' this. They got money troubles of their own."

"Then she must really care about you," Yvonne says mindfully.

"I should call her, just to-"

"It's already paid for. If you don't want to proceed, it'll be a waste of her money."

Glen sighs. She's got a point.

"So. What do you wanna know?"

Yvonne places her glass down on the small table between the chairs, then leans over and picks up her case. She opens it and takes out a yellow lined notepad and unscrews a fountain pen.

"Let's start with recurring dreams and nightmares. Do you have any that repeat, or feel like they are repeating?"

Glen takes a hefty sip of the bourbon and clears his throat, nodding his head slowly.

Yvonne scribbles something on her pad.

"Is it a good dream, or a bad one?"

"It's a nightmare."

"And how often does this nightmare occur?"

Glen sighs and looks out the window. Light flecks of snow falling outside. "Every six months or so."

"And for how long have you been experiencing this recurring nightmare?"

"Since my mid-twenties." He shrugs. "Not exactly sure what year."

"And how old are you?"

"Forty-two."

Yvonne does the quick math in her head. "So... you've been having this same nightmare every few months... for around, eighteen years?"

"No. I mean, yeah, I've had it since then. But not every six months exactly. That's only happened in the past couple of years. It started when I was in the service. During my two tours, and not for a while after that. I guess that period came with its own nightmares."

Yvonne vigorously jots notes on her pad for a minute.

"What are you writin' down?" Glen says, trying to peer over but the writing is scrawl he couldn't read even if his eyesight was sharper.

Yvonne grins, still writing. "Don't worry. This isn't an assessment. I need to know the ingredients of the soup I'm making if it's going to taste any good." She stops, then chuckles to herself and shakes her head. "I'm sorry. That was a piss poor analogy. I was trying to be creative on the fly, and as it turns out, I'm quite shit at that."

Glen smiles. He loves the way this lady talks.

She says, "Now. If you're comfortable doing so, I'd like to hear the nature of this nightmare. What happens and who is involved. Are there other people you know or is it people you have manifested?"

"Well, that's the weird part."

"I love weird. Go on."

"Um, so the dream is usually me and my brother, Joe. We're walking along a frozen lake. The ice breaks and he falls in. He drowns and I try to save him, but I can't."

"Uh huh," Yvonne says as she continues to jot information down.

"It's...," Glen takes a sip of his drink. "It happened in real life. When we were kids."

Yvonne stops writing a moment and looks up at him with a serious expression, then continues to scribble.

"The weird part is, lately, there's been this woman in my dreams. She doesn't exist. I mean, I've certainly never seen her before."

"Interesting. Does she resemble a famous figure? Like a politician. Or a celebrity. Someone you might see on TV or the internet?"

"What? I don't go on the internet."

Yvonne stops writing and picks up her bourbon, takes a sip and puts it back down.

"Sometimes when we manifest a person in our dreams, it usually comes from the subconscious. You might have seen this woman on the cover of a magazine, or in a movie you saw a little while ago. Does she remind you of anyone?"

Glen shakes his head slowly, taking a ruminating sip of his drink. "No, I don't think so. She just feels so… real."

Yvonne furrows her brows and taps the pen on the pad. "What exactly do you mean by real?"

"I dunno how to explain it. But when you dream, it's usually all over the place, right?"

Yvonne nods.

"When this woman enters my dreams, it feels like real life. I wake up and I don't forget it. It's like a memory. You know, when somethin' happens in day-to-day life, you remember it. You remember the details. Even the most memorable dreams seem to… I dunno… they turn foggy after a day or so. With her, it's like I'm actually there. You know what I'm sayin'?"

"I do. Are you attracted to this woman?"

Glen looks at her with astonishment.

Yvonne says, "Sorry, I should clarify. Are you heterosexual?"

"Straight as an arrow."

"Okay. So, when you see this woman… is it sexual?"

Glen bursts out laughing.

Yvonne raises her eyebrows and scribbles notes.

"It ain't like that, no. I mean, she's pretty an' all. But she's fuckin' nuts."

Yvonne stifles a smile.

"How does she make you feel?"

Glen stares at her, blinking slowly.

Yvonne changes her legs to cross over the other one. "You said she appears in your nightmare. Does she add to the tension, or does she bring you some kind of repose?"

Glen isn't sure what repose means exactly, but he assumes from the sentence that it means comfort or something like that.

"Well, thing is, first she was scared of me. Because, I kinda shot her in the stomach. But the next time she saved me from a well. I was stuck down there, and she got me out. She's a stress head. Obsessed with babies and shit. The funny thing is, every time she appears, it's like I'm entering her dream, and not the other way around."

Yvonne stops writing and takes a moment to contemplate while she has a sip of bourbon. She places her pad aside for a moment and folds her hands in her lap.

"This is going to sound a little...," she pauses, then smiles and says, "Have you been exposed to any kind of... accident, or trauma, recently?"

"Trauma?"

"You know, an accident. Like an electric shock."

Glen stiffens up, then takes a hearty swig of bourbon.

"Why electric shock, specifically?"

Yvonne shrugs. "Just curious."

Glen shifts uncomfortably in his recliner, looking out the window a moment, then back to Yvonne.

"About two or three weeks ago, a clap of lightning almost hit my car while I was driving in the Berkshires. It was so damn loud I passed out momentarily."

Yvonne sits forward eagerly; her eyes widen with anticipation. "Was it just you?"

"On the road?"

"Yes. Was anyone else present when the lightning struck?"

Glen goes to tell her about the other car that swerved off the road. Then he stops himself. He doesn't want Yvonne to know he drove off without checking if the person in the other car was alright. He especially doesn't want her that the drugs in the back of his truck were the reason he left the scene so quickly.

"No. It was just me," Glen says, nestling his back into the recliner while taking a sip of bourbon.

"Are you sure?" Yvonne says with a hopeful visage.

"Yeah. I'm sure."

Yvonne blinks, looking at the floor with disappointment. "I see."

"What's that gotta do with anything, anyway?"

She waves her hand at him and sits back, picking up her pad and pen again.

"Nothing. There's a school of thought… don't worry. It's silly. So, let's forget about the crazy baby lady for now. I want to know more about Joe."

Glen rubs his thumbs anxiously up and down his glass. He suddenly downs the rest of the bourbon and quickly stands up.

"I'm gonna have another. You want a fresh pour?"

Yvonne glances at her glass with a few good nips still in there but knew the answer anyway. "I'm good. Thank you."

Glen abruptly marches out of the room and into the kitchen. Yvonne sits patiently, listening to a few cupboards opening and closing.

The thin little smile on her face from knowing that Glen is stalling in there. After a few minutes he reappears in the living room with a refilled glass of bourbon.

"Sorry, had to find a new bottle." He plonks down in his recliner and rocks in it a few times. "So, what's this about electricity? You asked a specific question, to which I gave you a specific answer. Now I'm kinda curious where you were goin' with that."

"We'll touch on that another time. Now, let's not get sidetracked. I want to know why your brother is the key to your recurring nightmare."

Glen sniffs and clears his throat, staring balefully out at the falling snow through the front window. His expression darkening into a scowl.

"I told ya. He drowned. I was there. Didn't you write it down in your fuckin' notes there?"

"Now Glen, I'm just-"

"But I bet you already knew. My sister would'a given you the whole fuckin' lowdown."

"Janeen hasn't told me anything, other than she felt you were in some deep internal pain, that usually manifests itself in your sleep. She said that you're not exactly the opening up kind. That you wouldn't feel comfortable talking to friends or family about your struggles."

"She sure said a fuckin' lot for someone who told you nothing."

"It's perfectly normal to be that way. You have physically isolated yourself out here to make that clear, not just to others, but to yourself."

"Yeah, and that's the way I like it," Glen takes a hefty swig of bourbon. The liquid now giving him mild heartburn. He taps his chest with his fist a few times.

Yvonne says, "I did put two and two together about your brother and the drowning. But I'm not as interested in the event, so much as what you see in your dreams relating to him. A color. An animal. A specific plant or tree. The little details you might not think important. That's what I do. You can think of me as a detective. Your subconscious leaves the clues, and I piece it together and find the culprit."

"The culprit?" Glen scoffs and shakes his head. "I'd say the fuckin' culprit is my dead fuckin' brother. No, you know what? The culprit is me. I didn't save him, and he's dead because of me. I killed him, and that fact haunts me every goddam day. There you go detective. Case fuckin' closed." Glen slams his glass down on the coffee table and leaps off the seat to stand. "Here's another case for ya. Find the fuckin' front door and use it. And don't come back."

Glen huffs angry breaths from his nose, staring at her angrily.

Yvonne picks up her work case and puts the pad and pen back inside. She knocks back the rest of her bourbon and stands up, smoothing out her plaid skirt. Yvonne picks up her stylish trench coat and puts it on. She holds her case in one hand, giving Glen an endearing smile.

"I'm sorry if we got off on the wrong foot." She reaches into a pocket in her jacket and pulls out a business card, leaving it on the table next to her empty glass. "If you decide you want to talk further, I'll be ready and waiting."

With that, Yvonne turns on her heels and strides out of the room, keeping eye contact with Bullit as she passes him in the hall all the way to the front door, gently closing it behind her.

Glen waits until Yvonne's car starts and hears the gravel crunch under the moving tires before letting out a massive painful groan. He goes back to his recliner and sits down, sticking his face in his hands. His head pounding furiously to the point he can't think straight. White blotches in his vision, the same thing that happened just before he passed out in the woods. After a few minutes he removes his hands from his face. Blood smeared on his palms. He feels his nose, feeling liquid trickling from it. God damn it. Time to go back to the hospital.

Janeen and Brian lie in bed, both of them reading. Janeen is reading a murder mystery book; Brian is reading a beginner's book on gardening. He's had enough and places the book on his bedside table, removing his reading glasses and placing them on top. He turns the lamp off on his side.

"Turning in?"

"Yeah."

"Okay. Night."

"Night."

Brian lays on his back and closes his eyes. Thoughts begin running through his head. Mostly about seeding development and weed biology information that he just consumed. The thoughts on gardening turn to pictures he had seen on the internet showing plant biology labs. He imagines Sally at one of those desks, dressed professionally in a lab coat, and not in the ugly sweater and pants he saw her in. Then he imagines her wearing nothing. He thinks she would look good naked, and with some makeup on. Now he's becoming horny. He reaches down through his boxer shorts and feels his semi-erect penis.

Brian rolls over on his side face Janeen and reaches under the blankets to stroke her leg. She doesn't flinch, she simply keeps on reading. His stroking becoming more sensual now, she can't ignore it.

"You alright?"

"Yeah." He continues stroking, moving his hand closer to her crotch. She sighs and puts the open book down on her stomach.

"What are you doin'?"

"I dunno... I thought maybe we could... y'know."

"The kids are here."

"We can be quiet."

"Brian... nuh-uh. Not tonight."

"It's been… I can't even remember the last time we did."

"I think our last anniversary."

"No. We went for dinner. Got home, and you said you had a wine headache."

Janeen thinks about that for a second, then shrugs.

"So we'll make an effort next one."

"I have to wait all that time to-"

"I'm not in the mood Brian." She takes his hand and guides it away from her, then picks up the book to resume reading.

Brian lies there for a moment, filled with defeat. He rolls over to face the other way and closes his eyes.

He imagines Sally naked again. It won't leave his mind. He imagines her masturbating, looking at him while she does it.

Less than five minutes later Brian is in the upstairs bathroom jerking off while thinking of Sally.

CHAPTER FOURTEEN

AN IMPULSE
PURCHASE

Sally is checking out her butt in the mirror of a boutique women's clothing store changing room. The dress is emerald green, sleek and tight fitting with a V-neck plunge, the bottom flowy and falls to just below the knees. She didn't expect to go dress shopping today, but Rain insisted.

"How's it fit?" Rain calls from the changing room waiting area, looking at her Instagram feed.

"It doesn't have pockets."

"Stroppy, you are going to be hard pressed finding a lady's formal dress that has pockets. Trust me." She looks up from her phone. "And besides, why is that even a thing? Why do women complain about not have pockets all the time? What would you keep in there that wouldn't go in your purse or handbag?"

Sally jiggles her body trying to get her ass to move in the dress, but it seals her cheeks in tight. She slaps her butt. The sound a little louder than she imagined, and her face turns a little red.

"What was that?" Rain calls out.

"Nothing. Look, if there were pockets, maybe we wouldn't need handbags. I could keep my bank card and lip balm in there easy."

Rain laughs. "You really think that we could fit everything inside a couple of measly pockets? Dude, reality check. I mean, I know you're super low maintenance, but most chick's I know have handbags like Mary Poppin's little luggage case. You could furnish a bedroom with the shit in there. It's fucking endless. So no, they're not going to change centuries of fashion for some hairy taco muncher in Boston." Rain purses her lips apologetically. "Sorry, I didn't mean to use a derogatory name like that. I wasn't thinking."

"You never do," Sally says with a sigh.

"So that's your only issue with it? The lack of pockets?"

Sally turns to look at her butt from a different angle, stepping up on her tippy-toes and craning her head to obsess over her derriere. She's never had to look sexy for anyone in a very long time. Larissa likes her the disheveled mess that she is, always saying they're like Ying and Yang in that sense. Larissa is the one who dresses decadently. Sally looking like she got home from Burning Man when they go out to eat. Larissa loves the looks they get from other patrons.

"Hey, you still in there?" Rain says, then sighs and dumps her phone in her bohemian woven handbag. She rises up from the stool and strides to the stall Sally is in and whips the curtain open.

Sally responds as if she's naked for a second and covers her privates with both arms.

"You're a fuckin' unit," Rain says shaking her head with a smile. She looks Sally up and down a moment. "That looks great on you. It's hot."

Sally looks in the mirror again, placing her hands on her hips.

"Yeah. Green is my favorite color. But, I dunno. It's not really doing it for me."

"Then get out of it. We're moving on."

"Wait. If I just look at it a little bit longer...,"

Rain steps over and unzips the back. "Nope. If you're not wow-ed by it straight up, it's not your thing. When it comes to getting a dress that makes you feel hot, you gotta be impressed the second you lay eyes on it when you look in the mirror. If you can't sell yourself, you're not gonna sell anyone else. Come on. Off with it."

Rain swipes one of the straps off her shoulder.

"I can do it myself," Sally says stepping away from Rain's meddling.

Rain puts her hands up defensively. "Alright, alright. Don't get your knickers in a twist."

Sally strips down to her underwear. Granny panties and a bra that's seen the inside of a dryer so much it's hard to tell if the original color was pink, cream or peach.

"Jesus fuck. Okay, speaking of kickers, after we get you a dress, we are getting you lingerie."

Sally looks down at her shabby old underwear, now appearing quite embarrassed.

Rain says, "That is a crime against sexuality."

"Isn't lingerie expensive? I don't know if I wanna spend lots of money on something I'll only ever wear once."

"Wear once?" Rain scoffs. "Okay, I don't want to get too personal, but how is your and Larissa's sex life?"

Sally spins around to face her with raised eyebrows and an open mouth of shock.

Rain puts her hands up defensively again and says, "I don't mean to pry."

"Don't mean to pry?" Sally scoffs. "You're asking about my intimate details with my partner."

"I'm your sister, believe me, I don't wanna know how you two bump uglies. But after the baby comes, it's important to have healthy adult alone time."

"And you're the expert on post-birth child rearing?"

Rain's expression suddenly drops to one of sadness. Sally realizes she just invoked a painful memory and places her hand on Rain's arm.

"I'm sorry. That was rude and facetious."

"It's okay," Rain says with a forced smile. She's quick to change the subject back. "Just… trust me. I've seen it a lot. You're both gonna be stressed all the time, and sleep deprived. I'm sure you've been doing your research. But sexy time is what saves fatigued new parents. Buy some hot ass sexy lingerie. Not for this guy Brad. For Larissa. And most importantly, for you."

Sally gives her a weak grin, nodding a couple of times. "I guess it can't hurt."

Rain gives Sally a sleazy smirk. "Well, it can, if you discover new things." Rain follows that up with a cheeky wink.

"Like pegging?"

"You looked that up, huh?"

"Oh, I looked it up alright. Except I stupidly used Larissa's computer. She went to type something in Google that night and saw the search history." Sally's cheeks turn bright red. "Now she thinks I'm some perverted freak."

Rain bursts out laughing. It doesn't stop. She has to use the wall for support while she tries to control the snickering.

Sally puts her stone washed jeans and faded vintage Daisy Duck sweater back on while Rain tries to calm her laughing fit.

Sally says, "Alright, now it's getting a little weird."

Rain tries to get her words in short breaths between laughs. "I'm... just imaging you... on all fours... Larissa with a... big black strap-on...,"

"Yeah okay, now it's really frikkin' weird."

Sally shakes her head and marches out of the stall, leaving Rain in hysterics.

Sally and Rain meander down Newbury Street in downtown Boston, perusing all the decadent window shop fronts filled with mannequins wearing high end outfits and accessories. Rain licks her hand to get the melted ice cream that has fallen on there from the cone she's eating. Sally has a small container with apricot gelato, eating tidbits from the little plastic spoon.

"I think you should get two," Rain says, eying off a brown dress that she reckons would look dynamite on her.

"Two dresses?"

"Yeah. I mean, why not? You only have the one formal dress at home."

"I only wear it to Larissa's work thingies. It serves that purpose well and isn't falling apart or anything like that. I dry clean it all the time. It still looks like it did the day I bought it."

"But how many photos must there be of you in the same dress?"

Sally inhales a sharp breath. She is recalling an argument about this very thing she had with Larissa about six months ago. Larissa telling her that she's becoming embarrassed about Sally wearing the same fucking dress every time. They both have a good income, so money isn't the issue. Why is she acting like Marge Simpson from that one episode where she wears the same modified dress at functions with the same people. Larissa telling her at least Marge made an effort to change it up. Sally wears the same boring dress, over and over. Then the argument became about something else, as they always tend to do.

Sally says, "Look. I only wear that dress for events I'd really rather not be at anyway. They're a chore to me. I don't dress to the nines to do the dishes, know what I'm saying?"

"Sally, I know you're not really into the idea of fucking this guy. At least in the sexual sense. But you have to stop thinking about it like a chore. Cause it's only going to suck that way. Think of it, more as a challenge."

"Like a game show?"

"Shut up and listen. You wanna blow this Brad guy's socks off. Not because you want it to be romantic, but you should feel kick-ass. Dude's gayer than RuPaul, right? So what if you made him question his sexuality. How fucking cool would that be?"

"I just want to make a baby."

"Exactly. You want him to shoot a load so big that the sperms will be fighting like football hooligans to get in that egg."

"You're disgusting."

"But a disgusting genius."

Sally shakes her head with a grin as she sucks more gelato from the spoon. Her eyes widen and she stops in her tracks. Rain keeps walking ahead, talking about sex and unaware that Sally is stopped and staring at a shop front window display.

A white faceless mannequin is wearing a long thin red polyester cocktail dress, with a plunging neckline and thigh high side split. To Sally it's stunning. Simple yet sexy. It also reminds Sally of the dress that the alter-ego of herself in her recent dreams is wearing. It's almost exactly the same.

Rain now realizes Sally is no longer by her side and turns to find her gawking at the shop window. She power-walks back to stand by Sally's side, following her gaze to the red dress.

"You like that one?"

"It's perfect."

"But... you don't even like the color red. You always said it's tacky, and reminds you of blood and violence."

"It's just like the one from my dream." Sally turns her head to look at Rain. "Remember, the woman with the dogs I told you about?"

Rain nods her head and bites half the ice cream cone off in her hand, clearly not that much of a fan of this particular dress.

"You wanna try it on?"

Sally shakes her head slowly, like she's in some kind of daze.

"No. I don't need to. I've already seen it on me."

Sally hands her gelato to Rain and briskly strides into the shop.

Rain is busily licking the back of her forearm to catch streaks of melted ice cream that are running toward her elbow. She calls out with a full mouth of ice cream and waffle cone, "I'll wait out here!" Rain empties the rest of Sally's gelato on top of her half eaten ice cream.

A well-dressed lady walks past Rain, giving her a look of disdain from her hippie-like appearance and licking her arm with chocolate ice cream smeared all around her mouth.

Sally is less than five minutes. Rain watching as the store clerk goes to get her size out back. She offers Sally to wrap it up nicely, but Sally couldn't be bothered with that, and takes it as is in a shopping bag.

Sally comes out to find Rain stuffing the rest of the ice cream in her mouth, her cheeks puffed from overdoing it. Rain makes a painful face and says something, but Sally can't make sense of it because of how full her mouth is. She tries again.

Sally says, "I can't understand you."

Rain swallows a few times then says, "I got brain freeze."

"Well that's your own fault, isn't it."

"Let's go get you some fancy panties."

The two of them roam the shopping district, browsing lingerie and make-up stores. Sally tries a few lacy gowns and underwear on. It takes her nearly two hours, but she finally finds a matching red set of laced lingerie with sheer panels and delicate cut outs. Sally figuring since the dress is red and she has red heels at home, or rather Larissa's red heels she will borrow, she may as well make the color red a theme.

"Well Stroppy, I think we got just about everything we need to turn you from dowdy dyke to dynamite."

"Except courage. Where do they sell that?"

"About fifteen bucks from your local liquor store."

Sally grins. "I could use a drink right now come to think of it."

"I've got one better."

Rain reaches into her hefty handbag and fishes around a few moments until she finds what she's looking for. She takes out a small tin with glow-in-the-dark stickers on it that have long since lost their glow. She opens it to reveal four pre-rolled joints and plucks on out. She seals the tin and drops it back in her bag, then holds the joint in front of Sally's face.

"What's that?"

Rain smirks and gives her a knowing look. "Oh please."

Sally sighs. "You know I only grow plants, not smoke them."

"Yeah, well this is different. It's a strand of weed known as Frostbite. My boy toy Steve got it from his dealer. Way better than the government approved stuff. It's the mellowest ganja I've ever had. And as you well know, I've somewhat of a connoisseur on the subject. This shit will relax the fuck outta you."

Sally maintains her brisk gait and looks past the joint that Rain is defiantly holding in front of her and focuses on the people ahead on the sidewalk.

"Just take it and decide later," Rain says. "It can't hurt just to have it."

Sally remains determined with her stone cold visage.

"I won't take no for an answer," Rain says.

Sally exhales sharply through her nose and plucks the joint from Rain's fingertips. She drops it in the little shopping baggy with the lingerie inside.

Rain nods with satisfaction. "Good. Now. Did you read those books I gave you?"

"Sort of. I was actually on the train the other day and nodded off while it was open on my lap. Some creep thought I was a sex nut or something and leered at me."

Rain chuckles, then says, "Did it give you any ideas?"

"I fantasized about farting at him."

Rain blurts out laughing, slapping Sally's arm. "No, you lummox. I meant the book."

Sally screws up her face and looks at Rain. "Lummox?"

"It's an old word I'm trying to bring back. Stop changing the subject. Did you find any inspiration from the books?"

"Not really. It's all that Kama Sutra style stuff. I don't want do that, y'know, weird stuff."

They continue walking in silence a moment, passing Trinity Church on the corner of Boylston street and Clarendon street, then Sally says, "I just want it to be plain. Passionate, but plain. I'm baking a cake, not making tiramisu."

Rain shrugs haphazardly. "Suit yourself. But some of those melding techniques really get your juices flowing."

Sally nods slowly, watching a few nuns with fruit smoothie's crossing the road toward them.

"I was in this hostel once in Darjeeling. I met this guy," Rain smiles wistfully, "Aaron. I'll never forget Aaron. He taught me a few things you'll find in that book. The best was one was when he got me to lie on my back on the edge of the bed. I stuck both legs together and raised them, and he lowered his cock down from a standing position-"

"Okay that's enough."

"Don't you wanna hear about my mind blowing orgasm? And it wasn't just my mind that blew. Holy hell."

"Don't be disgusting."

"Says you, who just said she wanted to fart on some guy riding the train."

Sally sighs and shakes her head, looking back at the nun's and hoping they didn't hear any of that filth.

CHAPTER FIFTEEN

CLAIRE THE TELEMARKETER

Sally arrives home and dumps her shopping bags on the dining room table.

"Larry?"

No answer. She walks around the bottom floor of the house and looks for Larissa, calling out, then heads upstairs and does the same thing. Larissa doesn't appear to be home.

Sally heads back downstairs to the kitchen and makes a loose leaf green tea. She goes into the dining room and takes the clothes and makeup she bought, laying them all out across the varnished mahogany surface of the antique cabriole dining table. The dress laid out flat vertically on the table, the lace panties and bra neatly together, and the array of expensive new makeup lined up OCD fashion at the end of the table.

Sally stands at the end of the table marveling over her purchases. She's never been a shopping kind of girl. Most of her clothes she finds in thrift or vintage stores she happens past from time to time. Larissa buys all the décor for their house. She picked all the colors and styles during their renovations a few years back. Sally sips her tea intermittently, obsessing over how she will look when she puts all this on.

Then it dawns on her. The ridiculousness of this whole thing. Getting dolled up in all this nonsense she would never otherwise do. And for what? To please some guy she's never even met. A gay man, she's never even met. As if he's going to find her attractive no matter what she puts on. She could put holes in a garbage bag and wear that and it would still have the same effect. This is stupid. And more to the point, what if it doesn't work? She'll be left with the humiliation of prostituting her body to make a point about biological ownership. And using Brad's body on top of that. And that's not even taking into account the fallout this would have on her relationship. Technically this is cheating, even if Larissa gave her the blessing. It's downright cruel putting her lover in this position after all she puts up with. The anxiety attacks. The emotional baggage outbursts. Rain was right. If Sally is to buy this kind of intimate clothing, it should be for the one she loves. And even then, this isn't what Larissa wants. This isn't even what Sally wants.

"This isn't me," Sally says under her breath.

Sally marches into the kitchen and angrily pulls open a bottom drawer, whipping out a garbage bag, then strides back to the dining table. She opens the bag and walks around the table shoving everything in. The dress. The lingerie. The makeup. Once it's all in there she ties a knot to seal the bag and walks out the front of the house and shoves it in the dumpster.

Sally walks back inside and slams the door. She collects herself a moment, then figures she should go lie down for a while. Sleep off this nonsense and tell Larissa when she gets home that it's all off. Call Brad first thing in the morning and apologize for inconveniencing him.

Sally heads back upstairs and falls backward onto her bed, closing her eyes. She starts to drift off, then thinks about that hunter guy in her dreams. The coldness that he brings. The stress of the baby that he seems to exacerbate. No, she doesn't feel like experiencing that right now. Sally opens her eyes and looks on the other side of the bed. Larissa's laptop is charging. 'I should play some Solitaire until Larissa gets home,' she thinks.

Sally rises up and snatches the laptop, then sits down on the corner of the bed and opens the computer. She types in Larissa's password and, once entered into her operating system, opens the games section and plays a couple of games. A work email alert flashes onscreen. Sally dare not open it, and minimizes it. She wonders if the email is from Brad. Sally finds Larissa's contacts folder. She scours it for several minutes until she finds 'Bradley Young'. She finds his cell and work number. Sally checks the first lot of digits in the work number and compares it to Larissa's work number. Yep, they're the same. Sally gets up and walks the laptop over to the dresser and opens the drawer to find a pen. She shoves all the makeup and random crap around inside, but there isn't a pen to be found. Sally picks up one of Larissa's eyeliner pencils and briskly walks into the bathroom attached to the bedroom and rips off a square of toilet paper. She uses the pencil to jot down the cell number next to Brad's name, then signs off the computer and puts it back on the bed exactly how she found it.

Sally picks up her half drunken tea from her nightstand then dashes downstairs to the kitchen, dumping out the tea in the sink. She goes to the liquor cabinet and pulls out a bottle of vodka. She finds a shot glass and fills it on the kitchen counter. Without hesitation, she downs the shot. Sally pours another, then slams that back too. She clears her throat from the onslaught of bitterness and shakes her head a few times. She lets those two shots settle, then pours another. This time she slowly sips on it as she makes her way back to the front foyer.

She drinks the rest of her vodka shot then swipes her keys from the white French antique console table and is out the door and in her car in moments. She drives the streets until she finds a payphone. She smiles as she pulls up next to the dirty relic of the past, not sure if the alcohol is starting to kick in, or the fact that she's going to use a payphone for the first time since she can even remember. Most likely a bit of both.

Sally fishes in her pockets for her coin purse and brings it out, fingers the coins in her palm until she has the right amount, then picks up the receiver and dumps the coins in. She pulls out the toilet paper and reads the digits as she dials them on the phone's keypad.

A few moments of hearing it ring before the other end picks up.

"Hello?"

Sally slams the phone down. She closes her eyes and breathes successively long inhales and exhales. 'Come on, you can do this,' she thinks. She opens her eyes, finds more coins, and dials the number again.

The phone picks up with another, "Hello?"

Sally freezes. She wants to hang up but can't seem to.

"Hello? Is there someone there? I think you might have bad reception," the male voice says. Sally assuming that this is Brad's voice. He doesn't sound as flamboyantly gay as Larissa made out he was. His voice actually quite deep, and somewhat soothing.

Sally clears her throat and says in a lower voice than normal, "Uh, hi. I'm… Claire… from Geico. I was, uh, calling to see if your phone plan is-"

"How did you get my number?"

"E-e-excuse me?"

"I specifically paid more to my service provider to make my number private from telemarketers. So how did you get this?"

"I-I-I... I'm not a telemarketer," Sally's voice now comically lower as she talks. "I'm calling about, um, our new and better rates."

"That's literally what a telemarketer is you fucking imbecile. What is your name? Was it Claire?"

"Y-yes."

"Listen Claire. I'm usually a mild mannered individual. But you have caught me at a rather bizarre and stressful time. So if you want to stay on the line to tell me more about your new and improved rates, I'm going to berate you with every fucking insult known to the human vocabulary."

"Why are you stressed, Brad?"

There is a scoff at the other end, and a moment of silence, before he says, "Are you fucking kidding me?"

"What?"

"Why would you want to know why I'm stressed? And also, while we're at it, how did you know my name is Brad? Since this number is private, there is no way that, A, you should have it, and, B, the name that goes with it."

"I... I, uh, don't know."

"Who put you up to this?"

"Um, what?"

"This has got to be a joke, hasn't it? This is a prank call, right?"

"No."

"Okay, Claire. You wanna know why I'm stressed?"

"Yes."

"Because tomorrow night I'm going to have sex with a woman for the first time. Do you know why that's stressful?"

"Uh, no?"

"Because I'm gay."

"Oh... um...,"

"I'm fucking terrified, Claire."

"You... you are?"

Sally can hear the sound of Brad pouring liquid into a glass.

"Yes I am," he takes a lengthy sip. "I'm doing it to help out a friend at work."

"Did she pressure you?"

Headlights wash over Sally as a car drives past.

"No. Nothing like that. Wait. Was that a car passing by? Where are you? Shouldn't you be in a call center?"

"I, uh...,"

Brad takes a noisy slurp of his drink. "Man this wine is going down a fucking treat."

"You didn't answer me, Brad. Are you having sex with this woman because you feel you have to?"

"I mean, I am sort of benefiting from it. She's going to help me climb the corporate ladder. But that's not it. I guess... I'm curious."

Sally smiles. She covers the talking piece with her cupped hand as another car drives past.

"What are you curious about?"

"Look Claire. I don't want kids. They gross me the fuck out. I couldn't imagine a screaming little shit running around my high-rise apartment, touching my sculptures and wood veneer surfaces with sticky juice covered fingers. Having to watch the same Pixar movie a thousand fucking times. I adore the Hamilton musical, but I've only seen it twice and that's enough for a while, y'know? Then there's screaming tantrums in supermarkets. I look at those mother's desperately trying to reason with an arrogant three-year-old, and I pity them, as well as finding it both amusing and annoyed that I can't go over there and slap the little runny nosed shrieking brat."

Sally imagines all those scenarios as he says them and can't wait to experience these character building moments as a parent.

Brad says, "But the thing is, I want to know what a mini-me would look like. From afar. I'm curious to see how this child grows up, if the parents would let me, of course. My friend Larissa, the one who, shall we say, headhunted me for this prestigious task, has promised me I'll at least get updated pictures over the years."

Tears of joy form in Sally's eyes. Larissa never told her that part. Perhaps she was too scared Sally would find that weird or something. But she finds it absolutely adorable.

Brad says, "And that's all I want. Well, that and to make this couple happy. Larissa talks endlessly about her love. I think her name is Sally? Anyway, I only have career aspirations. I don't want a family. But I like to think that, through my actions, I can help others achieve that goal."

Sally sniffs and wipes her wet nose with the back of her sweater.

"Are you alright, Claire?" Brad says. "Sounds like you're crying."

Sally desperately waves her hand in front of her face to dry her tears. She covers the phone a moment so she can let out a few calm breaths to stop the weeping.

Sally clears her throat and says, "No, I have a cold."

"Well, anyway. That's the main reason I'm doing this. I couldn't care about an early promotion. I'll get that with a little time and elbow grease anyway."

"Then why are you terrified? You said you are terrified."

"Me and this... Sally? We're supposed to make a baby together. I don't just wanna stick my dick in her meat locker and cum, then leave her with a disappointing experience. I want this baby to come from some passion. Some fireworks. But seeing as how we're both gay, I'm not sure that's going to happen. And I'm terrified that they will never want to speak to me again on account of me being a dud fuck."

Sally giggles. Brad takes a hefty sip of his wine.

"I'm glad one of us can laugh."

"You'll be fine."

"No offense, Claire. But you have no idea."

Sally smiles. "Yeah. You're right. I don't."

"Well as fun as this has been, I'm going to have to decline your Geico phone plan offer, Claire. But thanks for the vent. Now I'm going to get rotten drunk and listen to 90's Madonna until I pass out."

"No problem, Brad."

The phone line goes dead. Sally places the receiver back in its place on the phone and moseys back to her car.

Sally arrives back home and strides to the dumpster. She takes the lid off and pulls out the garbage bag containing today's purchases, then heads inside. She takes out the dress and sets up an ironing board. Sally spends the next hour carefully steam cleaning the dress, unable to take the smile off her face. The half bottle of vodka she's been drinking helps as well. Sally aimlessly waltzes into the loungeroom and falls backward onto the couch. 'I'll just rest my eyes for a minute or two,' she tells herself, and before sixty seconds even elapses, she drifts off into slumber.

Chapter Sixteen

SWEET AND SAVORY

Sally rides a turquoise colored bicycle down a mountain trail on a gorgeous summer day. The bottom of her bright yellow sundress flaps in the wind behind her as she lets the bike glide her down the dirt road overlooking lush green meadows below. She closes her eyes and lets the wind tickle her face. When she opens them again, she's now on a road that cuts through a pine forest. The sun is no longer bright, and the air now dense and cold. She spots a car parked on the side of the road just ahead. A man is standing next to the car, staring into the cold dark woods. Sally pulls her bike to a stop and hops off it, deploying the kickstand so she can leave it upright.

"Hey Mister bullet man. Are you okay?" Sally calls out to Glen, who is wearing a woolen hat, khaki bomber jacket and dirty jeans.

Glen turns to face her.

"You again, flower lady."

"Hey. Last time you said Flower Girl. I like girl better. Lady makes me sound... old."

"Fine."

Sally looks around the bordering woodlands off the road with clumps of snow scattered all around.

"And it's winter again. Should have known you arrived when it got cold," Sally says with an unimpressed tone.

"My car broke down. It's the battery. Do you mind if I hook mine up to yours to get some juice?"

"Yeah. Sure." Sally looks behind to find her blue Honda Civic where the parked bike was. Without skipping a beat, she turns and strides to the hood and opens it. Glen is behind her with the jumper cables in his hand, already attached to the dead battery in his truck. Sally watches as Glen attaches the metal prongs to the appropriate terminals.

A noise in the forest makes Sally turn around. She spots someone skulking around in the trees. It's Glen as a young boy. Sally meanders across the road and into the start of the woods.

"Hey."

The boy stops and looks over at Sally.

"Wha'cha doin'?" Sally says.

He wears a perplexed expression, seeming somewhat afraid.

"It's okay. I'm not going to hurt you. My name is Sally. What's yours?"

The boy looks past her to older Glen fiddling around the engine of the Honda. A few moments later he says, "Glen."

"Well, hey Glen. I'm Sally. What are you doing out here?"

He shrugs with his hands still in the pockets of his denim jacket.

Sally looks him up and down. He's only wearing a thin denim jacket, sweatpants and sneakers. His cheeks and ears are reddened.

"You look cold, Glen."

"What?" older Glen calls out from across the road.

"I'm not talking to you," Sally says loudly without turning to acknowledge him. She keeps her eyes on young Glen. "Aren't you freezing?"

The boy shrugs again, then looks her up and down in her flowy sundress. "Aren't you?"

Sally looks down and realizes she is wearing less than he is. The kid's got a point. She turns around on the spot to look in every direction. The endless road that was there before is now leading directly to a log cabin. Sally immediately recognizes it as her grandfather's cabin.

"Hey! That's my family's cabin. There's always a fire going inside. Wanna come with?"

Sally holds out her hand for young Glen. He darts his eyes back and forth between her and the cabin. The stone chimney on the roof spewing thick smoke. He takes one hand out of his pocket and clasps Sally's waiting hand. She smiles warmly at him and they both head toward the cabin.

Older Glen is sitting in his truck having trouble getting it started. The ignition won't take. He hears dogs barking and snarling somewhere nearby and looks around. He can't see any animals. Behind him, shadows of huskies run through the trees. He spins around but can't see the dogs. They are all around him, howling now as well as barking. Glen begins growing unsettled. Now he notices Sally is nowhere to be seen.

Glen walks out into the middle of the road and looks in both directions. Nothing but road either way with seemingly no end in sight.

"Where'd you go?" Glen calls out. His voice echoing through the woods.

"I'm right here."

Glen looks over to find Sally, now in a fitted red cocktail dress, stepping out of the forest and onto the roadside in shiny red heels. Her hair pulled back and makeup immaculately done. Her juicy red painted lips are twisted into a confident grin. She's carrying a bouquet of red roses.

"Where are you goin' dressed like that?" asks Glen.

"Maybe it's not where I'm going, but where I've been," she says with a wink.

Glen rubs his grease covered hands together, looking her up and down, becoming captivated by her beauty and oozing sexuality.

"Alright." He shrugs. "Where ya been?"

"That's none of your fucking business," she says with her smile broadening.

"Fine. Have it your way," Glen says quietly, somewhat embarrassed. He turns and marches to his truck and swings his body into the driver's seat. He tries the engine again. No dice.

"Having a little problem getting things going, huh?" Sally's alter-ego says with an air of ribald cheekiness, standing right next to Glen now. She sticks her tongue slightly out the side of her mouth in a suggestive manner. "Maybe I can help you... get your engine going, if you know what I mean."

Glen tries the engine again, and says irritably, "No. I don't."

"You're coy, as well as handsome."

Glen turns around to face her with a scowl. She takes a step back, putting one hand on her stuck-out hip.

Glen says, "Listen lady, I have a delivery to make. I don't have time for this."

"Awwww, come on. Don't get your panties in a bunch. I'm just playing around."

Glen, now growing considerably flustered, turns his attention back to the car. He tries the engine again rapaciously. Again and again. It won't start.

"Fuck!" Glen slams his palms aggressively on the steering wheel.

"What's the delivery?"

"What?!"

"You said you had an urgent delivery." She motions to the bed of the truck that is covered with a tarp. "What's the cargo?"

"None of your fuckin' business."

Glen gets out of the truck and pushes past her, mumbling about how he thinks her car's battery is dead too. When he reaches the front of the truck he stops, looking around in bewilderment.

"Where's your car?"

The spot where Sally's car was is empty. The jumper cables gone too.

"What car?"

"The one you came in goddamit."

"I didn't come here in a car," Sally's ego says matter-of-factly.

"Yes you did. You just-," Glen stops himself, his face turning rage red.

Sally steps over to him with a sultry pout and speaks with a tone like she's addressing a kid with a tantrum. "Naw, look at you getting all hot and bothered. Want me to give you a wittle massage to calmy-walmy your-"

"What's the matter with you?"

Sally's ego touches her hair daintily. "What do you mean?"

"You don't normally act like this."

"Like what?"

"Like a... sex craved... creep."

Sally's ego throws her head back and laughs, then recomposes herself to stand rigidly with a perturbed expression and says, "Creep?"

The sound of snarling and barking again coming from the forest. Silhouettes of the big dogs appearing, running through the bushes, and disappearing again.

Glen looking concerned now. Scared, for the first time he can remember. He looks at the bouquet of roses she's carrying.

"Who are those for?"

"None of your fuckin' business," she says trying to emulate his voice.

Glen shakes his head and throws his hands out in defeat.

Ego Sally says, "Just kidding. See, it doesn't feel nice, does it? Getting a taste of your own medicine."

Glen is too busy paying attention to his surroundings, not wanting one of those beasts to jump out and attack him.

Ego Sally says, "Actually, they're for you." She holds out the flowers for him to take

"Very fitting, coming from you, Flower Girl."

Ego Sally's visage turns ashen. "I'm not Flower Girl. I'm Sally."

Glen reluctantly takes the roses from her outstretched hand.

"Ouch!" Glen cries out in pain. He looks down at his hand, which is now dripping with an abundance of blood. The thorns are long and thick and have stabbed into his skin. He looks up at Ego Sally, who is smirking mischievously.

"Hurts, doesn't it? Do you like pain? You do. I can see it all over your hands and wrists. Why do you love pain so much, Glen? Does it get you off? Does it make you feel alive? Or does it make you wish you were dead? Yeah, that's it, isn't it. Nail on the fucking head. Or, thorn in your side more appropriately."

Glen watches in horror as the blood now cascades from his hand, yet he still holds onto the roses. He wants to drop them, throw them even, but he can't.

"You wish you were dead, but you don't have the guts to kill yourself." Ego Sally's disposition now menacing. Her face sneering, her cold eyes boring through him.

Glen steps backward, edging further away from her with each step. He is afraid of her. He swallows hard. "What do you want?"

Sally's ego cocks her head to the side, with a hauntingly vacant expression. "To devour you."

※

"Are you hungry?" Sally says to Young Glen, who is sitting on the couch in the log cabin, staring at the roaring fire.

Young Glen looks at her, blinking innocently.

"Let's see what we got."

Sally opens the cupboards one-by-one, only finding pots, pans and other kitchen accessories. But no food. She opens the walk-in pantry, which is also devoid of anything remotely edible.

"Oh! I know!" Sally claps her hands together excitedly. "Cocoa!" She grins exuberantly. "You like cocoa, don't you? All kids love cocoa. Adults too, really. Is that being offensive? Would that be ageist? Or... child... ist?" She shrugs haphazardly with a goofy grin and makes a beeline for a tin without any label sitting next to a coffee percolator in the corner of the main kitchen bench. "This is where grandpa kept it, hopefully there's still...," she uses a spoon to pop the lid open and looks inside, her face beaming with a smile. "Yes! There's still some here. Alright, two cups of hot chocolate are coming our way."

"I don't like cocoa."

Sally snaps her head around to look at Young Glen.

"What?"

"I don't like the taste of chocolate, Sally."

Sally's eyes widen with shock. Young Glen looks into his lap, a little ashamed.

Sally makes a thoughtful face. "I've never heard of a kid not liking chocolate."

"Or candy. Or ice cream." He sticks his hands in his pockets and shrugs. "I like Dorito's. And cheese. And hock-a-rolly."

"Hock-a… oh, you mean guacamole," Sally says then grins. "The green stuff you eat with Mexican food, right?"

Young Glen sheepishly nods, staring into the fire again.

"So, you like savory, not sweet, huh?" Sally pops the lid back on the tin. "That's cool. I love cheese too. In fact, I love it so much it used to get me in a lot of trouble when I was your age."

Young Glen turns his head to look at her with confusion. "You weren't allowed to eat cheese?"

"Nuh-uh," Sally says while shaking her head.

"Why the heck not?"

"My family was vegan."

"Vee-gan?"

"It means you can't eat animals, or anything that comes from them. And, cheese is dairy. It comes from a cow. Or goat. Or whatever floats your boat."

Sally cackles at her little play on words.

"I know another name for that."

"Oh yeah?"

"Yeah. Sad."

Sally grins with a mindful look.

"Well, I know what you mean. But vegans find healthy satisfaction in helping their animal friends."

The sound of shouting coming from outside. Sally slams the tin back on the counter and races over to the window looking out over a rolling valley. She peers outside with wide eyes, her head bobbing around to find the source of the yelling. Then she sees it. It's Older Glen. He's running through the forest being chased by a pack of snarling dogs.

"Oh no!"

"What?"

"Your friend is in trouble out there."

"I don't have any friends. Except my brother Joe. But he's dead."

"Sure you do. The man with the rifle. Glen. I always see you with him. He's the one out there right now."

Sally squints to look out at the wilderness below. Glen keeps looking behind him as he sprints, yelling for the dogs to stop. No, wait. Not them. He's calling out to a woman to make them stop.

"He's not my friend."

Sally turns to look at Young Glen. "Then why do you hang around him?"

Young Glen lowers his head, fighting back tears. "I want him to be my friend."

Sally thinks about that a moment, then points out the window. "Well, if you want him to be your friend, you should go help him. And I'll help you." Sally peers out the window again. Glen and the dogs are nowhere to be seen. She creases her eyebrows with puzzlement. "Where did they go?"

Tears are running down Young Glen's rosy cheeks. Sally turns around and notices him crying. Her eyes fill with sadness, and she strides over to the couch and plonks herself down next to him. She slowly reaches over and gently places her hand on his shoulder, speaking softly.

"Hey. Hey now. What's the matter?"

"He hates me." Young Glen starts openly sobbing now.

Sally moves her hand up and caresses his chestnut hair.

"How do you know he hates you?"

"He's always telling me to fuck off."

Sally pauses, about to tell him he's too young to be cussing like that, but figures he should be free of those norms right now.

"Why would he do that?"

A piece of firewood pops loudly into sparks making Sally momentarily look over at the fireplace.

"Because I killed his brother."

The sudden change in kid voice to deep adult voice causes Sally to whip her head around. Older Glen is now sitting there. Sally gasps in fright. Her hand is still on his head. She quickly jerks it away and backs up a little on the couch. Her eyes filled with awe. Glen doesn't seem to be phased too much, except for his new surroundings.

"Hey, I've been here before." He looks over to frightened Sally. "With you."

"H-h-how did you get here? Wasn't there just...," Sally looks around the room, vaguely recalling talking to a little boy, but that feels like an ancient memory now.

Sally looks down at Glen's lap. His hands are resting in them, clutching a bouquet of roses. Blood smeared all over both hands. She puts her hands over her mouth like she's going to be sick.

Glen notices her sudden alarm, then follows her gaze to the flowers. He forgot he had them.

"Are you okay?"

"I think so."

"Who gave you those?"

Glen looks at her with bewilderment.

"Didn't you?"

Another pop from the fireplace as a log shoots out shards of burning embers. Sally looks over with horror to find a few embers have landed on the bear skin rug and have begun to start a few small fires.

"No!" Sally cries out and dives off the couch, crawling on her hands and knees to the rug, using an old magazine to slap the flames out of existence. She succeeds but another log bursts into sparks that fly all over the room, some landing on the dining table, some on the couch forcing Glen to dive out of the way.

"Help me!" Sally cries.

Glen uses the flowers to beat the embers on the couch, successfully stopping them from igniting further.

Ego Sally is at the window on the far side of the cabin. Her face is smiling with glee at the dire situation happening inside. Another log bursts into embers all over the cabin and she howls with laughter.

On the other side of the cabin, Young Glen watches the madness with an empathic, sorrowful expression. He puts the palms of his hands onto the windowpane with a visage that signals he wants to desperately get inside to help them.

Sally rushes around using cushions from the couch to whack the flames erupting from the embers. She rushes around the wooden slat floors on her kneecaps to any new fires that spring from the fireplace flak. Tears are welling in her eyes, moaning to herself in fear with each new flame that pops up somewhere else in the cabin. She looks up and spots her ego at the window, having a grand old time, pointing and laughing at her.

Glen whacks more embers by the kitchen with the bouquet, the roses now having lost half of their petals, and now no more than thorny stems with remnants of the flowers. He looks over to the window and sees Young Glen, watching him with a pleading demeanor.

"What are you doing here?!"

"I want to help!"

"You'll just make it worse!"

"The bucket!"

"What?"

Young Glen is enthusiastically pointing to a wooden bucket sitting next to the pantry door. Glen follows his instruction and spots the bucket.

The drapes by the window Ego Sally is at erupt into flames. Sally screams and dashes over to them, beating the flames manically with the cushions in either hand. She catches a glimpse of her ego outside making humiliating funny faces at her. Sally's face now streaming with tears, she ignores her ego outside and continues to pummel the curtains until she gets the fire under control.

The dining room table bursts into flames. The walls are all now alight. Every part of the cabin is on fire with massive flames all the way to the roof.

Sally lets out a bloodcurdling scream.

A whooshing sound followed by a long loud hiss.

Sally looks over to find Glen has doused out the fire. Thick plumes of grey smoke billow from the fireplace, the logs now wet and black. Glen holds the empty water bucket in his grasp.

All the fires in the cabin have now vanished.

Sally looks around in bewilderment at the fact the cabin looks like it did before the fires. Everything, from the drapes to the dining table, are pristine.

"You gotta stop the source of the problem," says Glen, dropping the bucket on the bear skin rug. "Otherwise it spreads further and further until you can't do anything but watch it destroy you, and everything around you."

Sally wipes the tears from her face with the back of her hands. "Thank you, Bullet."

Sally looks over at the window where her ego was. She's gone.

Glen looks over at the window where his child self was. Gone.

Sally blankly looks around the cabin again, her eyes narrowing with suspicion.

"Wait. I haven't been here since I was a teenager. My family doesn't own this place anymore." She steps into the center of the room and does a slow 360-degree turn. She scoffs a little chuckle.

Sally looks Glen dead in the eyes and says, "This isn't real." She picks up a vase from the coffee table and stares at it a moment. "This is just a dream."

Sally raises the vase above her head and hurls it at the ground, smashing it to pieces.

Everything around Glen and Sally whirls into a frenzy like they were in the eye of a tornado just as Glen realizes she's right.

CHAPTER SEVENTEEN

BRIAN'S DISCOVERY

Glen's eyes open slowly, his eyeballs roll around as he sits up in his hospital bed. His head feeling a bit groggy from the sleeping medication the nurses gave him to assuage the pounding headaches he was enduring last night. Glen hears a crinkle sound and looks down the side of his body to find he is holding a bouquet of half dead sunflowers wrapped in a brown craft sheet. He holds it up and stares at it with bewilderment. Did someone come and place flowers in his hand? Why would they do that? Glen notices a small purple card attached that is blank inside.

The curtain around his bed slides open and his doctor Adrian enters his space. Glen looks up numbly as Adrian stands there with a grin planted on his face.

"Didn't know you were a sleepwalker," Adrian says.

"I'm not."

Adrian chuckles. "Security cameras don't lie." He points to the dying flowers. "I'm surprised you made it to the dumpster downstairs without an orderly seeing you. Must have been quiet as a mouse."

Glen looks at the flowers in his hand with confusion, then places them on the nightstand next to his bed.

Adrian places the clipboard under his arm and rocks on his feet a little.

"So, any queries about tonight? Or do you think you're good to go?"

Glen wipes his hand over his bed hair and sits up a little more.

"Those headaches I've been gettin'. It's not going to make it worse, is it?"

Adrian sits on the end of the bed, then says, "Sorry, do you mind?"

Glen shakes his head.

Adrian says, "An MRI scan is basically a big magnet. A brief radio frequency sends your brain cells into a little flutter so we can see where the tumor is, and how big it is." He shrugs. "Then your noggin goes back to normal."

"Then I can go, right?"

Adrian smiles. "I know the food sucks. But hang in there. We'll get you home as soon as we can."

Adrian pats the bed next to Glen's leg and stands up.

Glen says, "Hey doc. The TV you got in here only has basic cable. The UFC title fight is on tonight. Any chance I could get something to watch it on?"

"I've got a tablet in my office that you could stream off."

"That would be awesome."

"Just don't get rowdy, there's another patient in the room," Adrian points in the direction of the other half of the room.

"You got it doc."

"And no more late night walks," Adrian says with a grin.

Glen looks genuinely concerned.

"I'm kidding, Glen. I know you can't control that. But the staff are on alert, just in case."

Adrian gives him an awkward finger-gun, then pulls the curtain back around so Glen is enclosed again.

Brian pulls up in his khaki colored 4WD in front of Glen's house and hops out, a green book under his arm. He can hear Bullit barking inside. It's been a long while since Brian has visited Glen's place, and when he has, they usually take Janeen's car. Janeen was supposed to come and feed Bullit while Glen is in hospital, but Kaylee got a pretty bad toothache, so she had to be taken to the dentist. Brian opting for the chore of feeding Bullit. The thought of getting out of the house and away from the family for a little bit of respite was a heavenly concept to Brian. Janeen has been stressed with work stuff, Alex is in one of his aggressive moods, picking fights with Brayden, who hit back and was punished with no phone or internet privileges for the day, and purposely doing his chores badly out of spite, making Janeen even more irritable. Good thing Charlie, their neighbor, was around to watch the boys for a little while.

Brian approaches the front door to Glen's house, Bullit still barking and carrying on.

"Hey Bullit, calm down, it's me. Brian."

The barking stops and is replaced with happy whimpering. Brian opens the door and is met with a wagging tail as Bullit runs circles around him. Brian smiles and gives him a good pet and scratches behind the ears.

"Hey boy. I know, I know, you're happy to see me. I'm just happy to be here."

Brian heads into the kitchen with Bullit in zealous tow. He searches the pantry until he comes across tins of dog food and a sack of dry kibble. He dishes a serving of both into Bullit's bowl, who wolfs it down in less than a minute.

"Hungry huh? Yeah, me too."

Brian goes to the fridge and opens it, immediately disappointed. There's not much in there. Nothing snackable anyway. A carton of eggs. Some out-of-date milk. Half a pack of questionable ham. A third of a loaf of bread. Brian wondering why Glen keeps his bread in the fridge. Weird guy.

Brian closes the fridge. He looks around the kitchen, wondering what to do now. He's fed the dog, the only thing required of him, so he's good to leave. Only he doesn't want to. That would mean going home already, and he's just starting to appreciate the alone time.

Brian walks around the house slowly and casually, looking for a mess to clean up or garbage to throw away. He meanders through the dining room with one plain table and some chairs. A room that clearly never gets used. In the living room now, he takes the rifle off its rack on the wall and holds it firmly, feeling the weight and appreciating the fine rifle. He points the gun at the window and looks through the scope to the outside. He places then gun back and walks to the center of the room, looking down at the coffee table which has scrunched up tissues bearing splotches of dry old blood. 'That's odd,' Brian thinks. Must have cut himself again. Janeen's told him about Glen's propensity to self-harm on account of his brother's death all those years ago. Poor bastard.

Brian sits in the recliner. Not Glen's one. That would be rude. He takes the green book he's been carrying and opens it to where he left off. The book's title is 'Principles of Horticulture'. He reads two chapters then gets up and leaves the book on the coffee table.

Brian moseys upstairs to Glen's bedroom but decides not to go in there. That's crossing a boundary. He opens the door to the two other spare bedrooms. The beds made impeccably. Brian recognizes the triple fold of the two top sheets. Janeen's work for sure. Must have been from when the kids last had a sleepover here. Which was at least a year back. Brian heads back downstairs, sliding his hand down the wooden banister on his way. When he reaches the bottom, he slaps his hand on the round knob at the end of the banister and it wobbles. Brian taps it again, making it move. Ah-ha. Found something he can fix. Brian, now with purpose to his step, looks around the back of the house for a tool kit. He soon discovers Glen doesn't keep tools in the house, at the end of which he realizes he is an idiot. The shed out back. Of course.

Brian trudges through the snow around the side of the house to get to the wooden shed. When he finds the door, he quickly realizes there are several padlocks on bolted latches running down the length of the door.

'Man is really paranoid about having his tools stolen,' Brian thinks to himself.

Brian heads back in the house and searches for the keys. It takes him a good portion of twenty minutes, but he finds a stash of spare keys in a tin box under the kitchen sink. Janeen calls on his way back out to the shed.

"Are you on your way home?"

"I wish. But I noticed the stair rail is falling apart. Gonna need to fix it."

Janeen goes on a rant about leaving Glen's house alone. He's a perfectly good carpenter and doesn't need Brian's shoddy skills to fix it. Brian explains that as an officer of the law it's his responsibility to report a Health and Safety breach, despite the fact it is not at all. Fortunately for Brian, Janeen doesn't know much about many branches of law enforcement and OHS procedures and doesn't want to know. She rattles off a few things she needs from the store that she wants him to get on the way home, and after agreeing with everything she says, Brian is off the phone and now unlocking the padlocks on the shed door.

Once inside, Brian marvels at all the weapons and hunting paraphernalia. He and Glen have been hunting together in the past, but not in a long time. And this shed certainly did not exist the way it does now when Brian saw it last. He walks around and feels the animal pelts hanging from hooks on the above beams. Brian now very keen on going out hunting with Glen to get his skills up to scratch. Looking at this setup, Brian feels it would be a great way to let off steam and get out of the house more. If Janeen will allow it.

Brian looks at the old Mustang in the corner a few moments. He can at least admire the relic a little, but not being a car enthusiast in any way, his interest quickly fades.

Brian finds the corner workbench housing all the carpentry tools. He runs his hands all over the tools neatly placed on nails stuck into cork boards. Claw hammers, chisels, mallets, backsaws. Brian now envious of Glen's collection. And even more so that he actually gets the time to use them.

And those paints. Brian ogles the shelves housing tins of different colored paints. Brian himself has been wanting to paint his house for years. Maybe he can offer Glen some cash to come and help him on weekends. He has been dreaming of doing a coat of white with brown windowsills and doors. It's been burned into his mind for years. 'Ohhhh, what's this?' Brian thinks to himself as he reaches for a tin labelled 'Bronze Pearl', pulling it by the handle off the shelf. The bottom of the tin is a little stuck to the wood shelf, so when Brian tugs it off, he has to use a little more force. He uses a little too much force and the can comes away easier than he anticipated, forcing him to lose his balance and stumble back a few steps. In the process he drops the can which lands on its side on the cement floor. The lip pops open and brown paint immediately pours out all over the floor.

"Shit!"

Brian is quick to get the can upright on the floor, though the runaway paint is finding its way across the floor toward the old worn rug next to the Mustang. Brian cusses under his breath several times while dashing over to a bucket of rags under a table, grabbing a few before running over to catch the paint before it ruins the already soiled rug. He dumps several rags on the traveling puddle of paint, then whips the rug up and out of the line of the paint. He manages to stop the mess from going further.

'But what's this?' he thinks to himself, looking at the trapdoor that is hidden under the rug.

Brian wipes his hands clean, staring at the hidden entrance with locks all over it. Brian wondering what the hell Glen has down there that he wants to protect so much. He thinks long and hard about trying the other keys on the spares. 'It can't hurt to take a little peek,' Brian reasons, then snatches up the chain full of keys and begins to try them on the trapdoor locks.

Chapter Eighteen
PIKKA-PIKKA

An Uber pulls up out the front of Boston Harbor Hotel on Atlantic Avenue just north of Chinatown. A valet opens the door for Larissa who steps out in a long waterproof tanned trench coat, the belt around the waist tied tight. She avoids the pouring rain barely as she strides steadfast through the front doors carrying a large black gym bag stuffed as far as it will go. She marches through the wide corridor of lounge chairs where folk sit scrolling through social media or corporate people on their phones writing emails on their laptops as they talk. Larissa glances at the austere framed paintings of copycat French Impressionist art, then is passing through the brown marble floored circular roomed lobby, her heels clickity-clacking as she strides up to the front desk in front of the window looking out at the grandiose Boston Harbor.

"Good evening, ma'am," the uniformed black make receptionist says with a welcoming smile.

"Yeah, hey. I've got a booking."

"No problem. If I can just have some-"

Larissa already has her license out and slaps it on the dark brown solid pine check-in desk. The receptionist smiles and takes it, quickly punching in her details on the computer in front of him.

Larissa taps her manicured fingernails on the desk while glancing around the room and her watch repeatedly, letting the receptionist know she's in no mood for dilly-dallying.

"You have the Honeymoon suite tonight," the receptionist says, handing Larissa back her license.

Larissa curtly nods with a forced grin, giving him a not-so-subtle hint she doesn't want to be questioned or congratulated in any way.

The receptionist does get the strong hint and picks up the phone, calling a valet to come and collect her luggage.

"That won't be necessary. I've just got the one bag, and I can, and want to, handle it myself."

The receptionist nods politely and calls off the valet. He hands over the hotel welcome envelope with the room's keycard and general information about the facilities inside. Larissa snatches it from his grasp, picks up her bag and power walks to a set of nearby elevators.

"Ma'am!"

Larissa stops and spins around to face the receptionist.

"The elevator to your suite is that way," he says, pointing in the opposite direction Larissa was headed.

She smiles and salutes him with the welcome envelope. "Ah. Thanks."

Larissa hotfoots it to the appropriate elevator. She presses the button for the top floor. Bing. The doors open and she uses the signage on the hallway walls to find the suite. Once she arrives, she slides her hotel key card and the little green light signals for her to open the door.

Larissa walks inside the massive suite to the main lounge area and drops the duffel bag on the floor. She glances to the large round coffee table in the middle of the room which bears an ice bucket containing a bottle of Verve Champagne and two glass flutes, a box of Belgium chocolates next to it, a bunch of roses on the other side with a teddy bear carrying a heart.

Larissa lets out a long exhale and says, "Hi-ho, hi-ho, it's off to work I go."

She strides to the kitchenette and finds a dustbin, taking it over to the table and tosses the roses, teddy bear and chocolates in. She pops open the champagne and takes a lengthy guzzle straight from the bottle.

Larissa moseys into the lofty bathroom and flips the switch on. She inspects the ornate jacuzzi with a large Renaissance painting print above it, bearing two cupids on a cloud with the words 'LOVERS' written in red ribbon.

"Ugh," Larissa says, then takes another swig from the champagne bottle.

Two towels are folded into a big heart shape. Larissa snatches them up and walks them to a cupboard and throws them in. She notices a dustbuster vacuum on the top shelf of the cupboard and grabs it, walking over to the king-size bed which is mottled with rose petals. Larissa fires up the dustbuster and vacuums all the petals up. She looks over at the large circular shaped bay window overlooking the harbor below. A long white silk banner runs across it that says 'Congratulations!' with hearts all around the writing. Larissa moseys over to it and tears it down with one hand, the other still grasping the neck of the champagne bottle. She tosses the banner into the dustbin. She goes to walk away, stops, then turns back and fishes the box of chocolates. She carelessly pries the lid off and drops it in the bin, then plucks out three chocolates and stuffs them all in her mouth at once. She swallows the large lump of chocolate and washes it down with champagne.

Larissa walks over to the gym bag and stoops down to unzip it.

Bing. The elevator doors open and Larissa walks out on the ground level with the empty gym bag and a tipsy gait. She strides toward the main reception area then stops dead in her tracks. She quickly dashes to a nearby pillar to hide, poking her head around the side for a gander. Her jaw literally drops.

Appearing through the hotel entrance is Sally. She's wearing her new red dress, red heels, diamond earrings, and clasping a red velvet purse. A knee length black gown hangs from her shoulders. The slit running down her left leg shows off her black pantyhose. Her hair is pulled back tight into a bun and shines under the chandeliers as she walks. Her lips are painted with bright red lipstick, resplendently complimenting her mascara and eyeshadow.

Sally looks like a 1950's movie star goddess to Larissa, who has never seen her lover dressed like this. Not even close.

Every man and woman in the general vicinity of Sally is gawking at her, both pleasing, amusing and angering Larissa all at the same time. Sally is completely oblivious to her admirers all around as she daintily moseys toward the reception area. One man in a lounge chair has to apologize to whoever he is on the phone to for the silence he just gave them while thirsting for the luminous looking Sally.

Sally stumbles awkwardly on her high heels, having barely worn these kinds of shoes before. Larissa giggles at Sally's clumsiness while trying to imbue and air of sexy confidence.

Sally reaches the reception area and looks around, spotting an information desk valet. She consciously steps to them and asks for directions to the hotel's seafood restaurant. The valet, clearly smitten with

Sally, offers to take her there personally, and Sally walks with him to the doors leading out to the harbor walkway.

Larissa now watching Sally's pert derriere swaying side to side in the figure-hugging dress. She shakes her head in disbelief and mouths the word "wow". She feels like she just fell in love all over again and knows that from now on she wants Sally to dress like this on occasion, even if she is wearing her jewelry. Larissa waits until Sally is out of sight then goes to the reception desk and tells the clerk that Sally and a guest will be coming to collect their room keys after dinner. With that, she makes a beeline for the front doors and orders an Uber on the way.

Sally sheepishly enters the opulent fine dining restaurant. Soft lighting from low lit lampshade chandeliers adorns the ceiling. French chic designed columns run down either side of the restaurant. The windows look right out to the harbor where the rain is beginning to ease. A maître d' wearing a dinner jacket and bow tie approaches Sally and asks if she has a reservation. A few moments as he looks her up and says for her to follow him to her table which is right next to the window which boasts a starched white tablecloth and a vase of fresh flowers. Sally takes her seat on the brass-backed chair with a salmon pink cushion. The maître d' beckons for the waitress who comes over and fills her water glass from a stainless steel pitcher. The waitress asks if Sally would like to see the wine menu, but Sally says she would just like a glass of a middle ground priced Pino Grigio.

Sally, now by herself, nervously plays with her hands under the table, staring at the vase of flowers, containing mostly white carnations and yellow daffodils. She looks at the lit candle in a crystal candle holder, then waves her hand over it a few times. Her eyes then dart around the crowded restaurant full of chatter, the sounds of forks hitting plates and soft Chopin music playing from unseen speakers. Sally bites her lip anxiously, then reminds herself she's wearing lipstick and puts a stop to that.

The waitress arrives with Sally's wine and asks if she wants some bread.

"No thanks. Not yet anyway. I'm, ah, meeting someone here shortly. I'll just wait for him."

That's when a tall, handsome young man walks into the restaurant. He looks lost and anxious. Sally is sure that this is Brad. The maître d' approaches him, and after a brief conversation, they both look over to Sally. Yep, it's him alright. She lets out a slow, silent exhale in an attempt to calm her nerves. It doesn't. Sally pretends to rearrange the flowers in the vase as the maître d' escorts Brad to the table.

"Sally?"

Sally looks up to find Brad now standing on the other side of the table. She smiles and nods.

"Brad?" she says as she stands up.

"Don't get up," Brad says. "I think that I am supposed to do that. Aren't I?"

Sally shrugs and smiles with clenched teeth. "I, ah, um, don't know."

Brad maneuvers to stand behind Sally and pushes her seat gently toward her back, hitting the back of her knees.

"Oh. I'm... supposed to sit... right," Sally says as she takes a seat.

"I thought this is how you, y'know, do this chivalry thing," Brad says as he rounds the table to take his seat.

"You don't need to bother with that shit," Sally says as she dismissively waves her hand. Her eyes pop wide open and she clamps her hand over her mouth. "Sorry for the language," she says through her fingers. "I've had a few drinks."

Brad chuckles, looking up at their waitress who is filling his water glass. "I would be lying if I said I didn't have a few Dutch courage chardy's before I left my place."

"Would you like to see a wine list, sir?"

"I'll have whatever the lady is having."

The waitress nods and leaves them alone.

"It's Pinot Grigio," Sally says as she sips her glass.

"Perfect."

They both look at each other awkwardly a moment. Sally trying to steal glances where she can at him. His dark blue suit is tailored, and she can tell he works out, especially with those arms. He is extremely well manicured, right down to his perfectly curved fingernails and perfect white veneered teeth. His tanned chiseled jawline is so soft and shiny, Sally feels if she got close enough, she could see her reflection in it.

Brad says, "I'm sorry I'm late."

Sally looks surprised. "You're not late."

"Enough for you to put a few vino's away, I guess."

"Oh. No. No, no, no. I had some at home. While getting ready."

Brad exudes a cheeky grin. "Ah. A pre-gamer. A woman after my own heart."

Sally forces a smile, feeling her cheeks redden. A little from the alcohol, a little from anxiety. She flattens the already perfectly flattened tablecloth, sweeping away imaginary crumbs.

Brad clenches his eyes shut out of disappointment, then looks at her earnestly. "You look very beautiful by the way. It should have been the first thing I said. I'm sorry."

"It's fine. You don't need to placate me." She takes a gulp of wine, realizing that sounded somewhat insulting. She smiles and says, "Thank you."

The waitress comes back and silently delivers bread in a wicker basket lined with a white napkin and places a menu in front of them both.

Another long, uncomfortable silence as they both look out the window at the harbor walk. The rain has stopped and a few stragglers meander along the lantern-lit boardwalk. The rested raindrops along the promenade twinkling in the lights.

"So… do you come here often?" Brad says with a badly imitated sleazy tone.

Sally looks around the restaurant. "I've never been in this hotel. But I've been to the Marriot. The one up the street. I didn't stay there, but Larry and I went there for a wedding reception once. Oh. I mean Larissa. I call her Larry. It's just a…,' Sally stops rambling and smiles, looking into her lap. "That was a joke, wasn't it? The 'do you come here often', like a pick-up line. I'm sorry."

The waitress arrives with Brad's wine and goes to put it on the table, but he quickly intercepts and takes it straight from her hand, mouthing 'thank you' to her before she vanishes.

"No. I should apologize. It was kinda lame," Brad says, then takes a hefty sip of vino.

They both chuckle uncomfortably.

Brad says, "Wait. Should I be drinking?"

"Why shouldn't you?"

"I just thought… you know… it might not help the chances of you becoming, uh…,' he makes a gesture with his hand signaling a big pregnant stomach.

Sally scoffs with a smile. "No, not at all. I mean, I'm half soused already." She wiggles her body to sit up straight, becoming animated. "How do you think most people end up pregnant in the first place?" Sally clears her throat and adopts a demurer expression. "I just… read that the statistics… of teenagers…,' Sally stops herself from saying more by bringing the wine glass to her lips. After a few small sips, she says, "Anyway. It's fine. Alcohol is fine. At this point, anyway."

Brad nods with a smile, then raises his glass to her. "Well, in that case, cheers."

"Cheers."

The two of them clink glasses and take a sip. Brad picks up a piece of sliced baguette bread and takes the small porcelain bowl inside the basket which has butter squares in it. He digs the knife in one to halve it and tries to smear the hard butter on the soft bread with apparent difficulty, tearing most of the bread.

"I hate that," Sally says.

Brad looks up from his bread-and-butter struggle.

Sally points at the bread and says, "Why does every fancy restaurant do that? They always give you super soft bread and frozen rock-hard butter. It makes no sense."

"Not just restaurants. Airlines. Room service. Hell, I've ordered take-out and had it delivered thirty minutes later. And guess how the butter arrived?"

"Like trying to lather a stone on water?"

Brad chuckles. "Exactly."

"There's no excuse. Refrigerated butter has been around for over a century. Do you know what else has happened over a century?"

Brad makes an open-handed gesture with the bread in one hand and the knife in the other.

Sally says, "We went from horse and carriages to cars. Calculators to smartphones. Writing letters to FaceTime. I can talk to anyone across the world from the palm of my hand, and yet, I can't go out to eat without turning my bread roll into a fucking hollow ring."

Brad lets out a hearty chuckle.

Sally places her hand over her mouth and looks out the window. "Sorry. I don't drink that often. But apparently when I do I speak like a surly dock worker."

"But I love the company of surly dock workers," Brad says, feigning a playful offended disposition.

Sally grins, touching the side of her hair for what feels like the hundredth time in the past twenty minutes, not being used to it confined by product.

"I guess we should look at the menu, huh?" says Brad, opening his.

Sally nods and opens hers. They spend a few minutes running their eyes over the options, turning pages.

Brad says, "Do you have anything you don't eat? Like are you a vegan or anything?"

"I grew up in a vegan household. All my family are, except me. I'm vegetarian though."

"You didn't want to go all the way?"

"Cheese. It's my weakness."

Brad grins and nods. "A lady of culture, I see."

"When I was younger, my brothers and sisters would sneak out at night to do drugs or drink booze. Me? I snuck out to eat aged cheddar."

Brad chortles.

Sally says, "No, seriously. You should have seen it. I would secretly buy a whole block of the stuff, hide it in the garage fridge, and go down to the creek at midnight and gorge the whole thing down. Straight off the block. No crackers. No bread. I would wolf the whole thing down like a seagull eating a dropped waffle cone."

Sally follows up by imitating a seagull swallowing something too big for its throat. She throws her head back and pretends to have a fat neck, making loud glugging swallowing sounds that attract the attention of the surrounding tables. The occupants expressing a mixture of visages from concern to disgusted.

Brad bursts out laughing, his whole body shaking. He has to place his wine glass on the table to avoid spilling any. Sally smiles with content. She can't remember the last time someone laughed this hard at her joke, or even the last time she told one.

The waitress reappears.

"Are you ready to order, or do you need more time?"

Brad wipes the laughter tear from his eye and looks up at the waitress. "We're still deciding, thanks."

The waitress nods and disappears.

"Did your parents ever find out about your late night fromage adventures?"

Sally is in the middle of drinking wine, and hurriedly swallows it so she can answer.

"Yes. They did. It's a little embarrassing."

"I love Pokemon."

Sally coughs from the wine going down the wrong way. She clears her throat and says, "What?"

"I'm a thirty-year old man and I fucking love Pokemon. I don't just love it, I own all the trading cards, watch the cartoons all the time. I even have a Pokemon blankie I rug up in at night. So if you're embarrassed eating cheese like a junkie, I've also got my crosses to bear."

"Pokemon…," Sally says as she thinks hard to remember what that is. "The cartoon, thing?"

"Yup."

"With that cute little yellow guy. He got those pointy ears and those adorable little dimples on his face."

"Pikachu."

Sally slaps her hand on the table. "Yes!"

"Pikka-Pikka!" Brad shouts, imitating Pikachu's little catchphrase.

Sally bursts out laughing and repeats even louder, "Pikka-Pikka!"

Everyone is looking over in their direction again. Sally and Brad obviously detracting from their 5-Star dining experience.

"So how did your parents find out about your naughty eating habits?"

"My mother is a dietician. Specifically for vegans. Basically for hipsters and hippies. You could say she is an expert with bodily functions. Well, she sniffed me out. Like, literally caught the downwind of my... uh... flatulence." Sally smirks bashfully and puts her wine glass to her lips.

"Your mother could tell you ate cheese because of your farts?"

Sally nods, sipping on her wine with a cocked eyebrow.

"That's... pretty impressive."

Sally places her glass gently on the table, now looking self-conscious. Brad picks up on it.

"What's the matter?"

Sally shakes her head. "Never mind." She takes a deep breath then locks eyes with him. "Sorry. It's just that... well, we're supposed to... you know," her eyes flick to the ceiling to insinuate the hotel rooms upstairs. "I'm supposed to be acting all sexy-like, and here I am talking about my teenage bowel movements."

Brad smiles and chuckles. He reaches across the table and gingerly puts his hand on top of hers. "Hey. Don't worry."

Sally looks up into his eyes. The candle flame reflection dancing on his brown eyes. He has a gentle, reassuring smile on his face. She starts to feel comfortable. Romantic, even.

Brad suddenly blurts out, "Pikka-Pikka!" followed by a loud fart sound from the side of his mouth.

Sally erupts into hysterical laughter. All the patrons staring at them with utter revulsion. The maître d' and a couple of servers looking at them from the front of the restaurant, talking in low voices. Sally noticing properly this time at their unhappy audience and tries to stifle her laughter, now bursting out of her nose in snorts, making Brad laugh.

Brad slams his menu shut. "You know. I think we should get out of here."

Sally closes her menu too. "I think you're right. I don't like the look of anything in this menu anyway."

Brad stands up and goes to her side, sticking out his elbow. Sally stands up and links her elbow with his. The both of them assuming an ostentatious stiff posture, and stride to the maître d' desk to pay for the drinks. Their chins turned up like they were royalty the whole way there. Sally trying her hardest to keep the straight face and not bursting into laughter.

CHAPTER TWENTY
TACOS AND CHER

Sally bites into her third black bean and avocado taco, bits of sauce laden tomato and lettuce falling to join the rest of the mess at her feet. Both her and Brad huddled under the covered portable heater tower next to the taco truck they found not long after leaving the hotel restaurant. The neon light making Sally's red dress even more exuberant on the eyes. Her black gown now snugly around her upper body.

Brad stuffs the last half of his pulled pork taco into his mouth, trying to talk while trying to contain the food in his overpacked mouth, spilling out small chunks in the process. Sally giggles hysterically, then sips her beer from the six-pack they split from the grocers across the street.

Brad twirls his finger in the air as he waits for the contents of his mouth to go down his throat so he can speak to make sense. "Best idea," he eventually manages to get out. "Tacos."

"Tacos are always the best idea, even when there are better options. Which there never is."

"Nice oxymoron."

"You're an oxymoron," Sally says, flicking a rogue chunk of tomato at him.

Brad gulps down a few hefty sips of his beer, then wipes his hands with a napkin. He looks at Sally stretching her fingers on her right hand, back and forth, crunching her hand into a fist then spreading out her fingers as far as they will go.

"What's with your fingers?" says Brad.

"Huh?"

"You've been doing that since we left the restaurant. Making a closed fist then flattening your palm all the way."

"Oh. That." Sally looks down at her hand which is closed again. She sticks her fingers out and wiggles them. "I had an accident when I was twelve. Severed the tendons and nerves in my right hand. Had to get surgery to sew them all back together."

"Does it always hurt?"

"No, not really. When it's cold out, it sometimes goes a little stiff. I just do some hand exercises to… I dunno, make it feel less stiff? It's more of a habit than anything."

"Must have been a pretty bad accident, that you feel it all these years later."

"Not necessarily bad. Just unfortunate. I mean, it didn't hurt much at the time. A lot of blood. But crazily enough, not much pain."

"Do you mind me asking how you did it?"

Sally takes a long sip of beer, looking across the street at a busker playing the saxophone for a moment. She looks back to Brad, now caressing her right hand with her left.

"I was riding my bike near our family property. One of my brothers thought it was funny to convince another brother to hurl a stick at the tires as I was coming fast down a hill. Well, he got a bullseye, because the stick managed to jam in the spokes of my back tire, locking it up.

The bike swerved under me, and I was thrown off onto the rocky dirt road. I landed and skidded on my side, ripping the back of my hand open on gravel and stones." Sally looks at her half-eaten taco on the little table between them, deciding she's had enough. She sips the beer again. "Anyway. I survived. Messed my hand up for a while. I couldn't paint, which was my favorite hobby. I was damn good at it too." She looks back at the saxophone player wistfully. "Never picked it up again. Even when my hand healed to the point I could do everything again like normal."

"Why?"

Sally shrugs. "I don't know. I turned my attention to plants. Being in the garden by myself was peaceful. You paint a painting, and it just sits there. You grow a plant, and you've created and fostered life. It serves a purpose. I didn't really think the paintings did."

"Surely you could have entered local competitions? Sold them on art websites or something? Creating art is a beautiful thing. It's got a life of its own."

"They weren't any good anyway."

"Says who?"

Sally swallows hard. A forlorn expression crosses over her face. She looks down at her hand, still caressing it with the other.

Brad rolls his eyes, and says, "Let me guess. The same brothers who caused your bike accident?"

Sally twists her lips from side to side, looking distressed now.

Brad says, "You shouldn't have listened to them then. And you definitely shouldn't let it bother you now."

"It was all my siblings. Not just them."

"How many do you have?"

"Six." Sally sips her beer, realizing the bottle is empty, then places it on the table. "Three brothers. Three sisters. And little ol' me."

Brad stoops down to his feet where the paper bag housing the six pack rests, and grabs a new one, uncapping it and placing it in front of Sally.

"Thanks," she says, picking it up and nestling it in her lap.

"Did you get along with the others?"

Sally shakes her head slowly, now staring at the flames inside the tower of the portable outdoor heater.

"Not ever?"

"Well, there's one who I've made a connection with, in my adult life. Rain. She's actually in town at the moment. In fact, she helped me pick this outfit."

Brad is looking a little concerned now. "Was it just you they picked on? Or were they shits to each other as well?"

"Oh God no. They were tighter than a nun's cervix." Sally's eyes pop open with embarrassment. "Sorry. The alcohol is loosening my tongue a little."

Brad smiles ear-to-ear, showing off his pearly white teeth. "I love it, and have already made the decision to use that phrase in future conversations."

Sally manages a little smile as she sips her beer.

Brad's smile quickly fades, his eyes furrowing. "So why was it just you they picked on?"

"I was the youngest. And I was adopted."

"So? Shouldn't that have made them more protective of you?"

"Evidently not. They were always ganging up on me. Playing pranks on me. I thought I was a bed wetter for many years. Turns out they were pouring water around my crotch while I was asleep. For years."

"Little fuckers."

"That's nothing. The boys were just assholes. The girls were plain evil sometimes."

"Where were your parents in all this?"

"They led busy lives. They left the older two in charge of us younger ones a lot of the time. I can never remember a time they were good to me. Except when they went too far and wanted me to keep quiet when my parents got home."

"And you did?"

Sally nods, gulping a mouthful of beer.

"Sorry... but... why?"

"Because I was afraid of what they would do the next time. Y'know, like in those prison movies how they shank the snitches. Except not shanking. More like tying me up to a tree in the backyard when they went off to play for hours."

Brad sighs exasperatedly and shakes his head. "I can't believe this. That's so fucked up."

"It wasn't all the time."

"Don't defend them. I don't care if they were kids. I'd throat punch them now if I saw them."

"Well you won't. And neither will I thankfully. They're not in my life anymore. Well, most of them anyway."

Brad sits back in his chair, looking off into the distance with an aggrieved expression.

Sally says, "I didn't know until I was at college. But my parents sat me down one day and told me why I was adopted. My natural parents died in a freak car crash when I was a baby. My adopted parents knew them from years ago. My adopted dad and natural father were best friends growing up. I guess they felt obligated to take me in. My new siblings kind of knew. Which was why they were so mean. My parents felt bad for me and gave me special treatment as a result. The siblings didn't take too well to their extra doting on me, especially since I wasn't 'real blood'," Sally using exclamation signals with both hands, "And in some ways, I understand."

"It doesn't make it right. Adopted or not adopted, you were their sister."

Sally gently places the beer bottle on the table, then kneads her hands together under the table. After a few moments, Sally bursts into tears.

Brad is immediately out of his seat and by her side, hugging her. He coos to her gently, squeezing her affectionately while rocking with her a little. Sally calms herself after a moment and pulls free.

"I'm sorry," she says, looking to Brad with wet mascara around her eyes.

"What are you sorry for? Don't apologize for anything. No matter what bullying you went through as a child, you are one of the sweetest, most sensitive women I've met. Despite your thorns, you bloomed into a rose." Brad creases his brows, looking away with disbelief. "Did I just say that Mills and Boone shit?"

Sally erupts into laughter, mascara infused tears rolling down her cheeks.

"I should write for soap operas with that nonsense."

Sally laughs again, using a spare napkin to wipe the tears and makeup from her face.

"Seriously though. I like you. You're smart, funny, and hot damn gorgeous to boot. If I was straight, I'd do you like-"

Brad stops himself, realizing what he's about to say. Sally looks at her lap awkwardly.

"Y'know what? Let's get drunk as skunks and sing Cher on karaoke at the hotel bar and not talk about this crap anymore. Let's have fun and see what happens. You down?"

Sally sniffs, wiping her runny nose with a napkin, and nods her head.

"I'd like that."

Brad now stands still to attention, once again offering his elbow for her to take in an old-fashioned escort manner.

Sally picks up the beer bottle and downs the whole thing, one large gulp after the next. She slams the empty beer bottle on the table and lets out a burp, immediately covering her mouth.

"Sorry," she says through her cupped hand.

Brad makes a determined face, convulses his chest a few times, and lets out a little burp to try and match hers.

Sally laughs and picks up her handbag. She stands up, taking his elbow with hers, and says, "Lead on, Sir Cher."

CHAPTER TWENTY

LET THEM GO

Glen is led by an orderly into a large spaced sterile radiology laboratory and told to hop up on the table attached to the Magnetic Resonance Imaging machine behind it. Glen, never having seen an MRI machine before, likens it to a big white donut with a cot sticking out of the hollow tube. The starched medical scrubs he's wearing making him itch his skin several times as he sits on the side of the bed, then swings his legs up so he's now lying down with his head rested on a curved headrest at the base of the machine's donut hole.

A few doctors and medical staff are looking at Glen get comfortable on the MRI bed through a wide glass window in the adjacent room. One of the doctors is staring intensely at three computer monitors that will soon show x-rays of Glen's skull and brain.

A whirring sound as the slab Glen is lying on is backed up a little by the orderly via a set of controls next to the MRI machine. The cot stops and Glen's upper body is now inside the MRI tube.

"Just close your eyes and relax. As we discussed, you won't feel a thing," one of the medical staff says through the intercom speaker from the monitoring room. "And remember to keep absolutely still if you can. That way the scanner can pick up clearer results."

Glen closes his eyes and lets out a long, silent exhale.

The door to the Honeymoon Suite opens, and a very tipsy Sally and Brad straggle into the main room with the circular couches and suave armchairs. Brad finds the light switch on the wall and turns on all the lights in the penthouse. Sally's jaw physically drops as she looks around the room.

"Brad. Turn the lights off."

Brad turns them all back off.

The room's decoration is nothing short of enchanting. The floor is sporadically covered in big, lush magnolia flowers, with little lit candles in the center of some of them. On the large middle coffee table rests a Buddha's head statue with lit candles and incense sticks all around it. Sally sucks in the aroma and smiles. Lavender.

Different colored Thai-inspired scarves are swathed around the walls and linked to one another. The king size bed has a thick sheep wool Moroccan rug spread over it. The red, white and brown patterns on the rug swirl and spiral into each other. A fat beeswax candle on each nightstand, giving the bed enclave a majestic glow.

Sally's eyes are moistening from oncoming tears of joy. She turns and dashes to the bathroom door. Instead of the Renaissance print that was there before, there's now a grandiose Indian mural cloth hanging over it. The jacuzzi underneath it is lit up by candles all around the basin, with Japanese water lilies floating on the water inside.

"Oh Larissa," Sally says putting her hand to her mouth.

Brad himself is extremely impressed by the New Age décor.

"Wow. Did the hotel do all this?"

Sally turns around to face him, remaining in the bathroom doorway. "Make yourself a drink. I'll... um... be out in a moment." Brad nods in understanding as Sally closes the bathroom door.

✻

Glen opens his eyes and stares at himself for a moment in the reflection of the radio frequency coils directly above his face in the MRI machine. The room's main fluorescent lights suddenly turn off and an electronic hum kicks in. Glen's face glowing from the machine's scanner starting to do its work.

Glen closes his eyes again and swallows a dry lump in his throat as loud whirring sounds emanate all around him.

✻

Sally stands in front of the bathroom mirror staring at herself. She holds the joint in her hand; the Frostbite one Rain gave her to save for a rainy day. She's halfway through smoking it, and already considerably stoned. It's the first time she's smoked weed since she can remember. Probably in her early twenties before the anxiety disorder really started to own her.

Sally blows out a long string of smoke from the side of her mouth, again fighting the urge to cough. Her ability to take in lungsful of smoke is impressing her. She had fought and won the cigarette quitting battle eight years ago, but on occasion has lit up a cheeky one when appropriately inebriated. Which is not that often. Except right now. The marijuana is countering the booze though. She's starting to feel relaxed. Like, really relaxed. Rain was right. This weed calms the nerves, not exacerbates them. Sally closes her eyes and smiles as she sucks in another long draw of the joint. She holds it in her lungs for a good fifteen seconds and lets the smoke puff out in short little bursts.

Sally giggles. The bathroom a haze of marijuana smog right now. The candle flames looking to her like torchlight in the fog from a lantern in an 1800's London street. For a moment she laments that she has never been to London, nor two centuries ago for that matter. She closes her eyes and giggles again.

She wonders if Brad is okay out there. Maybe he would like some of this Frostbite weed too? Nah. He's fine on the booze. More for her.

Sally opens her lazy eyes and looks at the joint. It's two-thirds done. That should probably do for now. She goes to turn the faucet on to douse the joint out, then hesitates. Rain did tell her this particular strain of weed is hard to come by. It would be a shame to waste it. Sally brings it back up to her lips and sucks in another lung filling toke.

Her head is feeling fuzzy now. A sudden jolt of light makes her eyes snap open. A few seconds later it happens again, this time making her flinch. She can swear she almost heard a noise. Like a mechanical humming sound.

Glen lies partially submerged in the MRI scanner with his eyes still closed. The sounds of the scanner, the gradient coils and the magnet all working together with the electronic charge are causing a cacophony of humming and buzzing sounds through his head.

A quick flash of a lightning bolt in Glen's mind causes him to flinch.

Another rapid flash and he sees Sally's face. It's only for a split second, but to Glen it felt longer. It looked to him as if Sally was looking at her reflection in a mirror shrouded partly by some kind of fog.

Glen's instinct on the sudden close-up image of Sally causes him to spasm again. It felt physical, and less dreamlike. Like he was inside her head looking at herself.

She whispers, "Bullet."

He whispers, "Flower."

One of the computer monitors in the MRI surveillance room shows schematics and x-rays of Glen's brain. One page displays black and white imagery, where another shows infrared-colored scans that mostly display blue and yellow signatures. The doctor standing behind the seated one is taking notes on a computer tablet, the only striking sound in the room is her tapping fingers on the oleophobic coated glass screen.

A small blip occurs on the black and white brain scan. It was so fast that it could have been missed in a blink. Not to the standing doctor.

"That was odd."

The seated doctor adjusts his glasses and turns halfway around on his chair to look up at her.

"What was odd?"

"You didn't see that?"

There's another blip on the scan. The female doctor's eyes widen, and she leans over and points at the screen.

"There. Again. The first one was in the Thalamus. Then there was another in the cortex."

The male doctor leans over and squints through his thick glasses at the screens, not himself seeing anything.

"Do you think it's a software issue?"

"It wasn't a glitch. It was like a… like a little explosion. I've never seen anything like it before. It looked the same in two different spots."

The male doctor taps the part of the screen showing a three-inch white ball in the pituitary gland. "So it had nothing to do with the tumor?"

The female doctor slowly shakes her head, then shrugs. "The first one kinda was. The second one was way off in the cortex."

"Must be the software playing up."

"There's another one!"

* * *

Glen is now in a state of sleep paralysis. Not quite Rapid Eye Movement, but not far off from lucid dreaming. He can feel the cold air-conditioning in the MRI lab and the goosebumps on his skin as a result. He can hear the clicking, whirring and humming of the machine. He can feel his teeth with his tongue and taste his hangover. But he can't control what his mind is throwing at him. Little flashes of places he was recently visited in the dreamscape. The frozen lake. The log cabin. The forest. The lavender field.

Then like an explosion in his consciousness the big huskie dogs feel like they are right in his face. Barking. Snarling. Foam dripping from their mouths. Their eyes fierce and full of bloodlust.

Glen's whole body flinches violently like he was having a min-seizure.

* * *

Sally is sitting on the edge of the jacuzzi, gently playing with one of the floating lilies holding a lit candle in it. She uses her index finger to guide it in circles around other lilies, watching the water ripples with a stupefied grin on her face.

She closes her eyes. The soft sound of the water ripples decreases. A flash of bright light explodes into her relaxed mind, quickly followed by the sound of barking dogs. It's the same vicious snarling she recognizes from her dreams.

Sally opens her eyes wide. She looks through the pot haze in the dimly lit bathroom. At the other end of the room a swirling portal of smoke opens up. Sally blinks. Her heart races. She wishes she didn't smoke that joint now. This is all feeling too real for her. She knows it is a hallucination, yet it feels like more than that. It's a dreamlike apparition, not a ghost, and yet it is just as scary to her. A black hole with several yellow eyes peering through at her.

Sally stands up. She tries to control her breathing. In and out in slow controlled successions.

Then *she* comes out.

Sally's alter-ego.

She's not wearing the red dress this time. She is completely naked. The tuft of pubic hair above her vagina matches Sally's. The barking dogs are on leashes that she holds, slowing their angry barking to grumbling growls. Sally's ego smiles. She steps across the tiles and is now right in front of Sally.

Sally hears a voice in her head. It is succinct and clear, and it belongs to Glen.

"They need to be let go."

Sally repeats it to her ego in a trancelike state. "They need to be let go."

The ego's smile quickly vanishes. She stares at Sally with a stone expression. She holds her hands out, still clenching the leads. She slowly opens her hands and lets the leads fall from her grasp. Sally is now terrified of the now freed canines. They begin to circle her. They don't appear to be ferocious anymore. In fact, the opposite happens.

They turn into big puppies, making whimpering sounds, licking her ankles and nuzzling her legs as they swarm around her in a friendly fashion. Sally's expression turns to joy as she looks down at the playful dogs. Her ego reaches around and undoes the zip on the back of Sally's dress. It's Sally physically doing it, but in her mind right now it feels like her apparition is unzipping her. She shimmies until the dress falls to her feet. She's now simply wearing the red lace lingerie she bought.

She kicks the dress aside like it was a dirt rag. She reaches behind and pulls the pin from her bun, letting her curled hair cascade down her back. The ego leans in and kisses Sally sensually on the lips. A moment as the two share a sensual moment, then the ego steps forward and liquifies into Sally, disappearing inside her.

Sally now feeling a burning sexuality she has never experienced before. Her libido on fire. It's not lust she's feeling. It's power. She has never felt this connected to her inner passion. She feels like she just found her goddess. Her hands aren't trembling anymore. She clenches her fists tight. Her breathing long and deep through her nose. Fuck everyone. Fuck anyone who has ever criticized her. Fuck anyone who ever belittled her. Fuck anyone who treated her like a crazy bitch. Fuck societal norms and expectations. And most of all, right now, she's gonna fuck the shit out of Brad.

Let's make this baby.

Sally's eyes bolt wide open. She turns swiftly on her red heels and strides purposefully for the bathroom door. She whisks it open making the candle infused smoke haze around her waft violently.

Brad is sitting on the edge of the bed, still in his suit and nestling a glass of scotch in his hands. He looks up as Sally marches toward him in her sexy lingerie and heels, her hair swinging back and forth across her back.

The huskie dogs surround Sally as she walks. Brad can't see them, but Sally imagines them walking in front, alongside and behind her, now feeling like a wild animal herself. Like she is one of them, and they are one of her.

Brad looks intimidated as Sally comes at him with a fierceness in her runny mascara fueled eyes. He gulps the remaining scotch and places the glass on the floor as Sally approaches him.

"Why are you still dressed?" she says with a cold, yet playful tone to her voice.

Brad stands up, gulps, and starts to loosen his tie.

It's already too long for Sally. She reaches over and takes the tie, pulling it hard and unravelling it with intensity. She tosses it aside and then grabs either side of Brad's shirt and tears it open; every button popping off and bouncing on the carpet around them.

Brad is too in shock to undo his belt and pants, but Sally is already on that task and before he knows it his pants and boxer shorts are at his feet. Sally shoves him hard in the chest with her flattened palm. Brad falls back onto the bed with a bounce and Sally struts forward and puts her knees on the mattress one-by-one, walking on her knees to straddle him in the cowgirl position, still wearing her heels. Sally having watched straight porn in the past week to pick up tricks and tactics, she did notice a lot of the female porn actors kept their heels on for the whole performance. Must be a thing, she thought.

Now sitting on top of Brad, Sally wriggles her crotch to grind on his. She can feel him getting hard and can't keep the smile from forming on her face.

*

Glen is twitching frenziedly inside the MRI machine. The sounds of crackling electricity and changing radio bandwidth sounds are overbearing. Flashes of images bombard Glen's consciousness. Lightning bolts. Sally. The huskie dogs. Sally's alter ago. The screaming baby. The deer.

Glen is now convulsing into a seizure as the MRI machine stops and starts, the lights on the control panel flickering.

*

The computer screen in the radiology lab observatory room is showing little blotches all over Glen's brain.

The assistant behind the seated doctor is watching with awe. "What the hell is going on?"

The seated doctor jumps up from his seat and races for the door joining the two rooms.

"He's going into a seizure! Stop the scanner!"

Sally's lace bra is off, and she hooks her finger into the panties material and tears them off. She feels around under her and finds Brad's erect penis, guiding it inside of her. Sally enters into a tranced ecstasy as she writhes up and down on Brad. It doesn't hurt like she thought it would. The sensation is weird, only ever really having used penis sized sex toys and not the real deal attached to an actual man. But Brad is well endowed. She's no expert, of course, but when you know, you know, she muses.

She closes her eyes. Her face dripping with sweat. Her ears are thrumming with a baseline. She's not enjoying the sex so much as she is owning it. She's never felt so alive and in control. Brad conversely has never felt so helpless. He's not enjoying the sex so much as watching Sally get into it. He is wondering if this experience might turn her sexuality into other directions. Then he starts thinking what would happen if Sally left Larissa to pursue men. Larissa would kill him. He can feel his erection waning and puts those thoughts out of his head, concentrating on how tight Sally feels. He reaches up and grabs her breasts, as he had seen the male porn actors do in his previous straight porn research. It must be a thing, he thinks. He closes his eyes and pictures a past lover. A Jamaican man by the name of Sharif. Man, that sex was phenomenal. Brad now reminiscing in detail of one of their particular encounters. It's working for him, and in turn, looks like it's working on Sally.

Sally cups his hands over her breasts and makes him massage them as she rides him more ferociously. Then she hears crackling akin to strong electrical currents. Images flash through her mind. Lightning bolts. The frozen lake. Young Glen. The screaming baby. The stone well.

*

The MRI doctor grabs the manual lever for the stretcher Glen is on and heaves him out so he is free of the machine.

Two orderlies run over with syringes filled with buccal midazolam while the doctor and an assistant try to hold Glen's spasming body from toppling off the cot.

Glen is foaming at the mouth while the doctor snatches the syringes from an orderly and squeezes a couple of small pumps of liquid out, then jams the needle into Glen's thigh, pumping the medicine in.

*

Sally is getting right into a rhythm as she speeds up the tempo for the climax. She is giving it all she's got for Brad to ejaculate. That is, after all, the whole point of all this. But she also wants to feel pleasured so the sperm connects to her eggs in the throes of passion. Part of her feels the pain of the penis inside her now, but the rest of her is in rapture. Thinking about that baby she's going to have. All hers.

Brad's face winces as he lets his seed explode inside Sally, then lets loose a little groan. That felt better than he had expected it to.

Sally throws her head back in satisfied victory, slowing her writhing down bit by bit until she's stopped altogether. She lets out a little moan of relief then falls to the side and collapses on the bed next to Brad.

The doctors and orderlies loosen their grip on Glen. His spasmodic surges have died down to minor twitching as the tranquilizer takes hold throughout his body. The head doctor takes Glen's pulse, then lets out a sigh of relief and regains his composure. He tells his assistants to take Glen to the stasis room for evaluation, then inspects the controls for the MRI machine, wondering what the hell caused that.

CHAPTER TWENTY-ONE

PILLOW TALK

The incense sticks around the Honeymoon Suite have all burned down to the stubs. Sally lies on the bed, staring at the ceiling in a euphoric daze. 'I did it,' she thinks proudly to herself.

Brad is now sitting on the corner of the bed, pulling his boxer shorts on. He stops for a moment, staring into thin air with a dumbfounded look on his face. He can't believe he actually just did that. It's really sinking in now, and he almost feels violated. Sure, he did cum, like he was supposed to. But now his seed is actually inside a woman and that seed is going to be a human being. It was one thing to plan it. It's another thing it happened.

"So... um... was it like you expected?" asks Brad.

"No."

"In a good way, or a bad way?"

Sally chortles and rolls onto her side, propping her head on her elbow.

"Bradley, dear. You can save the pillow talk. You didn't sign up for that."

"Huh? I didn't 'sign up' for anything."

"No offense, but unless you want to stick around and double bag the objective, we're kind of done."

"Are you okay?"

"What?"

"You sound like a different person."

"As opposed to the person you knew for a few hours beforehand?"

"You weren't acting like a bitch, that's for sure."

"How am I a bitch, exactly?"

Brad takes a moment to prepare a politely articulated response.

"Oh, you mean because I told you to get the fuck out," says Sally.

"Are you telling me to get the fuck out?"

"Well… I'm not, not telling you to get the fuck out."

"It's like you and Claire are completely different people."

"Claire?"

"I know it was you that called me the other night pretending to sell a phone plan," Brad says with a dry smirk. "You do the same low voice when you imitate people, like your family stories. You're a terrible actor."

Sally laughs, but it's not sincere.

"I wasn't going for an Oscar."

"Then what were you going for?"

Sally twirls her index finger around on the bed sheet and keeps her eyes on it. The smile on her face fades away.

Brad picks up his boxer shorts and slips them back on.

Sally looks up with an apologetic expression.

"You can stay," she looks back down at her fidgeting fingers, "If you want."

Brad now putting his shirt on, sighing with dismay that the buttons are no longer there.

"I gotta work early in the morning."

Sally laughs. This time it's sincere.

"So, this is what it feels like."

"What feels like what?"

"My straight girl friends have told me the old 'I have to work early' excuse, and ones with similar overtones."

Brad now putting his pants on, shaking his head with a grin.

"What?" Sally asks with offense in her tone.

"First you kick me out, then you ask me to stay, then call me a piece of shit bro-dude for wanting to leave."

"I didn't call you a piece of shit."

"And I don't have to work early."

Sally's lips curl into a devilish smile.

"Well, now you can't leave. The banter is starting to get real."

"Look, Sally. I did what Larissa asked me to. I did it willingly, and actually had a great dinner with you. But just because I'm a gay guy, I'm not a Ken doll with accessories. I don't have the expected razor-sharp acerbic wit. I don't like to trade insults for fun." Brad puts his dinner jacket on and secures the two waist buttons in an effort to mask the fact that he doesn't have buttons on his shirt. "I would much rather go home, drink some vino and play X-Box. Why don't you relax? Take stock of what we did. Maybe use that awesome jacuzzi in there. Smoke another doob."

Sally blinks in feigned confusion.

Brad says, "I could taste the weed on you as soon as you came out. Seemed like strong shit too. If I didn't have to partake in the odd urine test, I would have wanted in on that action."

"Why do you have to do drug tests?"

Brad looks out the window a moment at the twinkling lights of downtown Boston, then looks back to Sally with a caring smile.

"I hope it all works out for you. And Larissa. I hope…," he looks at his feet in sadness a moment, then turns and strides to the door, opens it and is quickly gone.

Sally lies on her back staring at the ceiling for a few minutes, then shimmies herself off the bed and saunters to the window, still wearing her red heels. She stares down at the headlights moving through the rain glistened streets. She places one of her palms on the glass and rests her forehead on the window, using her other hand to gently rub her stomach. After a few moments, she looks at her planted hand, then the hand on her tummy. They aren't shaking for once.

Larissa is nestled in the corner of the sofa in the lounge room, wearing a matching dark purple sweatshirt and pants. She sips her chardonnay as she highlights a few sentences in a legal case study copy, the booklet open in her cross-legged lap. She has a thought and places her wine glass down on the varnished oak stand next to the sofa, then leans over to the cardboard box sitting on the other side of her and rifles through the other case studies that fill the box. After several minutes she punches the box out of frustration, then leans over to the glass-top coffee table in front of her and snatches her phone from the surface. She scrolls down her contacts until she finds who she's after. The phone rings for several moments.

"Hello?"

"Who's the fucking paralegal assigned to the Roberts versus Kusz case?"

"Uh, let me check."

Larissa uses the opportunity to have another sip of wine, angrily slamming the glass on the wooden table.

After a few moments, the woman on the other end says, "Craig Zahn."

Larissa rolls her eyes. "Ugh. That fucking frat bro." Larissa sighs angrily. "He left out the Rochester case file. I specifically asked for that."

"Okay." An awkward pause. "I'm not far from the office. You want me to go look for it?"

Larissa pulls the phone away from her ear a moment to check the time. It's nearly two in the morning.

"No. You call that mother fucker. I don't care what time it is. It's his fuck up, not yours."

"Okay boss."

"Thanks Abby."

Larissa hangs up the call and languidly tosses the phone down the couch, then resumes drinking more chardonnay. The Tchaikovsky playing on the portable speaker on the coffee table is keeping her somewhat calm. She really wants to hurl the crystal vase on the oak table next to her across the room. It doesn't help her mood that her partner is off getting boned by her co-worker. She licks the chardonnay drops on her upper lip and reminds herself that this was her idea. Well, part of it anyway. She hasn't really thought through the repercussions of seeing Brad, day in, day out for the foreseeable future. It just seemed so convenient. But one thing she is betting on, is that Sally won't go through with it anyway. Her anxiety will get the better of her. They'll have dinner at a posh restaurant. Sally will be awkward as fuck. Brad will be too pretentious for her. She'll have realized what a mistake this all was. Boom. Back to the fertility clinic they go.

Larissa hears the front door close, and keys hitting the French table stand by the entrance. Wow, she's home already. Larissa half expected her to at least go use the hotel room for the night. Take some time to lament on the absurdity of this whole baby making operation.

"Twinkie?" Larissa calls out as she tops up her wine from the now lukewarm bottle of chardonnay sitting at the base of the sofa.

Silence. Larissa wondering if she went straight upstairs. Probably too embarrassed to talk about how she couldn't go through with it. That's fair enough, she doesn't need to-

"Hey Bunny."

Larissa screams and jolts in fright, spilling wine all over her legs and the couch. She snaps her neck around to find Sally standing right behind the couch.

"Jesus fuck! You scared the shit out of me," Larissa says, putting her hand on her beating chest.

"Sorry."

Sally is wearing an old baggy grey college sweater over her cocktail dress. Her hair looks like a bomb went off in a haystack. Her makeup is smudged all over her face.

Larissa wipes the wine that has now seeped into her sweatpants, then looks at the damage done to the sofa upholstery. Little splotches of wet are on the soft dark green fabric. Oh well. She'll get a steam cleaner or some shit. Larissa looks back up to Sally.

"So… how… did it go?"

Sally forces a little smile but doesn't say anything right away. After several long moments, and what feels like an eternity to Larissa, she says, "The room was amazing."

"I know, right."

"You did a wonderful job decorating."

Larissa smiles and grabs the wine bottle again, filling her glass. She speaks in a Southern accent for fun. "Why thank ye."

Another long moment. Larissa takes a long sip of wine, focusing on a pot plant behind Sally, who is focused on the crystal vase next to Larissa.

"I love that vase."

Larissa follows her gaze to the crystal vase, then looks back to Sally with pursed lips.

"So, how did it go?"

"Hmmm?"

"With Brad."

"Oh." She wistfully looks around the room like she's never seen it before, despite it being her who decorated it. "Um... yeah. It went well."

Larissa takes in too much wine and winces as she gulps it down, immediately wanting to puke it up. She clears her throat and can feel water in her eyes.

"That's it? It went 'well'?"

Sally shrugs. "Y'know...,"

Larissa waits for the rest, but it never comes.

"I'm tired."

"Okay."

Sally stands there, making Larissa a little uncomfortable.

"Well, I'm burning the midnight oil on this case. I'll be up for a while."

"That's okay. You do your thing."

Sally leans down and kisses Larissa on the top of her head, then turns and strides out of the loungeroom. Larissa hears her soft footsteps going up the stairs and stares off into thin air with a vacant expression. It feels like a million questions are going through her mind, none of which have anything to do with this court case.

※

Larissa is passed out on the couch with file papers scattered all around her.

BANG. CRASH.

Larissa wakes with a startle at the loud noises. She quickly surmises they are coming from the kitchen and she jumps up and races to the back of the house.

She runs into the kitchen to find Sally fully naked in the middle of the kitchen, pots and pans scattered on the floor all around her. She has a soup pot in her hand.

Sally's eyes are closed, and she says, "I can't control everything."

Sally pitches it across the room. The pot crashes into the wall with a loud CLANG.

"What the fuck are you doing?!"

Sally's closed eyes pop open and she freezes for a few moments than drops to the floor.

Larissa races over and drops down next to her, taking Sally in her arms.

"Are you okay?"

Sally nods slowly, then looks at the floor around her with cooking pots scattered all around the kitchen.

"What happened?"

"You were sleepwalking again."

"Again?"

"Yeah."

Sally is blinking erratically, still in a state of shock and confusion.

Larissa says, "I think it's time we got you back to that therapist."

CHAPTER TWENTY-TWO

THE SHADOW

Glen is in a hospital room staring vacantly at the ceiling, rigorously debating in his head if he should ask the nurse if he can have another pudding. The one he had earlier with his lunch was not bad at all.

Doctor Thomas pulls the sheet around his bed aside. He's carrying his clipboard as always.

"Morning Glen. How are you feeling?"

"Like my head's being held together by crazy glue and duct-tape."

"Well, at least your sense of humor is still intact."

Thomas pulls the chair next to bed over and faces it at Glen, then plonks himself down and takes off his glasses, putting them on the nightstand along with his clipboard. He crosses one leg and adopts a casual demeanor.

"Alright. Let's cut to the chase. You have a grade four Astrocytoma tumor. Not gonna lie, it's spread pretty quickly, and my charts show that its pace has picked up rapidly over the past few weeks. That part I can't tell you why."

"So I'm as dead as dinosaurs, that it?"

"Not exactly. But your chances of recovery aren't good." He shrugs. "That being said, you've still got a chance. So, there's that."

"A slim one."

"You got more than some people in here right now."

"So what do we do now?"

Thomas stands up and puts his glasses back on.

"You get a buzz cut and we try and cut this crap outta your brain. From the data we accrued based on the MRI results, this thing is aggressive so it's likely there will be a follow up session of surgery, depending of course how the first one goes."

"Sounds like a hoot."

"Due to staffing and availability, I can't get you in until a week from now."

"Cool. Do I have to stay here until then?"

"I'd rather you did. After the MRI incident, I would like to do more checks. Keep you monitored."

"But I can leave?"

Thomas sighs. "Yes, you can. But since you live alone in a remote location, I strongly advise you stay here under the care of medical professionals."

"No offense doc, but if it's likely I'm gonna be a worm buffet soon, I'd rather try to live a little if I can."

"But that's just it, Glen. If you are too active in any way, you may bring on more of these attacks. If you go into the woods by yourself again and not on the phone with someone, you might not make it out this time."

"I won't be doin' any huntin'. I was thinkin' of goin' fishing with my brother-in-law."

"As I said, I'd prefer if you didn't leave the hospital, but, if you are in good company that's something. I would also recommend having your sister check up on you if you don't answer your phone."

"I may be sick, but I ain't stupid."

Thomas manages a little lopsided grin, then resumes his serious demeanor. "And I think it goes without saying, if there's any more nosebleeds, come in immediately. But don't drive yourself obviously."

Glen chuckles and shakes his head. "I won't, doc. I won't."

"Alright. Well, you have my personal number. Contact me anytime you need, day or night."

Glen nods. Thomas nods at him with a terse smile then turns to leave.

"Say, doc?"

Thomas turns around. "Yeah Glen?"

"What happened. Y'know, last night?"

"The seizure?"

"Yeah, that. They said there might have been a malfunction in the machine."

"They did a maintenance overhaul on the MRI first thing this morning. They found no issues at all with the hardware. If you were planning on suing, I would advise-"

"No, no. Nothing like that. I've been having these dreams lately. This woman and her dogs. Sometimes there's a baby."

Glen notices the change in Thomas' face. He's trying to look professionally engaged but has a hint of 'are you nuts?' on there.

"Look, never mind all that. Forget I said that. But I gotta ask. Those MRI machines. They use a lot of electricity, yeah?"

Thomas nods. "Yeah. You could say that."

"What else could you say?"

"Well, the one you experienced uses phase three power. Four-hundred and eighty volts at two-hundred Amps."

Glen stares at him with furrowed brows.

Thomas grins and says, "It's roughly the equivalent of powering six houses."

Glen's eyebrows raise in interest. That's more his language.

"Why does this interest you?" says Thomas. "If you don't mind my asking."

"I'm just trying to figure out...," Glen scratches his head. "It just interests me, is all."

"Well, if you have any more questions, don't hesitate to call. Just don't call me at four in the morning with questions on medical hardware specs, okay?"

"Okay," Glen says with a smirk. "I gotta ask, though. If you say there was no malfunction on the machine, what do you think happened last night?"

"Honestly, I couldn't tell you." Thomas shrugs. "I'm a doctor, not an engineer."

Glen nods in understanding, then Thomas swiftly turns on his heels and strides for the door, stopping in the doorway.

"Hey Glen."

"Yeah?"

"Dinosaurs aren't dead. Technically chickens are dinosaurs."

Thomas winks and is gone.

"Do you have an appointment, mister...?" the plucky receptionist with square glasses says.

"Uh, yeah. I got a three o'clock. Name's Glen."

"Last name?"

"Oh, sorry. Bourke. Glen Bourke."

She taps away at her keyboard, squinting at the screen, then says, "Yes. Gotcha. She's almost ready. Take a seat over there and I'll call you when it's time."

Glen matches her polite smile then ambles over to a waiting area of seats, placing his backpack on the spare seat next to him. He glances at the mounted TV in the corner as he unzips the bag and takes out a book. The TV playing one of those soap operas with the soft lens and basic lighting. Glen zips his bag back up and opens the book to where he dogeared the page last. The book is called 'Your Brain on Electricity: A Guide to Understand Synapses Cortex Currents'. He's read over half of it in the past couple of days, not understanding large amounts of it due to all that complex math and scientific jargon. But the parts he wants to understand is how electricity influences the brain.

After nearly ten minutes the receptionist calls out, "Mister Bourke? Yvonne will see you now."

Glen puts the book back in his bag and zips it back up, standing and slinging it over his shoulder. He spots a door open in a small corridor behind the reception desk, and Yvonne steps out wearing a light blue pantsuit. Her hair wound up into a bun on the crown of her head.

"Glen. What an unexpected pleasure. Glad you came in."

Glen purses his lips uncomfortably as he approaches her. She motions for him to enter her office and he walks into the large room. There's a desk in the back, and several seats arranged neatly in the middle of the office. A dark blue classic French lounge, two faux leather wingback armchairs, a black high back sofa chair, a plain white plastic chair and a red deep teal velvet armchair.

"Take a seat," Yvonne says as she closes the office door.

"Which one?"

"Any one you want." She smiles genially. "Whatever speaks to you."

Glen takes a moment to run his eyes over the mostly ostentatious seats. He wants to sit on that Chez lounge but feels like it's somewhat cheesy to go sit in one of those shrink chairs while he's in a shrink's office. Also, it looks so comfy that he may just fall asleep. Since the MRI incident, he's been feeling a lot more fatigued lately.

Glen meanders over to one of the faux leather chairs and plants himself in it.

Yvonne making mental notes on this as she strides to her pinewood brown desk and retrieves her thick padded notebook, then takes a seat in the plain plastic chair opposite him. She clicks her pen and opens her book.

"Right. Let's get to it, shall we?"

Glen nods, haphazardly gazing around at the art on the walls. A couple of Picasso-inspired abstract paintings. One oil painting of a 1800's woman in a bonnet sewing at a spinning wheel. And a large, wide photo print behind her desk of a wild rural wheat field with mountains on the horizon. Glen stares at it a moment, feeling a growing relaxation the more he stays with it.

"My son took that," Yvonne says, following his gaze to the print.

"Is he a photographer? That's pretty fuckin' good." Glen clears his throat with a sheepish expression. "Sorry."

"You know terse language doesn't bother me. I want to hear your voice, not what you want me to think of you."

Glen nods slowly, looking at the art deco glass coffee table in the center of all the seats.

"And no, he wasn't a photographer. He was a long haul truck driver." She smiles with sadness in her eyes. "He loved being on the open road, seeing different parts of the country."

Glen creases his brows. "Was?"

Yvonne looks into her lap a moment, suppressing a memory, then looks back to Glen with a newfound determination. "Let's keep this about you, okay? That's what you're here for."

"Okay. Well, let's start with sleepwalking."

"You've been sleepwalking?"

"Like a mother fucker."

Yvonne grins as she jots down in her pad. "Do you have a history with it, like, as a child?"

Glen says, "I've never in my life done this shit. Now I'm doin' it nearly every night."

"Interesting."

"What would be even more interesting is if I didn't. I'm getting' fed up with waking up in different parts of the house. Holdin' somethin' new."

"You collect props?"

"Yeah. And the weird part is, whatever I got usually has somethin' to do with the dream."

"That's even more interesting."

"Aren't you supposed to, like, be in some sorta coma when you're fast asleep? Think I saw that on a TV show once or somethin'."

Yvonne places her palms flat on the pages of her notebook. "During REM, Rapid Eye Movement as it is technically called, our muscles become temporarily paralyzed. So, in effect, you are in a self-induced coma, yes. It stops you from physically acting out your dream."

"Apparently my brain didn't get the memo."

"Have you had any trauma's lately that might have brought it on? Any new medications, or illnesses? Have you had constant interrupted sleep?"

"All of the above, and then some."

Yvonne writing on her pad, says, "What would be your best guess of who the main culprit is?"

"Probably the giant tumor in my brain."

Yvonne drops the pen along with her jaw.

Glen says, "Probably should'a told you that off the bat, huh?"

Yvonne slowly nods her head and adjusts the glasses on her now very concerned face. "Yes. You should have."

"Sorry."

"Don't be sorry," she says blinking. "I'm sorry. Are you okay?"

Glen shrugs, leaning over to pour himself a glass of water from the pitcher on the coffee table. "Got a bunch of gnarly headaches. Migraines. Some blood noses. But most of the time I feel alright. Just tired. But I think that's mostly from the meds. I dunno." He leans into the back of the chair and takes a few gulps of water, then says, "But other than the erratic sleeping shit, I'm doin' fine, I guess. I'm having it cut out next week. I'm in good hands."

"Well, that's good."

"It's just… the dreams are really fuckin' with me lately. That's why I'm here I guess."

"The recurring dream you told me about. The one with your brother."

"That goes back a ways. A long ways."

"And the woman?"

"Huh?"

"You said there was a woman you vividly interact with. A baby, and I think you said-"

"Oh, right. Her. Yeah, she's pretty damn recent."

"Do you associate illness with any other woman in your life? I may have to get a little personal here, but did your mother, or sister, or daughter, niece, anyone close to you. Did they have any serious illnesses like you are going through?"

"Nope. Nothin' like that."

Yvonne is writing notes.

"Actually. I wanna talk about what you were askin' me at my house." Yvonne looks up at him with her eyes staring over the top of her glasses. "What was that?"

"You were startin' to talk about electric shocks and such."

Yvonne purses her lips and nearly rolls her eyes. "Oh, don't worry about that."

"No, I'm interested. You asked if anyone was there when the lightning strike happened?"

"Was there?"

"N-no. But hypothetically, what if there was?"

"It doesn't matter. Let's stick to the subject."

"But I want this to be the subject."

"We don't have time to go off on tangents."

"I'm payin' to be here." He raises his brows mindfully. "And a pretty penny at that."

Yvonne sighs and gently lays her pen in the middle of the open book. "Look. There's a wild theory, and I do mean wild, that if two people, or more, are subjected to a traumatic electrical outburst, that they...," she looks at the ceiling trying to articulate what she wants to say in her head, "That they become connected."

"Connected?"

Yvonne bobs her head from side to side a moment. "Like...," she stops moving her head and looks at him. "Okay. The brain is the most complex organism there is. It's made up of five key parts that all selectively concentrate on their respective tasks, which ultimately culminate in the overall big picture. Cogs in a well oiled machine, if you will. The average human brain contains roughly a hundred and twenty billion neurons which constantly send and receive information amongst one another in a tree-branch like appendages." She uses her hands to emulate a tree sprouting up. "All of which use chemical and electrical signals to message each other."

Yvonne pauses, watching Glen's face twist as he tries to take this information in, then continues.

"There is a belief, that an external punch of electricity can cause a fluctuation of the electrodes in the brain. There is another belief still, that if people within a close proximity experiencing the same burst, might connect, however briefly, to one another's brain signals. It might be for a few seconds, or it might be weeks, or even months." Yvonne takes a deep breath and straightens her posture. "But, it's really all conjecture. Such a thing cannot be proven categorically. Not yet anyway. It's an interesting concept, nonetheless. But in your situation, I would easily venture that this… tumor, you're experiencing, is the cause of your brain's erratic behavior. The migraines. The sleepwalking. The nose bleeds. All of it. I'm no medical doctor, but that would be my face value diagnosis. The lightning strike may well have exacerbated the tumor. But that's a good thing. Because now you're aware of it and can remove it before it does any more damage. The best thing I can do for you right now is to help steer your mental ship to confront the under-lying issues you face in the subconscious arena. That is, your dreams."

Glen finishes his water and plays with the empty glass, turning it around slowly in his palms with a thoughtful visage.

"Yeah. You're right. That does sound crazy."

"I told you." Yvonne puts her glasses back on and picks up the pen. "Now. Aside from this woman in your dreams, are there any other recurring prominent characters that stand out to you?"

"Me."

"Well, we are generally always the main character in our dreams."

"No. There's a different version of me. He's me as a kid. Around the age of twelve."

Yvonne scribbles away in her book. "Is he a positive presence?"

"No."

Glen's quick resolute reply prompts Yvonne to look up at him a moment, then continues writing. "Does he bring negativity? Anxiety?"

Glen squeezes the glass harder as he rotates it in his palms.

"He pisses me off, is what."

"Why?"

"Because the little fuck is always in the background, watching me. Every time I tell him to go away, he just sulks and walks to another spot. I try to get away from him sometimes, but he just follows. He's like a tick. The more you try to pull it out, it just digs deeper."

"He's your shadow."

"My what?"

"Jung coined the term in his dream research and dissertations."

"Who the fuck is young?"

"Carl Jung. He's a well known and respected psychiatrist."

"Never heard of him."

"Well, he's been dead for over sixty years. And unless you're familiar with psychiatric studies, it's not uncommon to not have heard of him. He's not Donald Trump."

"Who the fuck is Donald Trump?"

Yvonne looks up with furrowed brows.

"I'm kidding," Glen says with a smirk.

Yvonne manages a terse little grin and crosses one leg over the other. "Jung said that The Shadow is the manifestation of everything we do not wish to be."

Glen stops rotating the glass in his hands and stares into the bottom of it. "Well… ain't that the damn truth." He looks up to Yvonne with determination in his eyes. "How do I get rid of the fucker?"

"First thing's first, we need to dig right into your subconscious."

Glen shifts uncomfortably in his seat. "What. You mean I have to get into a gizmo, like an MRI, so you can scan with magnets and shit?"

Yvonne chuckles lightly under her breath. "No, no, nothing like that. It's not physical. We simply talk. Or, rather, you talk, and I listen. I need to know the dark recesses of your mind. And, on top of that, you have to start paying attention to your dreams. Record everything that happens as soon as you wake up. And you have about ten minutes to do that before you lose the specifics as they dissolve while your conscious mind takes over."

Glen leans forward with newfound interest. "Yeah, why is that? Why do you damn near forget your dream by the time you're outta bed and takin' a piss?"

"The subconscious becomes strong when you're in RMI, which is basically a self-induced coma. It's time to shine is when the main lights are off. The subconscious mind communicates infinitely better when there's no bells and whistles of everyday life. Your conscious mind is fraught with the complexities of existing in the real world. And I don't just mean the obvious stuff, like relationships, bills, work, house and home chores. Your brain is constantly mapping everything out for you, right to the mundane. Walk a few inches to the left to avoid colliding your hip to the dining table as you walk by. Putting one foot in front of the other while you walk. You may think that's an inherent trait you haven't had to think about since you learnt to walk as a toddler. But your brain is always reminding you of the basics even when you don't have to give it much thought. Its why really old people start to forget the basics, especially when traits of dementia start to appear."

Glen's mind flashes to his grandpa who died many years ago now. Glen remembering how his mind started to go in his late eighties. Dementia. He would often forget things such as how to walk properly, and topple over out of the blue.

"Your conscious mind also does not register your Shadow. The very existence of the Shadow is your conscious mind rejecting the qualities about yourself that you despise. All those unappealing emotions and memories are pushed so far back they manifest themselves into entries, or a singular entity. Like, in this case, your child self. And if you deny your psyche the ability to heal these damaging aspects, they can and often do, project onto others around you in your waking life. Or even worse, yourself in waking life."

Glen steals a quick glance at the many scars permeating his hands and wrists.

Yvonne says, "Aristotle believed there was a clear connection between dreams and one's physical health."

"Aristotle," Glen repeats with a thoughtful visage. He snaps his fingers and grins. "I know who he is. He was some kind of famous philosopher, wasn't he?"

Yvonne nods her head at him. "He was."

Glen nods his head holding onto his grin, proud he said something smart to Yvonne.

Yvonne closes her large black notepad in her lap and places it on the seat next to her. She leans forward and picks up a smaller yellow notepad and flicks through it until she finds the page she wants and flattens the book out in her lap with her palms.

"Let's start assigning you some activities to do before and after you sleep." She looks up at him with a subtle smile. "Think of it as home-work."

Glen rolls his eyes and leans back in his chair with a little grunt.

Yvonne says, "But first, we are going to talk about your brother Joe."

Glen takes a sharp breath in and swallows a dry lump in his throat. He starts tapping his foot anxiously.

✻

Glen drives down the highway back toward Great Barrington. He wipes his reddened eyes, having just stopped in a Burger King parking lot to cry. Not just cry, wail like a kid having a tantrum. Glen can't remember the last time he cried like that, or even at all. Probably when he was a kid having a tantrum. He didn't cry at his mother's funeral. Not that he didn't feel profoundly sad. Of course he did. He loved that woman. Even if she was too weak to stand up to his father and his abusive drunk behavior. But her death was caused by cancer, and they could all see it coming a mile away. He didn't cry at his grandparents' deaths. Not one of them. Probably some of it to do with keeping up some kind of macho appearance to his friends and other relatives. Janeen sobbed at all of them. She was doing the weeping for him, and he felt like he needed to stay strong for her.

No, the last time he cried, he reckons, is when Joe died. And Glen has not spoken about all that to a soul since it happened. Digging it all up for Yvonne earlier made him think about things he has been running away from his whole life. God damn it, he can feel the tears starting to come back now. Glen is eying off signs for upcoming gas stations or food outlets so he can pull in for another meltdown.

No.

Stay strong, asshole.

Glen pounds his fist on the steering wheel. He can feel his foot pressing on the accelerator harder, now going well over the speed limit.

Think about something else, goddammit.

Glen racks his brain thinking about other insights to that session with Yvonne. Aristotle. Glen now picturing an old man in a toga. Nah, that's not interesting enough. What about that Jung dude she was on about. The psychiatrist. Nope, not doing it. Then Glen remembers Yvonne talking about the electrical charge and the brain tree, and how lightning can make people connected.

Glen now thinking about the other car passing him that morning. What kind of car was that again? It was white, he remembers that. It was a hatchback of some kind, he vaguely recalls. Something Japanese maybe? A Toyota? A Suzuki? Honda, maybe? Damn, he really didn't get a good look. And his head was pounding like shit.

Glen wonders now, who was in that car? Was it the woman he sees in his dreams? Was it someone she knows? Was it even a woman?

"This is stupid," Glen says to himself, shaking his head.

Bolts of lightning and telepathy. May was well believe in the Easter Bunny while he's at it. And even, despite it being one of the craziest ideas he ever heard, if it were in anyway true, how the fuck would he find them?

CHAPTER TWENTY-THREE

SPEAKING PLAINLY

"Pass me another beer?" says Brian as he finishes screwing the bait worm on his fishing hook.

Glen reaches over to the cooler sitting next to him and takes off his glove. He shoves his hand in the ice, sloshing around until he grips a can of Busch, then tosses it to Brian who catches it with one hand and sticks it between his thighs. Brian holds the fishing rod up and flicks the line out into the large river. The baited hook plopping in the middle of the running water several yards away. Brian snaps open the beer, cursing as some of it sprays on his pants in his crotch.

"God friggin' damn it."

Brian licks the foamy beer off his fingers and tries to flick off the suds sinking into his pants.

The two of them sit on the shore to the upper Hudson River, just over the New York state line in the Livingston State Forest. A small piece of land juts out from the shore and is Brian's favorite fishing spot all year round. The skeletal bare branches of the Sugar Maple trees behind them covered with fresh snow. A small campfire burns between the two foldout chairs Glen and Brian are sitting on. The two men wearing thick waterproof parka's, jeans and hiking boots. Glen sporting a worn red baseball cap that's been through the dryer one too many times.

Glen feels a tug on his line and leans forward, gulping down the rest of his beer and crunching the can, dropping it to his feet so he can take the fishing rod with both hands. He quickly reels the line in, the top of the rod bending from pressure.

"Current's strong today," says Brian as he takes a sip of beer, watching Glen's fishing line struggling to bring in the catch. The fine pulling heavily downstream.

Glen is on his feet now, reeling the line in enthusiastically. As the catch gets closer to shore and out of the current, Glen can make out the fish being pulled through the water. He reels it all the way in and bends down next to the flopping Smallmouth Bass on the riverbank. Glen grips the speckled yellow fish with one hand, holding it down while he plucks the hook from its mouth. Once the bass is free of the hook, Glen picks it up with both hands and tosses it back in the river. Glen meanders back to his seat, fishing a beer from the cooler before he sits down.

"Hey, was meanin' to ask. You're driving the police truck today. You even allowed to do that?"

"It's one of the older one's about to be put outta commission. I signed it out, by the book, as always."

Glen nods and raises one eyebrow in a knowing fashion with a little smirk.

After a few minutes of baiting his hook, Glen says, "Do you believe in the supernatural?"

Brian side glances him a moment, then takes a sip of beer.

"What, like ghosts?"

"No… not really. More, like, telepathy."

Now Brian turns his head to look at Glen with a vexed expression. "Telepathy?"

"Yeah. Y'know. Seein' other people's thoughts n'shit."

"I know what it is," Brian says, looking at the river with a now concerned visage. "Science fiction nonsense. Braden watches one of them superhero shows. One of the characters does it."

Glen cracks open his can of beer. "Guess that answers the question," he says, taking a hefty gulp of beer.

After an uncomfortable minute, Brian says, "Do you?"

Glen sucks in cold air through his nostrils with a deeply thoughtful expression. He hesitates a moment, then says, "Maybe."

"Maybe you're a damn loon."

"I've been thinkin' a lot lately, Brian."

"Sounds like you should do less of that."

A sliver of a grin enters Glen's face and disappears just as quick as it arrived.

"Come on now, man. Just havin' some conversation."

Brian exhales hot air from his nose with a grouchy sentiment. He found Glen's setup under the back shed while he was cleaning up the paint he spilt. Brian had never felt so hurt and betrayed in his life. His brother-in-law, of all people, a damn drug dealer. The weed wouldn't be so bad, now that's it mostly legal. But the MDMA, acid and mushrooms, that's heavy duty stuff right there. Considerable jail time for the amount he has.

Brian wanting to spray the bunker with gasoline and set it all on fire. He came within a hair's length of doing just that. The hair off a buzz cut. He had to calm himself. He had to find out what the heck was going on. Was this man, who he has known and trusted since high school, loved as a brother the day he was married to Janeen, indeed a drug dealer? If so, Brian would have no reservation arresting him on the spot. The law is the law. And Brian is charged to uphold that law. It doesn't matter if the criminal is family. But he had to be sure. So he asked Glen to go fishing with him. Lay the cards on the table and allow Glen to explain himself. There could be a perfectly acceptable explanation. He rents the space out to someone and doesn't know what's going on down there. What if... alright, Brian knows he's reaching now. He just wants to hear Glen confess, and he'll put the cuffs on him right here. It's the real reason he drove out here in an official work vehicle. Save him the embarrassment of doing it in front of other police. Take him to the station and book him nice and quietly. Then go home and tell Janeen everything. God damn that's going be the hardest part.

Brian says, "Why would you ask me if I'm into that crap? You been smokin' the wacky tobaccy lately?"

"What?" Glen says, darting Brian an incredulous look. "Since when have you ever known me to smoke that shit?"

Brian shrugs, staring at the river. "You did it in high school. Right up until you joined the service."

Glen scoffs. "A million fuckin' years ago, sure." He throws his head back and chugs beer, promptly belching loudly right after.

"Look, I dunno man. You're in and out of hospital with these headaches and nosebleeds. Now you're yammerin' on about reading people's thoughts like you're one of them crackpot folk who believe in lizard people, or thought the virus wasn't real a few years back."

"I was just askin' a question," Glen says shaking his head with a little annoyance. "I'm not a fuckin' conspiracy nut."

Brian becoming more agitated he can't bring the line of questioning faster to where he would like. "Are you doing drugs or not?"

Glen tosses his fishing reel on the ground in front of him and stands up heatedly.

"What the fuck is your problem, bro?" Glen says, saying 'Bro' aggressively.

Brian sticks the beer can in the beverage holder on his chair and stands up as well.

"I'm gonna ask you again. And this time I want you to answer me. Truthfully. Are yo-"

"I'm not on fuckin' drugs, Brian. 'Cept the painkillers the doctor prescribed. You got a problem with that?"

Brian now breathing short angry breaths out of his nostrils, staring Glen down. He reaches into his jacket pocket to take out his handcuffs. If Glen's not going to play ball, Brian will end the game, right now.

Brian goes to say to Glen to turn around and put his hands behind his back. But before the first word is out of his mouth, Glen abruptly shouts.

"I've got a fuckin' brain tumor!"

Brian freezes, his hand gripping the cuffs in his coat.

"Stage four, astrotomia, or astroglycoma... astro fuckin' somethin'."

Brian slowly takes his hand off the handcuffs and takes his empty hand from his pocket. "Stage four? That's... not good... is it?"

"No, it's not. It's spread quickly and aggressive as hell. They're gonna cut it outta me but might not mean shit. There's a good chance I may die. That's why the blood noses and the headaches. So yeah, I'm on some heavy painkillers and such. You happy?!"

"G... Glen. I-I'm sorry. I dunno what to say."

"And as for the weird telepathy question, I've been havin' some fuckin' wild dreams lately. Might be the tumor, might be 'cause I almost got hit by lightning the other week. When you're on death's door, you start doin' some retrospective thinkin', you know? Open my mind up to other possibilities. Cause my mind's about to get opened by surgeons anyway, might as well get a little freaky." Glen tilts his head back and puts the beer to his mouth, guzzling the rest of the beer, then crunches the can in his fist and pelts it at the ground. "Anyway, you can thank Janeen for my wacky line of thinkin'. She's the one who sent the dream psychiatrist my way."

"A what now?"

"Yeah. A shrink who specializes in nighty-night. Ain't that somethin'." Glen marches to the cooler and rips another can from the ice, busting it open. "I'll tell ya what, though. She says some interesting shit." Glen guzzles more beer then wipes the foam from his moustache. "Never thought I'd ever say it, but therapy can be a little eye opening."

Brian not sure what to say now. Between the stage four tumor, the dream shrink, and the drug lab, he's not sure of who this man standing in front of him is right now.

Brian leans over and plucks the can from his chair and sips his beer slowly, watching Glen sit back down in his lawn chair.

"Do you need... is there anything I can do to help?"

"You cannot tell Janeen and the kids for a start."

"Janeen doesn't know?"

"If she knew, you'd know. And she'd probably sell the bowling alley to help me with the surgeries and recoveries. And I can't have that. It means too much to her."

"You mean everything to her."

Glen looks up at him sternly.

"I said don't fuckin' tell her."

Brian raises both arms up defensively. "I won't. Scouts honor."

Glen nods and looks at the river, sipping his beer.

"How are you gonna afford it... if you don't mind my asking."

Glen looks at Brian again. This time with an apprehensive glare. He holds that on Brian for several moments, then careens forward to pick his rod from the ground.

"I got some things goin' on."

"Like what?"

"Things. Don't worry about it. I can afford it. Trust me."

"You know you can trust me as well. You can tell me anything." Brian hopeful Glen will come clean to him.

"Well, I just told you somethin' no one else knows. And if you wanna keep that trust, you keep that somethin' to yourself."

Brian nods. Now he's thinking about it, he doesn't want to arrest Glen. Put him up on drug charges that he'll go down for and die in prison. The law is the law, but if those drugs are paying for his medical treatment, and it keeps Janeen from making rash decisions, which she no doubt will. But where are those drugs going? And what lives are they ruining? Brian sighs quietly. He's going to have to think long and hard about this. Brian slowly takes his seat back in the chair. "I won't tell anyone. Promise."

Glen nods. After a few minutes of silence, Glen turns to look at Brian.

"I'll tell her. Soon. I just don't want her or the kids to worry about it right now. There's nothin' she can do to change anything anyway. Let her have some blissful ignorance. If the operation doesn't go well, I'll... I'll tell her everything."

Glen's fishing line tugs again. He smiles and starts to reel the catch in.

"This is the third one in an hour. I guess it's my day, huh?"

CHAPTER TWENTY-FOUR

HUFFING AND BLUFFING

Teddy sits at the bar, staring languidly up at a TV playing SportsCenter. He drops the last finished buffalo wing into the pile of meat stripped bones and loudly sucks on his fingers one by one until every remnant of the hot sauce is gone. He can feel someone looking at him, so he turns his head to the right. He was right. Some old coot a few seats down, giving him an irritated stare.

"Fuck you want, old man?" Teddy says with a sneer.

The old patron blinks and looks back into thin air in front of him.

"Can I get you anything else?" says Janeen as she picks up Teddy's plate.

Teddy picks his teeth with his pinkie finger and says, "Another beer."

"Same one?"

Teddy wants to say a smart-ass retort, something along the lines of 'yeah, I'm doing a tour of all the shitty domestic beers you have', but this woman looks tough. Even if she's tending bar at a hick bowling alley.

"Yeah, same one," he says with a droll expression.

The echoing sound of balls hitting pins in the other room, the dated arcade games in the adjacent room, the stale carpet and the pathetic redneck patrons make Teddy want to bash his head against the bar top then start a fight with the biggest, dumbest asshole here. But he has a purpose. His number one supplier lives somewhere in this shithole town. He heard Glen mention he lives in Great Barrington once and committed that to memory for some reason. Now that reason is, he wants to know where Glen lives, so he can bust into his home when he's not there and find the formula for Frostbite. Then he'll be done with the man. Hell, he may even stick around, wait for the chump to get home and take him out for good. He gets all the other shit from a couple of other suppliers. Sure, the meth isn't quite as good as Glen's, nor is the DMT, but it's close enough. It's just that damned Frostbite he does so fucking well.

Janeen is back and plonks a bottle of Miller's on the counter in front of Teddy.

"You don't look like you're from around here," she says putting her hands on her hips. "Never seen ya before, anyway."

Teddy shrugs apathetically, looking at two fat middle-aged men walk through the front door with the bowling ball bags. "Passing through."

She nods slowly, eying him off a little suspiciously for a quick moment, then she heads down the bar to attend to other chores. Teddy watches her meander away with that fat ass. Teddy thinking he could do some work with that. And her melon tits. She's a bit on the old side, but he bets she's experienced.

Teddy looks at the shelves of liquor on the other side of the bar and sighs. He's not even sure how to play this out. What did he think? That he could just roll into town, see Glen get in his truck, and follow him back to his house? It sounded like a good plan a few hours ago. But

Teddy was high on meth and coke a few hours ago when he decided to get in his car and drive out all this way. It's a small town, sure. But it's not that small. This whole idea was stupid. Now he's pretty much sober, overpaid for shitty wings and is drinking beer he wouldn't even let his dog touch.

Teddy angrily swipes the bottle off the counter and downs nearly half of it in one go, slamming it back on the bar top a little too aggressively, making a few people look over, including Janeen.

"Hey," she passively says with furrowed brows. "Take it easy, huh guy."

Teddy gives her a wave that could pass a both an apology and a dismissive gesture.

Teddy thinking this was all a waste of time. He should just wait until Glen comes by for the next delivery, then follow the fucker home. Yeah, that's what he'll do next time. But Teddy doesn't want this whole day to feel like a waste of time. He has to give a shot while he's here. Being that this is somewhat a small town, there can't be too many drug dealers. Teddy figures that Glen must have a side hustle selling his shit to locals here. And this mean-ass bitch behind the bar looks like she gets on the gear. Those bags under her eyes. The unkempt hair. No-nonsense attitude.

"Yo," Teddy calls to Janeen.

Janeen finishes polishing a pint glass, puts it down, then ambles down the bar to Teddy.

"Yo," she repeats with a sarcastic attitude.

Teddy leans in a little, lowers his voice, and says, "You do drugs?"

"Excuse me?"

"I didn't stutter or nothin', did I?"

Janeen scoffs and chortles incredulously, looking around with a grin on her face.

"Do I do drugs?"

Teddy half nods, half shrugs.

Janeen grabs the beer bottle from in front of Teddy, then pours the other half of beer into the sink next to her.

"What's your fuckin' problem? I was just askin' a question."

"Get the fuck outta my bar, asshole. Or I'll call my husband."

Teddy smiles and huffs a little chuckle. "Call your husband huh. Okay. Tell his redneck ass to meet me in the parking lot if he wants to play." Teddy leans back into a relaxed pose. "I can wait."

"Oh honey, he doesn't play. He'll have you in cuffs and booked before you can get the rest of the chicken from between your teeth."

Teddy sits forward again, running his tongue over his teeth. Damn, bitch is right. He missed some.

Janeen leans on the bar with both elbows, and says, "That's right dipshit. My husband is a cop. And I can tell ya as sure as I know the sun'll be up in the mornin' that he won't take very kindly to strange gansta greaseballs askin' his wife if she does drugs, no matter what the context." She stands up straight again, hands on hips. "And he'll have your vehicle searched too. He's good at findin' probable cause."

Teddy isn't sure she's bluffing. Many women have said to him, especially the ones he raped, that their brother, father or boyfriend is a cop. Never turned out to be true though.

"You want me to call him now?" Janeen says, taking her phone from her jeans back pocket.

Teddy slowly rises from his stool, fishes out a wad of cash from his pocket, flips out a few notes, and dumps them on the bar counter.

"Keep the change," he says, turning to walk out the door.

As he heads outside and to his car, he realizes, cop husband or not, that she could pin him easily in a line-up once he's killed Glen.

That means he'll have to pop her too.

CHAPTER TWENTY-FIVE

HE'S GONE

"Can you count backwards from one hundred for me, Glen?" The anesthesiologist says to Glen, checking the reader on the anesthetic machine. A middle-aged woman with a stony face, she leans over and adjusts one of the machine's valves slightly.

Glen is lying on a bed inside an operating room at the hospital. The suction mask firmly cupped over his nose and mouth; Glen is starting to breath in the sevoflurane laced gas pumping through the plastic tubes attached to the machine. His head freshly shaved bald; he can hear the quietly casual conversations of the surgeons moving about the room out of his sight as they prep for surgery. The bright surgical lamps warmly beaming down on his growingly relaxed face, he thinks the two different beeping sounds coming from computers and machines somewhere in the room are starting to sound somewhat in tune with each other, and quite calming.

"A hundred. Ninety-nine. Ninety-eight. Ninety-seven. Ninety... six. Nin...," Glen's number readout starting to drift off into unintelligible mumbling as the vapored drugs take hold of his mind.

Glen's eyes flutter a moment, then they close out the heavenly glow of the lamps above to a welcoming blackness.

The heavily overcast sky blocks most of the sun from casting over the woodlands, making it appear dark and gloomy.

Glen's thick rubber boots trudge through the snow with a rhythmic crunching sound. He's wearing a hospital gown, his leather jacket and no pants. His rifle is slung over his left shoulder, and his head kept warm by a furry brown muskrat hat. He hasn't owned such a hat in years. It was his favorite hat until it was stolen from a bar one night. It doesn't seem out of the ordinary to him right now that he parted ways with the hat ten or so years ago, all he knows is that it is making him super comfortable right now out in these cold woods. He can hear a faint rhythmic beeping sound somewhere in the far distance, but he doesn't pay it too much mind.

Glen stops and freezes. A deer in the near distance, maybe twenty yards away. Glen is amazed it hasn't heard him and spooked. It idly stands over a clump of fresh plants and chews away at the luscious green leaves poking out of the powdery snow.

Glen slowly and carefully takes the rifle from his shoulder and lines up the animal in the target scope. He takes the safety off and wraps his index finger around the trigger. He takes a deep breath and exhales, then goes to pull the trigger, when the deer snaps its head up and suddenly bolts off into the thick array of trees.

"Damn it," Glen says under his breath. He wonders what spooked the animal. Certainly wasn't him, he was quiet as a mouse.

Young Glen steps out into the clearing and meanders over to the plants that the deer was feeding from.

"Fucking Christ," Glen growls out, slinging his rifle back over his shoulder. "Should have known you'd show to fuck shit up."

Young Glen simply stares at him with a guilty visage and a pouted bottom lip.

"Yeah, you just stand there and sulk like always, asshole." Glen shakes his head. "Pathetic."

"Have you seen Sally?"

"Who the fuck is Sally?"

"The woman who is always with you."

Glen thinks for a moment. "Wait. Flower? Is that her actual name?"

Glen marches on past Young Glen through the dark forest, now on the hunt for Sally. He keeps looking over his shoulder sporadically to find Young Glen is following him, ducking out of sight occasionally behind tree trunks and bushes. Glen quickens his pace. He strides over a pine tree dotted hill, then down the other side where a hint of light appears to be coming through the trees ahead. As Glen strides on, the brightness is reflecting off the snow powder and drawing Glen like a moth to a flame. When he reaches the edge of the forest, Glen pushes through thick foliage and steps out into a massive clearing. He feels his boots walk onto a hardened surface, making him stop in his tracks.

He's standing on the edge of the frozen lake.

Glen takes a couple of steps back until he is on solid earth again. 'Back we go,' Glen thinks to himself, then realizes the child is back there and doesn't want to run into him again. Glen looks around the vast landscape with desperation, realizing he doesn't want to cross the lake either.

Then he sees her. Sally. He could swear she wasn't there a moment ago, but a moment later it doesn't bother him. She's fifty yards away on the ice in the middle of making a snowman. She's dressed in an ornate red sequined ball gown and picks up clumps of snow with satin long gloves that end at her elbows. Her golden hair is several French braids gathered and swept up to sit on the crown of her head, with two long stands of curls falling either side of her face. To Glen, she has an air about her, like one of those olden days movie stars who oozed class and sophistication.

Sally glances over and spots Glen standing at the edge of the lake. Her face immediately lights up, and she rises to stand with a glowing smile, waving enthusiastically at him.

"Hey! Bullet!" She adjusts the bouffant skirt of her dress, fanning it out all around her. "Come over!"

Glen looks at the lake's ice sheet with trepidation. He looks back to Sally hopelessly.

"I've been waiting for you!" she calls out, then uses her hands to hike her gown up and strides over toward him.

Glen takes the rifle off and rests it against the nearest tree trunk on the shoreline. He looks over to find Sally is now running across the ice in bare feet, bunching up the ostentatious skirt in her fists so she can run unimpeded. She reaches him and purposefully tries to commit a suave skid to a stop but loses her footing near the finish and tumbles over and slides on her side to Glen's feet.

Glen immediately goes to her aid to help her up, to find that she's laughing uncontrollably. Her cackling echoing out over the lake. She eventually takes Glen's outstretched hand, and he pulls her to stand, watching as she dusts the snow off her dress. The remaining powder giving off a sparkle alongside the sequins.

After she gains control of her emotions and calms the laughter, she reaches both her gloved hands out to him, signaling for him to take them.

"Come on. It's great out here. Come and help me finish the snowman."

She looks back at the two balls of packed snow on top of each other, and realizes she needs props to make the face. She looks past Glen to the forest and suddenly dashes past him, collecting little rocks for the mouth and eyes, and sticks for the nose and arms.

She nearly has everything, then remembers she needs a hat. She spins around with her arms full of snowman props, wondering what the hell she'll use as a hat. Then her eyes fall on Glen, and his big furry muskrat hat.

"Can I use your hat?"

"For what?"

Sally makes a face at him like he's crazy. "For the snowman, silly!"

Glen looks down, processing for the first time that he's naked except for the hospital gown and leather jacket. He wonders for a second why the cold hasn't been harsher on his exposed legs.

"You can have it back. He just needs to wear it for a minute. He can't come to life unless you put a hat on him. Them's the rules."

Glen sighs and goes to remove his hat.

"Not yet," says Sally. "You can keep it on until we finish him."

"You're different, Flower."

"Different how?"

Glen shrugs. "Happier, I guess."

Sally takes in a deep breath of the cold air in her nose with a blissful smile. "Yeah. I think so too."

Glen glances at the snowman, then back to her. "No screaming babies. Ravenous dogs. Spontaneously combusting fires."

Sally rubs her tummy, thinking of the baby starting to grow in there. "I think I'm going to be fine." She puts her hand softly on his arm. "And your advice. About not being able to control everything. It worked. I've given up being a nervous nelly, and I feel… lighter."

The snap of twigs in the forest makes Sally turn around. She sees Young Glen trying to hide behind a tree but not doing a great job.

"He looks like he wants to come," says Sally.

Glen follows Sally's gaze to Young Glen watching on bashfully.

"No."

Sally sighs, then takes Glen's hand and forcefully pulls him out onto the icy lake. Glen is hesitant, but Sally's insistence wins.

"He's just a little boy," Sally says taking bigger steps to pull Glen out to the snowman.

"He's a murderer."

"I didn't kill him!" Young Glen shouts from behind, now standing on the ice several yards away. His lips trembling, his eyes forming tears.

Glen takes a heated step forward pointing out his index finger accusingly. "You killed *me!*"

"If I didn't run, you would have died too."

"You don't know that."

"I know I was scared. I just wanted to save you. Save us."

"There was a chance to save Joe. Just a little bit longer, and you could have saved our brother."

The sound of electronic beeps make Sally look up at the sky. A heartrate monitor noise echoing across the landscape. Then the sound of heavy breathing into an oxygen mask.

"Where's that coming from?" asks Sally, peering across every direction.

Glen ignores her and steps at Young Glen again. "You may as well died with him, for all the good it's done me."

Sally stops concentrating on the heart monitor and gas mask sounds, looking to Young Glen with sadness in her eyes.

"You can't expect an adult's bravery of a child's fear. You fought in a war. I played with G.I.Joe's."

A tear runs down Glen's cheek. "He's a coward." Glen wipes the tear away and angrily flicks it away. "I'm a coward."

Sally steps next to Glen, gently taking his hand in hers.

"There's nothing wrong with being afraid to die. Hell, up until recently, I was filled with that fear and anxiety. After all, life is a gift we're taught to protect as soon as we're old enough to walk." Sally motions to Young Glen with a head tilt. "You can't save everyone. And holding on to blame for comfort is not going to make you feel like could have been the hero you wanted yourself to be in that moment."

Tears are now streaming down Glen's face as he stares at his younger self, and he makes no effort to wipe them away. Glen takes a deep breath and clamps his eyes shut.

Sally smiles warmly and squeezes his hand affectionately. She puts her arm out toward Young Glen, using her fingers to signal for him to take it. Young Glen hesitates, pouting his lip, then sheepishly dawdles over and takes her hand. The three of them standing in silence a moment, Sally taking slow glances between the two Glen's. She leans over and whispers in Glen's ear.

"You need to let it go."

Glen opens his eyes and lowers his head to find there is a large hole in the ice. Water lapping peacefully around the circumference.

Sally gradually leans forward, pulling Glen and Young Glen with her.

Glen closes his eyes again as they fall forward into the gaping hole in the ice sheet with a splash.

Glen and Sally plunge into the clear blue water, big and little bubbles swirling all around them. Sally's large ball gown skirt billowing out in the water around her. Young Glen isn't with them anymore, just the two of them. Sally kicks her feet to swim around to be in front of Glen, using her now other free hand to take Glen's other hand, so they now face each other, hand-in-hand. Sun beams slice serenely through the crystal clear water around them as the ice surface disappears.

Sally is smiling at Glen's face just a foot away from hers, and he smiles back, both of them suspended tranquilly in the water.

Behind Sally, Glen notices a silhouette appearing in the near distance, floating peacefully through the water. It's his teenage brother Joe. His long brown hair swishing around him. Young Glen appears, breast-stroking through the water toward Joe. When he reaches him, he offers his hand to Joe, who takes it. Joe looks over to Glen and smiles, waving with his other hand. All Glen can do is watch with a melancholy gaze, managing a saddened smile. Joe and Young Glen turn around and swim off into the depths together, eventually disappearing through the sun beams and into the darkness below.

Glen turns his head to look at Sally. She motions with her eyes toward the surface. A moment later Sally kicks her feet to ascend, and Glen willingly lets her take him with her.

Sally's head pops out of the water and she takes in a deep breath. Glen surfaces beside her and fills his lungs with air. There's no ice. It's a beautiful sunny summer day, and the two of them wade in the middle of the lake.

"He's gone," says Glen.

Sally smiles at him.

"Holy hell, he's gone." Glen lets out a deep guttural laugh. He rolls around in the water so he's floating on his back, his face staring back at the light blue sky above.

Sally is beaming a smile as she watches Glen backstroke away through the still lake water. She too turns in the water so she is lying on her back, and leisurely kicks her feet so she drifts off in no particular direction, hearing Glen's laughter somewhere in the distance. She stares at the sun above, transfixed by the large angelic ring around it.

Chapter Twenty-Six

A FAILED EXPERIMENT

Sally opens her eyes. She's slouched over her work desk facing the bright bulb of the desk lamp in front of her, nap drool out the side of her mouth and running to her chin.

"Staring at the back of your eyelids, huh Sally?" says a male voice behind her.

Sally sits bolt upright, blinking erratically. She looks over her shoulder to find her boss Marcus standing there clutching a small stack of colored folders to his chest. A dry, almost condescending smirk on his face.

Sally clears her throat, then wipes the half solidified saliva from her mouth and chin. "Ah, yeah, um, sorry. I haven't been sleeping well lately."

"Bad dreams keeping you up?"

"Not bad, just... weird." Sally pats her hair to see if it's presentable. "There's this hunter guy. A character in my mind, I guess. It's like... he's really there, y'know? Like he's...," Sally trails off a moment, then notices Marcus's stiff composure and slightly irritated visage, realizing that she's rambling, and he's clearly not interested in where she's going with her story. "Anyway. It's stupid." She motions to her open laptop in front of her. "I was just in the middle of checking these samples. I think I'm almost where I need to-"

"Yeeeaaaaahhh, that's what I came here to discuss with you."

Marcus places the folders on a metal portable tray and sits on the edge of Sally's desk, cupping his hands together. A lump of dryness forms in Sally's throat, knowing by his demeanor that bad news is coming.

"We're shutting down the Urticaceae project.," says Marcus.

Sally swallows the dry lump.

Marcus continues, "We need your skills elsewhere."

"But I'm so close!"

"You've been saying that for two months now."

"The samples I was working on were showing signs of considerable positivity."

"Well, where are these samples?"

Sally sighs and looks blankly at her laptop screen. She knows if she tells him she was arrested for doing her research on state property, she will not have a chance at reinstating her project and most likely be reprimanded, put on probation, or possibly even fired.

Marcus says, "The economy was hit hard by another Covid outbreak, as you know. Our investors are impatient and want results yesterday."

Sally looks at him with raw determination in her wide eyes.

"I'll go get the samples. Right now. I'll show you how close I am."

Marcus taps the back of his foot on the side of the desk, looking down at his cupped hands. "Look Sally, I've already been given your next assignment." Marcus hops off the desk and grabs the purple folder on top of the stack he was carrying. "This is the outline here. Sounds interesting." He holds it out for her to take. "Hybrid grapes." He snorts a little chuckle out of his nostrils. "I even picked out the folder on purpose. See? Purple. Just like grapes."

Sally looks at it, performing a passive aggressive protest that only lasts five seconds, then gingerly takes the folder and places it on the desk.

Marcus says, "Do me a favor, and look it over this afternoon. Write a summary report for the nettle project. Make sure to be thorough so we can try to convince the top brass it wasn't a waste of money. Which it clearly was."

Marcus picks up the rest of the folders and hugs them to his chest, walking to the door. He stops and turns around. "And Sally. Wear your protective cap."

Sally pats her hair again, looking over next to her laptop where she placed the cap before taking a nap. She puts it on and looks back over to find Marcus has gone. Sally looks at the purple folder. She can feel the waterworks coming on but fights those tears back hard. She clenches her jaw so hard her jaw muscles visibly move around on the outside of her cheeks. She stands up quickly, snatches her car keys and handbag, and marches to the lab door.

Sally strides down the research institute's hallway with a determined face. She suddenly stops, grabbing her stomach with one hand. A dull pain. Cramps. 'Am I getting my period?' she wonders for a moment. No, that can't be possible. Maybe it was the sandwich from the cafeteria she had earlier. It did look like it had been sitting there a long time. The cramp subsides, and she continues on her mission.

✻

Sally speeds down the highway in the backwaters of Great Barrington, surmising at one point this was the spot that bolt of lightning almost hit her car nearly two weeks ago. She drives up through the hillside off-road, her tires kicking up mud as she rounds corners with impetus. She slams the brakes when she hits the clearing she knows.

Sally is out of the car and striding through the thick forest until she reaches the spot where her experiment was. She stops with a startled visage, then drops to her knees. After a few moments, Sally bursts into tears, then uncontrollable sobbing.

She collapses onto her side next to the dug out hole where her samples were. From the precise, neat way it has been removed, Sally knows someone with expertise has cut a large deep hole and removed a massive chunk of soil that contained her experiment.

CHAPTER TWENTY-SEVEN

ONE WAY OR ANOTHER

Two rugged up men in their 60's sit on a frozen lake, fishing from a hole in the ice they had cut there an hour ago. They both drink from their thermos coffee mugs, listening to a battery powered radio playing classic 1970's rock music. One of them slowly shifts his gaze to look over to the shoreline, where he can swear he hears a car loudly revving its engine.

"You hear that?"

"What?"

He turns the volume down on the radio.

"That. Sounds like-"

"A car engine, yeah I hear it now."

They both stare at the trees along the shore but can't see any car.

All of a sudden, a black 1976 Mustang bursts out of the foliage and swerves from side to side as the tires slip on the hard ice.

Glen gains control of the car by steadily keeping a good hold of the steering wheel. He puts his foot harder on the accelerator and the car rockets across the frozen lake. Glen hasn't been to this lake since Joe died here.

Glen pulls the handbrake and the car locks up and swerves into a double 360 degree turn, sliding to a stop. Glen pushes the handbrake down, revs the engine, and beelines across the ice again, repeating the handbrake pull a couple more times.

Glen hits the brakes and the car skids to a stop. He gets out of the car and strips off his clothes until he is completely naked apart from the surgery bandage wrapped around his head.

The two fishermen watch with bewilderment as Glen runs past them buck naked, laughing and cheering as he runs from one side of the lake to the other.

Sally sits on the toilet, her phone to her ear talking to Larissa, her other hand holding a pregnancy test stick that she's loosely shaking.

Larissa says, "I've contacted a few fertility clinics and made a few appointments. What's your work week looking like next week? Do you think you'll be able to get out early next Tuesday? The only appointment I could get was at three-fifteen."

"I'll check with Marcus, but it should be fine," Sally says drolly.

As Larissa keeps talking about their insemination prospects, Sally checks the result on the test stick.

Negative.

"Fuck!"

"What?!"

"Nothing. I just realized... I may have left a sample out in the lab." Sally tosses the test stick in front of her. It lands on the tiles and slides out under the toilet cubicle door. "I'm gonna have to go back into the office."

"Are you okay Twinkie?"

"Huh?"

"You sound a little drunk. You know how your voice does that thing when you're a bit pissy."

"I had a couple of wines with lunch. I'm not drunk."

"I think I should come get you."

"I'm not fucking drunk, okay?"

"Alright. Jesus. And what is it with you and the cussing lately? You never cuss, and all of a sudden you sound like a Bible Belt meth head."

"I'm having a bad week."

"Look… I get it. When you got your period the other week, and it meant your night with Brad wasn't a success, I… I know what it-"

"What the fuck do you know? Huh? What it's like to have a dick in you? Yeah, you sure know about that. You just loooove to brag about it. And it wasn't a waste of time. I had a good night with Brad. I haven't had good conversation like that since… since we were in our honeymoon phase. Then it's work, work, work with you. I want a baby, and I'm going to fucking get one. I don't want, or need your sympathy. Isn't there a case you should be working on?"

A long pause.

"You are drunk."

"Fuck you."

Sally ends the call by tapping the hang-up symbol aggressively like a woodpecker. She stands up, adjusting her tight black cocktail dress around her stocking-clad thighs, flushes the toilet, then marches out of the cubicle. She stops, looking down at the pregnancy test stick. She slams the heel of her black stiletto on it, smashing it in half. Sally walks to the sink, checks her makeup and neatly styled hair, then struts back out to the bar.

Sally takes her seat at the bar counter where she had been sitting the past hour and a half. The venue is swanky, low lit with velvet curtains swathed across the walls. The patrons around her mostly corporate types. Men in suits and women in power skirts and blouses.

The bartender approaches her and asks if she wants another martini.

"I'll have a Cosmopolitan this time," Sally says matter-of-factly.

The bartender nods and walks away to prepare the cocktail. Sally looks around the bar at the patrons, trying not to be too obvious she's looking to be looked at.

"Hey," says a voice next to her.

Sally turns her head to find a man in his mid-thirties standing there, holding a long glass of beer.

"Hello," Sally says coldly.

"I, uh, saw you when you first came in. I'm pretty sure the whole place did. Including the women."

Sally doesn't say anything, she just looks him up and down with a neutral expression, exerting an ice queen poise with her body language. While she is not at all attracted to men, she can tell at least that this guy is handsome. A bit douchey, but he's ruggedly hot. Good genes.

He'll do.

The bartender places the Cosmo in front of Sally, who daintily takes it and downs nearly half in one long sip.

"Damn. You don't waste time," says the man with good genes. "Can I buy your next drink?"

"You can buy all my next drinks."

The man smiles and takes a lengthy sip of his beer. He starts asking Sally what she does for a living, she tells him it's to do with plants and will probably bore the shit out of him. He feigns interest anyway, so Sally goes on to tell him about the grape project she's working on. He tells her he is a financial adviser for a software giant, and says it'll probably bore the shit out of her. She tells him he's dead right.

It's not long before Sally suggests they adjourn to the bathroom together. She takes him back to the cubicle she was in while doing the pregnancy test, hikes up her dress so the bottom is around her waist, and pulls her panties down. The man is shocked at how easy it has been getting to the chase with this gorgeous woman, but is thrilled nonetheless, and wrestles with his belt to hurriedly get his pants around his ankles.

Sally bends over the toilet and the man with good genes takes her from behind. Sally's too dry down there, so she tells him to get the lubrication gel from her purse, which he does promptly, and lathers his penis with it. He's gentle at first, but he builds momentum, so he is thrusting in and out of her at a frenzied pace. Because of the spontaneous excitement the man ejaculates inside her after a little less than three minutes. Sally feels it, her expression dull and tired. The man goes to pull his penis out of her.

"Leave it in a little longer?"

"What?"

"'I want to be sure."

"Sure of what?"

"Never mind, just stay still another minute."

The man awkwardly stands there looking at the back of Sally's head until she rises and pulls him out of her.

"Thanks. That was fun," Sally says apathetically.

Sally pulls her panties back up, readjusts her dress to fit around her thighs, pushes past the man and exits the cubicle, stepping over the busted pregnancy test stick on the floor. She walks past the bar where there is a third of a cocktail she didn't finish. She stops at the bar, downs the rest of the drink and marches out of the bar.

While she waits on the curb for a taxi, she looks back through the window of the bar. The man she just had sex with is standing at the bar, staring at her with a dumbfounded expression. Sally looks back to the street. This is the third random man in the past two weeks she has screwed in a bathroom, or the one in the alley next to the pub. She hasn't enjoyed a second of her promiscuous encounters. She knows she is simply playing roulette with her uterus and doesn't mind until she gets her desired outcome.

CHAPTER TWENTY-EIGHT

ONE WAY OR ANOTHER

Glen wakes from a dream and immediately rolls over to his bedside table to pick up a notebook and pen, hastily writing down specific details of his dream before he forgets. Furniture. Colors. Food and beverages. Everything he can think of before the details start to dissipate.

He puts the pad down and winces a little, feeling a sharp little pain in his head. He puts his hand on his head, which is half covered in bandages from the tumor surgery.

Glen visited Sally's cabin again in last night's dream, only this time she wasn't there. In fact, he hasn't seen her in weeks. Glen laments for a moment that he does in fact miss her. A lot. And after reading several books on telepathy, extrasensory perception, astral projection and remote viewing while in surgery recovery, he has become convinced this woman is out there somewhere. He also believes she was in the other car when the lightning struck. Which all says to Glen that if she is real, then the cabin must be real too.

Glen has breakfast, gets dressed, and calls Janeen to tell her he's going out of town for a couple of days to go up north to Maine.

"Why Maine?"

"Never been, and I hear there's good hunting reserves there. Never bagged a moose, and I've always wanted to. Also, now I have the Mustang working, I wanna find excuses to drive."

"Well drive safe. I'll see to it Bullit gets fed. Might even come grab him for a few days. The kids have been yapping on about gettin' a dog. So we'll see how they go with him."

"Thanks J."

Glen hits the road and drives north in his restored Mustang. He drives past Boston, up over the state line to Portsmouth, then up the coastline to Portland where he gets a hotel for the night. The next day he drives up to the mountain region. Sally had only mentioned the cabin was in Maine in the dream, so Glen did research based on the visuals. He distinctly remembers a mountain when looking out the window and narrowed it down to three possibilities. Mount Bigelow, Tumbledown Mountain and Saddleback Mountain. All three of which are near to one another. There might be another couple of possibilities, but Glen does not want to drive over the whole state chasing a hunch. These three will do, and failing that, he'll have to hope Sally reappears in his dreams so he can ask her flat out. He hopes that he hasn't lost her forever. That the surgery on his brain did something to cut her out somehow, or mess with the electric signals that caused her to be there in the first place.

Glen spends the morning driving around Tumbledown Mountain. No luck there. He drives up to Saddleback Mountain next. Again, no dice. He stays the night near there in a hotel, doing mind exercises suggested by Yvonne, and a few others he read about that might entice Sally back into his dreams.

Again, she is a no show.

The next morning Glen drives to Mount Bigelow, the one that looked most familiar in pictures. He drives around at the distance he surmises the cabin might be. After a few hours, he spots a cabin on a hill, just like the one from his dreams.

Glen parks out the front of the cabins in the small gravel parking lot and looks around the area. A few smaller cabins on the slope. His heart sinks. There were no other cabins in the dream. Must not be the place. It's going to storm soon by the looks of the sky, so this will be his last stop. Damn it. The view from here looks exactly like the one in his dreams.

"Can I help you?"

Glen turns around to find a lady in her late 50's, standing on the large gravel driveway in front of the main cabin.

"Hi there."

"Do you have a booking?"

"A booking?"

"Yeah, for one of the cabins."

Glen thinks for a moment. "Is this a hotel?"

The hotel lady also seems confused. "Sort of. Those cabins down there are for hire. It's low season and I got a couple spare if you would like."

"Maybe." Glen is staring at the main cabin she came out of. "What about that one?"

"That's where my husband and I live. It's not for hire."

"Have those other cabins always been there?"

She thinks for a moment, cocking her head to the side, then says, "Seven years nearly."

Glen strokes his stubbly chin. "Seven huh? What about the one you live in?"

She shrugs. "I don't know exactly. My father bought it about ten years ago."

"Can I see it?"

"Excuse me?"

"The inside. Can I have a look?"

The lady's mood now shifting from welcoming to annoyed and a little stand offish. She folds her arms over her chest and says, "It's not for sale."

"Oh, no, no. I'm not...," Glen wants to tell her the real reason he's here, but the lady would probably think he's a lunatic and call the cops. "I think it... see, I was driving in the area, and my family used to own a cabin in this area many years ago. I thought I'd see if it was the one. I haven't seen it since I was a little boy. I thought if this was it, I could tell my sister. Y'know. Nostalgia and all that."

The lady continues to stare at him suspiciously.

"It's okay if you... I can leave. Sorry. My name's Glen by the way. I'll get outta your hair."

She unfolds her arms and takes a more relaxed stance. "I'm Jeanie." She motions to the main cabin behind her. "I can make you a coffee is you want."

"That would be swell, thanks."

"My husband, Tony, is taking a nap. But he should be getting up now so it's okay if we wake him."

She leads him up a stone path and into the cabin.

Glen looks around as soon as he enters, while Jeanie prepares a coffee using a French Press.

"Milk and sugar?"

"Black is fine, thanks."

Glen's heart sinks again. It doesn't look like the one from his dreams. Two of the windows are not where they should be. The kitchen is up the back instead of by the front door. The stone fireplace is there where it should be, but the stones are different. These look more like stone brick, as opposed to the cobblestone look in the dream.

"So, is it the same place?" asks Jeanie.

Glen puts his hands on his hips. "I don't think so. Some things don't match."

Jeanie facepalms herself. "Oh, right. The fire."

"The fire?"

The kettle whistles and Jeanie pours water into the press, pushing the plunger down.

"Yeah, my dad got the place cheap because this cabin was half burned down. The previous owner, or the one before, fell asleep with a lit cigarette. It caught fire on the sofa and the whole place damn near burned down. The owner died as well." She puts her hand over her mouth. "Oh geez. I hope they weren't related… you said your family maybe owned it at some point."

"No, it's okay. Must have been the next owner. No one I know died here."

Glen's blood pressure rising with excitement. He remembers how Sally said in one of the dreams that her grandfather died here.

Jeanie says, "The person who bought it before us did serious renovations, then sold it to my husband. So yeah, it would look a bit different."

This is the place alright, Glen muses. Which means his hunch was correct.

Sally is real.

"Y'know, I think I might take you up on booking one of those cabins down there. There's a snowstorm coming by the looks, so it might be best I hunker down here for the night."

"No problem," says Jeanie, handing him a piping hot coffee.

Glen drinks his coffee while they chat. Her husband Tony wakes from his nap and joins them, and before too long coffee is replaced by whiskey. Glen eats dinner with the couple, and they share a nightcap. When he is shown to his cabin as the wind howls from the storm coming in, Glen does his pre-sleep mental exercises. Deep breathing. Sensory imaginations such as the sound and smell of the crackling fire in the cabin. Yvonne told him about MILD, Mnemonic Induction of Lucid Dreaming, where she encourages him to repeat phrases that manifest what he wants to see in his dream.

"Flower... Flower Girl... Flower... Flower Girl...," he repeats softly, over and over.

He figures that because he is at the cabin that Sally's family owned, there should be a stronger telepathic signal to her. That a part of her spirit might be here still. Or something. It occasionally bothers Glen how spiritual his beliefs are becoming. A month ago, if someone spouted the same stuff he subscribes to now, he would have thought they were fucking nuts and belong in the loony bin.

Glen falls into a slumber and has a very vivid dream. But unfortunately, still no Sally.

"Can I just add something?" Sally says to the judge.

Judge Cowan waves his hand indolently. "Go ahead."

The municipal court room has several bored people waiting their turns in the spectator area. Rain is three rows back, stoned and playing a snake game on her phone. Sally is representing herself at the council table, wearing a smart skirt suit and too much perfume, to disguise the smell of last night's alcohol binge seeping from her pores.

"I know what I did was wrong. But I honestly didn't know it was a protected forest. If I had I would have set up my experiment elsewhere.

And that's all it was, your honor. An experiment. I'm in the process of trying to grow papaya plants in sub-zero temperatures. If successful, the results would open doors for all sorts of botanical discoveries, and I'm conf-"

"I don't care about any of that. The forests are protected for a reason. To keep people like you from disturbing the fragile ecoculture in that region." He puts on his glasses and reads from a notebook on his bench. "The standard fine for trespassing in the state of Massachusetts is a hundred dollars. In your case, since I deem your activities vandalism, I'm issuing you a fine of three hundred dollars. For resisting arrest and verbally assaulting a police officer, I'm issuing you a two thousand dollar fine, fifty hours of community service, and six month probation"

The judge bangs the gavel and dismisses Sally. A bailiff comes to Sally and escorts her back to the spectator area.

Rain looks up aloofly as Sally calls her name in a low voice, giving Rain a head tilt toward the door to signal that it's time to leave.

Sally and Rain walk down the courthouse corridor for a couple of minutes, before Sally stops and takes a seat on a bench, sobbing into her hands. Rain takes a seat beside her, putting her large hessian bag on the other side of her. She puts a consoling arm around Sally.

"Hey, it's alright. You got off pretty light in my opinion. He could have given you jail time. Especially for the cop assault charge. Believe me, I've been there before. In three different countries."

"I've never had a criminal conviction before. This will be on my record forever. I should have hired a lawyer instead of arguing for myself. Stupid!"

"Well, I mean, you're not wrong."

"I was just so scared I'd get a lawyer who somehow knew, or knew of, Larissa or one of her colleagues."

"You didn't tell her?"

Sally shakes her head, wiping her snotty nose with the back of her hand.

"Why not?"

"I lied to her about driving all the way out to the wilderness. She doesn't like me driving long distances because of the medications I've been on." Sally shrugs. "And the two previous car accidents I've been in." Sally sniffs, wiping away tears on her cheek. "And if she told her friends… they already look down on me, for being some kind of hippie loser, weirdo. I can just hear them laughing about it over Thai food. Fucking assholes." She sniffs and assumes a resolute visage. "Anyway, it was my problem. Not hers. I don't need her to fight for my actions."

Rain's eyes widen slightly. "Oooo. Stroppy uses a swear word."

"Don't call me Stroppy." Sally clears her throat. "I fucking hate it."

"I've always called you that."

"Leaf and Meadow started calling me that because they teased me into being defensive all the time, saying I was always bad tempered. I hated it then, and I hate it even more now. Don't ever call me that again."

Rain puts her hands up defensively. "Okay, okay. I won't."

"Sally?"

Sally looks up to find Larissa's friend, Lynne, standing in the middle of the hallway in a dark green pantsuit, briefcase in hand.

"Lynne." Sally frantically wipes the mascara streaks from her cheeks and uses her thumbs to get the remaining tears from her eyes. "Hi. How are you?"

"Better than you by the looks of things. Are you okay?"

"Uh… yeah. I'm fine. What are you doing here?"

"I'm just helping out an old client of mine. She's just passed her bar exam and I'm giving her some pointers."

"I'm Rain, her sister."

Rain holds her hand out and Lynne shakes it.

"Oh, yeah, I think Larissa has mentioned you before. I'm Lynne, one of her best friends."

Rain's expression turns a little dour, knowing that if Larissa has mentioned her before, it probably wasn't in a good light.

Lynne looks back to Sally and says, "Are you sure you're good. You look like... you seemed a little upset just now."

Sally clears her throat and looks anxiously down both directions of the hallway a moment, then looks up at Lynne with a pleading expression.

"Look. Can you not mention to Larissa that you saw me here?"

Lynne beginning to look a little uncomfortable, her eyes flitting between Sally and Rain.

"Uh... sure," says Lynne, looking a little uncomfortable.

"It was my fault," Rain says. "I got charged with trespassing. I got a fine, it's nothing really. Sally just gets emotional whenever I get into trouble. It happens a lot."

Lynne looks at Sally's post-crying eyes, not convinced. "Oh, okay."

"I'm hormonal at the moment," says Sally. "Seeing Rain in court brought back some memories."

Lynne nods, now appearing somewhat convinced. She tells them both she has to run, she has a meeting with a client shortly. After an awkward goodbye, Lynne bustles off down the hallway.

"That was a good save, thanks," Sally says.

"Anytime Strop-" Rain quickly stops herself. "I mean, Sally."

They both stand and Sally recomposes herself before they both head for the exit.

"What can I call you now?" asks Rain. "I need a new nickname."

"How about, probation puta?"

Rain laughs. As they walk through the carpark Rain digs into her hessian bag and eventually pulls out a pre-rolled joint, holding out to Sally.

"Here. It's been a shitty day. Have it tonight to calm your nerves."

Sally looks at it a moment, then gets paranoid about being in a courthouse carpark and snatches it before anyone can see.

"Is this the same stuff you gave me before my night with Brad?"

"Yup. Frostbite. It's the best shit out there, so don't go wasting it."

Sally sticks the Frostbite joint in her purse as they approach her car.

CHAPTER TWENTY-NINE

SOILED SENTIMENTS

The front door chime sounds.

Larissa, working on a law case in the comfort of her bed, looks up from her document with confusion. She didn't order any food. She tosses her work documents aside and rips off the cover angrily, putting on her night gown, and descending the stairs. It's a weekend, so it can't be the postal service, she muses. And she's not expecting anyone. Sally has been at work all day, and she would have said if a guest was coming over. Maybe it's Sally, forgot her keys or something. But she knows there's spares under the rock in the garden.

Larissa reaches the front door. "If this is a fucking salesman or religious nut, I'm gonna-" She whips the door open.

Brian is standing on the front porch, wearing stone-wash jeans and a zipped-up khaki parka. His hands are in the jacket pockets.

"Hello ma'am."

Larissa looks him up and down, then looks over at the white iron outdoor table which has a large Styrofoam box sitting on it.

"Uh... hi."

"I was wondering if miss Field is home?"

"Miss Field?" Larissa makes a contorted smile with her lips, not being able to recall the last time someone referred to Sally as 'Miss Field'. "You mean Sally."

"That's correct, ma'am."

"Sally's not here. She's at work." Larissa looks past Brian a moment to the rolling overcast clouds in the sky, then back to Brian with an apathetic gaze. "I think she's at work, anyway. Who knows where she is these days."

Brian looks disappointed, taking his hands from his pockets and putting them on his hips.

"When might she be home?"

Larissa shrugs, pulling her nightgown tighter as she starts feeling the outside cold.

"Ummm... when am I.... what? Wait, hang on buddy. Who are you?"

"Oh," says Brian with feigned abashment. "Sorry. I'm Brian."

Larissa maintains her wooden face. "Uh huh."

Brian picks up on the fact that he's a strange man on this woman's doorstep who clearly is not dressed for a social interaction.

"It's fine. I'm with the Berkshire Police."

"Sorry, what? You're a cop?"

"Yes ma'am."

Larissa now finding the frequency and vocalization of the word 'ma'am' a bit irritating.

"And why are you wanting to speak with Sally?"

Brian, trying to get a peek of the inside of the house behind Larissa, snaps out of his nosy gaze and looks over at the box on the table.

"I wanted to give her that."

Larissa eyeing off the box suspiciously now. There's no label on it of any kind.

"Okaaaaay. What's in it?"

"It's hers. I mean, the contents. I did research on the subsoil based on details she left on my report. I was successful in digging past the roots to transport it-"

"Whoa, back up a second. Report?"

Brian looks confused a moment, then nods and acts like he was absent minded. "Oh, right. Yes, my report for her arrest."

"Her arrest? Is this a joke? What's this about? When was she arrested?"

"Nearly a few of months ago now. When she was out in...," Brian stiffens his posture to now appear more commanding. "I'm sorry ma'am, are you a family member?"

"We're partners. What did she get arrested for?"

"Business partners?"

"No, we share assets and we fuck." Larissa steps forward with her hands on her hips and a no-nonsense tone. "What the fuck did she get arrested for?"

"Ma'am, I'm going to have to warn you not to take that tone with me, I'm-"

"Oh shut it, I'm a lawyer. I know my rights, mister off-duty police officer. What's this fucking arrest over?"

Brian glares at her scathingly a moment, then manages a polite grin. "I think we're done here ma'am."

Brian picks the box up from the table.

Larissa for the life of her cannot fathom what Sally would have done to be arrested by this guy. She would rather put a spider in the garden than killing it.

"Stop calling me ma'am. And no, we are not done here. Because I'm gonna get to the bottom of this and have whatever bullshit charges you slapped on her dropped before the milk in your fridge goes sour."

"Have a wonderful day now," Brian says as he turns to leave.

"Hey. Aren't you going to give me the box?"

Brian stops, looking down at the box in his grasp for a moment, then turns and says, "I would much rather give it to her myself, in person."

"Fine. Whatever. Take it to her work. I don't really wanna have to converse with you again."

Larissa spins around on the balls of her feet and marches inside the house, slamming the door behind her.

Brian takes a deep breath, then continues out the front yard with a forlorn demeanor. He was really looking forward to seeing her face as she opened it to reveal her papaya plant experiment. He had done a lot of work to see that he dug it up properly and without causing any damage. That excitement now quashed by that confrontational woman at the door. And the news that Sally is a lesbian, which is the worst part of that interaction to him.

'You know what, to hell with this,' Brian thinks to himself.

He turns and strides back to the porch, and carelessly dumps the box at the top of the small set of stairs. He briskly strides back to his car on the street outside.

Sally fumbles with her house keys for a minute, trying to slide the wrong one into the lock, then drops the set of keys at her feet. She curses herself and stoops to pick up the keys, almost falling over from drunkenly trying to maintain her balance. She eventually gets the right key into the slot and shoves the door open, then slams it shut once she's inside.

Sally thinks of a meme she saw earlier today before she hit the bars and laughs out loud. She pulls out her phone and scrolls through the website she saw it on but can't find it and mutters a string of expletives as she makes her way into the kitchen.

"You're home early," Larissa says as she exhales a string of cigarette smoke, sitting on the counter next to the sink.

"Am I?"

"I was being sarcastic. Where the fuck have you been? It's eleven at night."

"Really? I thought it was eleven in the morning," Sally says with a condescending smirk.

"Fuck off," Larissa says quietly.

"You're smoking again?"

Larissa now staring at Sally's light blue Manolo Blahnik heels.

"Nice shoes."

Sally looks down at the shoes and back to Larissa with a dumb grin. "Oh, um, yeah. Lucky we're the same size, huh?" She uses the kitchen counter as support while she sticks one leg out. "Do you think they look good on me?"

"They look better on me. In other news, what the fuck did you get arrested for?"

Sally's playful mood sinks like a stone in water. She gently puts her leg back down.

Larissa says, "I'm just a wee bit interested, because I've barely seen or spoken to you in weeks. Most days I wake up and your passed out ass stinks like a brewery. I asked how the whole sex thing went with Brad and all you've said is 'okay'. Excuse me for not accepting 'okay' as an answer for having sex to with a guy to make our baby. And this morning, the only day I've been graced with staying in bed since I can remember, I get a knock at the door from some redneck cop with a box of dirt." She grins bitterly. "For you."

Larissa points to the Styrofoam box sitting on the round table next to the kitchen area. Sally follows her gaze to the box and stares at it quizzically.

Larissa says, "Now you strut around in my fifteen-hundred dollar Manolo's like we traded Barbie accessories." Larissa angrily stubs out her cigarette in the sink. "Who the fuck are you?"

"I... I don't know what to say."

Larissa slides off the counter and snatches a pack of cigarettes next to her half-filled wine glass, pulling one out and lighting it up.

"How about we start with those charges." Larissa scoffs, looking at Sally's tight cocktail dress. "Do they arrest people for bad fashion sense now?"

Sally leans her butt up against the adjacent counter, exuding a complacent smirk. "Well, I'm wearing your shoes. Does that make you an accessory to said fashion crimes?"

"Fuck off. You don't get to joke about this." Larissa picks up the wine glass and takes a hefty sip, slamming it back down on the marble countertop. "You're lucky I don't let you handle the court case yourself. Because I'm guessing I'll have to."

Sally folds her arms. "I already have. It was a stupid trespassing charge. And I lost. I have to pay a fine and do community service. It sucks. But it is wh-"

"How do you get community service on a trespassing charge?"

Sally shrugs haphazardly. "There's a little more."

Larissa rolls her eyes and shakes her head.

Sally says, "If I'm ever going to be a role model to our kid, I've gotta take responsibility for my own actions."

"Role model? Sally, honey, you're being a little bit complacent for someone who tried once. And it didn't work. I'm not saying it won't, but you're being a little bit-"

"Try four."

"Four what?"

Sally just stands against the counter with a knowing stare. It takes a long moment, but Larissa finally understands. Her eyes narrow and her lips purse tightly.

"Sally…," Larissa says, then swallows a hard lump. "Have you had sex with other men besides Brad?"

Sally holds her indifferent expression, then nods slowly.

Larissa's fists clench. She looks away a moment, catching a glimpse of herself in the kitchen window's reflection. She puts out the cigarette with shaky hands, then turns to face Sally again.

"You cheating fucking whore."

Sally pushes her body off the counter. "Excuse me? Do not call me that. How can it be cheating if it was sex I didn't want to have?"

"There's consensual sex, and there's rape. You consented. You cheated. Whether you enjoyed it or not."

"It's my body. And remember that you agreed I conceive our child with a man."

"Yes! One man. One we both picked and agreed to."

"One that you picked. And he didn't deliver. I wanted to try again."

"So you turn your pussy into a freeway for every swinging dick you meet. In a bar, I'm assuming." Larissa goes to get wine and chugs the rest of the glass, staring at Sally with disdain. "You disgust me."

Sally lowers her head, looking at her feet with a hurt expression.

Larissa says, "Y'know, just because you turn your body into a cum bucket, doesn't guarantee you'll get pregnant. Some people just aren't meant to grow life." She forces a smile and shakes her head. "Thank God for that."

"Fuck you."

"Get out. Get out of my house."

"Your house? That's really bold of you."

"GET OUT! Get out! Get out! Get out! Get out! Get the fuck out!"

Larissa storms past Sally out of the kitchen to the next room and grabs an umbrella from the stand holding and takes the pointed end of it, holding it like a baseball bat. She strides over to the foam box on the table and swings the umbrella so the handle smashes into the box, busting it open. Forest soil sprays all over the table and the floor. Larissa bashes the box again with the umbrella, completely smashing it to pieces. She drops the umbrella and grabs fistfuls of dirt, hurling it at Sally.

Sally reels back in fright as she is pelted with dirt. She turns and dashes out of the room.

The front door slams. Larissa collapses to her knees on the dirt laden floor, then drops into the fetal position, bursting into loud wailing.

CHAPTER THIRTY

HIDERS AND SEEKERS

The car radio blares The Cranberries as Sally steers her vehicle through random Boston suburbs. She's not sure where she's going, and she doesn't care. Anywhere to take her mind off the fight she just had with Larissa. She takes a swig of vodka from the bottle she bought from the gas station ten minutes ago, wincing from the strong aftertaste.

Sally guides the car through the outskirts of downtown, finally deciding she wants to go sit on a quiet wharf or pier. Maybe even Pleasure Bay. Yeah, that will do nicely. Sally drives through the Seaport District, doing her best to keep to the backstreets in case a cop pulls her over and does a sobriety check. She is, after all, now on probation. Sally hits the Summer Street bridge and cruises over, abruptly bursting into tears at the cruel things Larissa said to her earlier. She was the maddest Sally has ever seen her. Loud surges of static now intermixed with the radio music. She hits the radio aggressively, then changes channels. She slows the car down, realizing that it's not the radio pulsing with static.

It's her head. The high frequency sound now becoming unbearable. She clenches her wet eyes shut, tears still streaming down her face.

Sally spots a little park just off the end of the bridge and quickly maneuvers the car onto the sidewalk meant for pedestrians and pulls over under a tree. She screams as the static becomes so intense she can't hear her own thoughts. She pounds the steering wheel with her fist, howling with pain.

Her vision now turning hazy and filled with white splotches as she begins to lose consciousness.

"Bullet... Bullet Man... Bullet... Bullet Man...," she repeats over and over.

What she doesn't realize is, only one block away is the South Boston Power Plant. The energy surging there right now because of an array of sporting matches and events around the city.

Sally's eyes roll back and she slumps down in her seat, out cold.

Sally is walking down a long hospital corridor that seemingly stretches on to eternity. The white phosphorescent lights so bright it's ethereally glowing all around her. She hears crying babies. Many of them. Sally walks faster to the source of the noise.

Sally sees a large viewing window in the wall just up ahead and she breaks into a run to get there. Her legs not moving as fast as she would like, she feels like she's running uphill even though it's a flat surface corridor. She makes it to the window and peers inside, pressing her palms up against the glass.

Rows and rows of babies in cots. The room and everything in it sterile white. To Sally it looks like an endless maze of crying babies. The sound of them wailing is becoming overbearing to her, but she doesn't want to leave.

A nurse in a starched white uniform and meticulously tight hair in a bun comes into view and checks on the babies as she passes by the cots. She stops at one and picks up the crying baby from her cot, cradling it in her arms and rocking back and forth to calm her.

Sally knocks on the glass. "Excuse me?"

The nurse doesn't appear to hear Sally, or is ignoring her. She continues rocking the baby.

Sally knocks on the window harder. "Excuse me? Is that my baby?"

The nurse looks up this time, with an apathetical glare at Sally, then turns her attention back to the baby girl in her arms.

Sally bangs the glass with her clenched fists.

"Hey! Answer me! Is that my baby?!"

The nurse looks up at Sally again and smiles with smug indifference. The baby in her arms has stopped crying. The nurse gently places the baby girl back in her cot.

Sally uses both fists to pound on the window. "Don't ignore me! I want MY baby!"

The nurse turns her back on Sally and walks between the cots again, gently touching the babies as she goes.

Sally screams and protests, her bashing of the glass becoming more frenzied as she tries to bust it to pieces.

The nurse picks up a baby boy and coos at him while she holds him with one arm out.

"Give me a baby!" Sally screams.

The nurse turns and makes a 'shhhh' motion with her index finger vertically against her closed lips. This enrages Sally who now kicks and punches at the window. Sally runs out of energy and stops for a breather.

The nurse says, "You're not allowed to have a baby."

Sally growls with wrath and looks around her. She spots a metal chair against the wall behind her and dashes over to it. She picks the chair up and runs to the window, hurling the chair at the glass. It bangs against it and bounces off, clattering on the floor past Sally. She chases after it and picks it up again, throwing it with more force at the window. It bounces off the glass again.

Sally falls to her knees and sobs loudly and unabashedly.

Glen appears out of the glowing ethereal corridor lights. He is looking around with confusion, trying to figure out where he is. He spots Sally weeping on the floor and goes straight to her side, kneeling next to her.

"Hey, I've been looking everywhere for you."

Sally looks up at him through her reddened wet eyes. She smiles.

"Bullet."

"No. You can call me Glen."

"Glen."

Glen says, "What's the matter?"

Sally calms her sobbing, and after a moment, she says, "Life is so common in this world. I'm a woman and I can't even create it."

Glen puts a consoling arm around her, pulling her in for a hug, which she willingly accepts.

"Everything needs something to grow. Some things just need the right combination. I'm growing a plant that, technically speaking, should not be growing."

Sally sniffles. "What kind of a plant is it?"

"It's a marijuana plant." He smiles proudly. "I call it Frostbite."

A loud booming voice coming from above the corridor.

"Glen? You okay?"

Glen looks around frantically as the hospital corridor starts to dematerialize all around him.

"Glen?" The voice booms again.

"Frostbite?" Sally says, now giving it some serious thought.

Glen stands up, his fists clenched by his sides. "No! I can't go yet. I need your name!" He grabs Sally by her arms and squeezes her skin to keep her there.

Sally looks somewhat alarmed and frightened by his sudden panic and tries to pull free of his hold.

"You're real! So am I. I went to the cabin. What is your name?"

Sally vanishes right before his eyes.

"No! Please!"

Glen's eyes flicker open.

Doctor Adrian Thomas is standing over him, looking a little concerned. "Glen. Are you okay?"

Glen looks around. He's in his recliner in his living room. His pale skin making him appear sick. He's lost noticeable weight.

Glen clears his throat and sits up straight. "Yeah… I'm fine." He scrambles to pick up his 'Dream Notebook' he had developed with Yvonne and quickly jots down what he can remember of the dream he just woke from.

Adrian watches him quickly scribble, making out the words 'thousands of crying babies' and 'hospital', before Glen shuts the book and places it back on the coffee table between the recliners.

Adrian says, "I hadn't heard from you in a few days. I got a little concerned and dropped by to see if you're okay. I saw you through the widow, you looked…," Adrian stops himself, and manages a curt little grin. "Well, anyway, the front door was open. I hope you don't mind."

Glen looking around now. "No, it's fine. Where's my… Bullit!" Glen calls out, just as he remembered he gave Bullit to Janeen and Brian to look after while he was in Maine.

"Oh, right. Your dog," says Adrian.

"I just remembered I left him with my sister while I went to Maine for a few days again. Lucky for you."

"He bites?"

"If you give him reason to."

Adrian motions to the other recliner. "May I?"

Glen sweeps his arm to the chair in a welcoming manner.

Adrian nods politely and takes a seat.

"You want a drink, or somethin'?"

"No, I won't be staying long. Thanks though."

Glen nods, looking at Adrian's casual clothes. A light blue polo shirt, puffer jacket and jeans.

"What's in Maine?" asks Adrian.

Glen strokes his hand over his bald head a few times. "Oh, ah, there's a bed and breakfast place there. It's…," Glen now ruminating how silly the whole Sally story would be to a person who hasn't experiences what he has. "It's relaxing. It's the one place I can gather my thoughts. The owners are real nice people too."

"I hear ya. The wife and I go to the same hotel in Boston for our anniversary."

"Is it true that humans only use ten percent of their brains?"

"Like Bigfoot, that's a myth I can't confirm or deny."

"You're the brain surgeon, ain't ya?"

"We can measure, poke and prod the physical. But all the technology in the world cannot quota nature's sophisticated irrationality." Adrian crosses his legs to get comfortable. "Like the universe, the human brain has a vast array of possibilities. There are roughly a hundred billion electrically charged neurons, and a hundred trillion connections between those neurons." He shrugs. "Give or take a couple of billion. So, when you consider the amount of combinations between each and every electrical burst and the differing degrees of power of those bursts, most of us just use a snippet of what we've been given. For now, at least."

"So you think we'll evolve to be super smarter or somethin'?"

"Maybe. Or there's another school of thought that we will harness the ability to reach into other people's minds."

"Like telepathy."

Adrian smiles. "Sure."

"Do you believe in that stuff?"

Adrian stares out the window for a moment, watching water dripping off the stalactites above.

"No. I don't. But I also don't belittle people who do. There's a lot of research in that field, and if we are to believe just one of the case studies, then that's enough for one to delve into the possibilities. I have neither met someone nor even know of anyone who have experienced such things. So, I remain skeptical."

"Y'know, I used to think that shit was crazy talk. But lately, I've been learning there are two types of people. A hider, or a seeker. And they are based on fact and fiction. The fact is the world I see, smell, hear, taste and touch. The fiction is the imagination those five senses give me. The real trick is interpreting what's real and what ain't, when the mind throws curveballs at you. Now, I can say that every one of them balls is just my imagination, and I hit 'em as far away as possible. That makes me a hider." Glen checks to see if the empty beer bottles at his feet have anything left in them. After shaking the third one, he feels the sloshing of beer still in it and has a sip. "But one day you might miss that one ball, and it slams you in the gut like a boozed up trucker.

And you reflect long and hard about all them balls you previously hit out of the park, and think to yourself, I'm gonna find them and put them into one big basket, to have a proper look this time. That makes me a seeker."

Glen stands up, slower than normal, taking his time. He has become a little weaker now as well, not eating as much. He moseys over to look out the front window where he can see Adrian's black Audi parked in the front yard.

Glen says, "I've been hiding my whole life. But someone has helped me to seek lately. And the kicker is, I don't even know if she's real or not."

"The type of tumor you have been experiencing may induce some forms of hallucinations. It's perfectly normal."

"Well, whatever she is, man, I'm dyin' and I've never felt more alive."

Adrian coughs nervously, and switches legs to cross over. "Embrace your newfound lust for life." Adrian sucks in a deep breath. "Because I'm not sure how much you have of it left."

"I know it Doc. I know it."

"It's just moving so fast. It's the most aggressive one I've seen, to be honest."

Glen nods slowly, sucking the rest of the beer from the bottle as he continues to stare out the window.

Adrian says, "But I remain hopeful. You know why, Glen?"

Glen turns to look at Adrian.

Adrian says, "Because I'm a seeker too."

Glen smiles and nods.

The sound of a phone ring. Glen looks at the coffee table to see his lit up phone vibrating. He walks over to it and picks it up, looking to Adrian.

"You mind?"

"Go ahead."

Glen answers it, to hear Jeanie's voice on the other end. "Hi, is this Glen?"

"Yeah."

"This is Jeanie, from the Maine cabins."

"Oh, hey."

"So, I got some good news. I did a little digging around and found who owned the cabin previous to the last owner. The one who died in the fire."

"Excellent. I mean… you know what I mean."

A little chuckle on the other end. "I get ya. So, yeah. It belonged to a man named Roy Field. Big family apparently. They used to come here a lot. I managed to get a next of kin as well. He had three kids. One of them is Clayton Field. Him and his wife live on a property near Lowell, north of Boston."

"I know the place."

"If you got a pen and paper, I'll give you their phone number and address."

Glen looks around frantically, eventually finding a pen and an old magazine.

"Alright. Shoot."

CHAPTER THIRTY-ONE

BINGO

"What about my anxiety medication?" Sally asks.

"Are you still taking it?"

"No. But maybe it did some damage? Or maybe because I'm not taking it anymore my body has had some kind of reaction?"

"No, I don't believe so."

Sally bursts into tears as she cups her face into her hands.

Doctor Ayomi de Silva, a short Sri Lankan woman in her early 40's, stands up from behind her desk and tenderly places a box of tissues on the other side in front of Sally.

A collection of charts and medical results are splayed out on the desk in front of Sally. Sally rips one of the tissues and soaks up tears from her cheeks and eyes, then uses another for her dripping nose.

"I don't understand," Sally says with a quivering voice. "My eggs are fine. My ovaries are fine. My estradiol levels are healthy."

"They are, yes. But the liver is vital to hormone regulation. And yours isn't responding to semen."

"So I'm barren, is that it?"

"No. Not at all. The way your organs are reacting to each other, at this stage… you are, well, infertile." Ayomi sits back in her chair behind the desk. "My best guess is complications with your endocrine system as well. Especially with your history with anorexia. But I will continue looking into it."

Sally stares down at the results again. Right there, on a piece of paper, is an outline of her defeated dreams. Liver disease. Endocrine failure. If it really does stem back to her bout with anorexia and eating disorders, then it's her wicked siblings that are responsible for this. Especially the girls. Meadow and Jasmine. And sometimes Rain. She's tempted to find them right now and beat the ever-living shit out of them with a bat of some sort. Sally's misery turning to rage now. Her breathing heightening, her jaw clenches.

Ayomi can see the change of emotions in Sally and gulps, sitting forward and placing her hands palms down on the table.

"I strongly believe that this is treatable over time. First, we will look into getting you on a waiting list for a liver replacement."

Sally looks up with fresh determination in her eyes. "What about IVF? Maybe it's the sperm I've been… maybe it's just not compatible with my eggs?"

"We will definitely explore that avenue. But know this, Sally. There is a common misconception that IVF is the plan B to becoming pregnant. The last report I read had success at around twenty percent per cycle. IVF does nothing in the way of improving the quality of eggs or sperm. Only improving the overall state of health of the patient can achieve that."

"So my body is essentially garbage?"

The tone of Sally's scathing voice and glowering eyes are unsettling Ayomi.

"That is not the case at all. And don't think such things. Some of us just have to work a little harder to get the results we want, that's all. The human body is not a carbon copy of anyone else. We are all unique. You are unique. It is not your body's fault in any way. It may take two, three years, but I think we-"

"I don't have time!" Sally heatedly rises up, almost knocking her chair over. "Fuck this shit!"

Sally storms to the office door and promptly leaves. Ayomi sinks into her chair, taking a deep breath before letting out a long melancholy sigh.

Sally marches down the sidewalk in the southern end of the suburb Cambridge, past the Victorian era inspired exterior of the Cambridge Town Hall with its ornate gables on the top level and churchlike tower. Sally angrily pushes past a large group of tourists taking photos and selfies with the imposing government building. A lady calls out to her to mind her manners, and Sally gives her the middle finger without looking back.

Sally finds herself near Central station amongst a bustling array of restaurants and cafes, glancing at all the people laughing and seeming to have no cares in the world. Sally notices a young couple walking down the street toward her. The girl must be barely legal. She's covered in tattoos and piercings. The boyfriend looks like a right piece of shit, complete with ostentatious street wear to look like a well-to-do thug. Both of them carry scowls on their faces as they puff on cigarettes, completely disregarding those around by blowing smoke into the faces of -passers-by. But it's the pregnant belly on the girl that upsets Sally.

She spots an empty alleyway and ducks into it. She strides halfway down, stops and walks to a wall to stick her back up against, and begins crying uncontrollably. 'Why is this happening to me?', she thinks. She's an upstanding citizen. She pays taxes. Goes out of her way to be nice to people. Why should an asshole couple like those people be able to conceive? They looked like they didn't even want it. If they really cared they wouldn't be smoking. It's unfair.

Sally pelts her handbag on the ground, then gives it a hard kick. The handbag flies across the alley and smashes into an industrial bin, busting open and spilling the contents everywhere. Sally sighs despondently, wipes the tears from her eyes, and begins collecting the contents. A makeup mirror. Credit and loyalty cards. Chapstick. Tampons. Wait, what's this? She picks up the joint Rain had given her at the courthouse. The Frostbite, she called it.

Sally suddenly has a flash go through her mind. Glen's voice saying "Frostbite". 'Did she dream that?' Yes, she vaguely recalls the man from her dreams saying that. Now she remembers him saying something along the lines of growing what wasn't meant to be grown. Sally quickly gets everything back in her handbag and makes a beeline for the main street as she orders an Uber.

Sally is at her work laboratory, using a dissecting microscope to study the marijuana from the now emptied joint that she cleaned in the autoclave. She takes several notes on the structure and composition of the buds, then moves the sample over to the pH meter to study the acidity of the plant. After using a few other lab instruments to determine the marijuana's embryonic tissue. Sally correlates her results using computer software, the glow from the monitors highlighting the tired bags under her eyes.

Sally isolates the different plant cells and studies them individually, before starting to combine the different bacteria used in the primary and secondary growth process.

And there it is.

Bingo.

What she has been seeking for years; a plant that has grown in conditions not usually fertile for its development.

With a name like Frostbite, Sally can only gather that this marijuana is grown in sub-zero conditions.

Sally squeals with delight and stamps her feet rapidly on the floor. She jumps up from her chair and dances around the middle of the room.

CHAPTER THIRTY-TWO

HAVE A GOOD TIME IN OREGON

Knock-knock-knock… knock-knock-knock… knock-knock-knock…

"Alright," Rain says irately as she wraps a faded maroon bathrobe around her, marching down the dark corridor to the front door as the knocking persists.

Rain opens the door to find Sally standing on the front porch of the East Boston house.

"Sally?"

Sally has the wide eyes and demeanor of a kid who just got the candy jackpot on Halloween.

"I did it!"

Rain clears her throat and blinks the sleep from her eyes. "Did what?"

"I fucking did it!"

"Shhh!" Rain exclaims, looking at both sides of neighboring houses. "You'll wake up the whole neighborhood."

Sally lowers her voice and steps in closer to Rain. "Okay, so the Urticaceae project I've been working on."

"The uricake... what?"

"I'm sure I told you about it. Anyway. The nettles plant. Nettles are part of the Urticaceae genus of plants, which belong to the hemp family, to which the Cannabaceae family belongs to, which the cannabis plant belongs to," Sally says with unquestionable glee in her voice.

"Do you know what time it is?"

"I've been trying to grow nettles in sub-zero temperatures, naturally, with several different experimental aides."

"It's nearly five in the fucking morning. What the fuck do I care ab-"

"Frostbite. The stuff you gave me. It grows in snowy conditions. My research isn't a hundred percent, but my hunch is a hundred and fifty percent." Sally bounces from one foot to the other, barely able to keep her excitement. "I need more Frostbite."

"You're a crazy bitch," Rain says, shaking her head. "You can't just roll up at the crack of dawn and ask for pot. This isn't even my place. It's Steve's, and he has housemates. What's gotten into you?"

"This could open up all sorts of doors to bio-chemical research. I'll get a promotion for this. If I can prove where it came from."

Rain sighs and wipes her hand over her face. "Get inside before we get more noise complaints."

Rain guides Sally down a long wooden hallway with high ceilings to the ill-kept kitchen at the back of the three-story house. Dirty dishes on the cluttered counters and a linoleum checkered floor that hasn't seen a wet mop in a long time.

Rain puts on the coffee percolator and prepares two mugs while Sally takes a seat at the round metal table in the middle, that was once stolen from the outside of a restaurant.

Sally says, "I swear, it's some kind of sign, don't you think?"

Rain grumbles something as she checks the milk expiry, then opens the carton to smell it, wincing with disgust.

"We're having black coffee," Rain says as she throws the expired milk in the trash.

"Whatever. But don't you think it's serendipitous?"

"Huh? Oh, I guess. Keep it down or you'll wake Steve. We've been having some problems lately, and the thin ice we're on is breaking."

The coffee is ready, and Rain fills two mugs. Too tired and lazy to get the sugar, she takes it over to the table and sits next to Sally, sipping on her mug with a deadpan visage.

Sally cups the mug in her hands and leans in toward Rain. "I mean, you gave it to me. The Frostbite. You did. Then the hunter guy said it, just the other day."

"Hunter guy?"

"Yeah, the one in my dreams. I told you about him. Bullet."

"Oh... right. The hunter guy from your dream. Got it."

"Don't be a smart ass."

"Come on dude. It's butt-fuck o'clock in the morning, I'm a hungover mess, and you wanna talk about strange men in your dreams. It's not exactly a pressing issue."

"He said Frostbite. I'm not fucking kidding you."

"Well... yeah. You do realize there's a thing called the subconscious, right? The thing in our brains that stores all the information you receive and generally is strongest contributor to dreams while we enter REM."

"I thought you were spiritual."

"I am. But you're not making a good enough case here."

Sally gently places her mug on the table and puts hands on both Rain's knees. "You don't understand. These dreams are vivid. The most intense ones I've ever had. It's like I'm talking with a real person. I... I can't explain it, but it felt real. It always does when he's around."

"So you think you have a telepathic connection with this man?"

Sally takes her hands off Rain's knees and sits back in her chair with a scowl. "Don't be stupid. He's not real. It just feels like... never mind. I'm taking it as a sign."

"You do you."

"Well, that's the thing. I need you to do me too."

"I've done a lot of things, but incest isn't one of them."

"Shut up. You know what I mean. I need your help Rain."

Rain sips her coffee and sighs with exasperation. "What do you need?"

"Take me to your dealer. I need to know who the grower is. I need to know how they did it."

Rain sits up now, the coffee kicking in and Sally getting on her nerves now. "Now hang on a second there Stroppy. Sorry, I mean, whatever. This isn't a networking industry. You can't just waltz up to a dealer you've never met and ask for their source. That's insanity. There's a ladder you gotta climb. There's politics."

"I don't care about politics."

"You will when you have a gun in your face." Rain now leaning over and putting her hand on Sally's knee. "These are mean people, Sally. I can't do it. I'm sorry." Rain squeezes Sally's kneecap and leans back in her chair.

Sally lets out a drawn sigh and stares at the coffee mug on the table with a dispirited expression.

Rain says, "Do you want me to make us some breakfast? May as well now that I'm up."

"How much is, like, an ounce of Frostbite?"

"Expensive."

"How much?"

"Five hundred."

"An ounce?!"

"I told ya. Shit's expensive. It's not cloned or hydro, it's one of a kind, remember? Interest in it is huge, and growing."

Sally stands up and starts pacing back and forth a few moments. "Right... right. Okay." She stops and looks to Rain with determination. "I need to go to ATM."

"You're not gonna let this go, are you?"

"I'll make it worth your while."

"Oh yeah? How much?"

"Let's talk in the car. "

Rain drives Sally's Honda with herself, the only one in the car, and pulls up out the front of Teddy's house. She hops out on the icy sidewalk, getting out of the way as two joggers pass by. The mid-morning sun catching Rain's frosty breath as she makes her way up the stairs to the porch and knocks on the door.

A few moments later a voice from inside tersely says, "Come down the side to the garage."

Rain heads around to the driveway and strides to the garage where Teddy awaits at the door, sipping coffee and smoking a cigarette.

"I don't like you coming here without Steve," he says as he guides her inside.

Rain makes her way to stand in front of the desk at the back. She nervously smiles and says playfully, "You know I'm not a cop."

Teddy plonks down in his leather armchair and looks at her blankly.

"First of all, don't tell me what I know. And secondly, it's not what I said." Teddy places his coffee mug on the desk and leans forward to stub out the cigarette in an ashtray that has a mountain of butts already. "What I said was, I don't like you comin' here without Steve. Meaning, you haven't earned the right to make house calls. I don't even like most of the dispshit fuckers who already earned that trust. But at least I know them. I've met you, what, twice? Briefly. That don't even entitle you to a friendly wave on the street."

Rain is anxiously squeezing her fingers together. "I... I'm sorry. Look, I didn't mean to... I can just go." Rain motions for the door like she's asking permission.

Teddy leans back in his chair with a creaking sound, looking her up and down intimidatingly.

"Tell me what you want and get the fuck out."

Rain clears her throat and says, "I'm after Frostbite."

"How much?"

"All of it. Everything you have."

Teddy sits up straight again and crosses his arms on the desk.

"Why would you say that? You don't even know how much I have." He pauses, sucking his bottom lip in and out a few times. "You wouldn't be going to the streets with this now, would you? Selling it at a marked up price, some shit like that?"

"I'm going on a road trip to Oregon with a large group of friends. We can get weed anywhere on the way, but not Frostbite. I want to stock up, is all. Don't wanna run out and have to buy that West Coast skunk."

Teddy stares at her blankly for a long moment, running his tongue around his teeth a few times.

"If you got three... no, four, g's, you can have what I got."

"Four? You almost said-"

"I almost said shut the fuck up, bitch. Four g's. Take it or leave it."

Rain smiles and digs into her Hessian bag, pulling out an envelope with five thousand cash inside. She counts out four thousand with shaky hands, thinking that Teddy is going to take all of it.

Little does she know; he's thinking just that.

Rain stuffs the remaining money back in her bag and neatly lays the small stack of cash on Teddy's desk. He snatches it and counts it. He opens a desk drawer and tosses the money inside, then slams it shut. He lights up another smoke from a pack on his desk and gets up to mosey over to the safe in the adjacent corner. He stoops down and turns his head to look over at Rain.

"I catch you peeking, then you've chosen today as the day you die."

Rain nods her head and stares intensely at a poster of a nude woman straddling a gymnastics horse.

Teddy enters the code on the safe, opens it, and takes out the last two small bags of Frostbite marijuana, then closes and locks the safe. He meanders over to Rain, still staring at the breasts of the gymnast model, and taps her shoulder. She looks down at the two bags of weed he's offering her, and she takes it, sticking them in her shoulder bag.

"Are you sure that's everything you have?"

Teddy sucks on his cigarette and gives her a cold stare, indicating strongly that she's pushing her luck.

Rain more than gets the hint and nods at him with a pursed smile. "Thank you."

"If I find out you're re-distributing this shit to punters, I'll be paying you and Steve a visit with a few guys who don't just specialize in torture. These sick fuck's actually enjoy it. We clear?"

Rain nods enthusiastically. "No problem. Totally understand."

Teddy uses his head to lazily motion to the door. Rain turns and makes a beeline for the exit.

"Have a good time in Oregon," Teddy calls out to her flatly as she walks through the doorway.

Rain nods politely at him and closes the door behind her.

Rain briskly strides to Sally's Honda and hops in, not being able to help looking uncomfortable and shaken. She fumbles nervously with the keys for a moment to get them in the ignition then starts the engine and drives away.

Rain drives the car around the corner, travels two blocks then pulls to the side, parking behind a tanned restored Volkswagen van. Rain quickly gets out and checks both ends of the street with a paranoid visage. She takes a deep breath, then marches to the back doors of the van and opens them, throwing herself in and hastily slams the doors shut.

"How did it go?" asks Sally, who is sitting on cushions near the front munching on a bag of dried apricots.

"Guy creeps me the fuck out."

"Did you get it?"

"Yeah, yeah, I got it."

"All of it?"

"Fuck's sake, yes." Rain sighs and falls onto her side on the thin mattress in the middle of the van. "'I feel like I need a shower after that."

Sally leans over and positions the bag of apricots in front of Rain's face.

Rain waves it away. "No, I'm good." A quick moment later as Sally goes to pull the bag away. "Actually, wait. Gimme."

Sally offers her the bag and Rain sinks her hand in and grabs a fistful.

"So what's the plan?" asks Rain before stuffing several dried apricots in her mouth.

CHAPTER THIRTY-THREE
SUPPLY AND DEMAND

Glen puts on his boots and laces them up. A little extra spring in his step today, because he's going to meet Clayton Field, the man whom he believes is the father of the woman in his dreams. He called yesterday after he received the tip off from Jeanie. Glen didn't say what his business was, because Clayton most likely would have written him off as a nut job. He had told him over the phone that he had a business proposition and kept it ambiguous. All he really wants is to see a photo album with Clayton's children, to see if one of them is her. Glen knows he shouldn't be long distance driving on account of how sick he is, but he's got to know.

Glen's phone rings and he picks up.

"Heeeeey, Glen my man. How the fuck is you?" says Teddy.

Glen wipes his hand over his bald head, rolling his eyes.

"Teddy, what's up?"

"I know it's a little ahead of schedule, but I'm gonna need another delivery. Particularly of the Frostbite variety."

Glen sighs. While he does have a batch ready to go, he doesn't really want to see Teddy today. Can't stand the guy. But, since he is going near Boston today, he might as well kill two birds with one stone. And it will be his final delivery too. He's got his last batch of everything and shut down the drug lab. Cleaned it all up for good.

"You know, I'm sorta goin' by your way tomorrow morning. I can be at yours early morning. Around seven."

"Perfection, man," says Teddy sounding pretty stoned.

Glen hangs up the phone and goes to the shed to get the weed, MDMA, acid and DMT. He packs his car, feeds Bullit, then loads up his truck and hits the road.

All he can think about on the drive to Boston is the woman from his dreams and the overwhelming possibility of meeting her in person.

⁂

Sally takes a sip from her Thermos, watching intensely through the side window in the back of the van, which is parked in the next street over from Teddy's house. She's got a clear view of the front of his house from this angle.

"I'm bored already," says Rain, who is lying on the mattress playing a game on her phone.

Sally doesn't say anything.

Rain rolls over to look at Sally. "This shit is ridiculous. I mean, what if the supplier doesn't come for days? Teddy sells other shit too. Acid, MDMA, DMT, meth, coke."

"You said Frostbite is his biggest seller. Where there's demand, there's supply."

"The supplier may be away, or out of town. Hell, how are you even going to know the supplier if they show up? Do you expect them to have a shirt with big bold letters that say, 'I make drugs?' I mean, come on."

"I've already seen two people come and go. They looked like users. And they both walked in empty handed. The supplier, I'm guessing, will drive up to the garage where you were and unload the goods."

"Look at you. Miss 'I'm an expert on drug dealers' all of a sudden."

Sally breaks her stare on Teddy's house and looks to Rain with sad eyes. "It's all I've got left, Rain. Please. I have to at least give it a shot."

"Fine," Rain says and rolls over on her back again.

"We'll give it two... no, three days. I promise. I'll do the bulk of the watching. Remember, I'm paying you as well."

"Yeah, yeah."

Sally watches the whole afternoon, needing a bathroom break once, using the disgusting public toilets in the park down the road. She's seen a few gang-bangers come and go. A couple of college students as well, by the look of them. A prim and proper woman came, intriguing Sally a little bit. She looked like a housewife. She reasons that there really are no stereotypes when it comes to drugs.

Rain is in the middle of knitting a sweater, high as a kite from smoking Frostbite. Sally having to tell her to tone it down, as she will have to be with it when it's her shift. Sally watches into the night, swapping over with Rain while she gets some sleep. Rain almost dozed off a few times. Towards four in the morning, she becomes irate. She wonders what the point is of watching at this hour. No customers, or supplier, are going to come at this hour, surely. Around six in the morning Sally wakes and tells Rain she's going to the local mini mart to fill up her Thermos. When she gets back Rain is in the middle of blazing up a joint.

"Hey! I told you not to do that while you're on the job," Sally says as she closes the van's back doors. "You won't be able to concentrate."

"You're taking over now anyway."

Sally coughs from the thick secondhand smoke. "I'm gonna get high too now. Jesus. Blow it out the window."

"And risk being noticed?"

Sally sighs. She's got a point.

Rain grins. "Remember when we hotboxed in ninth grade?"

"I never hotboxed with you. Must be thinking about Jasmine or Meadow."

Rain thinks for a moment, then says, "Oh yeah."

Sally takes the seat by the window to begin her shift, filled coffee Thermos in hand. Rain finishes her joint and says she's going to the toilet, and possibly get a breakfast burrito, then slinks out of the van.

Sally does feel a little high now. It's kind of nice. She gets sidetracked for a little while watching birds flit from tree to tree, wondering what it must be like to be one. When she looks back at Teddy's house, she can see a silver Ford pick-up truck reversing down Teddy's driveway and disappears down the back. Her eyes widen. Could this be the supplier? She needs a better look.

Sally crawls into the front cab of the van and gets in the driver's seat, starting the engine. She cruises the vehicle slowly past Teddy's place, coming to a stop directly across the road. Sally peers through the window, seeing the back of a man who just got out of the truck. She can't tell from this far away, but the man seems to have a bald head. And is that a scar or something running down his head? She watches as Teddy greets him with a mug of coffee in hand. He points to the man's head and laughs, obviously mocking this guy.

A crackling radio-like sound creeps into Sally's head. Must be from the weed, she muses.

Sally watches as the man walks to the bed of his truck and pulls out two gym bags. The two men then walk into the garage.

Glen dumps the two bags on the ratty old couch in Teddy's garage.

"Man, seriously though, you alright?" Teddy says, closing the garage side door. "You look like shit. Way too skinny, man."

Glen sticks his hands in his coat and looks at Teddy apathetically. "This is it. This is the last of it."

"Last of what?" Teddy half sits on the edge of his desk.

"My supplies. I ain't growin' anymore, or cookin'. I'm done. Out."

"Why? We have a good thing going here, man."

"I told you a little while back I was thinkin' of gettin' out of the game. And here we are."

Teddy adopts a threatening grin. "You sellin' to someone else? That it?"

"Did you not hear me? I'm not growin' or cookin' anymore. For anyone."

"Well, then I don't see any problem with you giving over the Frost-bite seeds, or show me how you grow it. If you don't wanna grow no more, I got customers who froth at the mouth for this shit."

"I'm not gonna do that, Teddy."

Teddy slams the table with his bunched fist. "Why the fuck not, you dumb hick cunt!"

Glen maintains his impassive stance. "Can you just get me my money. I've got a long drive up north."

Teddy rolls his tongue around his mouth a few times, staring at Glen, then says, "What business you got up north?"

"My business. You just mind yours."

Teddy grins and lets out a little chuckle. "Alright man. You alright." He pushes off the table and gangly meanders to the safe, dropping down into a squat to punch in the code.

Glen watches Teddy open the safe, impatiently rocking back and forth on his boot heels.

Teddy stands up and turns around, holding a G47 Glock pistol aimed at Glen.

"You ain't goin' north today, my friend."

Glen stares at the gun for a moment, then locks eyes with Teddy.

"Really?"

"Yeah, bro. We really goin' on a drive back to your place. And you're gonna give me the Frostbite source." He shrugs. "Then we good."

Glen lets out an unimpressed sigh, shaking his head.

Teddy uses the gun to motion to the garage side door. "Put some hop into your step, chief. I'm not fuckin' around."

Sally watches two men exit the garage at the end of the long driveway, squinting to get a better look. They both get in the Ford truck and the back brake lights glow red. The truck backs down the driveway. Sally shimmies her butt down the seat and slides out of view as the truck hits the street. Sally peers her eyes over the windowsill and watches as the truck drives off.

Sally quickly starts the engine to the van and turns the vehicle around, driving off in the direction the Ford is headed.

Rain returns to the place where the van was parked, munching the last of a burrito. She turns around on the spot, looking for any sign of her vehicle. She walks to the next street where Teddy's house is. No sign of the van.

"What the fuck Sally?"

CHAPTER THIRTY-FOUR

GREEN FINGERS

Glen drives the truck down the 90 Freeway. Thick woodlands on either side of the road now they have entered a more rural area.

Keith Urban plays on the truck's radio. Glen loosely drums his fingers along to the beat of the song. Teddy is sitting in the passenger seat. His gun in his grip, lying in his lap and pointed at Glen.

"Yo man, we have to listen to this honky-tonk shit?"

"You've got the gun, man. You're the boss."

Teddy leans over and studies the car radio with furrowed brows. "Who still listens to the radio anyway? Don't you got Spotify or some shit?"

Glen manages a limp little one-shoulder shrug and keeps silent while Teddy tries to change radio stations, causing the odd static frequency sound that is causing Glen sharp little headaches.

"Come on man, just pick a station already."

Teddy holds up the gun for a moment. "I'm the boss, remember?"

Teddy continues changing stations while Glen hides the pain the radio waves are causing.

Sally drives down the highway, anxiously hunched over the steering wheel as she follows Glen's truck about forty yards ahead. Her eyes wide with excitement and consternation. She can't wait to meet this supplier and see how they grow Frostbite. On the other hand, she's terrified how they might react to a stranger rolling up to their doorstep asking about the drugs they grow. She figures she will cross that bridge when she comes to it.

She passes a sign that reads; 'Welcome to Great Barrington!'

They have been on the road nearly a few hours now, and Sally is surprised that Rain hasn't called to ask what happened. Sally ready to tell her she had to act then and there. It's only then that Sally spots Rain's Hessian bag in the back through the rear-view mirror, realizing that Rain's phone is probably in there. Damn it. Poor Rain. She'll understand though, because she kno-.

A deer suddenly springs out of the surrounding woodlands and in front of the van. Sally slams on the brake just in time and hard turns the steering wheel, causing the van to swerve off the road with a bumpity-bump on the rocky side of the road, then comes to a complete stop. Sally looks over to make sure she didn't hit the animal. She sees the back of it bounding into the adjacent forest. Good.

She looks back ahead.

"Shit! Shit, shit, shit, shit shit," Sally repeats to herself as she starts the engine again. She's lost sight of Glen's truck.

The van starts up again and Sally slams her foot on the accelerator, the tires spinning off onto the highway again.

She speeds down the highway, seeing the town of Great Barrington to her left. Something in her head tells her to bypass the town. Intuition maybe? She doesn't know, but she's feeling a pull to the outskirts of town. She passes rural houses, wildly looking for the silver Ford truck.

Her heart sinks, realizing she may well have lost them. Damn it, and she was so close. Tears start forming in her eyes as she cruises the outskirts, now driving down the very passage of road that she almost had an accident on, from that bolt of lightning.

Brian places the bag full of books on the counter. The lady behind the counter at the Goodwill store takes a brief gander at the stack of books inside, then looks at Brian.

"Giving up a hobby, eh?"

Brian is staring at the bag filled with horticulture and botany books, thinking about the waste of time it was reading all that material to impress that crazy bitch he arrested.

"Not into gardening anymore I see," the shop assistant says.

Brian breaks out of his daze.

"Huh? Oh, sorry, I was just... yeah. Turns out I don't have green fingers."

The lady thanks him, and Brian heads back out to his truck and hops in. His phone vibrates and a message from Janeen pops up; 'GET HOME NOW'.

Jesus, Brian thinks, what did he do now?

Brian drives back home, and as he pulls into the front driveway, Janeen is out the front door and storms angrily down the front path to the car wearing her bathrobe and slippers.

As soon as Brian opens the door she's up in his grill.

"You need to go talk to our son."

"Which one?"

"Brayden."

"What did he do?"

She shakes her head incredulously, then leads him inside to the dining room, where Brayden is sitting at the table with his head lowered in shame. In front of him is an open tin box with marijuana, molly capsules, a small ziplock bag filled with meth, and a small glass pipe.

"What the hell is this?" Brian says, looking back and forth between his son and his wife.

"Our son has discovered drugs, Brian."

"Where did you find this?"

"I was deep cleaning the house. Found this hidden in a crawlspace near the laundry."

"Mom, I said I di-"

"Shut your mouth, boy-o. I've heard enough from you. Now you can tell your lame ass story to your father."

Brayden looks to his dad and goes to open his mouth, then finds he is speechless.

Brian says, "Where did you get these?"

Brayden swallows hard. "Dad, I already told mom. I found it in the basement at school. I was going to tell you, so you could find where it came from, but then I got scared and-"

"Where did you get it?" Brian says coldly, his blue eyes staring at Brayden with intensity.

"Dad, I said."

"Where. Did. You. Get. It."

Brayden has never seen his father this chilling. He blinks slowly a few times, looking down at his lap with defeat.

"Randy knows this guy, who knows this dealer. I don't think he makes it. Just gets it off some supplier in town somewhere. That's all I know. I swear."

Brian's head is swimming with thoughts as his face turns red with rage. The main thing in his mind is Glen's face. That fucking bastard. Selling the drugs he makes, that ends up in the hands of fourteen-year old's. Fourteen, for Christ's sake. And his own son, no less.

Brian points his index finger sternly at Brayden. "You go to your room. When I get back, we are having a serious chat. You hear me?"

Brayden nods. Tears now streaming down his cheeks as he stands and marches up the stairs to his room.

Brian strides to the locked drawer at his desk in the spare room. He takes out his badge, handcuffs, and holstered sidearm pistol, and stuffs them all in his pockets. He dashes down the stairs to the front door.

"Where are you going?" Janeen calls out to him as she enters the little hallway to the door.

"I'm going to do what I should have done weeks ago," Brian says with determination as he puts on his thick jacket and zips it up. "I'll explain everything when I get back. I might be a little while. I'm making an arrest and will have to deal with paperwork. But I'll explain. Love you."

Brian is out the front door before Janeen can get a word in, the door slamming shut. She can hear the car engine start up and the truck speeding off down the street.

CHAPTER THIRTY-FIVE

FACE TO FACE

"This is it?" Teddy says with disappointment and growing anger.

"That's it," says Glen.

Teddy taps the gun anxiously on his thigh, staring at two tall marijuana plants, huffing hot air out of his nostrils loudly. They are both just under six feet tall and the stems disappear into a thick layer of snow.

"You don't treat it in a den, or lab, or some shit?"

"Logically, this plant shouldn't be growing in these conditions."

"What's your secret then?"

"Ain't you listenin'? I said it's an anomaly. It's nature's secret."

"What the fuck's an anomaly?"

"A mystery."

Teddy shakes his head with malcontent. "Fuckin' nature's secret." He sniffs loudly and spits. "Whatever. Get a shovel and dig this shit up. I'm taking the whole thing. I'll get my own people to get to the bottom of this fuckin' anombelly."

"Anomaly."

"Shut the fuck up. This ain't English class bitch. Get to work."

"I'll get a shovel from my shed."

"And I'll be watching every move. I know you is a hunter. Probably got an arsenal in there."

Sally is about to give up her pursuit of Glen's truck when she takes an outer road, thinking it's a shortcut to the highway. That's when she passes a large, fenced property and sees the silver Ford truck parked out the front of a two-story house. Another truck pulls up behind it, and Sally can just make out a man getting out and heading into the house. To her, he kind of resembles the cop who arrested her months ago.

But that's the sliver truck she's been following. This must be it.

Glen digs the shovel blade into the snow and dirt surrounding the Frostbite plant.

"How are you gonna transport this back?" asks Glen.

"I dunno man. You got a spare barrel or somethin'?" Teddy says, smoking a cigarette while he watches Glen get to work digging the plant out.

"Yeah, maybe."

"Hold it right there! Don't move, I have a weapon aimed at you!" Brian says as he rounds the back of the house, gun drawn and aimed at the back of Teddy. "Drop the weapon! Now!"

Teddy clenches. His arm holding the gun remains stiff by his side.

Brian quickly points the gun in the air and fires a warning shot then aims at Teddy again.

Brian says, "I mean it. Drop the weapon or I will be forced to open fire on you."

Teddy curses a few times under his breath and lets the Glock fall from his grip into the snow at his feet.

"Hands up, both of you!"

Glen drops the shovel and raises his hands in the air.

Teddy scowls at Glen. "Set me up, huh?" He sucks on his bottom lip a moment. "You're a dead man." Teddy calls out over his shoulder. "Whatever he's paying you, I'll double it."

"I'm a police officer, sir. Raise your hands! Now!"

Brian now right behind Teddy, gun aimed at his upper right back.

Teddy grins, then raises his hands. He's already thinking about calling his lawyers and sorting this shit out. He's done nothing wrong here. Glen is digging the plant. The gun is registered. Well, except the whole kidnapping thing. But Glen won't say shit, he muses. This is just an inconvenience.

"Alright homie, your play," Teddy says with an ominous smile aimed at Glen.

"What are you doin' here Brian?"

"I'm here to arrest you for manufacturing and supplying illegal substances." His eyes on the back of Teddy now. "Who is this?"

Teddy says, "I'm a hunting buddy. We was just about to go shoot some deer. Weren't we, Glen my man?"

Glen ignores Teddy, his eyes on Brian. "How long have you known?"

"A little while now."

"Why haven't you arrested me already?"

"I had a change of heart." He barks at Teddy, "Get on your knees, sir, and place your hands behind your head, then interlock your fingers."

Teddy slowly drops on one knee, then the other.

Glen says, "Look Brian. I was just about to destroy the basement under the shed. I'm not doin' it anymore. I can promise you that. In a couple of hours, it will be like it was never there."

"Tell it to the judge." Brian inches closer to Teddy, reaching into his pocket for his handcuffs.

Glen says, "Come on man, I'm your brother. I-"

"I don't give a damn who you are! You broke the law. Kids are getting' your stuff on the streets. And now my son is involved. Not anymore."

Brian clips one of the cuffs on Teddy's left hand. "Get on your knees and hands on your head, Glen."

SNAP. A loose piece of timber snaps behind Brian.

Brian spins around, filled with sudden fear he's been ambushed, and fires his gun out of panic.

Sally is standing several yards behind. Her eyes wide with shock. She feels her hand over her stomach. Blood seeping in a growing circle in the fabric of her faded pink pajamas.

Brian's hands start to shake while holding his smoking gun, in disbelief he fired his weapon without warning. Then he recognizes this woman.

"What… what are doing here?"

Sally's eyes roll and her legs buckle. She collapses to the ground.

Teddy has used the distraction to find his gun in the snow next to him. He turns around to fire at Brian.

BANG.

Brian hollers in pain as his shoulder takes a bullet and forces him to spin around and fall to the ground.

Teddy steps forward and aims at Brian's head.

Glen stoops down to grab the shovel at his feet. He dashes over and slams the business end into the side of Teddy's head, knocking him out cold.

Glen drops the shovel and dashes to kneel next to Brian.

"Are you okay?!"

Brian rolls over and grabs his shoulder, blood seeping through his fingers.

"It's a shoulder hit. I'll live. Go see to her."

Glen dashes over to Sally's side and immediately hooks his arms under her and lifts her up so she's limply cradled in his arms.

Brian is now standing, wincing in pain. "I'll call in an ambulance." Brian looks over at Teddy's unconscious body. "And back up for this piece of shit."

"No time. Stay with him. He's dangerous. I'll get her to the hospital." Glen turns to leave and stops, turning back to look at Brian. "You sure you're gonna be okay?"

"Yeah, I'll suppress the wound in your house and wait for the ambulance. Just get her to the hospital!"

Glen runs as fast as his weakened body will let him to his truck. He gently lays Sally on the passenger side, then gets in and drives off out of the property.

As he speeds along the roads to the hospital, he looks down to get a better look at the woman. For the first time he realizes who she is. He tries to watch the road but is also mesmerized by Sally being here with him in the flesh. He was right, dammit.

Sally lolls her head to look at him, her face now pale as the blood drains to her stomach wound. She stares at Glen, who is intermittently looking at her.

A smile slowly creeps across her face. "It's you." She coughs. "I'm dreaming." Her eyes start to flutter closed.

"No you're not! Stay with me! Don't you fall asleep, please!" Glen shakes her shoulder so her eyes open again. "Talk to me. What's your name?"

"Sally."

Glen smiles as tears form in his eyes. "Sally."

Glen swerves around sharp corners, speeding past cars who blare their horns. He talks to Sally about the cabin and tells her that he went there. She is slipping in and out of consciousness.

Glen makes it to the hospital and drives into the emergency drop-off, slamming the brakes. He gets out of the truck and races around to collect Sally in his arms, rushing into the hospital as nurses run out to intercept him.

The hospital staff places Sally on a stretcher and dash her off inside. Glen stands at the doors, watching helplessly with tears running down his face. He looks down to see Sally's blood is all over his clothes and hands.

CHAPTER THIRTY-SIX

THE DONOR.

Glen, now dressed in sweatpants and a zip-up hoodie he bought near the hospital, is arguing with the doctor overseeing Sally's surgery. He has told Glen that while they removed the bullet and have put her on life support, and that while she's still alive, her liver and intestines were badly damaged, and she's in a coma.

"I told you, give her mine!" Glen shouts at the doctor.

"Mister Bourke. I can't stress this enough. What you are suggesting is suicide. Do you understand?"

"You said there's no donor's that match her blood type. But mine does."

"In your condition, you won't survive long enough to get a donor replacement for yourself."

"I ain't got much of a chance anyway. She does. My head is fucked, but my organs are fine." Glen slams his bunched fist into the nearby wall. "It's my body dammit!"

The doctor sighs and folds his arms. "Even if I could make that call, I still need a referral from an appropriate surgeon."

"What kind of surgeon?"

"One who is familiar with your medical history for a start."

Glen stops pacing. His eyes fill with determination as he turns to face the doctor.

"Call doctor Adrian Thomas. Call him now."

Glen lies on a surgery table, out cold, with a breathing mask on which had administered the anesthetic.

Adrian and his assistants are in the process of cutting out his liver.

Once it is removed, it is placed in a Styrofoam box filled with ice.

The liver is collected by a nurse and taken swiftly from the room while Adrian prepares to stitch Glen back up.

The nurse carries the box of liver through the waiting area toward the operating room where they have opened Sally up in preparation for removing her liver and replacing it with Glen's.

Brian, who is sitting down staring into thin air with a distraught visage, breaks his gaze to watch the nurse carry Glen's liver away. His left arm is in a sling, having gone through surgery of his own to remove the bullet from his shoulder.

He hasn't had time to ask Glen why Sally showed up at his house, or even how the heck they know each other. Glen was quick to get this surgery happening, and between Brian's surgery and interviews with his police colleagues about the turn of events involving Glen, Sally, and of course, Teddy, who they found was a high-level drug dealer, there's been no time for answers. One thing Brian knows, though, is that cop-shooting bastard Teddy is going away for a long, long time. Brian almost manages a smile. But how did all this happen? Even Sally's girlfriend didn't know what she was doing there.

'Crazy,' Brian surmises. The doors whisk open, and Janine comes racing in with their three kids.

Post surgery, Glen lies unconscious in his hospital bed in his private hospital room. Janeen sits by his side, holding his limp hand, fighting back tears that she eventually loses the battle for.

The heart monitor giving off little blips next to her.

"Why didn't you tell me, Glen? Why?"

Larissa is by Sally's side in her hospital room, holding her cold hand. She's being kept alive by an array of life support machines.

Sally's surgery was successful, but she's not out of the woods yet. She had lost a lot of blood during the whole incident, and will need considerable time to recover, the doctors told Larissa.

She leans over Sally's face, her tears dropping onto the pillow underneath her.

"I'm sorry... I'm so sorry... you were reaching out, and I was too selfish to see it. Oh Sally, don't you leave me. I can't do this without you... I need you Twinkie... I need you...,'

Glen meanders through a sprawling lavender field, dressed in a flowing white kaftan, and sprinkles seeds along the rows of flowers.

The sky above is a giant collection of aurora borealis, shimmering displays of green and blue colored waves oscillate gently as far as the eye can see.

Glen stops, spotting Sally walking toward him, dressed in a white sundress and carrying her old-fashioned red watering can. She is watering the seeds that Glen has been sowing. She lifts her floppy brimmed sun hat up and peers over at Glen, exuding a big bright smile that lights her whole face up.

"There you are!" she calls out.

Glen also bears a resplendent smile. "Good. You're still here."

"Why, where else would I be?"

"You don't know, do you?"

Sally now standing in front of him. "Know what?"

Glen takes a deep breath. He's not sure if it's a good idea to let her know she was shot and is in a critical condition. During his research on dreams, Glen found that one should never wake someone who is sleepwalking as it might send them into shock. He figures this might have the same effect.

"Nothing. Never mind. How are you feeling?"

"I feel great, actually."

"Well, that's good to hear, Sally."

She cocks her head with an inquisitive face. "Hey, that's the first time you've used my name. Did I even tell you?"

"You sure did. But not here."

"Where?"

Glen looks up at the dazzling sky above. "Out there."

"Your name is Glen, right?"

"Yeah."

"I remember." She smiles. "You look like a Glen."

"What does a Glen look like?"

Sally softly pushes his shoulder. "Like you."

The beeps and blips of heart monitors and hospital hardware can be heard in the distance, making Sally look up and around with confusion.

"What's that noise?"

Glen shrugs. "Beats me."

Then it clicks for Sally. She now remembers the cop who arrested her for trespassing shooting her. She vaguely remembers the ride to the hospital, but knows it was Glen who took her. But why... oh, right, the Frostbite plant. The quick visions are cascading through her mind like hail in a thunderstorm.

She looks over at the tree in the middle of the field and begins walking toward it like she is in a daze. Glen follows her by her side. Sally takes off her hat and frisbee's it across the lavender field. The hat glides lightly through the air, ascending up to the glowing waves of color in the sky and disappears into it.

"Am I dead?" she asks.

Glen stares at her a moment, realizing she knows what's going on. "I don't think so. At least, I hope not. Because my effort would have been in vain."

"I could happily die right now."

"Why would you say that?"

They reach the tree, and Sally takes a seat in the large rubber tire hanging by a rope attached to a sturdy branch above. She swings on the tire, lifting her feet off the ground.

Sally says, "Because I've come this far, haven't I? The hardest part of dying is the pain. And I don't feel it here." She closes her eyes and sniffs the air for a moment. "When I'm here, I can make things come alive."

"This is your mind, Sally. And as beautiful as it is, you don't know what'll happen when it switches off."

"What was your effort?"

"Huh?"

"You said if I die, your effort would be in vain."

Glen looks off in the distance a long moment, trying to figure how to tell her.

"You were in bad shape. I... I'm...,' he rubs his stomach. "I'm healthy down here. And we match. Blood wise."

Sally stops swinging and steps off the tire to stare at Glen with a hurt expression.

"You didn't."

"I had to. I don't think you'd have made it otherwise."

"Glen... I... I...,"

Glen steps forward and embraces her. "It's okay. You'll be okay."

"But what about you?"

Glen kisses her on top of her head and continues to hold her for a long time, eventually saying, "How did you find me? Out there, I mean."

Glen lets go of Sally and she looks at him, blinking as she recalls the events.

"Frostbite."

Glen furrows his brows and emits a little chuckle.

"You wanted to buy weed?"

"No. I've been working on an experiment. I've been trying to grow tropical plants in sub-zero climates."

"What on Earth for?"

"It's my job. My hobby. My passion." She looks at him now with determination. "How did you do it?"

Glen shrugs. "It was an accident."

"I tried everything."

"Just because you've been given the gift to know how to create, doesn't mean you get to decide what to create. That ain't up to us. And it damn well shouldn't be."

Glen holds his hand out. "Come, let me show you."

Sally takes his hand. They turn around.

Now they are at the back of Glen's house where the Frostbite plant is. Sally looks around with foreboding, quickly realizing this is the place where she was shot.

"I don't like it here."

"It's okay. Look. Here." Glen points to the marijuana plant growing out of the snow covered ground. "Is this what you wanted."

Sally's eyes widen and a smile creeps across her face. "Yes."

The plant suddenly vanishes right before her eyes and a moment later an apparition of a slightly younger Glen appears, filling in a dug out hole. He finishes and turns to a wheelbarrow to pick up a wooden cross headstone with the word "Lily" inscribed on it. He kneels and hammers it into the ground.

Glen, standing next to Sally watching himself installing the headstone, says "A few months after I buried my dog Lily, a pipe I had installed for ventilation to my growing lab under this shed burst. It released several toxins into the surrounding soil. A month or so after that...,"

They both watch as the plant sprouts and grows in rapid succession.

"...the plant sprouted and grew healthy and strong. In freezing temperatures. I can't say how, or why, it just did. And frankly, I don't wanna know. It's special. Unique." Glen turns his head to look at her with a heartfelt smile. "Just like Lily. Just like you."

Sally turns to return his genial smile.

Glen says, "I can't explain how I know I'm dreaming right now, and that I know you're real. But knowing that ain't gonna take away that you made me feel alive for the first time since I can remember."

Sally turns and takes his arms in hers.

"Then let's go back together. Right now. There's so much we need to talk about."

Glen looks down at his feet with melancholy.

"I don't think I'm comin' back this time, Sally."

The sound of a heart rate monitor flatlining echoes all around them followed by thunderous crashes of lightning all through the sky.

A big white flash of light forces Sally and Glen to shield their eyes. When they open their eyes again, the two of them are in the log cabin. Lightning flashes through the windows from outside as howling gusts of wind threaten to break the glass.

Sally turns to Glen with a pleading visage. "Please, Glen. Come back."

"It's too late, I fear. I did what I did and there's no goin' back."

"I didn't ask for you to do that."

"I know. And you didn't have to."

Sally looks up at the ceiling where the timber planks are bending and buckling under the storm outside.

"Stop it! Stop what you're doing!" Sally screams to the heavens above.

Glen manages a little chuckle. "I think they're actually tryin' to save me."

The sound of a defibrillator zapping electricity into Glen as doctors outside try to save Glen. A massive surge of electricity and a window by the fireplace shatters into pieces.

Glen and Sally are now standing on a hill overlooking the lake. It is no longer frozen, but a serine body of water surrounded by lush trees and foliage.

Glen says, "You once told me that life is a gift we are to protect." Glen scans the resplendent scenery with fondness. "Well, my gift to you is that a part of me will let you live on. You'll find what you yearn for. I know it. Somehow, I just know."

Sally's eyes are filled with tears as she stares at him with quivering lips.

"Come on," says Glen, holding out his hand.

Sally takes his hand, and he dashes down the hill through the forest with her. The two of them making excited sounds of glee as they sprint down the slope faster and faster until they burst out of the bushes and back into the lavender field.

The colorful waves in the sky are now more intense mixed with the flashes of lighting and electricity bolts.

The two of them stop to catch their breath.

Glen says, "That's the true beauty of our universe, Sally. You can't control where you stand in it. Maybe it has a plan. Maybe it doesn't. But it made you and everything you love. And while it's brief, make the most of your time here. I wish I had done that more. But at least I got to experience some happiness because of you."

The sound of the heart monitor is now much louder and drops into a flatline long beep.

Glen looks down at his body to find particles detaching and flitting off into the air like dancing fireflies.

"It's time," says Glen, looking back to Sally. "If you meet my sister, Janeen. Can you tell her something?"

"Of course."

"Tell her, if there is an afterlife, I'll look after Matthew until she gets her ass there."

Sally's eyes fill with tears as she watches Glen evaporate into the air bit by bit.

She says, "This is where you'll always live. As long as I'm alive, you will be too."

Glen's smile is the last of him left, which then separates into millions of tiny specs that are wafted up to the resplendently lit up sky.

The flatlining noise stops.

The lightning dies down.

Sally walks down one of the rows of lavender where Glen had been sowing with seeds. Plants have begun to sprout, and they look exactly like the Frostbite plant.

CHAPTER THIRTY-SEVEN

THE FLOWER AND
THE BULLET

Sally's eyes flutter open from the warm morning sun coming through her hospital room window. She slowly moves her head to look over at Larissa, who has been sitting there for the past hour waiting for her to wake up.

"How are you feeling Twinkie?"

Sally smacks her dry lips and tries to speak but can't summon the energy just yet.

Larissa sees that Sally is thirsty and pours a fresh glass of water from the jug sitting on the nightstand next to Sally's bed. Sally sloppily drinks in big gulps, spilling water down her chest, causing Larissa to chuckle.

"You've been in an out of consciousness for the past day."

Sally groggily remembers waking up a few times and drifting back asleep.

Her eyes lock on the doorway to the room where Janeen is standing stiffly with her hands clasped in front.

"Hi there. I'm Janeen. Glen's sister. Is this a bad time?"

Larissa stands up and picks up the near empty water jug. "Not at all. I was just about to go get this refilled." She walks past Janeen with a polite smile and disappears into the corridor.

Sally motions to the now empty chair next to her bed. "Sit down, if you like."

"Thank you, but I won't be stayin' long. Got a million things to do including two sick children. It never ends."

Sally's face now exuding a wide grin. "I can see the resemblance. You and Glen have the same eyes."

Janeen slowly steps over toward the end of Sally's bed, looking around the room nervously. She stops, staring at Sally for a moment with intrigue, then sadness.

"You okay?" asks Sally.

Janeen wipes an oncoming tear away. "Look. I guess I just wanna know why my brother risked… well, gave his life. For you. As far as my husband's report goes, you didn't even know each other. Y'know, before the incident. I just… I guess I just want to know why."

"The thing is, we did know each other. Just not in the flesh. At least until I went to his house that morning."

"Yes, your sister said you followed him from the drug dealer's house. But that still doesn't make sense, as to why he gave his life for yours. And not only that, but he made a will where you appear. He left you a God damn marijuana plant."

Sally grins weakly. "I didn't ask him to do any of that."

"But he did it anyway."

Sally looks out at the window a moment, letting the sun rays warm her face. She turns to look at Janeen.

"Do you believe in higher forces?"

"You mean, like God?"

"God. Or Gods. Or just something... bigger. Like we're all sharing the same consciousness. We're all connected."

"No offense, but no. I don't believe in any of that nonsense."

"Well, until recently, I didn't either."

Janeen folds her arms. "Look, I'm tired and still upset. Glen's been gone several days now, and I don't think I'll ever get used to not havin' him around. I didn't come here to talk religion or higher forces, or the like." Janeen swallows hard and starts to back away. "I think I made a mistake, coming here. I'm sorry, as well, that my husband shot you. He wouldn't have... he was doin' his job."

Sally smiles. "I know. He sure takes it seriously."

Janeen chuckles and nods. "That he does."

Janeen purses her lips uncomfortably and curtly nods as she steps back to the doorway. "I hope you make a full recovery soon."

"Glen said he would look after Matthew. If there is a Heaven, or someplace like it."

Janeen stops, now taking a couple of steps forward. "How do you know about Matthew?"

"I don't know who Matthew is. He just told me to tell you that. Before he moved on." She pauses and smiles. "Well his exact words were, he'll look after Matthew until you get your ass there."

Tears now forming in Janeen's eyes. "When I was sixteen, Matthew was my son. For eight and a half minutes." She sniffs and wipes away her tears. "No one knew that except Glen and my parents. The dad was a high school boyfriend who died in a car crash while I was pregnant."

"I... I'm sorry. That must have been hard."

Janeen starts weeping, looking away while she does. "I wanted him so damn bad. There's a hole in my heart where he used to be."

Sally leans forward and opens her arms. Janeen looks at her a moment, then briskly walks over and they both embrace softly.

"Glen told me that right before he died."

Janeen slowly pulls away from Sally, looking at her with confusion. "How is that possible? You were in a coma for cryin' out loud."

Sally shrugs. "If you don't believe there's a higher force, God or no God, maybe some universal pipeline we'll never understand while we're here, then you won't believe a word I say. People say they've spoken to God in their sleep. Glen spoke to me in my sleep. And Glen is no God."

Janeen blurts out a laugh, wiping more tears away.

Sally says, "But he made me come alive. In a way, he saved me." She taps her head. "All in here. We opened up to each other in ways you couldn't in real life." Sally watches as Janeen gives this some thought with a confused expression. "I know it sounds hard to believe."

"It's just hard to believe that Glen opened up to anyone."

They both laugh.

Janeen steps over and sits on the edge of the bed's end.

"What was he like?" Janeen says, then taps her head. "In here?"

Sally smiles reminiscently.

*

The doorbell rings.

Larissa moseys from the kitchen carrying a glass of Pino Grigio and opens the front door to the house.

"Heyyyyyy'" Larissa says opening her arms and almost spilling wine over the rim of her glass.

"Hey yourself," says Yvonne with a radiant smile, coming in for a hug.

After they have a tight embrace and rock each other back and forth a few moments, Larissa leads Yvonne through the house, catching up on pleasantries.

As they pass through the main living room, Yvonne steals a glance at a large gold framed painting mounted above the main mantle. The showpiece of the room is a painting of Glen. He's wearing a flowing white kaftan robe and in the midst of seeding a row in a sprawling lavender field. His long hair down and a content smile on his face.

Larissa and Yvonne reach the back sunroom, where Sally sits in a high-backed wicker chair, an easel in her lap and paintbrush in her hand which is laying strokes on a half painted picture. The painting is a portrait of Glen, walking through the woods with his rifle slung over his shoulder and Bullit by his side.

A fourteen-month little boy in a cot next to Sally squeals with delight as Larissa and Yvonne enter.

Yvonne goes straight to the baby and makes the appropriate baby gibberish noises and squeezes his cheeks.

"Hey little munchiken! Look at you, getting bigger already."

Sally pats her heavily pregnant stomach, the scar from the liver operation on the side. "Little Aubrie is going to weigh more than big Joseph there, they tell me. I won't have a vagina left if we decide to have a third."

"Must be my eggs," says Larissa with a smirk. "You should see my mom's side of the family."

Yvonne chuckles as she moves to stand next to Sally, admiring the half done painting. "This is just as great as the last one I saw. How are they doing?"

Larissa sips on her wine and says, "She's selling them like hotcakes. She's had to go part-time at the university to keep up with the demand."

"That's wonderful Sally," Yvonne says as she squeezes Sally's shoulder.

"What about you, Vonnie? How's the book coming along."

"I finally finished."

Sally and Larissa yell almost in tandem. "Oh my God!"

Yvonne reaches into her handbag and pulls out a book. The title reads; 'Two Souls One Dream'. A picture of a log cabin overlooking a lavender field on the cover.

"My publisher tells me pre-sales are through the roof."

Sally opens the first page to see the dedication is to her and Glen.

Yvonne says, "In fact, you get the first copy. It's only fitting."

Sally gasps with joy as she takes the book and marvels at it.

"After all," Yvonne says, "it wouldn't have been possible without the Flower and the Bullet."

ADAM PATRICK FOSTER

Adam Patrick Foster is a filmmaker and author of three novels, produced screenplays, theatre writer and actor, television editor and radio broadcasting contributor, and offers you a plutonic love story between two fragile souls, experiencing loss, pain, insecurity, loneliness, desperation, illness, hope, frivolity, sexual awakening, friendship, trust, philosophical growth and new uplifting emotions over both their physical and transcendental worlds.